THE PRESIDENT'S CLUB

A Novel

Nancy Veldman

Nancy Veldm

Special thanks to my husband, Richard,
who has walked beside me in this endeavor
of writing words that might provoke you
to turn the next page

PROLOGUE

There is a certain time of day when the sun is coming up over the hill in the front of the house, and the trees are beginning to bud with the promise of new leaves, and there is a smell of fresh cut grass in the air along with a mixture of whatever is blooming at the moment . . . that I feel my family close to me. I remember always feeling safe, always knowing that everything was going to be okay, and never doubting for one second that my parents were solid as stone. I can almost see the porch light on when we were playing in the street at night, catching fireflies in the warm summer wind. We were a good family. We had everything we needed and I don't have one single solitary bad memory of my childhood roaming around in my head. But now, even now, staring at the summer sky that I love so much, I no longer trust anything. I am certain now that I did not know who in the world my father really was. And whatever I recall about my life at home, whatever I thought my life was, I see now that it could not have been further from the truth.

—Emily

CHAPTER ONE

"Emily"

The house on Olive Street was a two-story brick house with tall evergreens standing like guards on either side of the front door. It had dark green shutters and a high-pitched roof, and well-trimmed shrubbery forming massive beds in the front and back yards. There was a two-stall garage attached to the house on the right side and the driveway was circular. In the spring, the cherry trees bloomed like pink candy, but in the middle of winter, everything was shrouded with three feet of the whitest snow I'd ever seen in Washington.

It was that kind of day for a roaring fire in the hearth room, as Mother stood at the stove making chili. The aroma was causing stomachs to growl and Father had already taken his seat at the head of the table. Tea was poured, and warm cornbread was in a covered basket near Father. I sat down hoping to get a few words with him before the crowd landed in the dining room.

I supposed he knew I needed to talk, for he suddenly put the paper down and looked at me over his glasses. It was a very intimidating look but it got him nowhere. "You know I'm getting married in a few weeks. You have said nothing about Rob either way. So let's hear it. What do you think of him after three years of seeing him around?"

He cleared his throat. "It's obvious I have no sway, so what's the point?"

"So that means you don't like him?"

"Those were not my words, but yours."

"I would love your blessing, Dad."

"Either way, the wedding happens, right?"

"Well, if you have to be that way, yes."

"Okay, then. There you have it."

"What do you not like about Rob? He's a hard worker, halfway through pharmaceutical school, and so pleasant to be around. He has been good to me, Dad."

"Is that the parameter that you have based your decision on? That he treats you well?"

"Well, you could take some lessons from him, you know. He's quite the gentleman."

He laughed. "I see. Well, Emily, my dear, I do hope you two are happy. I would wish nothing else for you. But I've done some background checking on his family and some of it was a tad brow-raising."

"Oh, come off it, Dad. I'm not even going to listen to this."

"You asked me. I told you."

"Mother, are you hearing this crap?"

Mother had a smile on her face as she walked into the room carrying the chili in a huge bowl that would feed the entire Marine Corps. She liked it mild and Dad liked it hot, so it ended up being a middle-of-the-road chili that almost tasted good.

"I'm staying out of that argument. This is between you and your father. Frankly, you should already know better than to enter into a discussion with him about whom you have chosen to marry. Living with him is like living with the FBI."

"No joke. I guess I keep hoping he will be on my side. But when has that ever happened?"

Suddenly the room was filled with noise and a million conversations going in different directions. I loved that feeling of family, and we were at our finest sitting around the dinner table. I looked at Mother in between bites of chili and cornbread, noticing an expression of tiredness or stress, I could not tell which. But Jesse's loud voice interrupted my train of thought.

"What's this about you and Rob getting married? Doesn't anyone tell me anything around here?"

I couldn't resist. "Thought you already knew, Mr. OCD. Anyway, it can't be much of a surprise to any of you, since we've been dating for three years now. It's time we either commit or stop, and I really think he's the one for me."

Dad looked at me but kept his mouth shut for once.

"I'm not one bit surprised," Susan remarked. "I knew you would fall for him, Emily. And now he has you wrapped around his finger." Susan was more like Father than any of us. It got on my nerves.

"Oh, hush. You're just jealous. We aren't getting any younger, Dear. Are you planning to be an old maid?"

"Certainly not! But I'm not going to allow a man to control me like you do with Rob."

"Okay, girls. That's enough. A wedding is a happy time and we're going to support Emily in her decision. After all, she's the one who is going to live with him and bear his children." Mother sounded a little annoyed.

"Well, thanks for the support, Mother. I don't know why you all are acting this way. He's a perfect gentleman to me. And I'm fully aware that I'm high maintenance. I probably could use someone to hold me back. Take the edge off my expensive taste."

Laughter trickled around the table like a running faucet. It got quiet and everyone ate in silence, thinking their own thoughts. But I was saddened by the lack of enthusiasm about my wedding. I thought they would be happy for me, but in truth, they all were stuck in their own lives and probably resented me being happy. Finally, Jacob broke the silence with an intelligent question, which was shocking because he rarely even spoke to me.

"So I suppose you will be living in Rob's house on Terrance Lane? That neighborhood looks a little shabby, don't you think?"

"We're planning on buying another house after we marry. I'm not worried about that for now. It's not all that bad and there are a lot of children on that block. I love having other families around with small children, like this neighborhood."

"It's nothing like this neighborhood, Emily. The houses are deteriorating and I think you should encourage Rob to sell pretty soon."

"Since when did you become an expert in real estate?"

"I'm just saying—"

"Well, don't."

"Okay, enough. You two stop your arguing and let's clear the table for dessert. It would be wonderful to hear some good news for a change." Mother stopped and corrected herself. "Not that your wedding is not good news, Emily. I am thrilled for you! Paul, did Avery get her teaching position at Walter Miller Elementary?"

"Yes, she got it. Kind of nice to be at the same school. Well, I'm at the high school, but still. She's close."

"Any talk of children on your end?" I had to ask.

"We've discussed it. I would not want to steal your limelight."

"Too bad Susan and I couldn't have a double wedding! I would love that! Wouldn't you, Mother?"

That hit a button I didn't know Mother had. "Heavens no! Planning for one wedding will be enough. And you know Susan isn't even dating anyone at this time."

Susan looked up from her almost empty bowl of chili and glared at Emily.

"We are having peach cobbler with ice cream. Anybody ready for dessert?"

All hands went up so I went to help Mother in the kitchen. She was full of words.

"What in the world were you thinking, Emily? Are you trying to hurt your sister?"

"Relax, Mom. She didn't say a word. She doesn't talk that much about her private life and I was trying to get a rise out of her. I was also halfway getting back at Dad for being such a jerk earlier. He really is in a mood lately. Have you noticed?"

A look crossed her face that I did not recognize. It disappeared as quickly as it came, but I didn't let it go as easily. "What's wrong, Mother? Is there something you need to tell me?"

Suddenly she was all smiles. "Oh, no! He's fine. Just overloaded. He took on some large accounts and I am sure it is stressing him out. We could use the extra money but I don't want him feeling pressure. Now with the wedding, we need to be watching our money so you can have your day!"

"Well, that doesn't make me feel too good. I'll pay for what I can, Mom. This doesn't have to be like Diana and Prince Charles. I just want a pretty dress and some flowers."

"I know, Honey. Don't worry about anything. And ignore your father. He has his moods and who knows what is causing them. I stopped a long time ago trying to figure him out. And I'm sure he is thrilled about Rob being a permanent fixture in this family. It feels like he already is."

I smiled but I was anything but convinced. Dad had been grouchy and jumpy for quite some time. Mom had blamed it on everything but the weather. I think that was going to be her next drug of choice. The weather. We walked back into the dining room and Dad wasn't at his place at the table.

"Where's Dad?" I looked at everyone and they just shrugged their shoulders.

"Did he leave or what?"

Jesse answered quietly. "He got a phone call and said he had to go, that he would be late getting home. He wants his dessert put back for later."

"Mom, what is that about? It's 7:30. Who needs Dad at 7:30?" Jesse's explanation didn't satisfy me.

"I have no idea, Honey. But you need to relax. He'll be back later. Don't worry. I am sure it is a worried client that has something to discuss with him. Money is huge to companies. You know how he is always on call like that when he takes on big companies."

I accepted what she said, on the outside, but inside I was feeling something I couldn't put my finger on. We all ate our cobbler and finished the night without another argument. It had been good to see everyone and when I climbed into bed, I was full and happy.

I never heard Dad when he came in. But in the morning, he was sitting at the kitchen table all bright-eyed and cheery. Except for a scratch on his right cheek. I wasn't about to ask where that came from. And Mother seemed not to notice. So another day started with the Sinclair family. And I was as blind as the rest of them for years to come.

CHAPTER TWO

William Sinclair moved to Washington as a young man, eager to make a life for himself that was entirely different from how he had been raised. He had shown a deep desire for excellence in his college years, getting a scholarship to Yale and graduating at the top of his class. He was a mathematical wizard of sorts but lived life at both ends of the male interests spectrum. He was a great hunter and an expert marksman. He loved the outdoors and learned all he could as a young man about survival. He had trained as a Navy SEAL and risen to lieutenant and he'd led his platoon of men in and out of Afghanistan four times without a scratch. Most would say he was kind and gentle on the outside but on the inside, he was tough as nails. Someone to be reckoned with. Underneath his starched shirt there were muscles that body builders would die for. In his brain was information that you would not want to know about. He was six-foot-four, had hair as black as a raven's, and a deep commanding voice. He was a natural leader.

The oldest of six boys, Bill learned early on that men had to be tough to get by in this world. And everywhere he went in life, that fact was confirmed. He was a romantic at heart and loved the women, and he married early in life to his first love, Sharon. At the same time, he would be the one you would want around you in a life-threatening situation. When he married Sharon, he worked for a CPA who had his own office in the middle of town. He soon became partner, and he and Sharon bought a new house and had their first child, Jesse. Two years later, the twins were born, Emily and Paul. Within eight years they had five children and the need for a bigger home.

Bill made a radical decision to sell out to his partner and go to work for a larger firm: McCloud, Kenner, and Jones. He worked hard and moved up in the firm, took a substantial raise, and bought a larger home on Olive Street. As the years passed, the children grew up and moved out of the house. All except Emily. She was employed as a legal secretary at Holmes and Wentworth Law Firm and was in love up to her neck with Rob Hamilton. Bill suspected he wasn't what he claimed to be, but he also knew that the harder he pushed the more she would move away from him. And he could tell that Sharon was on her daughter's side. Two against one. It never worked out.

Bill had secrets. He lived with them every single day. He got a call one day from the White House that blew his mind. But he could tell no one. He never saw the face of the man on the other end of that phone but the gravity of what he was asked to do would remain with him until his death. A voice he didn't recognize told him "You serve at the pleasure of the President," and he had no recourse. Some sort of President's Club. Only he would never know who the other members were. He would take to his grave the secrets he carried inside.

No matter how strong a man he was, that alone would age him. He knew that. His mind was a solid as any man's on earth and he carried out his day job perfectly. Clients were drawn to him and he got so many referrals he had to pass them on to the newbies in the company.

But when his cell rang, his private cell phone, he no longer was captain of his life. He was asked to immediately respond without question. He was given orders and they had to be carried out discreetly and with dogged determination. Nothing, nobody, could stand in his way of obeying the order given. He had been told if he died while attending to the order, no one would know. Nor would they know how he had died.

He was a member of a team of twelve men whom he would never see in his lifetime. They did not know each other and none of them knew their leader. It had to be this way because of what they were asked to do. The plans were laid out, they acted without hesitation, and they reported to no one other than the voice on the end of the line. The group originated in the White House under the President of the United States, but once appointed, the members did not answer to the President or anyone in the cabinet.

The team and its leader worked in seclusion and darkness. The job was too dangerous for them to be exposed, and no one in the political world wanted anyone to know he or she was connected to such a group. Most in Washington did not even know it existed. The leader decided who was in, how long, and when a member was done. So it was not a lifelong occupation. You were used for as long as they deemed necessary, and then you were done. You knew nothing, so there was not much temptation to tell anything. But you alone had to deal with the ramifications of what took place, and you learned early to compartmentalize this secret life.

He learned quickly that it was purposeless to try to keep the orders in the forefront of his mind. But some of the things he was asked to do were horrendous things and it took mental fortitude to handle them. At first he was not sure he would be able to function, and he was shocked that he was capable of doing such atrocities. But he knew he would have to answer for it if he failed the mission. And he feared that his life would be on the line if he did not obey the command.

So the responsibility was epic and he always had to face the fact that his precious family could never know what he did underground. He prayed that he would not be killed and that they would have no reason to ever research their father's life thoroughly. Not that they could find out anything strange. Even if they picked up on something, they would not be able to nail down what it was. Sharon might have assumptions but they would only be half accurate. She would not go far enough. Deep enough.

He was pretty sure that the smartest thing he did, that no one would have guessed in a million years, was to record every single covert mission they asked him to do. Every conversation with that anonymous voice that went by the name "Command." And every single person he had to take out or torture. And that secret information was stored on several thumb drives that he placed in a location that only he knew about. Because he knew that he could no longer count on the American government to protect him or his rights.

And so, that was the way things were on a lovely morning a few days before his daughter's wedding. *To Rob, the idiot. Rob the nice guy.* He just didn't like the man.

He walked out on the huge porch that wrapped around the whole house and looked out over the valley. The house was sitting on an acre of land. Their neighbors were not too close. He liked that. He had a moment of quiet before Sharon poked her head out the door.

"I was wondering where you were."

"Sitting here just trying not to think."

"That sounds like fun. We are having a wedding here on the lawn in a week and you are sitting around trying not to think?"

"I was hoping she would change her mind."

"Not going to happen, Bill."

"I can hope."

"Why are you so against him?" He saw her roll her eyes.

"I checked on his family. I don't like what I saw."

"And what horrible thing did they do? How bad could it be?"

"More than I care for, and I'm not saying." He yawned.

"Then what is the point? Come on, Bill. Stop playing detective and just enjoy this time in your oldest daughter's life."

"Why won't she listen to me? She's so damn stubborn. Are we forever going to marry people who are not good for us? Is that the road mankind is going down? That's why there are so many divorces."

"You didn't do so bad, buddy."

He raised an eyebrow and cracked a grin. He knew he had hit a nerve. And he loved it.

"Oh, well. Yes. Some of us do hit it right. But obviously not many."

"You need to get out there and mow the lawn and trim the bushes. We have some tree limbs that need to be cut down, Bill. Things need to look good for the wedding. Emily has planned a simple one, but people will be here. We want it to look good for her special day."

"I'll mow the lawn, and dance with her, and give her away. But I will not be happy about it."

"Oh, Lord. I am sure this isn't the last word on the subject."

"I can keep my mouth shut if you like."

"Don't be a martyr, Bill."

"I wear that robe well, I think."

He felt her staring. He always worried she would pick up on something.

"I wasn't going to say anything, but the other day when I was washing your clothes, I found a spot of blood on your sleeve. Where in the world did that come from?"

"I have no idea. You should have said something right then."

"That's not the first time."

He turned and looked at her. She wasn't smiling. "I'm sorry. I need to be more careful shaving, I guess. What else could it be?"

She paused. "If I knew I wouldn't have asked you."

"I know. I'll be more careful. Now I guess I'd better get moving. I am glad fall is approaching; I am tired of mowing all this grass. I've been thinking that next year I'll hire it done. What do you think?"

"Whatever makes you happy. But you'll get lazy, and you won't be happy with how they do it. I know you."

He laughed. "I sure hope so. You've lived with me a mighty long time. I'd hate to think we were strangers after all these years." If she only knew.

He stepped off the porch and headed towards the garage. August was a hot month and he could not imagine getting married on a hot summer evening. But Emily had set the date, and like everything else in her life, she wasn't budging. He admired her and knew she was a lot like him. But this marriage was not going to last. There was no way. Rob was lazy and the history of his family was crooked. Things didn't add up. His dad was an alcoholic and had gotten fired several times because of his drinking and a DUI. His brother had committed suicide. Too many negative things going on, and she didn't need that in her life.

Sitting on the mower, he had plenty of time to think or to let his mind just wander. For some reason he couldn't get the last phone call out of his mind. He was aware, after a short time, of the evil in the government. This thing he was doing was so totally wrong. But when they approached him from the White House, they would not take no for an answer. He was too good at what he did, and they wanted him. So, he agreed and now they owned him pretty much. He wasn't sure how long, and he wasn't sure what would happen to him when it was time to pull out.

He felt the wind blow through his hair, and he smelled, for maybe the last time that season, the fresh cut grass that he was collecting in a bag on the back of the mower. It would take him a while to cut the lawn, so that was a nice respite for him. Even though he complained, it was about the only time he had to think and not have someone ask what he was thinking about. It was times like this when he wondered about the other men on the team. Who they were. What their lives were like. He mused that probably they all were similar in how they handled things because there really wasn't another way. Torture, murder, and anything else they had to do, was hard to just walk away from and return to your normal life. But that was what they all had to do. Or lose their frigging minds.

All he knew today was that the sun was out, he was mowing grass, and his oldest daughter was getting married to a man he would not have chosen for her. He smiled to himself. The house would be emptier and it would be just him and Sharon left to make the world go 'round. He liked that, in a way. She was his soul mate. But it might make it tougher to hide things. He would have less room for error because Sharon would not be as distracted without a child at home to care for. It would all work out. One way or the other. But this one day, he was just going to focus on the lines he made in the grass and the smell of the last days of summertime. Dog days, they were.

CHAPTER THREE

The television was so loud Paul never heard his wife coming through the door with both arms full of groceries. But he did hear her yell his name. She had a voice that could wake the dead when she was mad. Some of that might have been because she was a first grade teacher and there was a ton of frustration building inside from all the know-it-all parents who were questioning everything she did. Paul was enough like his mother in that he liked things done in a timely manner, but he did have a smidgeon of laid-back in his bones. He jumped up and ran into the kitchen to get the rest of the sacks out of the car.

"I was wondering when you were going to get off that dang sofa, buddy." Avery could sound tough when she wanted to.

"Sorry, babe. Didn't hear you come in. Did you clean the shelves off at the store? Geez, who are you feeding anyway? The whole football team?"

"Well, if it feels that way, look in the mirror. You're the one who has such an insatiable appetite. Not me."

He laughed. "That's because you are such a great cook! So how was your day?"

"What are you doing home so early? I thought you had practice."

"We moved it until tomorrow. I had some meetings at the school and couldn't get there in time. No biggie. The boys are ready. I've worked them hard."

"My day was great except for the emails I am getting from one parent in the class that thinks she is in charge."

"I wouldn't have your job for anything in the world."

"I am playing with that thought, myself."

"Hang in there. School has only been in session for a few weeks. You got a long way to go before you are done with this year's parents. I guess it doesn't matter what year you are in, the parents are the same year after year. Anything you can do to change it? Turn it around?"

"Wish I knew. Hey, what are we getting Emily for her wedding?"

"I was leaving that up to you."

"She's your sister, Paul."

"We need to decide. I hate waiting until the last minute."

"Let's eat dinner. I can't think on an empty stomach."

Paul was the best football coach Walter Miller High had ever had. He was tough on the guys and knew the game inside and out. His plays were spontaneous or seemed so when you were watching. Almost like he pulled them out of the air at the moment of contact. The team respected him, although they would all admit he was unbearable at times. He wanted to win. To say that another way, he was a poor loser. And he didn't want the players to get in a rut of losing, so he kept them on top. He'd seen teams before that started out playing well and then if they lost a couple of games, they could not turn it around. It was like a snowball going downhill. His quarterback, Josh Langley, had an arm that wouldn't quit. That ball left his hand and shot out like a bullet coming out of a

Remington AR-15. It hit its mark every single time. But that didn't mean it was caught every time.

Paul had played football in college and was good. In fact, he had wanted to go pro but hurt his leg, so his time was over on the field. But he made a great coach and there was talk that he'd been recruited to a college team but he turned it down. The kids at Walter Miller were part of his life; he had grown fond of them and put so much sweat and tears into them that he just didn't want to turn them over to someone else. They seemed to belong to him.

His cell phone rang. It was Josh. *Speaking of the devil.* "Hey, man. How's it going? Whatcha need?"

"My elbow is hurting pretty bad. I'm worried it won't be cleared up before our game next Saturday."

"Put some ice on it. I'll call you tomorrow to check on it. If you're still hurting, we'll go see the doc. Did you do anything? Or is it from practice?"

"Not sure. I woke up this morning with the pain. I've rested it, but it is still very sore."

"I bet the ice will do it, but let's see. Talk to you tomorrow, Josh."

Avery walked into the living room and sat down beside him with two bowls of soup and tall glasses of milk. "Who was that?"

"Josh."

"Anything wrong?"

"Elbow is hurting. I'll check on him in the morning. If he's not better, we'll go see the doc."

"Doc Eldridge?"

"Who else is there?"

She laughed, nodding. "He'd have a cow if you didn't bring the boys to him. He loves that."

"He does. But he's getting old. I don't know how long he'll be doing this. I keep thinking that this year will be his last, but he just keeps on going."

"I have some news, Honey. I was going to wait until after the wedding, so that I didn't steal her day. Her most important day."

Paul was quiet. She seemed so serious. She put her bowl of soup down, watching the steam rise and curl. "I know we said we were going to wait. And we have waited. I don't know how this is going to affect our lives, Paul."

"What? What is going to affect us? Stop talking in riddles, because this is not your classroom."

"I just don't know how you are going to take it."

"At this point, I'm going to explode if you don't tell me. Did you get fired? What is it?"

"I'm pregnant. We are having a baby."

Paul nearly choked. "We're what? A baby? Now?"

"Yes, now."

He grabbed her and hugged her, shaking his head. "Oh, my gosh. Are you sure?"

"I am dead sure. Went to my doctor to get him to check because my in-home pregnancy test said I was."

He pulled back and laughed out loud. "I don't know about you, but I am thrilled. I know we haven't discussed whether or not it was time, but I've heard there is no perfect time. I love it."

She looked relieved. "I love it, too! It was impossible keeping it from you. I've been dying to tell you. I just found out, but still, I wanted to call you from the doctor's office. We are really going to be a family, Paul."

He kissed her and grinned. "I know we are. I am so excited. How far along are you?"

"Six weeks."

"Wow. We got a ways to go. Maybe we wait until after the wedding to share our good news. What do you think?"

"That's my feeling, too. Now eat your soup before it cools off. And we still need to get them a wedding gift. I have no idea what to do."

"They are starting out, so anything will do. They have basically nothing, so something for the house or kitchen, I would think."

"Listen to you! Like you know anything at all about shopping. I'll talk to your mom and maybe she will go with me. But I hate to be around anyone for fear I'll let our news slip out!"

"Don't worry. Even if you did with Mom, she would be ecstatic. You have no idea how much she loves babies. Dad, on the other hand, well . . . I'm not sure how he'd feel. But it's our lives, not his. He has been a good father, but so elusive. Maybe because of what he's been through in the military. They say it really can mess you up."

"Does he ever talk about it?"

"Not a word. Maybe here or there, but nothing in particular. We were told not to ask. So I know nothing about his career in the military. What he really did. I think he was some kind of hero of sorts. A Navy SEAL. But we will probably never know what he went through."

"Wow. A hero. That's pretty strong, Paul. Do you think that weighs on him? Maybe too much to carry around?"

"I'm not sure he even thinks about it anymore. It's been so long. But he sure keeps to himself and works hard. He has provided us with a good living, so you can't fault the guy. I hope I do as well as he has, in my lifetime."

"Good point. I'll clean up the kitchen. You relax. Won't be long I'll be feeling that morning sickness and you'll have to wait on me!"

Paul watched her walk away. A baby. His mind could not wrap around that, and he wanted to concentrate on the game next week. But all he could think about as he watched his lovely wife walking into the kitchen, was that she was carrying a baby. That was a game- changer for certain. One that he had not counted on, but he was more than ready to tackle the challenge. This baby would be the firstborn grandchild. Of all his siblings, he would be the first to start this process and he was excited about that. The family was going to grow stronger, one child at a time.

CHAPTER FOUR

O n the outskirts of Washington, there were large neighborhoods that had been established long ago but were still pris-
tine and sought out by couples who wanted to raise their children.
Schools were near and plenty of churches. That was where Jesse
decided to set up his dental practice. He'd always wanted to be
a dentist, and now his dream had come true. The number of patients was increasing rapidly and he was planning on hiring another dentist to help with the load. Jesse handled every aspect of
dentistry, including root canals and implants. It was rare but he
got bored with mainstream dentistry and broadened his practice.
It made his patients happy because everything was handled under
one roof.

Jesse wasn't as tall as his other brothers, but he had a stout
build and worked out regularly. It helped him maintain control of
the deterioration of his neck and hands that usually plagued older
dentists. He had music playing in his office and televisions in every
room. He offered heated blankets for those patients who were going to be in the chair for extended periods of time. And there were

always fresh coffee and snacks in the waiting room. Most of his patients were adults, but occasionally he took a young child if the mother was insistent. He had a way about him that drew people to him and removed their fears about sitting in a dentist chair. Even though he was an excellent dentist, he was very shy when it came to women. Especially pretty women. And this morning, his first patient was a woman.

"Good morning, Maryanne. I hope you are doing well."

"I was before I came in here."

Jesse winced. He was so tired of people hating dentists. "Oh, it's not so bad."

"That's because you're on the other side of the drill."

"I've sat in your seat before. I know what it feels like."

"I've heard there is a new drill out that goes so fast you don't have to use novocaine."

He smiled. "Not sure where you heard that, but I seriously doubt that there could be a drill that existed that would go fast enough for you not to want novocaine."

She attempted a grin. Her mouth was already getting numb. "I didn't feel you giving me a shot."

"That was intentional."

"You're pretty sneaky for a dentist."

"I have to be. It comes with the job."

She was a gorgeous woman. He could hardly fill the cavity he was so captivated by her eyes. He was also afraid she would notice, so it only made him feel more awkward while he was trying to finish up the filling. Her eyes were a chocolate brown, almost black. And her hair was like long silk. Very shiny in the bright light above her head. He noticed her nails were painted a pale pink and her toes matched. He finally finished and sat the chair upright. She stood up slowly, wiping her mouth with a clean cloth, glancing up to see if he was watching. He caught the look, but looked away quickly.

"I think you will be fine. If you have any problems, let me know. Your tooth may be sensitive for a few days."

"Thank you, Dr. Sinclair. It was pretty painless."

"I do my best."

"It may sound odd, but I hope I don't see you for a while."

He grinned. "You have good teeth, Maryanne. Just take care of them and we will remain distant friends."

She laughed and he lost his mind.

"That was a good one. Have a great day." She walked out of the room, taking every bit of strength he had with her.

Another patient was waiting in the next room, and as he moved in that direction he turned his head to watch Maryanne walk away. She wore jeans. She was a jeans girl. He loved that part about her. Dressed up in jeans.

She was soon gone from his view and he walked into the next room, greeting the man lying back in the chair. His day moved fast, one patient after another, and at the end of the day he found himself sitting in his office with the door closed, thinking about Maryanne Millhouse.

A full day of patients was exhausting. He was tired. But right now he was remembering her. Not many women had captured him in his practice like this one lady. Maryanne was different. But he knew the line that was drawn in the sand. She was a patient of his. He could not ever let her know how he felt unless he was willing to give her up as a patient. It was a dilemma that all single dentists faced. He was ready for a relationship and had to admit that he did not know her well. But he wanted to. That was the problem. He really wanted to ask her out. He decided on a whim to ask Emily her opinion. It was either that or lose himself to daydreams and never have them be a reality.

"Emily? Jesse. You busy?"

"What do you think? I am getting married in a week. Of course I'm busy!"

"Well, I have a situation."

"Really?"

"Don't make fun of me, Emily. It's an awkward situation and I want your opinion."

"Go. I'm all ears."

"You're not making this any easier."

"Enough already. What is the problem?"

"There's this woman—"

"I knew it!"

"You did not. Now listen."

"I'm all ears."

"I'm going to hang up if you don't stop."

"What about this woman?"

"She is one of my patients. Has been coming to me for a short while. I want to ask her out but I will lose her as a patient. I have never had to deal with this before but what if I ask her out and she turns me down, and then feels uncomfortable coming in to see me as her dentist?"

"You're right. You have a dilemma. I don't know what to tell you to do, Jess. You are thirty years old. It is way past time for you to find someone and experience a good relationship. I would say it is worth the risk. You cannot keep putting it off."

"It's not like I am choosing to be alone. I just haven't met anyone I am interested in. Until now."

"Ask her out. You can discuss the situation with her if she says yes. If she turns you down, well, at least you tried."

"You know I don't like any hanging participles around. I'm very logical in my thinking and it's either black or white, this or that. I don't like maybes."

"Jess, we are talking about a person here. Not figures on a piece of paper."

"Oh, I'm aware of who I'm talking about. I am dying to ask her out."

"Well, do it, then. Geez, Jesse. At your age, this should be a no-brainer."

"I am very protective of my practice, my patients. It has taken years to build my numbers and I don't want to mess that up just because I want to take someone out on a date. It may not ever move past the first date, and then I've lost her in every aspect."

"You are making this way too hard. Just do it. It's every bit worth the risk if you are that attracted to her."

"I am definitely that."

"Okay. End of conversation. Now have a good night. I've got things to do."

"Thanks, Em. I'll let you know how it goes."

"I'm sure you will. Now take a deep breath and call her. I'll be around."

"Bye, Em. Thanks again."

Jesse took a deep breath and blew it out. That was nerve wracking. He looked up Maryanne's number and wrote it down on his notepad. He didn't even know how old she was. He pulled out her file and looked. She was twenty-eight. Perfect. He got some hot coffee, a little cream and sugar, and sat back down to dial her number.

CHAPTER FIVE

Maryanne Millhouse was a contradiction in terms. Absolutely gorgeous and very talented. She could dress a room to the nines, but her own car was an absolute mess. She had issues with organization, but somehow could turn a barn into a fabulous wedding reception given enough money. *Money* being the key word. She was low on money at the moment and was looking for more interior design jobs. As she thumbed through the public records, searching for new home buyers, her phone rang. She almost let it go, but decided she needed a short break and hit the answer button.

"Hello, Maryanne? This is Jesse Sinclair. Am I calling at a bad time?"

"Dr. Sinclair? Uh, no. I was just trying to find new clients. Is there something wrong?"

He could tell she was surprised at his call. How often does one get a call from their dentist?

"I'm sorry. I'm calling you as Jesse, not Dr. Sinclair. I was wondering if you might be interested in going out to dinner with me on Friday night. There's a new Chinese restaurant in town and I thought it might be nice to try it out."

He could feel her hesitancy. "I don't know what to say. This was the last thing I expected to happen today."

"I realize how awkward this must feel to you. But I don't know another way of doing it. I have wanted to ask you out for a while and just decided to call you today. The downside is that I cannot or rather I should not date my patients, so you will lose me as a dentist if you go out with me."

"That sucks, really. Because I have just learned to trust you as a dentist."

"Well, think about it, Maryanne. I know it is a tough thing to decide, seeing as how you don't really like dentists. But I sure would like to get to know you better. We could try one time and see how it goes. If we don't get along or you don't enjoy yourself, then nothing is lost."

"How about if I text you the answer later tonight? That will give me some time to think about it. Do you have another dentist in mind for me, if I say yes to the date?"

"Yes, I do. Katherine Wilson. She's a very good dentist and I think she will be attentive to your needs. And your fears."

"Okay, good. I'll let you know what I decide and I'll try not to take too long to make up my mind. I am flattered that you called. That was nice of you."

He blushed. "I hope you will go out with me. At least to give us a chance to see if there is something there. Talk to you soon. Have a great evening."

He hung up and found himself shaking inside. He hated asking someone out and then being rejected. But that was the only way he was ever going to date so now he had to wait it out. He had no clue which way she would go, so he tried not to think about it for a while. That was like forgetting you felt nauseous. Next to impossible.

⟞⟝ ⟞⟞

Maryanne had decorated her apartment in neutrals and it was a peaceful place to live. She loved all the new pieces of furniture and also her new cat, Lola. The cat was stretched out on the floor on the last spot of sunshine coming through the window. It was warm there and she obviously loved it. Maryanne sat on her linen sofa looking at the public records, but her mind kept returning to the phone call.

Jesse was a nice man and she really liked him as a dentist. But there was a part of her that would also like to see what he was like on a date. What a decision.

Maryanne decided to call her best friend, Courtney, and ask her opinion. She anxiously dialed her number and sat back, waiting to see if she would answer. Sometimes she was not in the mood to talk; one never knew.

"Hello?" She sounded awful quiet for Courtney.

"Courtney? Are you okay?"

"Sure. What's up, Maryanne? Haven't heard from you in a few days."

"Are you sure you are okay? You sound unusually down."

"Oh, it's nothing, really. Ned is driving me crazy."

Courtney was a real blonde, but unlike the jokes going around, she was a brain. However, her body was fabulous and her husband was usually wrapped around her finger. So something must have happened to break that spell.

"I'm sorry. Anything you want to talk about?"

"No. I'll get over it. He has decided to take up hunting in a big way. So that means he will be gone with the guys when we usually would be in New York. Like I said, I'll get over it."

"The woes of marriage, I guess." Maryanne sat down on the sofa and sipped her tea.

"Exactly. Now what's going on in your design world?"

"I have a tentative date on Friday night. I knew you would want to know."

"Oh, my gosh! Are you kidding? Who in the world is it?"

"Hold on to your panties; it's my dentist."

"Seriously? Is that even legal?"

Maryanne laughed out loud. "Of course it is. But I'll have to change dentists if I go out with him more than once."

"Hmmm. How much do you like him as a dentist?"

"I just got really comfortable with him. I'm such a baby. But he is handsome. And I have no one on the horizon right now to go out with."

"I guess it won't hurt anything to go out with him one time. I am amazed he had the nerve to call."

"He probably has tons of women after him."

"Well how good looking is he, anyway?"

"Very. But I never thought of flirting with him. Good gosh! He's my dentist. He was just nice to stare at while he was working on my teeth."

"That is funny, Maryanne. I' m sure the thought never crossed your mind that he might be a hot date."

"Not once. But now that he has called me, I am allowing that thought to cross my mind."

"Oh, go for it. What do you have to lose? And who knows, you two may just get along famously. Wouldn't that be nice?" Courtney laughed.

"It would be a frigging miracle."

"No joke. Now don't be too picky, for heaven's sake, Miss OCD. You know how you were with that last man you went out with, the guy who was a friend of Ned's." Courtney's mood had greatly improved.

"That wasn't my fault."

"Oh? So the first night out of the pen you started picking him apart. His hair, the way he dressed, the shoes he had on, and what he ordered. The man didn't have a square chance with you being so critical. I didn't recognize you that night. It was ridiculous."

"He just seemed odd to me. Nothing felt right."

"Did you ever think it might be you? That you were too critical?"

"I didn't think I was. Do you think so?"

"I think you're afraid you might just like someone. I think you are doing that out of fear."

"I never thought of myself like that. I don't feel afraid."

"Well, frankly, you scared him off. He was a nervous wreck by the end of the night. He couldn't please you to save his life!"

"Was I that bad?"

"You even made me nervous, and Ned was about to blow a gasket. So don't do that on Friday night. Just sit back and see what he is like. For heaven's sake, you don't have to marry the guy."

"Mother said not to date someone you didn't think was a potential husband."

"Were your parents happy?"

"Not really."

"So there you go. Why would you listen to her?"

"I see your point. I'll relax. I guess I'll text him and let him know the answer is yes. Now you've made me nervous about going."

"Well, better you be nervous than make him nervous. You two already sort of know each other. Now just have a good time."

"I'll let you know how it goes."

"Great. It better be good news. I want to see a smile on your face. A little blush would not hurt, either. Don't wear your hair pulled back, and put on some perfume. And don't call your mother to talk about this."

"Bye, Courtney. Talk to you soon."

Jesse sat with his phone in his lap, afraid he would miss the text. He was a wreck thinking about whether she would go out with him or not. It had been a while since he'd had a decent date. He really had forgotten how to act on a date. No one likes dating. But he hated it. *Gold Diggers* was on the television and he almost dozed off, but suddenly his phone made a noise. He picked it up and saw that a text had come in. He opened the text and it had one word typed. *Yes.* He jumped off the chair and shouted out loud. She said yes! He was so happy he didn't know if he would be able to go to bed. But he had a full day of patients tomorrow and needed to be full of energy and clear headed.

She said yes! Wow. He texted back a smiley face and told her he would pick her up at 7:00. He climbed into bed but couldn't settle his mind. He may be losing a patient, but he could be gaining the love of his life. Well, he was going to kiss her no matter what. Easier to ask for forgiveness later than permission on the front end. Unless that was being too forward. And frankly, he couldn't for the life of him think of anyone he could ask that question.

CHAPTER SIX

Mccloud, Kenner, and Jones were building momentum. Clients were coming out of the woodwork and Bill Sinclair was part of the reason. His magnetic personality and attention to detail were irresistible. He also had an uncanny knowledge of the law and saved thousands of dollars for the larger corporate accounts. Jeff McCloud was about to stand up in the board meeting and ask for a vote to make Bill Sinclair a partner in the firm. He had no doubt that the vote would be unanimous, but he had to follow the protocol.

Jeff was a large man, not only in height but also in weight. He was turning gray at the temples, which only made him look distinguished. He had started the firm twenty years ago and had helped to build it to what it was today, with his sound, logical thinking. But he was also unafraid to take chances with people. And today it was with Bill Sinclair. All three partners were sitting at a massive walnut table with leather chairs. They all wore gray suits and white starched shirts. Their company was built on professionalism and they never changed when corporate America went casual. It seemed to sit well with their clients, so they held tight to their original form.

"I call the meeting to order. We have a few things to cover so let's get started." Jeff cleared his throat.

"I have a few things to discuss. I think we need to look at more office space. We are growing by leaps and bounds. The conference room just isn't large enough anymore." Les Kenner spoke up in a quiet, firm voice.

"I agree, Les. But do we build on or make a move?" Jeff raised an eyebrow and looked at Blake Jones, his right hand man.

"I am not sure. If we build, we are cutting into the already small parking lot. I think we may need to look for a place in one of those massive buildings downtown. Most of our clients are corporate, anyway."

"Good point, Blake. What do you think, Les?"

"I think that is a good idea, but we all know the cost will be high. We won't own our space anymore. And we'd have to sell this building. Although, there was a small law firm that had shown interest last year in this building. I had lunch with one of the partners a couple months ago. A Mr. Ted Aimes. I could give him a call and see if he's still interested."

"Let's vote on that right now and get it off the agenda. All in favor of moving into larger office spaces raise your hand."

All three men raised their hands, and the secretary nodded. Suzanne had been with the firm for years and was part of the wallpaper. She knew everything about every client and had a memory and body like an elephant. They could not run their office without her.

"Good. Now I have something to talk to you about. We all admire Bill Sinclair. He has become very valuable to this firm in the last couple of years. He is a strong individual and has brought us tons of business. His clients love him and he is bringing in a substantial amount of money. I would like to make him a partner, if he is interested."

"I had never thought about adding a partner to our group, Jeff. We have been happy with the three of us for many years. That's a big step in my opinion." Blake frowned.

"I agree that he is a valuable asset to the company. But does that mean he needs to be made a partner?"

Les shifted in his chair and wiped his mustache. He wanted no dissention between them. "We've been this way for years. Maybe we need some fresh blood in the group. He's proven himself over and over. He is making us a ton of money. But do we know he is interested?"

"I have no idea. I haven't said a word to him, because I needed to bring it before the two of you." Jeff replied honestly, sipping his coffee and taking a huge bite out of a donut on the plate in front of him.

"Let's vote. Then Jeff, you can speak to him since it was your idea. Let us know what he says." Blake spoke up.

"All in favor of bringing Bill Sinclair in as a partner to McCloud, Kenner, and Jones raise your hand."

All three raised their hands, and Suzanne nodded, even though no one was looking at her. It was done. Bill would now be approached to see if he was interested. Jeff felt sure he would be. What reason did he have to turn this down? He would get better pay and also benefit from the profits of the company. It was a perfect time to make the change since they were discussing moving the practice to a larger building on the floor of one of the huge corporate buildings downtown. Possibly One Franklin Square. It was a lovely building constructed in 1989. He personally hoped they would end up there. It was prestigious.

⊷⊰╋ ╋⊱⊶

Bill Sinclair entered his office at 8:10am, opening the blinds on the huge picture window behind his desk. He loved to let the light in. It felt fresh and energizing to him, and as he sat down in his huge leather chair, he glanced at his agenda for the day. He had a full schedule of clients coming in. He was used to that and it didn't stress him out. It actually was welcomed as it got his mind off of things that weighed him down. He hated having two lives, especially because he would never be able to share that other life with anyone. Not that he wanted to. But it was tough to always know it was there, hiding in the shadows. Lurking. The stench of it was overwhelming sometimes. But he smiled and carried on. It was his way and he knew he had to act like this firm was his whole life. He loved his job and the partners he worked for. He just wished he could have kept his life simpler.

Waiting on his first client to arrive, Bill leaned back in his chair and sipped his coffee. He was not expecting Jeff McCloud to come knocking on his door. Not this early.

"Morning, Bill. How's your day looking so far?"

"Come on in, Jeff. Good to see you!" He stood up to shake Jeff's hand.

"I'll only be a moment. I know how busy you are. I just have something I want to discuss with you and it won't take but just a second."

"Sure, Jeff. What's on your mind?" They both sat down.

"I know you like your job here, Bill. And you've done a tremendous job and have brought the firm a substantial amount of money during your years here."

"There's no need for 'Atta boys' with me, Jeff. I do my job to the best of my ability and I love doing it. I have a great group of people I work with and I respect all of you."

"I'm not here to congratulate you, Bill. I have a question for you. Would you like to become a partner in the firm? And you can take your time deciding. I just wanted to approach you this morning so that you could be thinking about it."

Bill was shocked. He had no idea they were even willing to consider adding a partner to the firm. He wasn't sure how he felt about it, but it was something that would give him pause. He stood and walked around his desk.

"Why, I am flattered, Jeff. That's a very nice thing for you to offer to me. I'll sure give it some thought and talk it over with Sharon. When do you need to know?"

"Take your time. It won't be that huge a change for you, Bill. Only the money will be better and you will have a vested interest in the firm. We would love to have you aboard as a partner. I really admire you and feel like we've developed a great friendship over the years."

"I'll take it very seriously, Jeff. Thank you again, and I will get back to you before the end of the week. How does that sound?"

"Perfect. That's just perfect. Now you have a great day and let me know if you have any questions."

"I sure will, Jeff. And every day here is a great day."

Bill sat down in his chair and blew out a deep breath. He didn't know what to think. Even if he spoke with Sharon it would not help him make the best decision. He had to ensure that his life was private. No matter how close he got to the partners, he could not give them so much of a place in his life that they might suspect anything unusual going on. That was the tough part with having friends. He always had to be sure he covered himself.

Because he never knew when he was going to get one of those phone calls, it was difficult to always be able to come up with the right excuse as to why he had to disappear for a few hours. Or a whole day. No one at the White House cared what his "other job was. The person on the end of that phone sure didn't care how much his life was inconvenienced. They just wanted the job done and that was it. They didn't care what he had to do to accomplish it.

He pulled out the private cell phone and checked to make sure he hadn't missed a call. It had been too long since that phone had rung. It worried him about what was coming next.

On impulse, after checking his watch, he called Sharon. He just wanted to let her know what was offered to him. She would be surprised and would probably see no harm in accepting the partnership offer.

"Hey, Honey. Are you busy?"

"I'm in the middle of a meeting, Bill. Can I get back to you?"

"Sure, sweetie. I just wanted to tell you that Jeff approached me today and offered me a partnership in the firm. Just think about it. We can talk more about it when I get home tonight."

"I'm surprised and so happy for you. Yes, I can't wait to discuss it tonight. Have a good day, Honey. Love you."

She was always supportive in everything he ever wanted to do. She hardly ever questioned things, but her input was always intelligent and carefully said. He had first fallen in love with her mind, actually, rather than her looks. She was a pretty woman, but her mind was something to be desired. She could see all angles of a situation and size things up quickly. That came in handy when dealing with the abusive situations she saw daily. But it also could be a snag because of what he was being asked to do for the government. He was petrified that she would suspect something. He was amazed that she had not already caught on.

His first client had arrived so he turned his attentions towards saving a corporate business some big money, and laid his fears aside for now. That was, until the cell phone rang in his pocket. Then it was a whole other ball game.

CHAPTER SEVEN

Jacob was sort of the black sheep of the Sinclair family, so to speak. Not that he wasn't a smart young man with a promising career in the world of insurance. But he had a sneaky side to him and he almost squelched any chances he had with a woman because he just couldn't help himself. He was sarcastic to the bone and sneaky. Those two traits were a bad combination. It sort of went with the salesman image, but more like the stereotype of a used car salesman. Not the trusted insurance man. He should have gone in that direction because he loved cars almost to an obsession. But insurance was where the money was, so there he was in his small cubicle at State Farm, on the phone with a possible customer. It just happened to be a woman this time, and she sounded like a very pretty one, at that. He had no idea for sure, though, because he couldn't see her. And he was giving her the best sales pitch known to man.

"So, Miss Stevens, I understand you want homeowners insurance with us. And I have the perfect package for you. We also carry auto insurance. You get a savings of one hundred dollars if you put your car with us, too. Can you come in so I can write up a proposal for you?"

"Well, I just needed a —"

"I'm sure we can meet your needs. Just drop by tomorrow morning at your convenience; say around ten, and I'll have this drawn up for you. I will need the make of your car and the VIN number."

"Sure, I can give that to you. But —"

"Now, don't worry, Miss Stevens. I'll take care of everything. You can trust State Farm to give you the best deal. I've been here for five years and this is where I would tell my family to go for all their insurance needs."

"I'll be in tomorrow, then, Mr. Sinclair. Thanks for everything. By the way, my car is a Ford Taurus. VIN number 1FLM207689S."

"Thank you very much. See you in the morning."

Jacob was next to the youngest in the family and seemed to have a wandering mind. He could not focus to save his life, always thinking he would find something better around the corner, just out of his reach. He seemed frustrated and charming at the same time. It was an odd combination and always left people around him confused. He was dating Jane Hill, and hoping to keep that going. But he was already picking her apart. She was a little over-weight, but fun to be around. She made him laugh. She had pretty hair full of curls and a great smile. She was an O.R nurse at Sibley Memorial Hospital and was doing very well. He admired her tenacity and courage, as there was no way he could have taken the blood. But she loved to talk, and sometimes it got on his nerves. He liked to control things entirely too much, and didn't quite know what to do with such a chatterbox.

He wasn't making that much money yet. He lived in a small apartment in Midtown and loved his time alone. So that wasn't conducive to having a girlfriend who wanted to move in. And Jane was hinting at that very thing. He wanted her to be more romantic yet slower in getting too serious. He hated that feeling of being closed in. But he was twenty-six and did want a family.

So, there was always a conflict going on inside of him when it came to being responsible and settling down. Why did that always feel like he was giving up something? Everyone else did it with such ease. He fought it like the plague. At the same time, he would die if she started dating someone else. So what was that about? The "I don't want you, but don't want anyone else to have you" syndrome?

He scratched his head and leaned back in his chair. His dream was to be manager of the office he was in now. The current manager, James Peterson, was getting old and talking about retiring. Jacob was young but very motivated. He was vying for that position against several other agents who were more experienced. But he was hoping his personality and results would outweigh the years they had over him.

He acted tough and hard to get close to, but when the phone rang and it was Jane, his insides turned to butter. So he guessed that pretty much meant he really liked the girl.

"Hey, what's up? Am I calling at a bad time?"

He grinned in spite of the rules of no personal calls. "Not at all. You at work?"

"Yeah. Just had a moment. Wanted to hear your voice. I got nine people waiting for surgery today. So I won't be talking to you until late. Your day good?"

"It is now. I got plenty of things to do. But good to hear your voice. Hope we can have a date on Saturday night. You have your schedule yet?"

"I asked off for Saturday. Unless all hell breaks loose, I'll be free. You never know about things around here. Gunshot wounds out the wazoo. I am reconsidering my position on gun control."

He rolled his eyes. She was naive to think that gun control would stop the shootings. Gangsters, kids in gangs, would always have guns. Even if you made it illegal. "Let's not go that far. Now you have a great day and I will talk to you when you get off. Don't fall for one of those geeky doctors, okay?"

She laughed her silly laugh and he fell farther into the well. "I won't."

He hung up grinning. But then, he did like to be around her. He just wasn't ready to buy a ring and make it permanent.

Just as he was about to take a lunch break, a lady walked in dressed in jeans, cowboy boots, and a tight black t-shirt. Her hair was golden and her teeth as white as a star on the darkest of nights. She had a Southern accent that would charm Satan himself and a cute little girl on her arm with the same golden hair.

"Hello, sir. I am interested in getting some car insurance. Can you help me, or do I need to talk to someone else?"

Jacob was caught staring, with his mouth ajar. He stood up quickly, nearly knocking over his coffee, and stuck his hand out. She shook his hand loosely and smiled. His used car salesman personality kicked in and he found some words to speak. "Why sure, Mrs.?"

"Gail Bailey. And I'm recently divorced. Thus the need for car insurance, you see."

"Yes, of course. Please sit down. I am sure I can take care of you. I mean, your insurance needs, of course."

She grinned and sat down, holding her little girl in her lap and hanging her purse on the back of her chair. "I have a BMW outside. I need insurance on the car, and maybe later a house. I just haven't gotten settled in yet. Still looking for that right place to buy."

"Do you have your driver's license And also, I will need to get the VIN number on your car."

She pulled out her license and scooted her chair closer to his desk, where she looked at the form he was filling out on the computer. "I'm an attorney. So I like to make sure things are done right, you see. I'm from Memphis, Tennessee but have been here in Washington for about five years now."

After getting all the information, checking her driving record, establishing the deductible, he quoted her a figure, and she signed the papers and stood up to leave.

"Miss Bailey, thank you so much for coming in today. I know you are going to be busy looking for a place to live, but if I can be of any help to you, just give me a call. I've lived in this area all my life and I know a lot of people in the real estate business."

She turned and smiled that starlit smile, shaking his hand again. Only this time he found himself not wanting to let her hand go. "I really appreciate that," she said. "You've helped me already with the car insurance. Say, where's a good place around here to get a bite to eat? Lily is hungry and I'm beginning to feel that way, too."

"I know just the place. It's down the street. Max and Benny's Cafe. If you like, you can follow me there because I was just about to take off for lunch when you came in."

"Well, that's nice of you, Mr. Sinclair, but I better find a place where Lila can eat. You've been very nice and I am so relieved to have the auto insurance taken care of. I'll let you know if I need anything else."

Jacob nodded and watched her walk away. She was so cute. But it was probably a good thing she said no. He had no business having lunch with her. Jane would have had a heart attack if she knew. Why was he so fickle?

He walked out the door and headed to the cafe. It was a beautiful day and he was hungry. He pulled up to the front of the cafe and parked the car and walked in. The place was pretty crowded but he found a small booth in the far right corner and sat down, pulling out his cell to check for messages. He was lost in the cyber world when the waitress walked up.

"Can I help you, sir? What would you like to drink?" She laid a menu in front of him and wiped the table with a damp cloth, smiling at him. He noticed she was chewing gum and had a tattoo that was barely showing on her right arm.

"I'll just have water with lemon. Thanks."

"I'll give you a moment to check the menu. Our soup today is lobster bisque."

He picked up his phone to answer a few messages and then looked over the menu. Before he could make up his mind, the waitress was back with her pad, ready to take the order.

"The turkey club panini is excellent, sir."

"That is perfect. And a cup of that lobster bisque."

He leaned back against the back of the cushioned seat and watched the cars whiz by. Suddenly he caught site of Gail Bailey and her daughter getting out of their car. They were going to eat at the cafe after all. He decided quickly to just keep his head down. He didn't want her to feel like he was watching her. But she was beautiful and he couldn't help but glance in her direction when she sat down in a booth near the front door.

His food came and he started eating, checking his Facebook account and messages. Jane had sent him one on her lunch break. It was short and sweet. He dared to look Gail's way for a moment and she was looking back at him. He smiled and waved and glanced back down. It wasn't two seconds later that he heard her walking towards him. Her cowboy boots were clicking on the tile floor.

"Mr. Sinclair. We decided to take a chance and eat here, anyway. I think Lila likes the red seats and black and white checkered floor. It smells wonderful in here which means the food can't be too bad."

"I'm glad you're gonna give it a try. The food is great and it's always packed in here at lunch time."

"I can see that. We're lucky to have gotten a seat. Well, just wanted to say hello. It was nice seeing you again."

"You, too. Remember, if you need anything, just call. My cell number is on my card."

"Thanks. Enjoy your lunch."

He watched her walk away. Her hips swayed with the music that was playing. Her hair was bouncing as she walked. She had to be his age or close to it. Too pretty to be going through a divorce. He sure didn't want that for his life. He'd seen so many of his friends from high school going through a divorce and knew how destructive it could be. She sat down and ordered her lunch and looked his way several times. He pretended not to notice. He was thankful for his cell phone because it was a good screen to hide behind. His mind was racing, trying to figure out why he was so attracted to women in general and especially Gail Bailey. He didn't know anything about her except that she was a lawyer. Big stinking deal. He looked around the room and wondered if other men were fighting the temptations that he was. He was still single. It was okay for him to look. But every time he saw another woman he thought was pretty, Jane's face came into his mind. He didn't want to hurt her. But he wasn't ready to marry her, either.

He gobbled down his sandwich and soup and paid the waitress. As soon as she made change for a tip, he got up and walked out of the cafe, only nodding at Gail as he closed the door. The sooner he got back to work, the better. He shouldn't be allowed to go out alone. It was ridiculous. He laughed as he climbed into his car and drove the mile and a half back to the office. The grass always looked greener because you were looking at it from farther away. Jane was close up and real. He knew all about her. The ups and downs. Gail was just another pretty girl. Well, sort of.

CHAPTER EIGHT

Sharon Sinclair was a very active woman, involved in the community and darn good at tennis. She loved her family, enjoyed cooking great meals, and loved her husband. She had been raised a Baptist and her beliefs strongly influenced her decisions in life. Her faith was important to her.

Bill, not so much. He believed in God but had not gone any further in his search for answers about the spiritual side of life. He was happy going on occasion to the North Hill Presbyterian Church, which was a compromise they had both made when they got married. Baptist and Episcopalian. So the Presbyterian belief was sort of in the middle.

Sharon put her children first while they were young. But now that Emily was the only one left at home and was about to be married, she wanted to stretch her wings and develop herself even more. As soon as Emily left the house for good, she wanted to redecorate all the bedrooms and change a few things in the hearth room. It was a large home and they'd certainly lived in the house.

Really lived in it. So now was her chance to freshen things up, give it a new look. A new feel.

Her position with the Montgomery House, a charity for abused women and unwed mothers, was one of counseling. Even though she was not formally trained, the girls seemed to gravitate towards her. And she was full of information that she could share with them to give them the tools they needed to move forward in their lives. Her warm demeanor drew them in and they immediately found that they trusted her with all of their secrets.

She worked three days a week at the House and played tennis during season on Saturdays. But she was always home to cook a good meal for Bill, her first love. They'd been married a long time now, but she loved him the same. Even more. She was proud of him for working his way up the proverbial ladder in spite of the compromises they had had to make. Now he had a chance to be a partner in a firm and she wanted him to take it.

He was coming in the door just as she came in from the back-yard and was washing her hands after pulling some stubborn weeds. "In here, Honey." She wiped beads of sweat from her brow.

Bill walked into the kitchen, taking a seat at the table. He stretched is long legs out and yawned.

"Been a long day for me. How about you?"

"I've been pretty busy today. The women were pretty needy to-day. But that's not unusual with that bunch."

"No. I can understand that. After all these years, you'd think it would get easier, but I know it doesn't. You get a new set of women in there every six or eight months and it starts all over again."

"Not to change the subject, but we need to talk about this part-nership offer. You up to that?"

Sharon pulled out a chair and sat down, blowing out a huge breath of air. "You have my full attention."

Bill raised an eyebrow. "Seriously, we can wait until later, after we've had dinner. I know you are tired, too."

"I always have time for you, Dear. Now what exactly is on the table?"

"It's pretty simple for now. They've offered me a seat at the partner table. That would make four partners. I'm not sure if there is room on the door for another name."

She laughed. "It's an honor. But you've put your time in. I know there are others who have been there longer than you, but not by much. I'm not surprised, Honey. As much time as you spend even after hours working for clients. You need to be rewarded somehow for that."

Bill shrugged. "Comes with the job, Honey. But I am excited about this. It sort of ties me down more. Gives me more responsibility because then I would care about how much the firm was making each year, instead of just how much I was making."

"Yes. The focus would be on the whole, not the one."

"Exactly."

"What are the benefits of being partner? Just a cut of the profit at the end of the year?"

"Well, I would be in on all of the decisions, also. The partners meet any time we are asked to take on another large corporation's financials. It's a ton of work but it brings in the most income. Guaranteed income."

"Would your pay go up?"

"Yes. I believe it would."

"What is the downside? Anything?"

"Not really. I am pretty private, though. I don't like to have to talk about what I'm doing all the time. They've pretty much allowed me to come and go as I please. I don't like having eyes on me, and I don't like anyone owning me."

"You haven't squirmed too much about being married. That's pretty confining."

It was his turn to laugh. "Little too late to bring that up, isn't it?"

"I guess so. Well, Bill, what do you want to do?"

"I guess I'll take it. But I sure hate to give up my freedom."

"How will that change?"

"I'm not sure. But it makes me leery."

"I think you're big enough to handle it. Just don't allow them to own you. But think about this. You will know everything they're doing, too. You need to look at the books and see if they are sound enough for you to join them. Hopefully they just have one set of books."

"Oh, that's brilliant. Not."

"Just joking."

"So it's settled. I'll take the partnership offer, after checking out the books. We're good with that, right? I shouldn't have to work anymore than I am working now. I doubt you will even notice a change."

"Sometimes I don't like you having to be at someone's beck and call at all hours of the day or night. I do get tired of you being called out right in the middle of dinner."

"You've never said a word."

"That's because I'm generous with you."

"And now?"

"I'm just saying I'm getting tired of that."

"I've told you that I have no choice. It comes with the job."

"I know. Your clients are first. Over everything. Unless I die, I guess."

"Yes, I'll put your funeral first, of course!" He laughed and grabbed her arm.

"I know you are joking. But I'm sorta serious. We're about to be empty nesters. This would be our time to go places, do things we haven't done. And that doesn't seem to happen. Is that because you may get a call?"

Beads of sweat broke out on his forehead. She noticed.

"No. We've been pretty busy for the last few years with the kids. With our jobs. Your charity. Not much time to just take off into the wild blue. I want to do some of that, too. And I'm sure we will once Emily is gone. I'll try to handle the calls better. But I really feel I don't have much of a choice."

"I don't know why you can't tell them you are busy. That you will meet them later."

"It doesn't work that way. And hey, you didn't say a word until now. It couldn't have been that bad or you would have said something before now."

"I give you room, Bill."

"Yes, you do. And I appreciate it."

"But there is a line. And you are fast approaching it with these late night calls."

"Let's focus on the partnership for the time being. Maybe the calls will be few and far between. I mean, I don't get them that often even now."

"Okay. Enough for now. I'll start dinner; we both are getting hungry. You relax and I'll have dinner made shortly."

"Thanks, sweetie. What would I do without you?"

She smiled weakly. "I hope you never have to find out."

Bill went into his office and sat down, taking a deep breath. Things got a little sticky during that conversation and he felt the heat. He leaned his head back against the leather chair and closed his eyes. He was sick of having to jump when they called him. He had no idea who was in charge and he felt so alone in it. No one debriefed him after asking him to take someone out. Kill them, to put it bluntly. Or the torture. It was horrendous. They knew he was trained and prepared, and that was all that mattered. He was well aware that if he made a mistake, a bad one, they would probably take him down. Or . . . he wasn't sure what they would do. He hoped he never found out.

Just as he was about to doze off, his other cell went off in his pocket. He jerked and hit his knee on the desk. A pain shot down through his shin.

He answered the phone and immediately noticed the voice on the other end had changed. It wasn't the same voice.

"You alone?"

"I am." He'd been told to always answer briefly. To the point.

"Things are changing in Washington. Security is getting tighter. You have to make sure you are aware of your surroundings at all times. Do not lose your cover. Leave nothing behind linked to you. It is imperative that you do this. We fear there is a weak link, and I don't want it to be you."

"I understand. Nothing gets by me."

"I am counting on it. The White House is counting on it."

"Is that all, Sir?"

"That is all. Need I reiterate that there is no room for error?"

"You've made that perfectly clear."

"I'll be calling you soon. Be ready."

"I have no choice, Sir."

"You have a problem with that?"

"Would it make a difference if I did?"

"I don't like your attitude."

"I will get the job done. I always do."

"See to it that that doesn't change."

"That is why you chose me, right?"

"We've talked too long. Just be ready."

The phone went dead on the other end. Bill hung up and shook his head. He was getting angry because he felt helpless. He had absolutely no control over any part of this. He was at their mercy. And the bad part was not knowing how long it would last.

How long they would ask this of him. He somehow didn't feel like he was serving his country like he did in Afghanistan. This might be equally important but it felt like murder. Just plain murder.

Sharon stuck her head in the door. "Dinner is ready, Honey."

Bill sat up straight and forced a smile. "Sure, Dear, I'll be right there."

She turned to walk away and he wiped his face again. He just had to be extra careful and make sure she never found out what he was doing. It would not only scare her, but it would kill her to know what was taking place. What they were asking him to do. It would go against everything she stood for. It was hard enough on him, although he was trained to do it. But he never knew the reason why. Or he only knew partially. When he had to interrogate people, he knew some but not all. He knew just enough to get information out of them that was needed. But the murders, the taking people out, was all on the blind. He was working blind.

He sat down at the table and picked up a fork. His hand was shaking. He knew Sharon saw it but didn't say a word. He was thankful. For he hated lying to her. He had secrets that he could not share. Odd that a stranger could open up their guts to her and he had to do just the opposite. He couldn't ever tell her what was going on. The secrets would go to his grave with him. And that thought, that truth, took his appetite away. It was all he could do to eat what she had so graciously prepared.

CHAPTER NINE

October was known for its sunsets. And this night was certainly a postcard evening. The sun had set but there was a pink light shoving itself up against the horizon. It put a glow across the lower part of the sky. Certainly was a plus for a romantic evening. Jesse pulled up into the parking lot of the apartments and got out of his car. His legs were a little weak but he was excited. He knocked on her door and waited, hoping she was half as excited as he was. Maryanne opened the door and Jesse stood there staring at her. It was a casual date, and she was wearing blue jeans with a lacy white blouse. Her hair was down and she had on gold earrings. Since he wasn't talking, she spoke up.

"Hey, Jesse. Seems weird not to call you Dr. Sinclair."

He paused, swallowing a football down his throat. "I hope you get used to it. I like it."

"Want to come in?"

"I made reservations, so we probably need to get going."

"Well, come in for a minute and let me get my purse. I want you to see the view I have."

He walked into the living room and stood there looking out huge windows at the skyline of Washington. "I had no idea you had this view. It's magnificent."

"Some days I don't want to leave home. And at night it's breathtaking. When you've had a tough day, this is better than any prescription drug."

He walked up next to her and stood for a moment. "I hate to ruin the moment, but we really need to go. This place I am taking you is a packed house every night. They frown on late arrivals."

"I'm ready. Let's go."

He walked her to the car and she slid in, not without his noticing her legs. The air was chilly and they both had jackets, but he still put a low heat on in the car.

It was silent for a moment and then they both started talking at once.

"I couldn't believe you said—"

"Uh, sorry I was so late in responding last night."

They laughed and the tension slipped out the cracked window on Jesse's side of the car. It was an old habit from his smoking days.

"No problem. I was worried there for a while, but when I got your text, it made my night."

She laughed easily. "I'm so glad I decided to come. I would have always wondered what tonight would have been like."

He reached over and squeezed her hand. "Nothing to worry about. We're just going to have a good time. I think you'll like this place, if you haven't already been. It's Graham's Fish House, on the west side of town. Closer to where I live. They have a great jazz band there tonight. You like jazz?"

"I like all types of music. All genres. It sounds great."

Jesse found a parking spot and pulled in, nearly clipping the car behind him as he pulled up to the curb. He could tell it was getting crowded by the number of cars in the lot. He took her arm and they walked into the dimly lit restaurant, and the maître d' seated them at one of the tables for two near the windows. There were only a few tables sitting empty, and he was silently glad he'd called to make a reservation when he did.

"Isn't this nice, Maryanne? Looks like the band is setting up now."

She looked around and nodded. "It's cool. I really like the atmosphere in here. I can't wait to hear the band. I hate to share this, for fear of sounding dorky, but I used to sing in a band when I was in my early twenties."

He looked surprised. "Are you serious? What kind of band?"

"It was country/western. But I listened to all kinds of music growing up."

Before Jesse could comment, the waiter came to the table dressed in black jeans and a crisp white shirt. "May I take your order for drinks, sir?"

"Yes. Maryanne, would you care for a glass of wine?"

"That would be great."

"We'll have a glass of merlot then, thank you."

He looked at her and cocked his head. "So, let's hear about your music days. Were you guys any good? Did you play in bars or what?"

"We played in a small lounge called 'The Waterhole' in Memphis, Tennessee. Nothing special, but I always loved the people who were in the audience. Kind of a laid back group."

"Sounds like fun. Wish I'd known you then."

Maryanne blushed. "We were okay. Good enough to pull our own weight, but no record labels were after us. Not even close. We were known for our tight harmony and could get a job anywhere. But we all were in college and our dreams were scattered. We were not focused enough to work hard and push to become famous. But we did enjoy the popularity we had in the small pub circuit."

"I would never have guessed that in a million years. Well, I will share something with you. I played saxophone in my younger years. So I sometimes sat in with a band when they needed a different sound. It didn't always work out because I had to study. It seemed like I was in school most of my youth."

"I have heard that from other dentists that were friends of mine."

They ordered their meals and sat listening to the band that had kicked into full swing while they were talking. Jesse reached over the squeezed her hand but did not hold it long. He didn't want to push things too fast. But she was so pretty. He really was enjoying her company. The food came quickly and as he took a bite, he glanced up at her. She was staring at him, smiling.

"What?"

"I was just watching you attack your food. You were hungry!"

"Yes, I am. I hope you're enjoying your dinner. It's very good."

"I really love this restaurant. I'm so glad you chose this one for our first date."

"First date? Does that mean there are more to be had?"

She laughed and he nearly choked on his food. Her teeth were so white, and she had a way of throwing her head back when she laughed. He loved it. But tonight he pretty much loved everything she did. It was sickening, but he was smitten.

"It may mean that. Some things are nice to leave unsaid. Don't you enjoy surprises?"

"This whole night is a surprise to me. I am so glad we are giving us a chance."

"I'm kinda sad about losing my dentist!"

Jesse laughed and raised an eyebrow. He reached over and touched her hand for a moment. "I'm thankful for tonight. That's all I want to say for now."

"Talk to me about your family. I want to hear all about your life."

"I have a big family. Five of us kids. My father is a CPA and mother stays home but is involved in charity work big time. We were a close-knit family that had great dinner time discussions each night. We battled things out over our dinner plates. It was fun and engaging. Sometimes it could get tense, but most of the time we ended up laughing. I have no big complaints about my childhood. Dad was there most of the time. However, now he seems to be busier than ever with his work. Taking on large corporations. I am proud of him, though. He has taught me much about good work ethic. Going beyond what is expected."

"I like the sound of that. You must have had to work hard to become a dentist. I know those courses are tough. I feel I could have done more with my life so far, but we both have a long time ahead of us to really become."

Jesse was surprised at how open she was being with him. It was refreshing. "My life wasn't perfect. I mean, I got in my share of trouble with the parents, skipping school a time or two, and staying out too late with the guys. Normal stuff that teenagers do. It was fun having twins in the family, Emily and Paul. They were funny to watch and had a great connection that the rest of us didn't share. But now they have moved on to develop their own lives. I am sure that connection is still there, but we just don't hear about it anymore."

"I've always wanted to be a twin. It is very interesting how connected they are subliminally."

"My mom is the greatest. You could not pull anything off without her knowing about it. She has the 'eyes in the back of her head' thing going on big time. My dad has even said he could not hide anything from her. I am not sure where she gets that, maybe a deep caring heart. But she is something else."

"I am happy for you, Jesse. You have some good grounding in your life. I didn't have that so much."

"I want to hear about you."

Maryanne sighed. She might as well say it now, instead of him finding out all about it later. "My family was wealthy. Very. So that explains my rich taste. But we were not close like your family. I have one brother who is an attorney. He is brilliant but was a rebel while we were young. Always pushing the envelope.

"My father was into diamonds. He made millions. I frankly think he was Mafia. It feels like it, anyway. Always a dark side. The secret phone calls. The black limousines and black suits. Hair slicked back like a gangster. Ugh! I hated it growing up. It was embarrassing. He talked like a gangster. I don't know what Mom saw in him, except that he could turn a penny into a million in one day. She liked nice things. She liked being wined and dined.

"I am just the opposite in some ways. I do love my apartment and lovely furniture and surroundings. But I hate people who are fake. And they surrounded themselves with that false society all my life. What was abnormal became the norm, if you can relate to that. I heard things as a child and didn't understand. I love my father and never dreamed he was doing anything wrong. Like killing people. But it seemed at that time that he was involved in some pretty shady dealings. He never went to prison, but I am certain his team of lawyers allowed him to escape several times when other men would have been sentenced for life."

"That's pretty heavy, Maryanne. You didn't have to share that with me if you didn't want to. All families have skeletons in their closets. I'm sure ours does, too."

"I bet your dad never killed anyone."

"Well, he was a Navy SEAL, so he may have put some people down in his lifetime. But I know we probably have some pretty scary ancestors. You never know what's in the closet until you open up the door. I have never dug into our past like that."

"True. Some doors are better left unopened."

Jesse asked for the bill and pulled out his wallet. He smiled at her and picked up his wine glass.

"Here's to a wonderful evening with you. Our first date."

Maryanne raised her glass and touched his and smiled. "Yes, our first of many. I have much more to share with you. And I believe you do, also. We've just begun this journey and I am looking forward to finding out where it goes."

Jesse was surprised but tried not to show it on his face. She was much easier to talk to than he'd dreaded. Or maybe he was relaxed around her and that brought it out in her. Either way, it was working.

"Let's go. I'm ready for a little alone time with you before I take you home."

"Sounds good to me. It's a lovely night out. Rather warm but I do feel the nights are getting cooler. It's nice out there now."

There was a huge moon in the sky and she was doing her thing, shining across the small lake where Jesse had parked the car. "This is the place I come when I want to wind down. It's quiet and usually no one else is around. You like?"

She grinned shyly. "I feel like you are going to give me my first kiss. Like high school."

He reached over and pulled her face towards his. "I am going to kiss you. It is our first kiss."

She sank into him and he kissed her fully on the mouth. He didn't want to stop. But he knew less was more on the first date. So he backed away and stared into her eyes.

"I am so glad we had this time tonight. I really did want to get to know you better. And I like what I have seen. You are so beautiful."

She glanced down at her hands. And his. She reached over and wrapped her fingers around his and looked into his eyes. "I trust you, Jesse. I already had begun to trust you as a dentist. But now I am getting to know you as a man. And I, too, like what I see."

He reached over and turned on the radio to an '80s station and they sat back holding hands and listened to the music, singing to some of the songs. The moonlight was shimmering across the still water, the frogs were croaking loudly, and off in the distance a dog was barking. But inside the car, Jesse was unaware of the passing of time or anything else, for that matter. It was the first time in a long time that he'd felt happy, really happy. And he wasn't going to let anything ruin the moment. He grabbed her hand and smiled, and he slipped into the pools of her eyes for what seemed like a lifetime. And if he were honest, he really didn't want to find his way back home.

CHAPTER TEN

The air was dry and there was a slight breeze swaying the great oaks in the backyard. A wedding was taking place at 4:00, and everyone was busy preparing for the crowd. There was a large white tent set up for the dinner, and flowers were everywhere. The tables were being set with fine white linen tablecloths and fine china, and there was a small section of the yard set off by posts and roping for the quartet that was going to play during and after the wedding. Of course, all weddings start out small in the planning, and this one was no different. But Sharon held the reins and put a limit on the wedding party. A hundred people would fill the yard and house, but that was enough for Emily and Rob to feel they'd invited the most important people in their lives.

The day had finally come, and Emily was so excited. Worried about her hair and writing her vows. She'd waited too long, and now she was in a panic to get it right. Rob, on the other hand, had written his weeks ago. He was home, keeping himself out of the way, and honoring the rule that he could not see her until the ceremony. But cell phones made it easy for them to communicate constantly.

"Mother, you have to help me with these vows. I am clueless. I don't want to sound corny."

Sharon raised an eyebrow and walked over to the sofa where Emily was piled up on the pillows with a pad of paper and a pen. "Honey, just relax. Don't make this so difficult. Just say what is in your heart."

"I don't want a bunch of rules. I just want us to love each other unconditionally. To create a safe room where there are no doors or windows, so that we can know that we are committed for life and that we have to work things out, no matter what."

"That sounds good to me. Good luck with that theory. I think you should say that if that is what you want your marriage to be."

"You don't think it's possible to have that room?"

"I have never seen it before."

"That is how you and Dad are, isn't it?

"I don't think we have ever spoken of a room." Sharon grinned.

"Well, you have lived together for a long time. How did you do it?"

"Stubbornness, I guess. And the fact that I didn't want another woman to end up with your father"

"I guess I can see that."

"It's harder than you think. Things come up that hurt you. Or you do the hurting."

"I guess I need to just write how I feel. That is what he is doing. We really don't have to say anything except "I do."

Sharon smiled. "That's about it. It is your special day. Enjoy it, Emily. You've waited a long time for this marriage. It's really just up to you and Rob to make it work. Somehow.

"We will, Mom. I know we will. Thanks."

Sharon walked out of the living room shaking her head. Young people always thought there was another way. A special thing you could do. But what marriage took was stamina. Determination.

And love. But even that seemed to come and go during a marriage. Or the feelings of love. She still had plenty of questions for Bill that she would never get answers for. The late night calls. The tiny blood spots on his shirt. The cut on his cheek. She had avoided asking because maybe she really didn't want to know the answer.

Bill came rushing in the house, sweating and talking loudly. "Sharon, the cake is here. Where do you want it?"

"What? They were supposed to bring it later in the day. I guess they will have to bring it in here. We can't leave it outside in the heat of the day. That means you and I will have to carry it outside around 3:30. I guess we'll have plenty of help by then."

Bill nodded and ran back outside. She opened the door and waited for the baker to bring the cake through the door. It was huge and he looked like he was straining. He had brought a helper with him but it was a very large three-tier cake. Beautiful. They'd done a great job.

"Emily! Your cake has arrived too early. We've put it in the kitchen until this afternoon because of the heat outside. So stay out of the kitchen."

"Yes, Mother. I've written my vows, so I am going to the salon to get my hair done. I have my phone with me if you need anything."

"Okay, Honey. Have fun."

Bill stuck his head back in the door. "The cake look okay?"

"Yes, it looks lovely. Bill, come here a moment. I need to talk to you."

"I'm pretty busy outside, Sharon."

"I know. But I have something I need to talk to you about. It won't take but just a second.""

Bill walked in and sat down at the bar. "Okay, I'm all ears. But let's make this quick."

Sharon felt nervous but wasn't sure why. "Well, last night I found a tiny speck of blood on your shirt collar again. What was that from?"

"I don't know, Honey. I could have nicked myself shaving or something. Are you sure it was blood?"

"Well, no. I assumed it was, because it was red. I guess it could have been ketchup."

"I have no reason to think it was blood, Honey. But next time, point it out when you see it, so I can see what you are talking about. Otherwise, I won't know what I ate or what may have happened."

"It's nothing to worry about. I was just curious, is all."

"No problem. I think things are coming together outside. Emily is going to be pleased."

Sharon stared into his eyes. He never seemed flustered about anything much. Even when she questioned him. He was always cool, calm and collected. It was almost irritating. "I'm sure she will be happy. We have really pulled this off with less trouble than I had expected. But one hundred people coming into our house and yard are going to be tough to handle. It's hard to think of everything, Bill."

"You'll do just fine."

"It's good to know you are in there right in the middle of things."

"It's our last child leaving home. A major time for us. We'll be empty nesters now."

"I'm looking forward to it. At least I think I am."

"Well, now it's time for you to develop yourself to the fullest. I know I am busy enough in my job, and with this offer to be partner, I will even have more responsibility."

"We'll work through these things, Bill. It's just a change. A simple life change."

Bill walked outside, wiping the sweat from his forehead. This was not good. Sharon had noticed another speck of blood on him. He could not let that happen again. It would be hard to explain more than once. She would not buy the reason he could come up with. This was crucial to his job. His agreement with whomever it was on the end of that phone. Thank heavens it had not rung lately and he'd had a reprieve from the horrors of that job. He hated it, but he was good at it. Made no sense at all. But in order to not get caught or killed, he had to keep it from his wife. His precious love. The one person he could trust in all the world and he had to lie to her. He tried to tell himself that he was fine with it, because he had to be. The White House didn't care what it took. They just wanted total silence, invisibility. He knew how to achieve that, but somehow he had slipped some because of the blood showing up on his collar. He reprimanded himself and headed towards some workman who was constructing the gazebo where his daughter would stand with Rob to say their vows. He had about fifty things on his mind, and he needed to shake all but one. This was the last time his daughter would be at home. She was about to fly. And he didn't want to miss one single moment of it.

CHAPTER ELEVEN

"Emily"

The proverbial "day of the wedding" nerves were setting in. I was sitting on my bed. My hair was done and I was waiting to do my makeup until the last minute. I leaned against the back of the bed, thinking of all the years in the house I'd called home. All the family dinners and laughter. The sharing that took place across plates of food, and the looks I'd seen passed between my parents. They were all loved. I'd had a good life, and I was thankful. But now it was my turn to step out and fly, and I was nervous as a cat about leaving home. It was time and I was ready.

I loved Rob more than anything. But it was a big step in my book, making this relationship permanent. It was what I wanted deep down, but Rob was the one pushing it to happen now. He was ready for me to move in with him and be his wife. I kind of liked being my own woman. He wanted input on what I did, where I went. He could be a bit controlling dressed in shy clothes. Sometimes the quiet one was the strongest.

Susan came through her door talking loudly, a grin on her face. I simply shrugged. So much for private time.

"Hey, Sis. How you doing in here by yourself?"

"Just thinking things through, is all."

"What's there to think about? You're marrying the love of your life."

"It's not all about the love of your life thing, you know."

"I realize that. But you are happy, aren't you?"

I frowned. For some reason I was feeling irritated. "I'm fine. Did you need anything?"

"Come on, Emily. This is your special day. Mom has worked her butt off trying to make this special for you. What's with the attitude?"

"I've just got some things on my mind. You wouldn't understand."

"Try me."

"Oh for heaven's sake. I just needed time alone to sort through things. I am feeling pushed all of a sudden. Like the time has narrowed down to two hours and I am feeling rushed."

"Do you need help? What is bothering you?"

"You cannot help me with this; no one can. I have to work it out on my own. I am certain all brides go through this on their wedding day. I'm no different."

"What in the world are you talking about, Honey? This is your wedding day. You and Rob have been dating for a century. Or it sure seems like it. So what could be a surprise?"

"Nothing is a surprise. But I am concerned about how he is. Controlling. Nosy. A bit possessive. It has not been an issue really, but now that I am going to be living under his roof, it may be. I was just trying to sort it all out."

"He doesn't abuse you, does he? I'll kill him if he does."

"Nothing like that, at all. But he does like to know all the details of what I'm doing, where I'm going, what I'm thinking. I'm not sure if it is concern or insecurity."

"You're a pretty independent woman. I am sure he knows that by now. So what's the problem?"

"That's just some of what's bothering me. I don't want to be under his thumb. And I like to make some decisions independent of him. What about when I have children? Is he going to dictate everything? The name of the child or if I breast feed? I mean, we need to talk about all of this. And it's too late today to bring it up."

"What the heck have you guys been talking about all these years? You've had plenty of time to discuss all the details of marriage and a relationship. Surely you've done this."

"Oh, some of it, yes. But I haven't really confronted him about how controlling he is. I need to go talk to him now. We need to at least have touched on it so it won't ruin our marriage."

"I would think you would have already had a few arguments on this subject by now."

"We've had a couple. But I didn't make a big issue of it because I wasn't under his roof. Tied to him, so to speak. I could come and go and do my own thing. Now that won't be possible."

"Call him up. See what he says. You really should not see each other before the wedding. That is a rule. I don't know who made up that stupid rule, like most rules. But it is so."

"It's a retarded rule. I am sure there was a reason that seemed validated at the time, but things have changed over the centuries. No telling what things were like for women back then."

"We've come a long way. But apparently not far enough." Susan laughed out loud.

"It's not funny. Just you wait. You're not even dating right now."

"Exactly. I am taking some time off to clear my head so I won't make the same mistake I did with Frank. He was a real ass. But at least I didn't marry him. I would be miserable now. No, I take that back. I would be divorced or dead."

I couldn't help but smile about the drama. "You are a piece of work. Leave so I can call Rob. I need to talk about this to him before we face each other at the altar, so to speak."

Susan got up and walked to the door. "Don't hold back. But don't ruin your day, either. Unless you are not in love with Rob. If that's the case, then I get the top layer of your cake."

"Get out."

"I'm going."

"Rob? It's me."

"What's up, Honey?"

"I'm getting nervous."

"Well I have issues with my stomach, too. But it's coming down to the hour, so we need to get our heads on straight. Pretty soon we will be saying our vows."

"I wanted to talk to you about something that has been on my mind. You got a few minutes to chat?"

"I got a lifetime to talk, but is this the time to do it?"

"I think this needs to be said."

"Shoot."

"I feel you are very controlling, Rob. I worry how that will make me feel when we marry."

"You are bringing that up now? The day we get married?"

"You sound like Susan."

"Well, she and I agree on something then."

"I just worry that you are not going to like my independence once we're married. You like to know every single thing I'm doing, and when and where and how much money. It drives me nuts. I am a strong-willed person. I don't like being under your thumb."

"I have no desire to keep you there. But because we are not married and living together, I have had to ask more questions. We can work this out, baby. I love your strength. You are going to be a handful to live with, but I am used to it now. I think I can go with the flow pretty well."

"So if I tell you to stop controlling me, you will listen?"

"I will try to be flexible."

"The word *try* is pretty large here."

"I mean that. I will try. What else can I say?"

"I just want to be sure we understand each other. I love you and want to be your wife. But this thing about *obey* bugs me. I see us as equals. How do you see it?"

"Honey, where is this coming from? We aren't even saying the word *obey* in our vows, are we?"

"I didn't think so, but I have been worrying all afternoon about it."

"Would you relax? We've dated for a long enough time so that if anything was way out of balance it would have shown up a time or two, don't you agree?"

"Just don't try to control me. Love me, be involved, but do not try to hold me down or control me."

"I get it. Now get your makeup on, and your lovely dress, and let's say 'I do' and get the heck out of Dodge. I am ready to start our honeymoon."

"Where are we going? You never said."

"It's a surprise."

"We aren't going to Biafra on a mission trip, are we?"

"No, Dear."

"Not building a house for Habitat?"

"Nope. Not even close."

"Okay. I'll relax and try to enjoy our day."

"Call me if you need another pep talk."

"Do you love me, Rob?"

"I wouldn't be marrying you if I didn't, Emily."

"This is a forever kind of thing we are doing. You can't just quit, you know."

"And the reason for this statement is?"

"I want us to have a safe room. Where there were no windows or doors to get out. So that means that we have to work things out. There is no choice."

"Hmmm. That sounds claustrophobic."

"Rob! I thought it was beautiful."

"Well, I'll consider it. But don't put me in a room with no doors or windows. It might as well be an insane asylum."

"It's a metaphor. Not an actual room."

"We are wasting such precious time here, Emily."

"What? My makeup and dress will take fifteen minutes. This is the rest of our life that we are talking about."

"I think we will be on the road long enough to cover just about any fear you have for the next fifty years."

"I didn't mention you are sarcastic, did I?"

"No, I don't believe you did."

"I'll see you soon. I know this is our wedding day. But the marriage will take work. Good old fashioned work and flexibility. Are you ready for that?"

"I was, until you called."

"Bye, Dear. See you shortly."

I smiled and sat down at the dressing table to put on my makeup. Maybe things were going to be okay. If Mother and Father did it, then we can. Why did it make me so nervous to commit to one man and know that it is forever? I feared I was losing myself.

Just as I was putting on my dress, Mother knocked on the door.

"You need some help with the back of that dress?"

"I think I do."

"Honey, you look lovely. And stop worrying. Everything is going to be all right."

"So you're happy after all these years, Mom?"

"Sure I am. We have our ups and downs, but neither of us is going anywhere."

"That's not what I am asking. Are you happy?"

"Emily, it's not about being happy. It's about loving the person no matter what. Some days you are happy, some days you are not. But in the end, you love each other through all of it. Would I change some things? Yes. But if I cannot change them, then I let go and just live."

"Okay, I'll let it go. Just remember we had this conversation. Down the road, we may need to revisit it."

"You'll be fine. Trust me."

I stood and looked at myself in the mirror. I made a pretty bride. The dress was killer. Everything was perfect; the cake, the tents, the dinner, and all my best friends were outside waiting on me. I turned and looked at Mother and there was a tear running down her face.

"Mom, are you sad?"

"No, Honey. I'm good. Just happy for you. Now go and have your special day. And enjoy every moment of it. Life is going to happen soon enough."

I walked out of the room with that sentence echoing in my brain. Life was going to happen. Maybe that was what I was afraid of. Life.

CHAPTER TWELVE

C louds were forming on the horizon. Rain was not in the forecast, but when did that ever mean anything? The tent looked
lovely with the tables set and the draped white fabric that touched
the ground. It was a perfect setting for a wedding, for two people
to get married in the back yard of the parents of the bride. How
perfect could it get?

Paul stood at the ceremony watching his sister get married.
His twin. He didn't realize it but he missed her terribly. They had
been inseparable when they were kids. Even in high school he
watched over her. But somehow, after he met Avery and got married, they lost touch. Inwardly. Seeing her there in her wedding
dress looking all beautiful and grown up, he found himself feeling saddened by the fact that she was leaving home and wouldn't
be so reachable. Not that he'd tried in the last few years. Oh yeah,
at family dinners they had the usual ribbing going on. The mind
reading. But not like when they were children. He always sat next
to her at the table, and they whispered things to each other and
laughed, making the whole table wonder what that was all about.

It was almost like a secret club that no one else was invited to join. But now, she was getting married. Pledging her love to another just like he'd done a few years ago. It felt like their connection was being torn apart. He wondered if she felt the same way, or if she was just over it.

Avery squeezed his hand. "Honey, where are you? Your sister's getting married and you are off somewhere in your head."

He looked at her with a solemn face. "I am here. Just thinking about my twin."

"You should be happy. Emily has waited so long to marry. I want her to be happy."

"I'm sure they love each other."

"Aren't you happy for her? What's going on in that head of yours?"

"It's all about us being twins. I just realized I miss her. I feel like today I am losing her for good. Hard to describe. We were so close when we were growing up. If you aren't a twin, you just can't get it."

Avery winced. "I understand how close you were, I think."

"You mean well, Honey. I'm not trying to exclude you from anything. But she and I were best buds, and it was internal not external. We were bonded in a way even we didn't understand. When I got married, it didn't seem such a big deal with Emily. She seemed glad for us. But I wonder if she wasn't feeling the same thing I am feeling today. Like I am losing her. I wished we had talked. It's too late now."

"Honey, it's not too late. You can call her after the honeymoon and you guys can have lunch. Talk it over. I am sure she would love that."

"Maybe. But now, this moment, she is pledging her life to another. And I feel shut out. It's stupid. Just don't listen to me. I'm a grown man with a wife and a child-to-be. It's not like I'm unhappy." He squeezed her hand and leaned over and kissed her lightly.

"I realize this has nothing to do with you and me. I could be jealous; I guess the whole family could, with the relationship you guys had. I feel sad that you feel it is gone."

"Thanks, Avery, for trying to understand. Here they come down the aisle. They look happy. Her hair is so thick and pretty. The dress is killer. I bet she said that, too!"

Emily locked eyes with Paul as she walked by and winked at him. He smiled and nodded, reaching out to touch the tips of fingers as she walked past him. For a moment, a brief one, she looked into his eyes and he thought she understood what he was feeling. His eyes watered and he looked down.

And then they were pronounced husband and wife. When he looked back up, she was all the way to the end of the rows of chairs. They were going towards the tent where the food was being laid out. It had just started and it would be over in no time. Weddings were like that.

Bill walked up to Paul with Sharon right behind him. He was grinning from ear to ear. A proud father. "Hey, Son. Doesn't she look beautiful?"

"Yes, Dad. She does. Hope they are happy."

"You don't look too happy."

"Come on, Dad. Just a little sad, is all. I'm fine."

"Let's go eat. Your mother is fighting back the tears. I have to keep her moving or she'll cave on me."

Paul laughed and watched them walk towards the tent. Maybe everyone was struggling.

Susan, Jesse, Jacob, and the two sets of parents came around the table and stood, looking for their names. Emily had decided to have the dinner and then cut the cake. It seemed a smart move, because it looked like everyone was starving. Bill waited until all the wedding party was seated and stood up, to make a toast to his daughter and son-in-law. The talking stopped for a moment as he began to speak.

"I raise my glass this afternoon to toast this wonderful family and group of friends, as my daughter, Emily and her new husband Rob start their new life. We are fortunate to be witnessing the very beginning of their life together, and I want to say a few words before we eat. Emily and Paul were twins, and we all had the joy of watching them grow up in a very unique relationship. It was special because they communicated in ways we did not understand. So Paul was the first boy in her life, and he taught her well. She learned how to do all the things he did, and they were very competitive."

Laughter trickled down the table.

"Now, Paul is married to Avery, and we are watching Emily today with her new husband. Time is moving forward and this will make Sharon and I empty nesters. We are so looking forward to all the grandchildren you all will give us in the future, and we also will enjoy the memories we have of you children through the years we were all together. Let's toast to Rob and Emily and bless their new lives together. Here's to a wonderful marriage and many joyous years ahead."

Everyone raised their glasses and drank, talking loudly and laughing. Emily and Rob stood and clinked their glasses together and kissed. Dinner was served and everyone dug in. Paul glanced towards Emily and she was staring at him. He winked this time, and smiled at her. She nodded and raised an eyebrow. For a moment it seemed like time stood still and they were small again, connected in a secret way.

Then just as suddenly, the spell was broken as a cell phone rang. It was Bill's. He turned red and reached into his pocket and cut the phone off. He knew it was a deadly move. The phone was never supposed to be off. But this was his daughter's wedding and how in the world would he explain that he had to leave. There was no excuse good enough for that. So he took the risk and kept the phone off during the whole dinner and the cutting of the cake.

The photographers were eating cake and taking pictures of the whole family as well as many separate ones of the wedding party. It took about three hours and then the back yard began to empty. Emily and Rob left in their car, full of tin cans tied to the bumper, and "Just Married" written on the back window in shaving cream. The wedding was over, and everyone was talking, laughing, and heading home.

Bill walked into the house and went to the bathroom. He reached into his pocket and turned the phone back on, and it rang immediately. He dreaded answering. The voice on the other end of the phone was very angry.

"So you just decided not to answer the phone?"

"My daughter got married today. I was at the wedding reception when you called. How in the world do you expect me to explain having to leave right in the middle of all that?"

"The deal is that you answer no matter what. You could have told me what was going on."

"Next time I will."

"I got something you need to take care of."

"What's up?"

"The Tower Building. Fifth and Ninth. 7:00 PM."

"Who is it?"

"Dial 7335 and you will get all the info you need. Remember, we need info this time. Nothing else. Make sure you are not seen entering or leaving."

"Always do. I will take care of it."

A dead line.

Bill put the phone back in his hidden pocket in his trousers. His family was coming through the door and he had to tell them he was leaving. He knew Sharon would be upset. It was the wrong time for this to happen and he felt the anger swelling up in him. He no longer owned his life. He belonged to them, whoever they were. He was getting tired of it, but he didn't see a way out just yet.

He was working on it but at this point he pretty much had to do what they asked.

"Did I hear you talking on the phone, Honey?"

"You won't believe this, but I need to leave. Centerfield Inc. wants to discuss something and I really need that account. I won't be long. Will you tell the kids for me? I'll be home as fast as I can."

Sharon shook her head and looked at him. "This seems odd that they would call you this time of night. What is that damn important?"

"People always think what they need is more important than what you are doing. They do not care about my life, Sharon. I am at their beck and call."

"Sure seems that way. Well, hurry back. The kids love visiting with you. And we got some great photos."

"I'll look at them in the morning. Or over dinner tomorrow night with you. I'm sorry, Babe. I'll be home soon as I can."

Bill turned, grabbed his jacket, and walked out the door that led to the garage. He cranked the black Chevy Silverado pickup and pulled out of the driveway before Paul could catch him. His mind was already on what he had to do. He drove through traffic slowly, making sure he didn't get stopped by the police. No one would help him if he did. And he sure didn't want to be late. Timing was everything. He reached the address he was given and parked, dialing the code number.

Instantly a voice came on the line and stated the name: "Fred Ashton. Information concerning who is on board with the agenda he is involved in to stop the President's deal with Iran. Photos are attached. Go to any lengths to get this info. He is gay and does not want this out. And he has a wife and three children. Use what you need to use."

Bill winced and hung up the phone. Everybody had skeletons in their closet. It seemed that the ones who made the most noise politically had the most skeletons. Or the worst. Of course, who in their right mind would want a spotlight shone on their life? No one.

The building was pretty dark except for the lights on the tenth floor. He pulled his mask on and got on the elevator and rode to the seventh floor, got off, took the stairs for three flights and opened the door to the tenth floor. No one was there. It felt empty. He walked slowly down the partially lit hallway and found office 1012. He cracked the door and looked inside. One man was sitting at his desk with his back facing the doorway. He was looking out the window, talking on the phone. Bill tried to listen but had to make his move quickly before his reflection showed up in the windows. He approached the man quickly and pushed down on the button on the phone base and disconnected the call. Fred Ashton looked at the receiver and then turned around. Bill was right on him.

"Keep your hands on top of the desk."

Fred was alarmed. "Who are you? What are you doing in my office?"

"I'm only going to say this once, Fred. Stop your agenda. Do I make myself clear?"

"Who sent you?"

"We know what you are doing, Fred. All of it. You have to stop or you won't like what is going to happen."

"Are you threatening me?"

"Yes, I am."

"You're crazy if you think you can stop me. I have people behind me."

Bill opened his phone and pulled up a photo of Fred with his lover. A man. He showed it to Fred and heard a gasp.

"Who took that photo? How did you get that?"

"What's wrong, Fred? You look white as a sheet. Now you believe me?"

"That cannot get out. It will ruin my life. I have a wife. Children. You can't ruin my life like that."

"Stop the agenda and this will disappear. Is that clear?"

Fred was pacing the floor now, sweating like a hog. Bill could almost see his mind working. His life would be ruined. His job, any political aspirations he had would be flushed down the toilet. His hands were tied. How did they obtain that photo? He was careful. For years he had been careful.

"You got five minutes to tell me who else is involved. Now, Fred."

"I could get killed telling you this."

"You could get killed either way. Now name them."

Fred wrote down two names on a piece of paper and handed them to Bill.

"Is that it?"

Fred nodded, sweating.

"If I hear anything, anything at all, you're gone. You will disappear and this photo and many more will come out in the paper. I wasn't here, Fred. You spoke to no one. But this better be the end of your agenda, or I'll be back. And I won't be near as friendly next time."

Bill stuck the paper in his pocket and walked out the door.

He was gone in a nanosecond and Fred picked up the phone to dial out. There was no dial tone. He grabbed his cell and thought better of it. He didn't know what to do next. He didn't want those photos out. His life would be destroyed. His wife would die if she knew. There was nowhere he could go. They were watching him. So any conversation he had from now on had to be made on a paid cell phone that could not be traced. He was going to have to get smart or drop out altogether. Because he knew one thing—this character who had just visited him meant business. He was not one to be pushed around. The best thing he could do was go purchase a cell phone at Walmart and put minutes on it. And then he needed to go straight home. He would have to contact the other people on the paid cell phone. They would not understand the threat against him personally. But they would understand the death threat. This would be a pivotal moment in his life. He would never sleep soundly again. He realized then that no matter what he did, it better be something that could be seen by the world. For at this point, there were no secrets they could not find out. His life was an open book.

CHAPTER THIRTEEN

Bill walked back to his truck, making sure he wasn't followed. He pulled out of the parking lot and drove around the downtown area to make sure no one was behind him. He dialed the number on his phone and reported the information he'd gotten from Fred. He felt sure he would be making another visit to someone in the next day or two. His mind was racing and his adrenaline was high, almost like a hunter's after he had shot a deer. The only difference was that he was hunting humans. And he was pretty sick of it. The pay was phenomenal. He didn't know how the government could afford paying eleven men what they paid him. He was assuming, of course, that they all got paid the same. Maybe it depended on the level of training they each had gotten, or other factors he couldn't guess at. He had opened up another bank account and the deposits were made electronically. Money never changed hands. He saw no one. He knew no one. It was the strangest thing he'd ever done in his life. And he had no way out just yet. The President had two more years in office. Maybe it would end then.

Of course, he might run for office a second term. So he wasn't sure what was down the road.

Sharon was waiting for him when he got home. It hadn't taken him as long as he feared it would. In fact, Paul was sitting on the sofa with Susan and his mother, when he walked in the door.

"Hey, Dad. How'd it go? You're back earlier than we thought you would be."

"Hey, Son. I'm doing great. It didn't take too long. What you guys doing? Eating again?"

"Heck, no. We are stuffed. But we were sitting here going over old times. I was sharing how much I missed Emily. The connection we had. And now she's on her way to a new life."

"Where's Avery?"

"She is already at home. Wasn't feeling too good, so I sent her home."

"Hope it's not the flu. That's going around."

"No, it's not the flu. So how do you feel Dad, about marrying off one of your daughters?"

"I'm pretty geeked about it, frankly. Proud of her. I am not dead sure about Rob, but I won't go there. I promised your mother I would shut up about it. He's a nice guy, but he'd better treat her right or he'll have to answer to me."

"Whoa. That wasn't what I was expecting. You've been tough on all the guys your daughters have dated. But she married him, Dad. Lighten up."

Sharon rolled her eyes and waved to Bill to sit down by her. It was family night. He relinquished his role as father for a moment and sat down meekly beside her. She leaned over and kissed him, and snuggled into his shoulder. It was going to be nice having the house to themselves. He knew she was looking forward to it. But there were going to be days when the house was just too empty. Neither one of them liked the sound of that. There would have to be more family dinners. More gatherings.

"We've got a game coming up Friday night, Dad. You coming?"

"Wouldn't miss it for the world. How's that quarterback?"

"His arm was bothering him but I think he's gonna pull it off. He's pretty tough."

"I know he handles that football like a bullet. He could thread a needle with it, if you ask me."

"Uh, I don't recall asking. But yes, he's got an arm on him."

Bill laughed. It felt good to laugh. The stress was killing him and he was tired. "Hope you win the championship this year. You have worked so hard, Paul."

Paul's phone rang. "You okay, Honey?"

"I'll be right home."

Paul got up and stretched. "Avery's not doing well. Throwing up. So I'm going to head home and see what she needs. Mom, thanks for a beautiful day. We will remember this day. I miss her already."

Sharon got up and hugged her son. It felt like she was hugging a bear. "It was fun, sad, and thrilling to see her getting married. Making this commitment. We need to help them all we can, because it's tough getting started. They both have good jobs, so it should be fine. Give her a call after the honeymoon, Paul, to see if she needs anything."

"I'll do that. You guys get some rest."

Bill walked Paul to the door and stopped him before he walked out. "There's nothing serious wrong with Avery, is there, Son?"

"No, Dad. She'll be fine."

Their eyes locked. "Is there something you're not telling us, Paul?"

Paul swallowed. "Uh . . . not really. I need to run, Dad. She's feeling pretty rotten."

"Okay. I'll let you go. But I think you're holding out on us."

Paul looked surprised but turned and walked to his car. When he pulled off, Bill shook his head and laughed. She was pregnant. He just knew it.

Susan was sitting with her mother on the sofa talking about her job and the fact that she wasn't dating anyone. "I know you think I am too picky, Mom, but I'm sick of going out and being so disappointed."

"It's going to happen. But eventually you will find someone you really enjoy being around"

"I'm beginning to wonder. It's pretty bad when going home after work and eating supper alone, watching television, sounds better than going out on a date."

"It will pass. But you can't stop looking, Susan. You don't want to live your whole life alone."

"I never thought Emily would marry before me. She's older but I was the one who dated the most. It seems weird that she's married now. Here I am, an old maid."

"Stop that. You are lovely and any man would be lucky to have you."

"Well, I would not be lucky to have any man. I think all the good ones are taken."

"You will find him, Honey. Or he will find you."

"I need to find someone like Dad. Except not so stubborn!"

"Let me know when you do, and I'll marry him."

"Oh, Mother. I need to go. You and Dad are tired, and I need to grade some papers."

"Okay, Honey. Be careful going home. We'll have dinner together soon."

She turned toward the open study door. "Bye, Dad."

Bill didn't answer.

He must be on the phone again, Sharon thought. She got off the sofa and walked Susan to the door.

"See you soon, Honey."

Sharon poked her head into the study. "Bill, you could have said goodbye to your daughter."

Bill put his hand over the phone. "I'll be off in a moment, Honey."

Sharon turned and walked out, leaving the door open, and went into the kitchen to clean up some dishes that were left from the wedding. She was tired, but it was a good tired. She decided to take a long hot shower and walked back to the bedroom. She turned on the water, laid her clothes on the bed, and stepped into the steaming shower, wrapping a small towel around her hair.

⋙⊹ ⊹⋘

Bill was still in his office when the house phone rang again. He ran to get it and was shocked to hear a police officer on the other end. At first, he was worried that he'd been found out, but the officer had something else to tell him.

"Is this Bill Sinclair?"

"Yes, it is."

"This is Officer Parker Jones. I hate to inform you that your daughter, Susan Sinclair, was involved in a terrible accident tonight on Madison and Fifth. Can you come down to the emergency room at Sibley Memorial? We need you to identify her."

"Wait. She was just here. I'm certain it's not her. She was just here with us."

"I'm sorry, Sir. Please come down and we can talk about it."

"How could it be my daughter? She just left the house. Where was the accident?"

"On Madison Avenue."

"That's two blocks from our house."

"Mr. Sinclair, we're pretty certain this is your daughter. You need to come down. I know it's tough, and I hated to have to call you. But it's best if you and your wife come down right away. There's no easy way to do this."

Bill slammed the phone down and screamed. Sharon was just finishing up in the bathroom and heard the terror in his voice. She ran, nearly tripping over the shoes she had left in the doorway of her bedroom.

"Bill? What's wrong? Are you okay?"

"Sharon! Come here! Something horrible has happened. Oh, Sharon. How could it be?"

Sharon rushed to his side and he hugged her tight. "Honey, there's been a terrible accident. Susan has been in an accident. Oh God, how could this happen?"

Sharon pulled away, crying. "What do you mean, Bill? Our Susan? Is she okay? Is she still alive?"

Bill held her close and they sat down in the two leather chairs in front of his desk. Suddenly it was cold in the house. He was freezing. "Honey, Susan is gone. I don't know what happened; must have been a hell of a wreck. But she's gone. They want us to identify her body. We need to go to Sibley Memorial right now."

"I can't breathe, Bill. Wait. You are saying she's gone. Are they sure? It can't be. She was just here. We just saw her."

"I know, baby. I know. I'll get your jacket. We need to leave now."

Sharon started shaking. She stood up and walked into the bedroom and threw on some jeans and a sweater. Bill was waiting at the door with her jacket and they both headed out the door. Bill dialed Paul right away to let him know.

"Paul, there's been a terrible accident. I just got a call from the police. Susan was involved in a car wreck on Madison Avenue and was killed. We are headed to Sibley Memorial right now. Call Jacob and Jesse for me. You might want to meet us there, but leave Avery at home. She will get too upset."

"Dad! What in the world! She's gone? Are they sure?"

"She is gone, Son. Meet us there. We are on our way now."

"Okay, Dad. I'll be right behind you."

The silence in the car was broken only by the sound of Sharon crying. Her sobs were not normal. Nothing was normal. Just the drone of the tires on the road, the blinker clicking when they made the turn into the hospital parking lot, and the pitiful moaning of his wife crying. This might be one of the hardest days of his life, but Bill had to hold up for the rest of the family. He was made of steel. He was used to death. So why were his knees turning to jelly, and his blood running cold? He called Emily and Rob to let them know. This was going to halt their honeymoon.

He opened the door for Sharon and held her arm as they walked into the ER. Nothing after that was reality. Nothing made sense after that. It was the emptiest night he'd ever lived and he just had to make sure they got through it somehow. The one thing that kept gnawing at him as he waded through the horror was that he never said goodbye when she left. Why was it that words left unsaid seemed to haunt you more than saying too much? Or perhaps it would have been impossible either way to have done enough of anything that would have made this nightmare palatable.

CHAPTER FOURTEEN

A chilly wind was blowing and everyone was dodging huge rain drops as they dashed from their cars into the funeral home. It was a small funeral, but many people had already stopped by the house to give their condolences.

As the preacher began his solemn talk about the deceased, the bottom fell out of the sky. Bill sat like a statue in the pew, next to Sharon. He had no words for this day. He could barely sit up straight on the bench, for his body felt broken. All his family was beside him, wiping tears from their eyes. It was the worst day they'd ever experienced as a family and no one could really accept that Susan was really gone. She was gone.

"I don't know if I can sit through this service, Honey."

"Bill, we have to."

"It's ripping my guts out to know she is in that casket. Her life is over."

Sharon took his hand and squeezed it. Susan had been so much like her father. Strong-willed.

"If we can get through this day and maybe tomorrow, things will go forward. They have to, Bill. They absolutely have to. We have other children still alive who will need us in the days ahead."

"I cannot see past today. I really can't. I would have never dreamed we would lose a child. Not us. Not our family. God help us."

"He will, Bill. He will."

Soon it was time for Bill to stand up and talk about his daughter. It felt like an impossible task, but he knew he had to do it. There was no one else that could speak at this point. The whole family was broken, frozen in time. Remembering when they last saw her.

He swallowed a lump that had been forming in his throat. He dared the tears to even think of showing up. The grizzly part of him dug in. And the words came out almost like someone else was saying them.

"This day will go down in history as one of the toughest days my family has ever had. Any family could have. It is our worst nightmare, burying a child or sibling. We all believe we will live forever and we do the things we need to do to make that happen. But some things, some ugly things, are out of our control. We don't live in a perfect world. Things happen to good people. We have all heard of that cliché and it seems to make us sick when we are the ones that are experiencing such tremendous grief. But in fact, it is the truth.

"My daughter stood similar to me on this earth. Both of us being a little stubborn, strong in stature, and opinionated. She was beginning her life as an adult and the thing I hate the most is that we, none of us who loved her, will have the joy of seeing what she would have made of it. I will miss her alongside me. But the rest of my children will stand in her place, as well as my lovely wife. We will hold this family together and make it even stronger for the sake of the one we have lost.

"I didn't tell her goodbye the night she left our house to go home. But I am kind of glad, looking back, that I was preoccupied. For I would not want the last word that I ever got to say to my precious daughter to be goodbye. She knew of our love for her. That, I am sure carried her home to that better place we call heaven. Whatever God has constructed for us when we leave this world, I am certain it is better than what we experience now. And I speak for all of my family in saying that I am counting on the fact that we will see her again. Whole and well, smiling that beautiful smile that would stop a freight train. Thank you for coming today to celebrate her life with us."

There was an applause that he thought would never end. He walked back to his family and they rose and walked out of the church. As the people filed out of the chapel and got into their cars to drive to the cemetery, Bill got his umbrella out and opened it over his head and pulled Sharon close. They got into the black limousine that was carrying the family and led the procession onto the main highway. When they arrived, all of his children were lined up in seats under the tent, beside him and Sharon. Everyone got out of their cars, getting drenched, in spite of their huge black umbrellas that dotted the grounds like gigantic mushrooms. It was uncanny how it rained at almost every funeral. Almost like the earth was weeping for the loss of life. One more person leaving the earth, to spend eternity in heaven. So many people living on earth, you would think no one would notice one person leaving. But Bill kept saying her name over and over to himself. Hoping in a sick way to wake her up. But knowing she would not, even if he screamed it.

When it was over, he and Sharon stood up. He felt dizzy. But he grabbed her and dashed to the limo and watched as his children and wife climbed in and rode the rest of the way back to the funeral home in silence. The blackness of everything overwhelmed him. Even the cars. It was so dreary. So depressing. He watched as everyone left the grounds, shaking their heads and wiping their eyes. He was ready for something different. Maybe a drink. But he knew he would have to go home and spend time with the family, trying to hold them together, and finding in the midst a sense of normalcy for them all to hold on to. It felt lopsided not having Susan around. No one was able to deal with it.

They all got into their own cars and drove back to the house. When Bill got out of the car, he saw Jacob and grabbed his arm.

"Son, you okay? This is tough on all of us."

Jacob frowned and shook his head. "No, Dad. I'm not okay. I'm shaking inside. This hit me blindsided like it did the rest of the family. There was no preparing for this. It just happened and boom, she's gone. It will take me some time to digest that one fact. She isn't coming back. How do you deal with that?"

"No one can, Son. It's tough and we just have to walk through these days until it gets a tiny bit easier. I am choking down so many emotions and so is your mother. It is awful to bury a child. I don't know how to tell you or the rest of the kids how to make it. We will find out one step at a time."

"I know, Dad. I just meant, how does anyone get through death? Sudden death. It's one thing if someone was ill and dies. But she was young. Had not lived that much of her life. It's scary."

"Death is scary, Jacob. I know that too well. Believe me. I have seen many people die. But it is so different when it is in your own family."

Bill walked past Jacob to Emily and Rob. "You two cancelled your honeymoon to be here. I know this is a heck of a way to have to spend time together after your wedding. I am so sorry you have had to deal with this, Emily. We all are sick about it and there is no easy way to walk through these next few months."

Emily laid her head on her father's shoulder. She whispered in his ear. "Dad, how do we go on without her? She was my sister. Yes, we fought, but I loved her. How in the world do we all go on like she was never here?"

He hugged her and pulled away. "Honey, she will remain with us in our thoughts. She will never completely leave this family. But it will be painful always to remember her. I don't think that leaves. I just hate this put such a downer on your beautiful wedding and honeymoon. You can leave tomorrow if you want to. We will all understand."

"I think we will. I need to get away and think. There is nothing here to do, and I think Mom is going to need some time alone to deal with it. I am thankful you will be here with her."

"I'll be here. Don't you worry about anything."

She grasped Sharon's hand as she said, "Mom, I know this has to be difficult for you and Dad. I am so sorry you have to deal with this."

Paul shook his head and put his hand on his mother's knee.

"It's hard for all of us, Paul. But we are a strong family. We'll get through this. I just pray that we all are more careful. I could not stand to lose anyone else. I still cannot believe she is gone."

Emily and Rob stood up. "I think we're going to go home, Mother. If that is okay with you. We both are exhausted and I told Dad earlier that we might leave tomorrow on our honeymoon. We will do no one any good hanging around. And I think it will do us good to get away."

"Of course, Honey. I want you to go. We all will have to deal with this in our own way. But this has come at a time when you need to be happy about your marriage. We all want you to go and enjoy a few days away. It will be good for you, Emily. You and Rob need that."

"Thanks, Mom, for being so understanding."

Sharon and Bill stood up and hugged them, and sat back down on the sofa. Everyone was numb. Paul and Avery stood up to leave, and Jesse and Jacob. It was time for their parents to be alone, so that they could mourn the loss of their daughter. The two brothers walked out arm in arm, talking quietly. Sharon hugged Paul and Avery and they left quietly.

"Honey, I don't even know what to do next. I am frozen inside." Bill sat up on the sofa and reached out to her.

"I feel the same way. This is our worst nightmare. One of our children is gone."

Bill held her and they rocked back and forth and cried until there were no tears left. And then a silence came over them that nearly drove them mad. It was late when they finally gave up and went to bed.

"I'm glad we decided not to allow anyone come to the house after the funeral. I really needed this quiet time to cope with it all." Sharon reached over and put her hand over Bill's.

"Me, too. I don't know how I'll sleep. For some reason I want to stay awake and think about Susan. It makes her feel close. Like she's here with us. But then again, sleep would be an escape from all the horrible sadness I feel. It's choking me."

"I feel the exact same way. Let's try to sleep, Honey. And pray that tomorrow we will not feel this heavy weight on our hearts. But I have a feeling that it will be there for quite some time. We just may grow accustomed to carrying it around."

The clock in the main hallway of the house was ticking loudly. The rain was coming down in a steady pattern, drumming on the roof. Water was gushing out of the gutters. It was a miserable night outside. Chilly and damp. The night just had to pass quickly, giving way to a new day. Something had to give. For it just might be the longest night of their lives. Bill knew only too well, and he couldn't share it with his wife lying beside him, that the silence of death could be deafening.

CHAPTER FIFTEEN

The sound of a football game could be heard from the porch where Sharon was sitting. Bill had dozed off with his feet propped up on the coffee table, a half empty can of beer on the end table, and two chocolate chip cookies were on a plate balanced on his lap. Sharon sat in a rocker outside, wrapped in a wool throw, listening to the wind blowing through the trees. The leaves had turned and she sat staring at all the color, wondering how her life could feel so dull. So empty. Losing Susan had caused her to become a hermit, a prisoner in her own home. She didn't feel like seeing anyone and just didn't have the energy to deal with the comments and sadness on people's faces. It was time to let it go. Susan would not want her to be sitting around depressed. But today, this day, she was allowing herself the pleasure of just being. Not thinking about anything at all.

Her friends had come around her after the funeral, but now, in the throes of November, they were busy with their own lives and families. Sharon was lost in her own thoughts and didn't hear Bill walk out on the porch. She suddenly became aware of being stared at, and jumped.

"I was trying hard not to wake you. You looked so comfortable in there."

"I missed the last half of the game, darn it. Slept right through it."

A smile nearly crossed her lips but slipped away. "You probably needed the rest. You don't get a nap often, Bill."

He nodded and walked up to her slowly and knelt down. "Honey, where are you with Susan's death? Are you still mourning, or what? Tell me where your head is."

Sharon stood up and walked towards the railing on the porch. The wind had kicked up a bit. She was getting chilled. "I don't know where I am, Bill. I think that's the issue here. I feel lost. I know I have all my other children, but for now, I am over focused on not having Susan. I am sorry. I know you are ready for me to snap out of this. I guess I am, too. But I can't get the energy to do it. To let it go."

"I know how you feel. I don't want to stop thinking about her. It keeps her close. But she would be angry if she knew you had dropped out of sight like this. People are asking about you. Calling. Your charity is waiting on you to return. Your life is waiting."

"I'll be back. I just need a little more time. Thanksgiving is around the corner and that is our first holiday that she will not be there. That will be difficult for me, Bill. For this whole family. How do we have celebrations without her?"

"She is in a safe place, Sharon. And we cannot call her back. So we have to keep on living, one day at a time, until it is our turn to go. I don't know another way."

"It sounds so simple. Cut and dried. But my body doesn't want me to go forward. It is fighting me tooth and nail. Maybe I need to see a doctor and get a med for this. I thought I would be farther along in the mourning process. I don't think I have moved an inch since we buried her. I think a part of me died that day, too."

"We both lost something, Honey. Come on, let's go inside. It's getting too cold to be out here. I don't need you to catch cold on top of you being depressed."

Sharon turned towards Bill and leaned into his chest. Suddenly she cried out loud and the tears came again. Bill held her for a few moments and slowly walked her into the living room where he had a small fire going in the fireplace.

"Sit here by the fire in your favorite rocker, and I'll get you some fresh coffee. We're going to get through this, Dear. I promise you that. But you may have to do some things you think you're not ready for, to break this cycle. I am not comfortable with you staying in this house day after day. It's not good for you. You need to be around people."

"That's exactly what I don't want to do. They'll ask how I am. They'll say they are so sorry for my loss. I will have to pretend I am fine."

"No, you don't. You can be honest and say you are still trying to cope with it all. No one expects you to be a martyr. You are human. You've helped so many people get through things. Now it is your time to use the help of your friends and co-workers to help pull you through this."

Sharon looked at her handsome husband and stared into his eyes. "What would I do without you, Bill? What would I do?"

"Well, I don't want to find that out. It would mean you would be looking for another man, and I am not sure I could handle that."

"I don't think I would look."

"Oh, boy. Men would be on you like flies. You look like a million dollars, even now. Depressed as you are."

"I do not. Don't try to butter me up."

"I'm being honest. I see men look at you. 'Stare' is the better choice of words."

"I am not aware of that."

"Baloney. You would have to be blind not to see it."

She chuckled and laid her head against the cushions on the rocker. "I wish I did have men looking at me. I see the women staring at you, like vultures. Waiting on me to die or leave so they can get their claws into you."

"So now I'm the bad guy."

"You are too handsome."

"And that means what?"

"Mother told me not to marry a looker. That other women would be after my husband all the time if he was a looker."

"Your mother told you many things that are not true."

"Probably so."

"I think we both have aged well. That is a plus."

"I feel old today."

"You look old sitting bundled up with that old wool blanket."

"Tact is not your strong suit."

"I think we should change the subject."

"I think I could maybe eat a bite of something. Do we still have some of that soup left that Avery brought us?"

"I gobbled that up earlier today. Let's go out and get a bite. The fresh air would do you good."

"You just said it was too cold."

"Sharon. You are fighting me at every turn. Now get dressed, comb that hair of yours, and let's go get something to eat. I don't care if it's a hamburger."

"Okay. I'll try. But don't expect me to be much company."

"Why is that?"

"I just don't feel like talking."

Bill shook his head. "You could have fooled me."

"What was that?"

"Nothing. Just get ready. We need to get out of this house fast."

Bill walked into his study to get his glasses. His phone buzzed in his pocket. He pulled it out and the voice on the other end gave instructions.

"Wallace Enterprises. A front for a spy operation. At 10:00. You will find a Mr. Jay Stern there. Take him out quickly. On the corner of 7th and Court Avenue. Don't be late. We have surveillance. Swap weapons at the designated place. Any questions?"

"Does it matter?" Bill was keeping an eye out for Sharon.

"Don't be a smart ass. We hired you to do a job. You serve at the pleasure of the President of the United States."

"I'm aware of who I serve. But can I ask why I'm putting this man down?"

"You don't need to know that."

The line went dead. Bill wiped the sweat off his brow as Sharon walked into his office.

"Anything wrong, Bill?"

He turned and pasted a smile on his face. "Not one single thing, Honey. Let's go."

Rosie's Cafe was busy. Bill was relieved in a way. He wanted people around so Sharon could experience being social again in a positive and cheery place. They were seated quickly at a small two-seater booth with red faux leather seats. There was duct tape on Bill's seat. He squeezed his large frame into the seat, smiling at Sharon. She had a look of fear on her face.

"What's wrong, Honey?"

"Nothing. I just don't want to see anyone I know."

"Chances are you won't."

The waiter brought them menus and they ordered burgers and Cokes.

"Feels like a date, doesn't it?"

Sharon nodded but wasn't paying attention.

"I bet Avery's belly is growing now. Do they know what the baby is, yet?"

"I think they find out at the end of the week."

"I am excited for them. New life will bring some freshness to our lives, don't you think?"

"I'm sure it will. A baby cures a lot of ills."

"I'm going to have to tell Jeff McCloud that I am honored to accept that partnership offer this week. I wanted to wait until after the funeral and now weeks have gone by. He left me alone at work, because he knew were going through a difficult time. But I know he is waiting on my answer."

"I think you should do it. It was nice of them to include you, Bill."

"I guess. I just don't want to be tied to them and have to report my every move. I do better if they leave me alone."

"You need to work by yourself. You should have kept your own business; you think?"

"I make more money working for them. I haven't had to worry about overhead or employees. That has been freeing, to say the least."

"Always a price to pay."

"Isn't this nice, Honey?"

"What? Getting out again?"

"Yeah. Something like that." Bill rolled his eyes.

"I get it. Yes, it is nice. Sorry that I am such a downer, Bill."

He reached over and touched her hand. "We're good, Honey. Just want you to smile. To let yourself enjoy being out."

"This is a huge step for me. It feels good in a way, if I am honest. I'm not thinking about myself, or Susan."

"Yes, that is good. Now enjoy that burger and we'll get out of here before the real crowd comes in."

"It's already packed. How could it get worse?"

"Trust me, you don't want to be here when the younger crowd comes in. It's so loud you cannot hear yourself think."

"You know me so well."

"I think I do."

⊷⊶

At 10:00 that evening, Sharon was in her pajamas and dozing on the sofa, halfway listening to the news. Bill checked his watch and leaned over her gently. "Sharon, I'm running out to get some more milk and cigarettes. Be right back."

She nodded and closed her eyes. Bill hurried out the door and closed the door quietly. He changed into dark clothing in the car and took off, not wanting to waste any time. The drive to Seventh Street went smoothly, and he found a parking place near Wallace Enterprises but far enough away as to not be noticed. He looked around him and tried to find the surveillance vehicle but saw nothing. He had made sure that he wasn't followed and he pulled up his mask as he got out of the car. It was dark, and the lights around the building were dim. The door was locked but he used a thin blade to open the door. No alarm was set. He looked around and spotted a light on in an office in the back of the large room. The building was spacious but all one room with dividers. There was what looked like a private office in the back and that was where he thought Mr. Stern would be. He crept along the wall leading to the office, trying to see in the door. When he reached the doorway, he called out the man's name.

"Mr. Stern?"

The man sitting at the desk raised his head and looked at Bill. When he saw the mask he yelled out in anger and fear. "Who are you? What are you doing in my office? There are cameras everywhere. You'll be caught. Now get out!"

Bill raised his arm and aimed his silenced .45. He pulled the trigger and the man shot backwards against the wall and his chair went with him. Bill paused for a second to make sure he was gone, and left the building quickly. He swapped weapons in a can behind the wheel of his car and pulled away without looking around, knowing that whoever had placed the can behind his wheel would immediately pick it up after he was gone. He ran in to the closest gas station and grabbed a gallon of milk and his cigarettes and headed home. He wasn't gone longer than thirty minutes tops.

When he came in the door, Sharon had already moved to the bed and was out cold. He sat down on the sofa and laid his head back. It was a friggin' miracle that she didn't suspect something. He wondered when his luck would run out. He wouldn't mind telling her that he was in the President's Club. But he would not relish the idea of sharing what he had to do to be a member. It was a mess. A sickening mess. And he also wondered how many Presidents had used this Club during their time in office. It surely didn't start with the current President. He wasn't that clever. But he was enjoying the benefits of it, that was for sure.

He got up and went into the bedroom, brushed his teeth, and climbed in between the cold sheets, shivering as his body sought to warm up his space. His wife was breathing deeply, sound asleep. He closed his eyes and was out cold.

He didn't give much thought to the man he had put down— it was just another job—but it was a nightmare in and of itself. For Mr. Stern was lying dead in his office with red blood running down his body and onto the floor. Someone would find him dead in the morning. But no one would ever know who killed him. Well, almost no one.

CHAPTER SIXTEEN

Every once in a blue moon, everything in the universe lines up, two people meet, and it just works out. It goes smoothly. But Jesse was skeptical about it. Hopeful, but scared he was dreaming. Or not seeing things clearly.

He was in his office preparing for the day, which was booked solid. He had a few extractions, a root canal, and plenty of fillings. But he loved his work, the only drawback being that his back and neck hurt at the end of the day. He tried to stretch in between patients, but often, there just wasn't time. His mind was on Maryanne this morning. Beautiful woman that she was. He had to pinch himself because it was just too hard to believe. Nothing in his life had gone this smoothly. Without a hitch. There had to be a catch, he just knew it.

After the first date, it was a whirlwind. He asked her out again, and soon they were seeing each other three or four times a week. It suited him just fine; he loved being around her. But he wondered sometimes if he was smothering her. She never complained, but he just didn't want to move too fast. He had always taken the angle of going slow, rather than rushing things. But this relationship seemed to have a mind of its own.

After several conversations, he discovered she was brilliant. Her looks were the first thing that snagged you, but her intelligence was mind boggling. She knew her stuff when it came to interior design and was developing some very rich clientele. He was proud of her, but didn't feel comfortable hob-knobbing with rich people. She, on the other hand, seemed to love it and showed no signs of feeling intimidated. Maybe it was a man thing, but he hated the empty conversation. The chit chat. The name dropping.

He dialed her number to see how she was feeling, as she had recently come down with a bad cold. The phone rang too long.

"Hello . . ." Her voice trailed off in a raspy whisper.

"Uh-oh. You don't sound too great."

"Thanks. Just what I needed to hear."

"Oh, Honey. Are you really sick? You sound so rough."

"I'm dying here and you are telling jokes."

He smiled. She was dry. Very dry. "I am calling to see if I need to bring you anything. I'm swamped today, but I will make time if I need to bring you some chicken soup from the deli down the street."

"No, I'm fine. I have soup here. But you are sweet to call, Jess."

He loved it when she called him Jess. "Are you sure? I hate you feeling bad."

"You are keeping me up too late at night."

"I am? I thought it was you who loved to sit up and watch late night television. I didn't even know half of those shows existed until I met you."

"This must be the flu, because I am chilled. And I have a very important meeting I need to attend tomorrow. The way things look, I may not be up to that and I could lose the client."

"I'm sure they will understand you are sick."

"They are a very rich couple, used to being wined and dined. They want it now and they want the best. If I can't deliver, then they'll move on to someone else. I have learned that the rich are not loyal to anything. Very fickle."

"And this is who you want to deal with on a day to day basis?"

"I have no choice if I want to make this business profitable."

"How rich do you have to be?"

"Well, I have rent to pay, you know. Car insurance, clothing. I have to have a certain image."

Jesse shook his head. "I'm not used to that, Maryanne. It sounds so false to me. But I totally understand that you have to impress people. I would think that if you do the work and they like it, then that is all that matters."

"For most people that is fine, but these people like to name drop. They want to be associated with only the best in town."

"I have to run. I don't want to wear you out talking. Get some rest and I'll call you later."

"I know you are not into the high society crowd. I'm not really, either. I could live in a log cabin, Jess. But if I'm going to be in the business I am in, I need to at least have a group of wealthy people buying from me so that I can make a good profit. The other people I deal with cannot pay the prices that it takes for me to stay in business."

"I am not fighting you, baby. Rest and get over this thing. I miss kissing you."

"Oh, you are such a male."

"I see that as a good thing."

"Thanks for the call. I feel better just hearing your voice."

"That's more like it. Talk later."

Jesse hung up the phone and smiled. She was a handful. He had to strain to keep up with her sometimes. He didn't know where her energy came from and her drive. She was a very determined woman, and would go at any length to get what she wanted.

He leaned back in his chair, rubbing his chin. This could be an issue down the road, because he was not interested in living that lifestyle. He knew they were going to have this conversation at some point, and it could be the deal breaker. His heart was getting involved; he really liked her. But he was a simple man. He liked a simple life. Maryanne, on the other hand, seemed to shine when she was running with the heavily jeweled women with rich husbands, cars, boats, and three homes. It made his head hurt to think about it.

The odd thing was how easily they had gotten to know each other. She was a lot easier to talk to than he'd imagined. But she had not met his family yet. And he knew Jacob and Paul would give him a difficult time. A hard way to go. They would say he didn't deserve such a beautiful woman. That he just got lucky. They would make fun of him and try to embarrass him in front of her. And his dad would be asking her ninety questions about her family and background, like he worked for the FBI. Only his mother would be happy for him. And she would love Maryanne.

He walked into the room for his first appointment and met Gail Bailey. Funny how things worked.

"Good morning, Mrs. Bailey."

"Hello, Dr. Sinclair."

"I see you are here because you're having issues with one of your teeth on your right upper?"

She pointed to the tooth and frowned.

"I think we need to do a set of X-rays to see what is going on here."

"Are you related to Jacob Sinclair? The insurance salesman?"

Jesse smiled and shook his head. His younger brother had not been too successful with girls for most of his young life. How in the world had he met Gail Bailey?

"Why, yes, I am! He's my younger brother."

"I met him the other day. About some car insurance."

"Hope he was helpful."

"He was very nice."

Jesse decided not to go there. "Laura, let's get those X-rays taken so I can take care of her quickly. We have a full day."

Laura nodded and pulled the X-ray machine near the chair.

It appeared Gail wasn't through talking. "How many siblings do you have? It's odd that I would run into one of them after being here such a short time."

"There were five of us kids, but we just lost our sister, Susan."

"I'm so sorry to hear that, Dr. Sinclair."

He nodded and walked out of the room to check on the patient in the next room. Laura quickly took a full mouth of X-rays and set them up on the computer screen on the desk near the door.

"He'll be right back to check your X-rays. Do you need any water?"

"No, I'm fine. Is he always this serious?"

"Pretty much, when he is working."

Jesse walked back in the room and looked at the X-rays and nodded.

"I see that you have one cavity in the upper right molar."

"Just one?" She sounded relieved.

"Yes. It won't take long to fill this. It's a pretty small cavity. Was it giving you trouble? Pain?"

"I felt a twinge when I drank something cold. Just wanted to catch it before it got worse."

"Glad you came in."

Jesse filled the cavity, keeping quiet while he worked. But he felt her watching him. Staring into his eyes. Usually it didn't bother him at all, but she was very attractive and it made him feel self-conscious since she'd met Jacob. He wondered if Jacob had flirted with her at all. He was pretty serious with Jane. Surely he wouldn't take a risk and mess that up.

"So did Jacob help you with some insurance?" He asked as he cleaned up her mouth and raised her seat up.

She smiled and shook her head yes. "Yes, he got me some decently priced car insurance. He was very helpful."

"Good, I'm glad. Well, you are all fixed up here, so let me know if you have any other issues with your teeth. Glad you came in this morning. Have a great day."

Gail stood up and shook his hand. "It was more than a pleasure to meet you, Dr. Sinclair. Please give Jacob my best."

Jesse nodded and walked out of the room. Women were hard to read sometimes. He was so glad that Maryanne was in his life. Or that little lady whose tooth he had just filled could be some trouble. Big trouble. She was friendly but there was something about her that bugged him. Maybe he was doubtful that she was sincere. It was hard to tell with women. But he would call Jacob when he got off work, just to check his temperature out about Gail. She was cute, and very friendly. Most men would not be able to resist her. He hoped his brother had done just that.

CHAPTER SEVENTEEN

"Emily"

Looking out my window, considering there was no actual glass in the window, my view was breath taking. Never dreamed in my lifetime that I would spend the night in the Bahamas with the man I loved. But this morning I awoke to coffee, breakfast in bed, and the sweetest breeze pushing the white gauzy curtains on all the windows. I felt spoiled. And Rob was lying next to me with a smile like the Cheshire cat in Alice in Wonderland. It felt like Wonderland, actually.

"I have to say you have outdone yourself, Mr. Hamilton. This is more than I expected, knowing what we've just been through lately. I am having to pinch myself."

"Well, you need to feel spoiled. I know losing your sister has been terribly hard on you and your whole family. I cannot imagine how that feels. But I wanted to make you feel special on your honeymoon, and I think this is just the place for that to happen."

I wiped my eyes, because I had not cried near enough over Susan's tragic death. I even felt a little guilty having a good time with Rob. She was gone. Her life was completely over. "I am not over it yet, by a long shot, Honey. But this is a good place to begin the restoration. My spirit feels a bit broken. I cannot imagine what my parents are feeling."

Rob sat up and stretched, grabbing his coffee off the tray and swallowing the hot liquid with a smile on his face. "There is no magic way to recover from this loss. It will take time, and even then you will have days when it feels like it happened just yesterday. Life has an ugly way of going on without us. I hate that part. All of us do. We would like to think that things come to a stop and the world mourns your loss. But it is not that way at all. I think it would do your parents a great deal of good to get away, just go somewhere. That house has tons of memories. They need a moment away from it all."

"Never going to happen with Dad. He is hooked to his work. I've never seen him so tied up with phone calls and staying out. They seem to own his very watch. It's crazy. No matter what we are doing together, if he gets a call, he jumps. Seems a bit weird to me, but I don't understand the corporate world. I work for attorneys and that is as corporate as I want to get."

"I don't know quite why he has to jump when it rings, but he knows what he's doing. I will say that when I met your father, I felt like he was one of the most intelligent people I'd ever come across. I'm sure he would not say that about me! But we had some unusual conversations and he was amazing. His mind is like a steal trap. He forgets nothing."

"He was a Navy SEAL. He was trained by some of the best. I think he still carries a lot of that with him, no matter what he is doing. He researched you, I am sure, when he found out we were getting serious."

"Oh, Lord. No telling what he found in my family background."

"What? Like robbers and thieves?"

"I have no idea. I'm sure there were some questionable characters in my family. My father was a drunk. He hid it but he was definitely an alcoholic. I decided long ago that I would not drink; I didn't want to discover that I was an alcoholic, too."

"I'm sure we wouldn't like our distant relatives, either. Everyone has skeletons in their closet. But Dad loves digging things up on people. I swear he could work for the FBI. He is so anal in his thinking. Detailed to the max. Maybe the SEAL training caused that in him. I have no idea. But it can get a bit much if you live with him."

Rob laughed. "I don't take him that seriously, like you do. Of course, I don't have to live with the guy. I respect him from a healthy distance. I don't feel he really likes me or thought I was suitable for his daughter. Although that may be true, I think I can hold up my end of the bargain here. And I do adore you."

He grabbed me and threw me back on the bed. We made passionate love and then showered and took a long walk on the beach. It was nearly empty, which felt good. We spent the next few days lolling around on the beach, eating, drinking fancy nonalcoholic drinks, and swimming in the clear water. I was totally relaxed and beginning to enjoy the idea of being married. Rob seemed to wear his ring with a smile on his face, and we talked about everything under the sun. Everything but children. And that was coming up right now.

We were lying back on huge cushions on the porch, on a swing that was gigantic and held up by thick ropes. We were full and lazy. A perfect time to discuss an avoided subject.

"Honey, I was wondering. You have not ever said to me that you wanted children. I guess we should have talked about it before now, but I was wondering how you felt about that."

Rob was noticeably shifting in his seat. He looked up at me and there was no smile on his face. "I guess we should have talked about it. I figured since you didn't bring it up, that you were not sold on the idea, either."

I sat up quickly, breaking out in a sweat. "So you thought I didn't want children?"

"Sort of did."

"I never said that, Rob. We never discussed it. What gave you that impression?"

"Most women talk about that the first date. You never even hinted at it."

"Well, we were getting to know each other. I wasn't thinking about children then."

"And you are now?"

"I want to be able to discuss it, yes."

"On our honeymoon you want to talk about our having children?"

"What difference does it make where we are? I just wanted to know that you do want them at some point in your life."

Rob stood up and looked at the ocean. "I think it would be a great time for me to take a short walk on the beach alone. We will finish this talk when I get back. Can you deal with that?"

I was getting angry. I could feel the blood rushing to my face. "Are you saying you don't want kids? Has this upset you?"

"Don't go Manson on me, now. I just want some time alone to think this through. For your information, I had not thought about it much. I want to sort through my feelings."

"Oh for heaven's sake, Rob. We just got married, and you are not sure if you want kids together. Raise a family. Why would you get married to me if you didn't want to have a family?"

Rob walked over to me and pushed my hair back. "You said you didn't want me to control you. Well I don't want you controlling me. Give me a moment to sort out my thoughts. We have never even talked about having a family, raising kids, or anything. I need some fresh air. Just give me a moment without going postal on me."

I sat down on the porch swing and shook my head. "This was what I didn't want to happen with us, Rob. You take all the time you need. It caught me blindsided. I had no idea this would be an issue."

"It's not an issue, baby. I just need to sort through how I feel about having children. I am not saying I don't want them. I am saying please let me think about it a moment. I'll be right back."

An hour can seem like a day when you are waiting for someone. I was second-guessing myself about having brought up the matter of children on our honeymoon. Maybe that wasn't the time or place. It had ruined a good portion of our day already. And I loved being here. I just had no idea he would react like that. I went for a long walk the other direction on the beach and passed some other obvious honeymooners walking hand in hand. They smiled and I nodded. It felt like my disappointment was written all over my face. The sun was lowering and I walked for a while back towards the house we were staying in, picking up large shells and watching the water come in and go out. It was lovely. I could see small fish in the water and waded out to feel the cool water on my feet. I was getting a good suntan and the breeze kept me cool. But I was wondering all the while about Rob, and what he was doing. What was on his mind?

He showed up after about two hours. I acted like I didn't notice how long he'd been gone. He saw me standing by the shoreline and walked up to me.

"You're collecting quite a pile of shells there, aren't you?"

I nodded. "It's a beautiful afternoon."

"The water is so clear. I waded out several times just to cool off. That sun is warm when you are just walking on the beach."

"Rob, I—"

"Don't say a word. I've been a real jerk about this whole thing. I want to apologize to you, Emily. You have every right to want children, and if I was in my right mind I would want them, too. It just caught me off guard and I said the wrong thing. I reacted too quickly. Do you forgive me?"

I hugged him and kissed his warm mouth. "I forgive you. But it has worried me ever since you walked off. I thought we would be of the same mind about this."

"I do love kids. I never thought about having my own, to be honest. I've been busy with my own career, and just didn't allow myself the luxury of thinking about kids of my own. Well, until you, I didn't have any reason to. I'd dated some but not fallen in love with anyone until I met you. And you pretty much nailed me at 'hello.'"

I couldn't help but laugh. "That is so typical. I cannot believe it. I don't think men give it that much thought when they are younger, and maybe even after they marry. Women, on the other hand, think about having children as soon as they reach puberty. We are drawn to other women's babies. I guess it is the way God made us. I don't want to get pregnant today, of course. But I just liked the idea of us talking about raising our own family one day in the future."

"I will talk about anything you want to talk about. I adore you and would be honored to father our children. I am a bit selfish, having lived alone for several years. You have been at home with your parents. I have had to think of no one but myself. Now we are married and you will be in that equation. So I just need time to adjust, and to just enjoy you. Us."

We held hands and walked inside the small thatched roofed house, relishing the shade and ready for a short nap. We lay next to each other, laughing and talking quietly about our families and dozed off to sleep. I woke first and walked into the kitchen to fix a small tray for us to snack on. I was hungrier than I realized, and sat on the porch eating some fresh grapes and walnuts. The sound of the ocean was hypnotic.

It suddenly occurred to me that I had not received one text or phone call since we'd left home. It felt good to be that detached from the world. Suddenly I looked up and Rob was standing in the doorway staring at me.

"Gosh. you are beautiful!" He stood there smiling.

"You are dangerous standing there like that."

"Why?"

I walked up to him and kissed him long and hard. We ran to the bed and made love, and it felt so good to be so free. To be loved by him. I knew that we would have to face the world again in another day or two, so I was trying my best to enjoy this time alone.

"I had no idea I married a tiger."

"You have no idea about a lot of things, mister."

"I will find out, I bet."

"I'm sure you will. Now let's go eat dinner. For some reason, I am starving."

We dressed and walked to the outdoor restaurant. The temperature was lowering as the sun had set, and it felt so good to be outside. Some other couples were scattered around the patio, talking low as the band played some Reggae music. We could have been anywhere in the world. It was so beautiful. I reached over and grabbed Rob's hand. He turned and looked into my eyes. I had made a good choice for a husband. I knew that now, more than ever. The fear of being married was gone for now. And I hoped it never came back.

"Where are you, Honey? I know you are lost in your thoughts."

"I'm here with you, Rob. And there's no place I'd rather be."

CHAPTER EIGHTEEN

Nothing was ever as it seemed in Washington. No matter what the news anchors spouted about the latest and greatest of what was going on, it wasn't even the tip of the iceberg. Had the public really known what was going on, they would have committed mutiny. An upheaval like Americans have never seen would have taken place. But that wasn't going to happen. For centuries Washington had held its secrets very well. Like a master sleeping giant, things were done in the darkness. In the shadows. And it would not matter who you asked, or who you listened to, no one knew a spit about the reality of politics and the power it had underground.

For underground was where Walter Hagan worked his magic. He was head command in The President's Club. For centuries that honor had been secretly passed down. Uncanny how it had remained such a secret all these years. Twelve men and one leader. Answering to no one. Ever.

You might look back in history to notice that there were people disappearing in certain presidential terms. People you suddenly heard nothing about. It was like they had never lived. They simply disappeared. It was done professionally, of course. But there was also torture like you've never seen. Perhaps similar to war times.

Well, it was war on some level. And Walter Van Hagan was nothing but a professional at what he did. He chose the best and demanded their best at all times. No questions asked, ever. Just complete the task at hand and disappear back into society. Of course, he was only as good as the men he chose. Their ability to do their job was in direct proportion to their ability to keep a secret career from their families. For no one could ever discover The President's Club existed.

Walter often went underground when something big was taking place. He always knew what was coming. That was his job. Today he was pacing in his small office waiting for a call back. He'd put in a call to Bill Sinclair, who had an uncanny way of avoiding calls when he was busy. The pressure on these men was huge and Walter knew it. But there was nothing he could do about it. They were trained to do things most humans would not or could not do. They were almost inhuman at times. But he sensed that Bill was hesitating. He didn't like that. It was dangerous. It could cost Bill his life. He wanted to talk to him, but it had to be over the phone, for no one was allowed to see Walter in person.

He had left a call back number for Bill and was waiting patiently. That word really wasn't in his vocabulary because usually when something had to be taken care of, it was immediate. It was time sensitive. Someone could be seriously injured or it might affect the security of the nation; it depended on what the action was that needed to happen. Walter had access to everything the President did, said, or even thought he wanted to do. He had access to computers throughout the White House and anyone the staff spoke to, emailed, or texted. It was a full time job that he took very seriously.

When Walter was hired, he did face the President once. One time only. He was told that this would be the last time he would ever speak to the President or any of his staff except the national security advisor. The Presidency might change but the agenda of the President's Club would never change. He was to protect at all costs what the President of the United States wanted to accomplish and the security of the United States. If anyone got in his way and would not adjust their agenda, then they were taken out. Information was retrieved from others at all costs.

In times of war, such as during the war in Afghanistan, many covert operations were taking place that no one knew about. They felt similar to a the plays of a football team moving down the field, with men being taken down so the runner could carry out his agenda of making a touchdown. Men dropped like flies on the field, so that the touchdown could be made.

In real life, there were people who lived to interfere with what went on inside the White House. Those people were watched 24/7. Nothing slipped by because it could mean the President would lose his life. Or lose the war. Either way, the loss would be too great. The national security advisor was connected to Walter through a private phone that had a code. He contacted Walter privately whenever something had to be done either internationally or domestically that was not made known to Walter through his regular text, phone, or email.

Walter's phone finally rang an hour after he'd sent Bill Sinclair the call back code. He was about to lose his temper, but needed to stay calm during this conversation. Usually it was very short and to the point. Today more words would be said. Things needed to be made clear or this wasn't going to work out.

Walter picked up his phone and spoke. "You've been weak in responding to my calls. Is there something I need to know about? Is there a problem at home? Does your wife suspect something?"

"It is difficult for me at times to answer your phone call immediately. I always get back to you as fast as I can. We just married off my oldest daughter, which was wonderful, but we also had to bury my other daughter, which is more than we could handle at this point. This is an issue that I have been wondering about this whole time—why I would be called to do this job, when you know I am married."

"It was your training that attracted us to you. We need you and we felt you could handle the situation. It appears we may have been wrong."

"I have only done that one time. Maybe twice at the most. I'm doing the best job I can do for the President."

"Are you emotionally sound?"

"I don't like what I have to do but I was trained to do it. So—"

"You pulled it off as a Navy SEAL. What's the difference?"

"If felt like war then. I guess this is war on our own land."

"Exactly."

"I will try to do a better job. But know if I do not answer, there is a good security reason."

"You are given jobs that I feel you can handle. And you know you aren't the only one."

"That doesn't make it any easier. It goes without saying that I will do what you ask. But I don't have to like it."

"Nothing goes without saying. I need to know if there is a weak hole. We cannot allow for weakness here."

"Yes, sir."

"When I call, answer as fast as you can. It is critical in nature most of the time. Time sensitive. I do feel there is a leak somewhere. Watch your back; make damn sure you aren't being followed. Go out of your way to be invisible. There can never be any trace of you anywhere."

"I was told that in the beginning."

"It is more critical now."

"I understand."

Walter hung up the phone. Something about Bill he liked. But he could not tolerate any weakness because it might mean that

Bill or the other eleven men could lose their lives, or that The President's Club would be compromised.

His phone rang again and he answered. This time it was the national security advisor. And he didn't sound too happy. "The last time we spoke I told you that I suspected a leak on your end."

"Yes. I am taking all precautions."

"You're missing something. We had a known spy we were tracking and someone leaked about our operation. We had set a date and time. It was a dead ringer. Someone scared him away. Now we have to track him again."

"It can't be my men."

"It has to be. I've checked with the CIA and they swear they are solid as a rock."

"They're lying."

"They have been known to."

"I will recheck my men. I am watching like a hawk. Any sign of weakness and I am addressing it."

"Whoever it is, is going down. This is treason. We have to find out who it is."

"I suggest you look in the mirror. In other words, the CIA. They have a looser code than we do. We are nearly invisible."

"I am aware of both operations. We have to stop this now, before it gets worse. Someone is going down for this. It cannot happen again."

"My eyes are on the field."

"See to it that they are."

A dial tone. Walter sat his phone down and sat at his desk rubbing his face. Sometimes this job could get to be too much. Or was he just getting too old? He leaned back and took a deep breath. He was so careful about choosing his men. They were impeccable. All of them. But a rat can come across as your best man, and then he'll turn on you in a nanosecond.

He had his eyes on all twelve. Bill was out. He knew it wasn't Bill. A gut feeling. But the other men, well, he would have to be more vigilant. Or perhaps set a trap. This just could not happen on his watch. He would not allow it. That alone could be reason to get rid of him. And he knew too much for them to allow him to live. He knew almost everything.

When he had taken the position, he had known what it meant. That he was not allowed to make a mistake too big. You might get away with killing the wrong person or breaking into the wrong computer system, but if you were found out, it was over. These men could not ever have their identities known. So the rat was taking a huge risk in allowing himself to be so vulnerable. He would pay a price for sure. But Walter didn't want his neck on the line. He sure wasn't going down for some stupid soul who thought he was larger than the United States government, the CIA, and the FBI. People who were risk-takers had an agenda that caused them to be blind at some point. He was waiting on that blindness to come to the light.

CHAPTER NINETEEN

B ill was watching the news. Russia was rearing its head in Syria and there was tension in Iran. The President had met with Putin but nothing seemed to get accomplished. There was no way Putin was going to budge. The Middle East was in a state of unrest and immigrants from Syria were fleeing. America was attempting to take them in, but there was a danger in doing so because there was no way of knowing who these men were, if they were ISIS or just people fleeing their country. Bill expected his phone to be ringing because of all the unrest. He knew there would be people trying to block what the President wanted to do. He didn't always agree with the President, either. He wasn't all that fond of him. But he was hired to do a job, so he put aside his own feelings to a point.

He had had a full day at work. Signed on two new conglomerates that wanted to hire his firm to do their accounting. It was a huge success and he knew these two new clients would bring in a lot of money. The partners would be happy. More than happy. Elated. They already liked him; he could tell. But he had a knack for signing large companies and that was where the big money was.

Sharon was coming in the door after spending the day with her charity for abused women. They had been able to construct a new home for unwed mothers or abused pregnant women so that they could deliver their babies in a safe environment. He was proud of her for pushing that through. The fund-raising was ruthless. But she got the job done.

"Hey, lady! How's your day been?"

She blew out a huge sigh. "I don't know about you, but I am worn out."

"I feel the same way. Want me to pour you a glass of wine, and we sit out on the porch? I will light up the fire pit if you like."

"That sounds like heaven. It's definitely getting colder out there. I don't know how long I can sit there, but let's give it a shot."

Bill got up and poured two glasses of wine and carried them out on the large screened porch and sat them down on a small round ottoman in front of two comfy chairs and a small sofa. He lit the fire pit and sat down, waiting on Sharon to take her place beside him. It was nice having the house to themselves. They could set their own schedule or have no schedule. Dinner was when they were hungry. She walked outside and sat beside him, snuggling against his chest. It was chilly and she was wrapped up in a blanket with socks on her feet. She picked up her glass of wine and took a long sip.

"Taste good to you?"

"Very. How was your day?"

"Busy but turned out fantastic. I signed two huge companies today that will bring us a good amount of income."

"Partners will like that."

"Yep. I am sure they will."

"I had a good day, too. Several new women came into the center and signed up for the new house we have nearly finished. I am so excited that we have this wonderful new place to bring these women. I feel so good about it."

"Took a ton of work on your part. Glad that is over. You were really clocking in the hours."

"Speaking of clocking in hours, you do that yourself. I hate that you are always on call. Will that ever change, Honey?"

"I hope so. Not in the near future, but it will let up at some point."

"I would love to be able to go on a short trip, Bill. Not now, maybe. But at some point. After the holidays. Think about it. See what you can do."

He kissed the top of her head and leaned back against the chair cushion. He was tired, too. But the way the country was going, the direction the President was heading, pretty much nailed down the chances of his getting out anytime soon. In fact, he felt like there was going to come a time when his phone rang more often. And the commands he would receive would be more and more about death than information. The possibility of a leak did not sound good, but he knew he wasn't being followed. He also knew he would never do anything to inform anyone about the existence of such a club or anything about the White House that would threaten the President or the United States. He hated what he was doing, but then, he had hated war. So maybe Hagan was right. It was war even now.

"You lost in your own world, Bill?"

Bill shook his head. "No, Honey. Just tired. Enjoying this moment with you. I will see about us taking a vacation. But not anytime soon. I just told the partners about my acceptance. It would not look good for me to take off just yet."

"I understand. Just something for us to think about." She paused. "Avery wanted me to go shopping with her tonight."

"This is the first I've heard of that."

"I forgot, actually. I'd better go change and call her. I totally forgot."

"It'll do you good to get out with her. I know you're tired, but she loves you to death."

"We do get along, don't we?"

"Go have a good time. I'll be right here. If I have to go out, I'll let you know."

"Surely not tonight. But thanks. I'll call you on my way home."

Bill sat alone for an hour, listening to the news and changing the stations to get different angles on the same subject. They ran things in the ground and focused on situations in ways that were redundant. It tired him to hear it. But his thoughts were interrupted by the phone vibrating in his pocket. He grabbed it quickly.

"There is a warehouse on Fifth and Central. You have twenty minutes to get there. The three men there are armed and dangerous. You will be on your own this time. You have the surprise element working for you. They won't be expecting anyone and that will be your way in. But once inside, you will find a huge room and only one way out. So they will be cornered when you enter. You'll have one chance to shoot all of them. Your weapon will be waiting for you. Discard it immediately and disappear quickly. I do not believe these men work alone. This is one of the most dangerous coups you've been involved in short of Afghanistan. Be careful. Watch your back."

"Three against one. That's bad odds."

"I wouldn't send you if I didn't think you could do it."

"Sure would be nice if one of the other men was around."

"That isn't how this works."

"We have masks on. I wouldn't know who he was."

"It isn't going to happen, Bill."

"I better go. My twenty minutes is going to be cut short as it is."

"If you don't think you can do it, better speak up now."

"I have no choice, do I?"

"Not really."

The phone went dead.

Bill grabbed his gun and ran to the car. Changing his clothes quickly, he sped down the road, choosing side streets to avoid the cops. He parked two blocks away from the warehouse and as he was walking he received a text telling him where the machine gun was hiding.

He found the garbage can and grabbed the loaded gun and walked slowly up to the side door. He was constantly aware of his surroundings. His whole nervous system was in high gear. All of his SEAL training came rushing in and he knew when he opened the door, he was going to have to come in shooting. He would only have seconds to detect their location and shoot. He had to ensure that he hit all three because once he started shooting, they would come alive. These were no ordinary men. They were after something and would stop at nothing to get it. He was at a great disadvantage but at this point there was no other way to deal with the problem. His task was to take them down and that was what he was going to do.

The street was unusually quiet. It felt like he was being watched. He put his gloved hand on the door and turned the knob. It opened easily. His gun was aimed at the three men standing in the center of the room, near a few tables and chairs. One was smoking a cigarette. The other two were standing with their arms by their sides, talking low. All three turned towards him as he began to shoot. He saw one reach for his gun, but Bill was able to gun all three down seconds before the other man could fire.

He had to be sure they were dead. So he kept on shooting until he could walk up to them to check their pulses. As soon as he knew the job was done, he walked away. He knew anyone near the building would have heard the shots fired, so he pulled off his mask, gloves, and dark shirt and stuck them into his briefcase, leaving a beige polo underneath. He slapped on a ball cap and walked out on the street, whistling.

Luckily, no one was walking by and the traffic was minimal. His heart was racing but he was amazed at how easy it had gone. The surprise entrance had worked out well. They had obviously never dreamed anyone would come through the door.

He ditched the gun in the garbage can, found his car, and pulled away. He slowed way down and drove around some neighborhoods, and then he typed the code into the phone to let Command know it was done. He got no response back, so he figured he was good to go. Job done.

He stopped and got some coffee at a McDonalds drive through and slowly drove home, allowing the hot coffee to settle his nerves. Another possible death avoided. His own. He was playing Russian roulette. He knew it well. But again, he had no choice. These men were planning to kill. But he killed them first. Did that make it right? He hoped it did. He had to believe it did or he would not be able to live with himself.

The weird thing about these jobs he was asked to do was that they were over so quickly. He was living his normal life, and then boom. He was asked to go torture someone to get information or to take their life just like it was nothing odd. A normal activity. And then he had to pretend like it never happened. He had to erase it from his mind. He was trained to do that, like the other SEALs and any Special Ops troops. The Green Beret. But this was on home ground.

America wasn't at war in the way he liked to think of war. It was a silent war, going on underground. But it was growing by leaps and bounds because of the country's open borders. Because they could fly in, walk in, or be born in the U.S. and plot and plan right under their neighbors' noses. The world was changing. Nothing was like it was years ago. But Bill knew that he was part of a new war where the enemy was hidden; hard to distinguish. And America would have to fight the same way. Hidden. Watchful. Not trusting much of anything at all. It was a hell of a way to live in the land of the free. The power struggle, religious wars, and pure greed were taking over the world. He hoped he never met the guy on the other end of the phone. That man was carrying a weight that no one should be asked to carry.

CHAPTER TWENTY

J acob was pretty private. Especially about the women in his life. He'd never had good luck with the girls and hated to be teased about it. Jesse, on the other hand, was Mr. Romance in comparison. So the phone call that was about to take place would pretty much ruin Jacob's day.

"Jesse? What you calling me about? This just about never happens in the middle of the day."

"That's a little defensive, don't you think?"

"So, I got things to do. What you need?"

Jesse laughed. "I just wondered how in the world you met Gail Bailey?"

Jacob blushed. "She walked into my office not too long ago, wanting insurance. What's it to you?"

"She walked into my dental office talking about you."

"She didn't. Why are you doing this?"

"She bragged on you. Could hardly stop talking about how nice you were. I was just hoping you would tell me that you didn't step over that proverbial line with her. She's trouble, Brother."

"I'm dating Jane, remember?"

"I'm well aware of her. But were you, when Miss Gail was in your office?"

"Frankly, I wasn't aware I had to answer to you, buddy."

"You don't. Relax. I'm joking around but I'm serious, too. She's trouble. That's all I'm saying."

"I don't know what you mean by trouble. She seemed pretty nice to me. She and her daughter."

"Don't be fooled by her looks, man. She could be a problem in your life if you don't watch out. I don't know how locked in you are with Jane, but tell me you won't touch this woman with a ten-foot pole."

"She's not my type."

"Bull. She's most men's type. That's the problem."

Jacob nearly choked on his laughter. "So you're saying you were bothered by her?"

"No, but I'm not blind, either. She was hot."

"Yes, but I didn't go over any lines with her. Just tried to help her with her insurance."

"All right, Buddy. It's just me, Big Brother, looking out for you. Otherwise, everything else good in your life?"

"You mean, besides us losing our sister? Yeah, other than that, things are just great. Where is your brain today? I can't believe this whole conversation."

"Just had to satisfy my own curiosity about Gail Bailey. It would not have surprised me if you had asked her out. She is a nice look-ing girl. But I feel trouble. And when that happens, I'm usually right."

"You have a high opinion of yourself, don't you? Look, I need to get back to work. I don't know about you, but I work for a living."

"Have a great day, Little Brother. Just me looking out for you."

"Bye, Jess. And thanks for the call. Not."

Jacob hung up the phone and shook his head. What were the odds? He walked back into his office and took care of some paperwork and waited for a client who was coming in at 2:00. He had written several policies that morning that were going to get him a raise. His boss had been pushing him, and now it was paying off.

He had a reason for wanting more money. Jane had been hinting at their living together. He really wasn't ready to get married, but if push came to shove, he would do it. He loved her but if he were honest he was a bit afraid of commitment. He believed in marriage; his parents had shown that it could be done. But for some reason, he felt like he would be giving up something to marry. He had no life other than work, and maybe going to the gym to work out. Jane was who he spent all his spare time with. He had not been in any kind of rush to marry her, but he knew he was going to have to get his act together or he would lose her. The idea that he was attracted to Gail Bailey was a joke. Granted, she was very attractive. But that didn't mean he wanted to date her at the risk of losing Jane. Jesse was out of line calling him like that.

At the end of the day, he called Jane. "Hey, Sweet Girl. How has your day been?"

She sounded tired. "We've worked our tails off today. So many people sick with the flu. It's going around. You and I don't need to get that, you know."

"I have no intention of getting it."

"So how is your day? I met someone who knew you."

"I'm afraid to ask who."

"Her name was Gail. Gail Bailey."

Jacob shook his head. This was not going to be good. "What do you mean? She was at the hospital today?"

"Well, not actually. I was walking out of the hospital to grab a bite to eat. I am sick of eating hospital food so I was going to Subway to eat a sandwich. Some of the nurses ordered sandwiches and I was going to pick them up. I saw a lady with a little girl who was crying, right outside the door of the hospital. I walked up to her to see if I could help. She said her daughter had been stung by a wasp and it was swelling slightly. I checked it and it looked normal for a wasp sting. We got into a conversation. She said she knew you, and also had met Jesse. I thought that was odd."

Jacob was shaking his head. "That woman gets around. I swear. She will eventually meet the whole dang family. What is going on with her?"

"I thought it was funny. So she bought insurance with you?"

"Auto insurance. And then Jesse took care of a cavity for her."

"She must think everyone she meets is related to you."

"I guess. I'm getting tired of hearing about her."

"Are we still eating together tonight?"

"Yeah. I thought we would go out. I know you're tired and I am too. Let's just grab something out."

"Sounds good to me. Will be great to see you. I missed you today."

"I thought of you, too. I'll pick you up at 6:30. That way we won't eat so late."

"You sound like an old maid."

"Thanks. I'll be there to get you with my cane."

CHAPTER TWENTY-ONE

Bill lay there in the dark, waiting for the sun's rays to burn through the open window. He had a zillion thoughts going through his head, but he was also aware that Sharon was staring at him.

"What in the world are you doing awake at this hour?" She sounded grouchy and had such a frown on her face.

"I was thinking. And I know I didn't wake you up. That's one thing I can do quietly."

A slow smile skittered across her face. Not a real smile. "I was already awake. I've been thinking about making a quick trip to North Carolina to see my sister, Anne. She's been on my mind lately, and she has called so much to see how we are doing. Don't you think that's a good idea?"

"Perfect one. When you want to go?"

"Tomorrow. I know it's sudden, but now is the time. I feel it."

"Then go you shall. What can I do to help?"

"Nothing. I will pack today and get what I will need at the store. I'm going to drive. I like to be in control of my time. And that will give me some alone time to think."

Bill smiled. "I seem to be able to do just that while lying in bed. Imagine that."

She punched him and got up to put her robe on. "We are fast approaching the holidays. I want to see her before that, because it's so busy here and I want to come back and get some shopping done before Christmas.

He watched her walk into the kitchen to start the coffee pot, and he turned over and faced the window. His last conversation with the Godfather (he'd assigned that name to the voice on the end of the phone) was bugging him. A leak; a weak link. Who in the world would leak what was happening underground. It could put all twelve men at risk. The job was already harrowing. Now to have a traitor in the midst just added to the stress.

He heard Sharon in the kitchen. She needed to go somewhere. He was glad she'd decided to visit her sister. Something needed to snap her out of this depression she'd been in since Susan's death. It was even hard to think about a child of his being dead. So he pushed it back, way back, into a compartment in his mind. But Sharon, being a mother, could not do that. She wasn't capable of it. So it was perfect for her to leave and have someone else on her mind. She would be good company for Anne, who had enough issues of her own to deal with.

As he walked into the kitchen, he could smell the bacon and eggs cooking on the stove. It was chilly and the hot coffee warmed him as he sat at the table waiting for his breakfast.

"I'm glad you decided to go. I think it's a great idea. The timing couldn't be better."

"I'm happy you agreed to it. I think it will help me, and I'm sure she could use the company. Her husband has been gone for three years, and I think she is lonely. We'll find great things to do. It is so lovely there. I've missed the fall colors, but it's still beautiful this time of year."

"How long you thinking about staying, Sharon?"

She looked at him with a blank face. "I have no idea, Honey. But it really doesn't matter. I won't be in a rush to come back and sit here depressed. And I know you are busy. You don't mind terribly, do you?"

"I think it's grand that you are going. I want you to look forward to it. We don't have that much anymore to look forward to, and you love Anne. So it will be good for you both."

"Good. Now let's eat while the food is hot."

While Sharon was in the shower, Bill got a call. This time was different.

"I know you have family, but this time I need you to leave the house for a few days. We have reason to believe the leak is one of the twelve. One of you. It's impossible for me to wrap my brain around it, but we are pinning it down and will need you to act on it. Are you available tomorrow?"

"Actually it couldn't have come at a better time. My wife is leaving for a week or more."

"Good. Not that it would matter. But it makes it easier on you. This is serious stuff. You cannot make a mistake. When you have a good shot, you take it. Don't even think about it. I'll give you the coordinates tomorrow; the location and time slots that you might be able to get a good shot at him."

"I'll be waiting."

"I have to ask; how do you feel about doing this? Knowing it's one of the twelve."

"It would take a sick idiot to turn on the group. For what reason? What is being accomplished? What made him turn?"

"He could be having second thoughts. He is doubting the validity of what we do. Or he was a spy in the first place. That is always an option."

"But he was vetted, I'm sure. We all were."

"Within inches of your lives. But things can slip through. Some people hide things incredibly well. But this is what we do. We find what's hidden. We missed this."

"I'll get him. Don't worry."

"That's why we picked you."

"Let me know the coordinates."

"Tomorrow."

"Did I hear you talking to someone?" Sharon came out of the bedroom, dressed and ready to pack.

"Yes. A client. Seems like I'll be busy while you are gone."

"I figured. You stay busy, Bill. I've never seen anything like it. What I don't get is how they own you once you take them on. They absolutely own you."

"It's corporate life, hon. I don't know how long I can do it, but while am strong enough, we're making good money. We need that for when I retire."

"I know. I understand that. But you answer calls all hours of the night and day. No matter what we're doing."

"I'm sorry it has inconvenienced you and us. And I appreciate your patience."

"It's wearing thin, I think. So this getting away will mend my lack of patience, I think."

"Then it's even a better reason for you to go."

Bill finished dressing and picked up his briefcase. "I've got to go, Honey. You finish your packing and pick up anything you are going to need for your trip. Have you called Anne?"

"Yes. She's thrilled I am coming."

"Great. I'll call you later to check on how things are going."

He walked outside, started the car and headed to the office. Finally alone, his thoughts went rampant about what he was about to do. The pressure was building and it appeared that so much of what he was taking care of was relatively close to the President.

This next one made no sense. A possible traitor. But what if it wasn't? What if the guy just couldn't believe in what he was being asked to do? The thought had crossed Bill's mind a time or two. It was wrong on so many levels, and on the outside if this were done, a life in prison or the death penalty would ensue. The other eleven men involved had to feel the same way, unless they had become ruthless with all the killing they'd seen in Afghanistan or Iraq.

He entered his office, closed the door, and sat in his leather office chair, turning around so that he could look out the huge window. His view was of the skyline and he could see for miles. But the new offices would give even a more powerful view of Washington's skyline. He'd always loved serving his country. He believed in America and didn't mind giving up his life to protect the freedom of the people at home. But this crap was Mafia-style politics. He really wanted no part in it. Of course he couldn't speak of that to anyone. He had to remain silent about all of what was taking place, along with his opinions. The White House wasn't paying twelve men for their opinions. Quite the opposite.

He tackled his paperwork with a vengeance. He pretty much kept to himself all day long, except for the random phone calls he received from a client or two. But in between the figures and computer programs he was running on his screen, his mind kept going back to the man who had decided to rat on the government. It would feel so freeing to just let it all out. To tell the world. But not today. And he wasn't sure it could ever happen.

CHAPTER TWENTY-TWO

"Emily"

I t was a lovely winter day, with December fast approaching, and I realized I had not called Mother in several weeks. I rang her, wondering how the depression was going. I had not been as close to Susan as I should have been; we'd always fought as children. But it was still difficult to swallow that she was gone.

"Hello, Mother? I' m just calling to see how you are. To see how things are going."

Sharon sounded preoccupied. "Hey, Em. I'm doing fine. Going tomorrow to see Anne. I am packed and ready to go."

"Was this a sudden decision? You haven't mentioned that this was something you wanted to do."

"It was kind of sudden. But she has been on my mind lately and has called several times to check on us."

"I'm not saying I don't think it's a bad idea. Nothing like that. Just didn't know you were up to going. That's quite a drive."

"I'm looking forward to it, frankly. I need to get myself out of this house and this way, I have hours in the car to think. Be alone."

"How's Dad feel about you going?"

"I don't think he cares, either way."

"Now, Mother. Don't say that. He adores you and has been worried sick."

"I'm sure he has been. But he doesn't say much. In fact, he seems more and more preoccupied with work."

"He does seem to be very busy. We've all been worried about you, though."

"No need for that, Emily. I'll be fine at some point. It's hard on a mother to bury a child. Takes a while to sort all that out. I haven't completely compartmentalized it yet, but I'm getting there. I don't want it to swallow my life up. The grieving. Your father is probably tired of my moping round. I haven't wanted to do one single thing."

"Maybe some fresh air, new scenery, will be just what you need."

"Anne has her own issues. It will be nice to think of something else for a change. And we'll have fun shopping."

"I won't keep you, Mother. But let me hear from you. How long do you plan on being gone?"

"I have no idea. No agenda. I'll see when I get there. Anne may want me to stay several weeks, which would suit me fine."

"Are you okay with Dad, Mother? Is something going on that I don't know about?"

"I really don't know. I'm not privy to what goes on in Bill's world. Not that I ask. But he is very busy and very private. So that is our life now. I know he's trying to make a good living and prepare us for retirement. I appreciate all that effort. But we need to enjoy life some, too."

"It will all fall into place. You have a great time and don't worry about anything at all. Dad will be fine. I'll stop by and check on him for you."

"Well, maybe you can get something out of him, Emily. I don't have much luck on that end. And I'll let you know how long I'm going to be gone, after I arrive and see what's going on in Anne's world."

"Sounds good, Mother. Love you and be careful on the road."

I recalled Mother talking about the "safe room" in her marriage. I hadn't been so lucky as to establish that in my own marriage. But so far we were doing fine. With my parents, it was hard to step back and see them as just people. Dad was very serious about his work; in fact, I hadn't seen him this attentive in years. And when that phone rang, he jumped. Which was unusual in itself. No one had been able to punch his buttons, ever since I was a child. But now, someone had his number. Someone, or a group of people, was controlling his time. It didn't seem right, didn't feel right, but he said it was corporate, so I believed that. But Mother's well- being was at stake, so I was going to tackle getting him to talk while she was gone. Not that I had my hopes up. He was pretty closed mouth about his work and personal feelings. I think that came from the SEAL training. What he had to do in the war. Men in general were difficult to read, but Dad was a heavyweight in keeping things to himself. And somehow he made you feel like a fool to think you could even begin to get him to open up. Which just made me want to try harder. I dialed his number while I had some courage in me.

"Dad? How's your day going? I just spoke with Mom."

"I guess she told you about her trip tomorrow."

"In fact, she did. That's why I am calling you. You think she's strong enough to make such a trip?"

"I think it'll be a perfect time for her to get away from everything, even me, and let her mind relax. Anne will be good for her."

"We'll see. I'm not as sure as you are. How about dinner tomorrow night? Rob would love to see you."

He paused. I felt him suck in a breath. "Actually, I'm going to be busy for the next few days, Honey. Can we take a rain check on that?"

I already knew he was going to avoid the dinner invite. "I'll hold you to it, Dad. Sounds like Mom is going to be gone for a while. I'll stick my head in from time to time just to check and see how you're doing."

"I'm a big boy. I'll be fine."

"No telling what you're going to eat while she's gone."

"She has spoiled me, that is true."

"I'm a phone call away, Dad. Would love a nice chat with you."

"I'll make that happen."

How did I know that my father would never open up to me? Guess it was obvious. My own life kept me pretty busy. The law firm was adding another partner soon, and business was growing by leaps and bounds. I was busier than I wanted to be, with only one thought on my mind. Would I ever reach a point when I wanted to have children? It was time. Well I had a few years yet. But Rob and I never finished that conversation and it sort of took the want-to right out of me. For a while I craved having a baby. And then suddenly, after he nixed the idea over and over, I dug into my work and let it go. When it surfaced now and then, I felt a twinge in my gut. Or my heart. But was it worth fighting for?

I saw Rob walking up to the front door. He'd parked in the circular drive in front of our house. "Hey, Dear. I'm home. Kind of thought we'd eat out tonight. Left the car in the front."

"I noticed. How was your day?"

"Tired of travelling. Selling. These doctors make you wait. I've learned to wiggle my way in, but some of them have bulldog receptionists out front who just won't let you in."

I laughed. "Oh, you are so handsome; I bet you could talk most of those girls into anything."

"Used to could. But not anymore. I'm losing my edge, I think." He smiled. I loved that smile.

"Okay, I'll get my purse. I have something to talk to you about, again."

Rob rolled his eyes. It was like he already knew.

We drove to the Harbor House Restaurant in Midtown and took a seat in the back. It was quiet; people were still getting off work. I ordered my usual small filet and waited for her to bring us each a small glass of Chardonnay. Rob sat there waiting on me to dig up the dead horse again.

"I know you know what I am about to say. But let's get it over with so we can go on with our night."

Rob nodded with a straight face.

"I was wondering if you had changed your stand on having kids, yet. I sort of have you cornered where you can't just walk out. Or at least, I hope you won't. We've come a little way in our marriage and I just wanted to broach the subject again."

"How did I know you were going to take about babies tonight?"

"I guess from time to time you know it's going to come up."

"Well, I've been doing some thinking on my own, lately."

I raised an eyebrow but thought better of speaking. Better to be silent and wait this one out.

"All the time we've eaten at your parents' house, and I see all your siblings sitting around the table talking. Granted there are words spoken that are a bit rude or downright crass. You don't always get along. But there is still a feeling of camaraderie and warmth that I did not have, being the only child. I am not used to sharing space. I like a lot of alone time. But, given all the facts, I think it might be kind of nice to have a couple of children to carry the name."

"I'm afraid to speak."

"Well, leave it alone then. Do what you will about it. I'm just saying that I'm open."

"You've made my day, Rob. Absolutely blown away."

"Good. I haven't done that in a long time. So this should be good for quite some time, don't you think? I don't have to try to come up with anything that will blow your mind for a long time."

"Centuries."

"Good. Now let's eat. I have some work to do when we get home."

I was smiling so big that I could hardly chew my meat. But now the ball was in my court. I had to decide whether or not I was serious about it or just trying to get my way. We women could be fickle. I didn't want this to be one of those times.

CHAPTER TWENTY-THREE

It was a rainy morning and Bill could hear the water pouring out of the downspouts on the side of his house. The forecast was for rain the next few days. He didn't care, but it might make his maneuvering a little more difficult.

He had showered, eaten breakfast, and was waiting for his phone to ring. He hated the waiting this time. And because he didn't know the location yet, there was no way to plan his set-up. He read the paper and turned on the morning news. Nothing good was ever on the news but he listened out of duty. He needed to know what was going on. The news media reported things with a certain slant, and the public only knew what they read and heard. Which was very little. They dramatized things that were not a big deal and minimized the actions that were critical to the country's well-being. When he had gone to Afghanistan and Iraq he had found out firsthand that what the news was reporting was insignificant compared to what was taking place on the ground. What was told was what would draw ratings. The truth sometimes just didn't cut it.

He was changing channels when the phone rang. He grabbed it and spoke quietly.

"Hello?"

"Are you ready, Bill?"

"As ready as I can be when I have had no information given."

"Well, I'm going to give it to you now. Is your wife gone?"

"Left this morning early."

"Good. The location is the Commerce Building on 8th Avenue. He usually works 9:00 to 5:00 but lately hasn't been regular in his hours. Which has us all concerned. Since we are convinced he is the leak, we are working overtime to understand what his next move is. There will be eyes all over the place but you won't see them. Don't even look."

"That goes without saying."

"We are assuming he is heavily armed. But he won't be expecting you, that's for sure. Now, the time we want you to be there is 8:00 at night. He's been returning to the building each night around 8:00."

"How will I know it's him? I mean, he's not the only person at this office, is he?"

"At the time of night that you are going to be approaching the building, so far, he is the only one we've seen coming and going. Now things are subject to change. So you will have your phone on vibrate and will be alerted if there is a change. It could take place quickly so you are going to have to be flexible. Frankly, we don't know how many others are involved in this scheme. We are winging it here, Bill."

"That puts the risk totally on me, again."

"Well, you didn't have any issue with that overseas."

Bill swore under his breath. "I'll be wearing a vest but that doesn't keep them from killing me. Especially if I'm greatly outnumbered. I understand you want me to just take him down. Is that correct?"

"Yes, without any discussion."

"What if there is more than one person in the building? How do you want me to handle that? I want to make sure I get the right person."

"If there are more people there, then you will have to take them all out. Because we are certain that if they are with him at that time of night, then they are part of this faction that is working against what we are trying to accomplish."

"I understand you are saying to take them all out."

"Correct."

"If for some reason there are women there or children; I'm saying worst case scenario, then what do you want me to do?"

Bill heard a sigh. "I'll let you make that call. Once they see you, they will know they've been had. Your life will be a great risk once you are seen. I doubt you'll have much time to make a decision as to whether or not these people are linked to him or would add to your risk of being killed."

"I don't know if I can shoot innocent children to take this man out. I would rather wait another night and find him alone."

"You mean you would abort the mission if women and children are present?"

"I'd be tempted to, yes, sir."

"Bill, I need you committed one hundred percent here. If you abort, they will still be alerted that we know what is going on. You cannot take that risk. Then our whole operation will be at risk. All twelve men involved will be at risk. And most likely the President."

"Whoever started this thing is aware of that."

"You have no choice but to take them down. "

Bill paused. He felt trapped. "I have no choice."

"That's correct. If anyone else is in that room, they have to be taken out. We have no choice in this matter. The man who has departed from serving his country and is helping the enemy, so to speak, is to blame. Not us. We cannot allow him to interfere like this with no consequences."

"I understand the principle of the maneuver. But I cannot see taking innocent lives."

"We are talking scenarios here. We have no idea what you will find. The probability of anyone else being in that room is slim and none. But if there is, you will have to take them out fast. You won't have time to think, Bill."

"I'll do my best."

"You have to take care of this, Bill. Once they know they have been discovered, it's all over."

"It will be done."

Bill set his phone down, but his hand was shaking. He was getting angrier and angrier about the whole situation. Killing people like it was nothing. He was done taking out people who were innocent. Especially women and children. He just hoped that when he walked into the room, there'd be one man standing there. He could take him down and leave. Done. But if there were others there, he'd have issue with that. On the other hand, he had no information on how big this rebellion was. How many others were involved. If there were a large group of people in this act of treason, then that was another ball game altogether. With so much in the air, he didn't feel sure about the mission. It was definitely high risk.

He got his gun out, knowing he would have to pick up another gun on the way into the building. But he still wanted his to be ready. It didn't hurt to have two weapons when so many things were questionable.

He sat down and relaxed, thinking through several possibilities. He pulled up GPS to look at a map of the city to get clear in his mind what the surroundings would be like. So the FBI was probably going to be hanging in the trees. On other floors. Around the corner from the building. Probably on the roof. He couldn't worry about where they were, because once he walked in, they would be of no help to him. The only help they would be was if the subject tried to escape and somehow got past him. That had never happened in his whole career. He had never failed to take someone out before. But there was always a slight chance and he had to be prepared for the worst.

The one single thing that was hanging up in his mind was that whoever this man was, he was one of the twelve. Why would he turn? He had to admit he wanted out, himself. He didn't agree with this sick way of eliminating people just because they were against what the President or government was trying to accomplish. Certainly there was a better way.

As the time approached for Bill to leave the house, he noted that the rain had subsided slightly. It was pitch-black out which aided his ability to maneuver around the streets without being seen. He parked far enough away so that his car would not be seen anywhere near the building.

The gun he would use would be hidden in a tall cedar on the side of the building. As he approached the building he could feel the hair standing on the back of his neck. His blood pressure was up and he could hear his heart beating in his ears. He didn't feel good about this mission at all. In fact, he was having big doubts when he reached for the gun and neared the door. They wanted him to enter shooting. He wasn't sure he was ready to do that. But he also knew he could be shot down the moment he opened the door.

Bill put his hand on the door handle and turned it slowly. He was an expert at quiet. As he pushed in with his shoulder, his gun was up and ready to shoot. He opened the door and there was a single man sitting at a desk near a window. The light was bright in the room and it took a moment for his eyes to adjust. He was moving in slow motion but he tried to squint to see the man's face. Before he could pull the trigger, the man yelled out, and at the same time, Bill recognized him

CHAPTER TWENTY-FOUR

"What are you doing in here?" The man's face turned red with anger and fear as he shakily pulled a drawer open and reached for something.

"Wait! Charles! Don't shoot." Bill tried to keep his voice down. He knew the FBI or whoever was outside watching the building, would be listening for a shot to be fired. He aimed his gun up at the ceiling and fired. It was like an explosion going off in the room and they both ducked down to avoid getting hit by the debris that fell out of the ceiling.

"Quick! Cut the lights out." Bill said in a low voice.

Charles quickly moved to the wall and turned off the lights. "Who in the hell are you? What are you doing in here? What do you want from me?"

"I'm one of the twelve. Like you. They sent me here to kill you. I recognized you from Afghanistan. We fought over there together. I am sure they never thought we'd meet."

"Take off your mask. I can't tell who you are by your voice." Charles' movements were still self-protective because he couldn't see Bill's face.

"It's better for you if you don't know who I am. Why are you turning against the Command? What are you trying to accomplish? Talk fast. They may come rushing through that door any second."

Charles walked towards Bill, slowly. "I despise this culling of humans to suit their agenda. It's sick and cannot be hidden any longer. Do you realize how many years this has gone on? How many Presidents have used it to control any opposition?"

Bill shook his head. "I'm aware of that and was hesitant to join. But they gave me no choice. I am certain you were the same."

"Oh, they acted like I had a choice. But when I hesitated, they informed me that I had to serve at the pleasure of the acting President. I had to do it. Bottom line, I felt threatened."

"Same here. But at the moment, we both are at risk standing in this room. They think you are dead. We need a plan."

"You are risking your life by not killing me."

"I knew that going in. I had no choice. When I saw your face, there was no way I could shoot you, unless you had turned spy on the United States government."

"No way. I love my country and risked my life more than once to fight for her. But this is not fighting. This is sick. A Hitler mentality. It has to stop. I wanted it to stop with me."

"We got to get you out of here without being seen. I'm going to run out of here now. Give me a few minutes and go out the back way. I am parked two streets over on Melbourne. A black Lexus. We don't have but just a second before they discover you are gone. I'll have to get you a passport so that you can leave the country. They will hunt you down when they discover there is no body."

"You'll be shot because you didn't kill me."

"I'll tell them I thought you were dead. Now give me a second and then head out the back and run a couple blocks as fast as you can. I'll wait a moment before I take off. This has to work, Charles, or both of us will be dead."

Bill busted through the door, ripping off his mask and pulling off his black shirt. He ran his fingers through his hair, ditched the gun in the cedar tree, and walked quickly to his car, not looking around to see if he was being followed. He didn't want to draw any suspicion by acting like he was afraid. He covered the two blocks quickly, found his car and started the engine. Two seconds later, Charles jumped into the back seat and Bill took off. He slowly drove around town, stopping to get a paper at the closest BP Gas station. When he got back into the car, his legs felt weak.

"I don't know about you, Charles, but that was too close. I know I was being watched going in. I have no idea if they hung around after they heard the shot or not. They usually don't get rid of the body, but this time, you being one of the twelve, I thought they might."

Charles took a good look at Bill and nodded. "I recognize you now, Bill. What a hell of a situation, you and I facing each other with guns when we fought together for the freedom of our country. Nearly lost our lives a few times over there. Good to see you again. But not under these circumstances. Bill, there is a movement right under our noses—states are sick and tired of big government. I've been working underground with some politicians who want to take action to stop what the President has been doing. There was no danger or threat to his life, and there isn't now. We were planning on finding a way to convince a few more states that his agenda concerning the overthrow of the Fifth Amendment, saying it was misinterpreted, has got to be stopped. It's no longer a government for the people. It has its own agenda. There are some states forming a Convention States; all we need is one more state."

"I'm with you on that, but they were watching me like a friggin' hawk. I knew I had to do what they said, or my family's lives would be at stake."

"Well, I'm not married. Had some PTSD issues from the war and just decided I'd better figure all this out on my own without dragging a woman into the mix. We live in a crazy world. I didn't want to make her life crazier."

"My family has no idea what I'm involved in. They would freak out. To top it off, I lost my daughter recently to a car accident. She left our house to drive home and was dead in a matter of moments."

"You sure it was an accident? They have their ways of getting you to do what they want."

Bill sat back in his seat. He'd never thought for one moment that the government was involved in the death of his daughter. But come to think of it, they were afraid there was a leak.

"I wonder if that was a warning from them, because they feared there was a leak; someone right under their nose. When they found out it was probably one of the twelve, we all were at risk of having their murderous hands in our lives. Do you think they killed her?"

"I'm just laying it out there as a possibility. It's strange that it happened a block or two from your house. Where do you live?"

Bill looked at him solemnly in the rear view mirror. He trusted this man with an awful lot, when he was supposed to be dead already. "On Olive Street."

"That's not a very busy part of town. Where was the wreck?"

"Madison and Fifth."

"I have no idea if they caused the accident, but it certainly is a possibility."

"Where am I taking you? Home?"

"Yeah, drop me off at the corner of Lincoln and South Cherry Street. I'll walk the rest of the way."

"What will you do now?"

"I'm not sure. The easy thing would be to leave the country. But since when do we do the easy thing, buddy?"

Bill laughed. "Will these politicians help you in any way? You need some people watching your back."

"We both do. They're going to come down hard on you for not taking me out. And what will you do when your next order comes down the pike?"

"Good question. I think I'm going to have to talk to my wife. Because this isn't going to stop. It's only going to get worse."

"You may be hearing from my group, too. They're going to want to talk to you."

"Damn. That may have to take place outside my home and work. I can't get them all involved in my daily life."

"Command may take away your daily life if they find out you are talking to me. Or anyone who is against what they are trying to do. Can you imagine changing the Constitution at this point? It's insane. But they are determined to do it. They say it is time for a change. That America is changing."

"Oh, it's changing all right. But we better fight to keep what we can. For once it's gone, there's no limit to what will happen. It will affect the rest of the world, if we allow this to go on.

Charles opened the door and turned to Bill. "Thanks for giving me a chance to talk to you. I still can't believe you didn't shoot me down."

"If I had not recognized you, I would have taken you out. There's no doubt about it."

"I'll be in touch. Good luck in telling your wife. I can't imagine that conversation."

"Neither can I, Charles. Talk to you soon. Watch your back."

CHAPTER TWENTY-FIVE

The phone beside him rang loudly. He was dead to the world and jumped when he heard the ring. He knew before he answered that it wouldn't be good.

"What's going on, Bill?"

"I did my job."

"You may have, but they found no body."

"What? That's crazy. I saw him go down. And the weapon I used had to have taken him out. It blew out half the ceiling."

"You better hope someone removed his body. I would be very disappointed if he turned up alive and well."

"I can't control what happens after I walk out."

"I'm aware of what you can't control."

"Were you responsible for the death of my daughter?"

"You expect me to answer that kind of question?"

"If I find out you did, you will have to answer a lot more questions."

"You don't threaten Command, Bill."

"And you don't kill my family and expect me to sit by and take it."

"I have no idea how your daughter died."

"And I'm to believe you?"

"Frankly, I don't care what you believe. We are capable of taking out anyone. As you well know. You have been a big part of that."

"To my demise, I am afraid."

"There is always a risk on both sides. But if you were the leak, or if we even thought you were, things would happen around you. We will find out one way or the other."

"Is there anything else you need?"

"Just letting you know there was no body. You better pray it shows up somewhere. A funeral needs to be taking place or heads will roll."

Dial tone.

Bill sat up in bed. Sleep was not on the agenda tonight. He walked over to his desk and sat down, opening his computer and searching Convention of States and read all he could on the subject concerning the overreaching of the government. He knew this was part of a big problem that the United States was facing but there was more. This agenda to take people out that were against what the President was doing was such Mafia mentality. No negotiations. Just death. .

As Bill was sitting there, he knew he had to get out soon. Even while he was in, he was not safe. They were watching him and the other men like hawks, waiting for some weak moment when they were faltering on their loyalty to this sick agenda of theirs. What he wondered was how the President's Club had lasted so long. Maybe their agenda was different long ago. Maybe it was needed in some other way. But it had certainly taken a turn, a wicked turn that meant there was no democracy any longer. It was the President's way or no way.

He moved his chair back and sat there thinking about what he was going to do. He needed to talk to Sharon, but was she safer with her sister than at home with him? Was he going to become a target and then his whole family would be at risk? So many questions and no one to ask.

He lay back on the bed and closed his eyes. Morning could not come soon enough. It would be refreshing to work with clients and get his head into the numbers again. That was his real world. This other was a parallel universe he lived in. A crazy world that he prayed didn't become a reality for everyone. How did Hitler kill so many people? He lied to them. And that was happening now in America. Lies and deceit. Murder. Bad decisions. A socialistic society where the hard-earned money of the rich was given to the poor or the lazy. A Robin Hood syndrome that never worked.

He must have dozed off because he was awakened again by the phone ringing. Only this time it was Sharon.

"Hope I didn't wake you."

"No. I was just lying here thinking."

"You've been doing a lot of that lately."

"Yes, too much of it. How are you? Are you having fun yet?"

"Oh yes. We are having a ball. You would be bored, but we are enjoying flea market shopping, decorating, and eating at all the hard to find lunch spots. I had forgotten how well we got along. I think I am doing her some good, too."

"I'm certain of that. You just enjoy yourself and take your time. There's no hurry coming home for now. I am working hard and even though I am missing you here, I am so glad you are happy. Laughing for a change."

"I am. It feels good, Bill. Haven't thought about Susan once while I was here. Maybe I am at the end of my grieving. Or at least the tough part."

"It never all goes away, baby. But we do get farther from it. I think the pain dims a bit as time goes on."

"That is my goal. How are you? Are you eating enough?"

He shook his head and then realized she couldn't see him. "Yes, I am doing fine. Just a little stressed. But don't you worry. I better get showered and off to work, Sharon. Call me and let me know what you're doing and what great things you are buying."

"I love you, Bill. I'll be home before you know it."

"Take your time, Honey. It's good to get away sometimes. It puts everything into perspective."

"Talk to you soon."

He hung up the phone, wanting to talk to her about everything. It was so tempting to call her back but he resisted the urge, showered, dressed, grabbed some hot coffee, and headed to the office. Once there, he closed himself off in his office and dealt with the pile of folders on his desk. He had three appointments before noon, and then a full afternoon meeting with two clients at their offices.

It was good to allow himself to get lost in the numbers and forget about everything else. His brain was tired of trying to solve an issue that seemed an enigma. As long as he could keep his partners happy, then he was doing fine. It was the secret world he lived in that was breaking him down. He was hoping Charles had escaped the long arms of the government but it didn't sound like he was going to run. He wanted to talk to him but there was no way possible for that to happen. He was certain now that they would be following him and probably had tapped all of his forms of communication. Except for his computer at work, and he couldn't really count on that. He was in a worse mess for helping Charles, but there wasn't a chance in hell that the event could have turned out any other way. He had recognized the guy immediately so there was no way he was going to pull the trigger. He would have to bide his time. Wait for the right moment. But who would he shoot in the near future that might be a terrible mistake?

It was a long day, and he knew he'd be facing a quiet house when he got home. He pulled up in the driveway, halfway expecting someone to be there, but it was quiet. He went in and laid his briefcase on his office desk and looked around, trying to see if he could tell if someone had been inside. He checked the lampshades and air conditioning vents for bugs, but found nothing. That didn't mean anything. The way technology was progressing, they might be using his own computer to watch him. He swore to be more vigilant in what he said at home and also made a note to purchase another phone in case he needed more privacy. It wasn't going to get easier.

He turned on the television and sat back, resting his feet on an old leather ottoman that Sharon had threatened to throw out a hundred times. The news was on but Bill was barely listening. Suddenly, he sat straight up in his chair, staring at a news flash that was running across the bottom of the screen. The announcement read "Charles Miller, former Special OPS Lieutenant, found dead in his home. Possible suicide. More to come at six."

Bill was overcome with emotion. He paced the living room, talking under his breath. What could he have done differently? How could he have protected Charles better? They hunted him down! Of course, the first place they would have looked for him was his home. Bill didn't understand why Charles wanted to go home. He knew they would come after him.

Something didn't feel right, but there was no one he could talk to about it. He certainly couldn't ask the voice of Command. He was already under a microscope now, so he was going to have to be even more careful about what was spoken at home. He didn't know whether to tell Sharon or not. He sure didn't want her life to be in jeopardy, but if he withheld all of this information from her and something happened to him, she would not understand. It would be too frightening. And now, with this situation with Charles, his life was on the line even more. The odds of him getting shot in some random way were higher than ever.

He sat back down in his chair and put his head in his hands. Since Susan's death, things had gotten out of control. He no longer recognized the man he saw staring back at him in the mirror every morning. He had to make a plan. Somehow, he had to disengage himself from this group of men bent on destruction at any cost. And he didn't want to be their next victim

CHAPTER TWENTY-SIX

One Franklin Square. The new address of McCloud, Sinclair, Kenner, and Jones. Bill and the others worked hard for two solid weeks getting their offices in shape. All the partners stayed late every day to put together one of the most prestigious accounting offices in Washington. It was sitting in a sought-out location, and they all realized that they might be acquiring more clients than their small staff could handle. They ran an ad immediately for associates. There was already a line a mile long down the hall and in the foyer of the new office composed of applicants for the job. Some were dressed in business suits and others like they were going to play nine holes. But after hours of reading applications which had been placed online earlier, the partners narrowed it down to twenty people to interview.

A massive mahogany desk was centered in Bill's office. Tall windows ran across the back of the office, where he could see most of the skyline of Washington. It was breathtaking and would win over many clients taken in by the view. Bill sat down and turned his chair towards the windows. It took some getting used to, staring across the great expanse of concrete mixed with massive trees. Man had certainly made his mark in Washington. Famous architects painted the sky with tall towers and steeples, while the drugs and dealings of the underground took place below sea level.

The city was a mixed variety of people, which is what attracted people to live there. But it didn't attract Bill anymore, even if it had in the past; the club that Bill had been forced to join had colored his view of the where the President resided. It left him with a sick feeling and dread. Hardly the emotions that most people held when thinking about the White House.

Bill began the arduous task of interviewing twenty eager, would-be associates one at a time. It kept his mind off his secrets. They were a motley group of mixed intellects: techie geeks, numbers people, and an uneducated few who had no chance. One woman and the rest men.

The first one he interviewed was a winner from the get-go. Freddie Martin. College graduate majoring in accounting who also knew the computer systems they used at the firm could probably hack into the White House if needed. He was hired on the spot.

The second person was Miranda Jones. Simple girl with long hair pulled back like a schoolmarm. She wore glasses and could not have looked plainer. But her brain was larger than her fashion sense and she knew her stuff. He liked her no-nonsense approach to things and was impressed with her resume. He hired her and went on to the third interview, which was a complete and utter joke, a guy named Jamie Winters who did not care to wear anything but tennis shoes and ripped jeans. He would not fit into the corporate world even if Bill had purchased him a new pair of jeans.

It was the next young man who impressed Bill the most. Marshall Whitman was dressed in a cheap suit but still looked good. He was polished and spoke intelligently, handled himself like a professional and was ready and eager to do the job. He knew accounting better than most and understood figures. He also had a personality, which was rare in CPAs and accountants. He had an easy smile and looked hungry for the job.

Jeff poked his head in the door after Marshall walked out, and grinned at Bill.

"How's it going?"

"I've sent several home and hired three. We got one great one, and the other two will be easy to train."

"Sounds good. I think one more, and then you're done."

"Okay. Send another one in."

Jeff left and in came a guy with long hair pulled back in a ponytail. He reached out to shake Bill's hand and Bill noticed he had a strong grip.

"Hello, Mr. Sinclair. My name is Jim Sneed. Thanks for seeing me today."

"Nice to meet you, Jim. Sit down."

Jim sat down and looked Bill in the eye.

"What do you know about accounting, Jim? Any experience?"

"Quite a bit. My father is a CPA. I have helped him as long as I can remember. I've always had a way with math and loved numbers. He started me early and I have learned a lot from him."

"You out of college?"

"Yes, sir. Two years. Worked in a small firm but it died. Not enough clients."

"It can happen. What do you see yourself doing in ten years?"

"I'd like to own my own firm one day. But everyone in the field knows who McCloud, Kenner, Sinclair, and Jones are, and when I heard that you were hiring, I couldn't get here fast enough. This would be the ideal job to learn all I need to know. And I want to get my master's. Don't have too much more in order to achieve that."

"We need some sharp people here that learn quickly and do a good job. I like you, Jim, but this is a serious job. Do you have what it takes to put in the hours and handle the challenge? We have some big accounts and we cannot lose them by making mistakes."

"I'm used to working under pressure. And I have nothing else going on in my life, so working long and hard suits me just fine."

Bill stood up and nodded. "Okay, you're hired. You start Monday morning with the other three people I hired today. I'll be here to get you started. I may even want you to work for me. I could use some help."

"I would love to work for you, Mr. Sinclair. It would be an opportunity of a lifetime."

"See you Monday, Jim. Eight o'clock sharp."

Jeff and Blake walked back into Bill's office and sat down.

"How do they look to you, Bill? You find some people who are ready to work hard?"

"Jeff, I did the best I could with what you gave me. I picked the best four. I think we'll do fine."

"We need some good help; people who understand real numbers. I'm tired of finding errors in the work our regulars are doing."

"I picked one for myself. Hope you don't mind. Jim Sneed. He seems sharp and knows his stuff. I'll train him. You guys might want to check out the other three. It helps, I think, if we train them instead of leaving them on their own to learn how we want things done."

They both nodded and walked out of his office.

Bill's phone rang. The private phone in his pocket. He got up and closed his door and answered in a low voice.

"You don't usually call me at work."

"You owe us for messing up that last deal."

"I owe you? I thought he was dead."

"Well, we took care of it. But we have another situation. We found someone we can get information from who knows about the group Charlie was involved with. It has to do with the Convention of States they're trying to convene. We need you to get some names for us."

"So when is this supposed to happen?"

"Tonight. Ten o'clock. We have his home address. He lives alone."

"You sending me the address?"

"I will send a code for you to retrieve it. Don't mess this up."

"I got it."

"You have said that before. Next time you will not get by with a warning, Bill."

"You threatening me?"

"It's part of the job. You can't make big mistakes."

"It wasn't on purpose."

"Could have been."

"Hell, if you don't trust me, then why are you sending me on another mission?"

"I could take you out now. I have reason enough."

"Then do it. This is tough enough for me with my wife and family without the threats."

"We need you to take care of this group. To find out enough information so that we can control it."

"Consider it done."

"The code will be the next thing you receive. The next thing I will hear from you will be the names we want."

Dead line.

Bill sat back in his chair and wiped beads of sweat from his brow. He felt like running. He was so tired of Command owning his life. And this was something he didn't ask for. He hated it.

He sighed. It was a wasted conversation he was having with himself. He had to learn to save that energy for something that mattered. And something he could change.

⟢ ⟣

Walter hung up the phone and swore. Bill was slipping away. He felt it. But he really needed Bill's expertise, if there was any way possible to turn him around. He was getting more and more difficult to deal with, and that meant that he wouldn't apply himself fully to the job at hand. It could cost Bill his life and it could blow the whole operation. No one man was worth that. He knew if there was one more error on Bill's part, he would get a call from the national security advisor. And that conversation would not go well. He could lose his position and Bill could lose his life. Neither outcome was acceptable.

CHAPTER TWENTY-SEVEN

It was pitch black outside, with clouds covering the moon. At precisely 9:45 PM, Bill received a text with a code number. He dialed the code and was told the address where the hit, a man named Doug Langley, lived. He jotted down the information and walked outside to his car. The thought occurred to him that it was a good thing that Sharon wasn't home yet from her visit with Anne. It made is much easier for him to get out at night and complete his mission. For a few moments, he sat in the dark inside his car and just took a deep breath. He wasn't looking forward to the job he was about to do. It could go easy or it could get ugly. Really ugly. He was prepared either way. But he would rather the guy just give up the names on the get-go. That wasn't going to happen.

When he arrived at Doug's home, there was a single light on in the living room. The rest of the large house was dark. Bill turned on his small flashlight and looked in the window of the garage. One car was inside. Doug was most likely alone. He pulled on his mask and carried only his briefcase with him to the door. When he passed the window facing the front of the house, he could see

Doug sitting at his computer. He walked quietly up to the front door and turned the knob. He was surprised to find it was not locked. Of course, Doug wasn't suspecting anything. He had no idea what was about to take place.

Bill opened the door and Doug jumped up from his computer desk and yelled. Bill aimed his gun as he spoke in a stern voice. He saw the panic in Doug's eyes. "Just take it easy, Doug. This will go easier for you if you stay calm. I'm not here to hurt you. I just need information. Now where can we sit and talk that's not in front of an open window."

Doug wasn't taking the intrusion well. It was obvious he was scared and angry. "What the hell are you doing here? What do you want from me?"

"Do you have an office where we can talk? Or I'm going to have to close those curtains on your front window."

"I need to know who you are. Who sent you?" Doug was a short man but came towards him with his fists ready to fight.

"Hold on a second. I'll tell you more when we get away from this window."

Doug turned and walked into the next room, his office. It was small, with one lamp on the desk. Doug sat behind the desk and Bill stood in front of the desk. Doug's cell phone rang, but he knew better than to answer it. "Turn that thing off until we're done. I don't want a reason to hurt you."

Doug looked up and Bill noticed his face had turned white. "What do you want from me? I've done nothing wrong."

"I'm not after you, Doug. I need some names. I know you are involved in this group supporting the Convention of States. I need the names of those who are funding this thing. The big money people. And don't tell me you have no idea."

Doug smiled nervously. "Of course I know who they are. But they've done nothing wrong. This isn't illegal what we are doing here. It's all perfectly legal."

"We don't give a crap if it's legal. We want those names and tonight you are going to give them to me."

"What are you going to do, shoot me?"

"No. I'm not going to kill you. I'm just going to make you wish you were dead."

"Come on, man. What are you trying to do? This movement is too big to stop. The people of the United States are sick of the way things are going down. Even if you take out some of the money people, there will be more who step up in their place."

Bill laughed. "They won't be so eager when the people suddenly disappear. Now start talking or I'm going to get out my tools."

Doug was sweating. "Have you thought about what you are doing? Do you realize what you will have to live with the rest of your life?"

"We're not talking about me. Now give me the names, or you're going to be missing some fingers. Maybe a limb." Bill opened up his briefcase and pulled out a small hatchet. He aimed his gun at Doug's head.

Doug swallowed and stood up. Bill knew he was trying to think of some way to get out of this mess. He also knew Doug realized there was no way. "Don't even think of running. Now, it's your choice. Either talk or I am going to take something away from you. The longer you delay in giving me the names, the more you're going to lose."

"I—I can give you a few names. But I want to be protected. No one can know who talked."

"You're worried about your reputation, and I have a gun aimed at your head?"

"I have to make a living. I know you don't care about me at all. But I do have to make a living."

"I'd say that's the least of your worries, right now. Talk to me."

"Why me? How did you find me?"

Bill knew he was stalling. And the longer he was standing in this man's study, the bigger the chance this thing could go south. He had to get him to talk. "Put your right hand on the table."

Doug yelled out. "No way! Just a minute. Why are you in such a hurry?"

Bill grabbed his hand before Doug could pull away, and slammed down the hatchet on his little finger. Doug screamed out and blood went all over the desk.

"Now you believe me? Start talking."

Doug pulled a handkerchief out of his pocket and wrapped it around his hand. He was shaking now. And Bill had his attention. "Fred Williams. CEO of Brigham Warner Investments. He's a big donor."

Bill wrote the name down and looked up with a raised eyebrow. "Now that wasn't too hard, was it? Give me some other names."

"Morgan Whitman Productions. Jimmy Simms. He's the finance guy there. One of the largest movie production companies in Hollywood."

"You're doing fine. Now who else is involved that is dropping the big money?"

Doug shook his head. "I don't know anyone else. I swear I don't. They don't tell me everything."

Bill stood up and grabbed his other arm. "You want this arm? Because I've been here too long already. I need to get out of here. For your sake and mine. Now talk or this arm is coming off, Doug."

Doug yanked back and nearly fell over his chair. "I said I didn't know anyone else. What do you want from me?"

Bill was getting impatient and also tired of the game. "He aimed the gun right at Doug's head and yelled out, 'Give me the names now!'"

Doug sat down and put his head in his hands. "I give up. If I don't tell you, you will kill me or cut off my arm. If I do tell you, they will find out somehow and I'll be dead anyway. People with money can be just as tough as you."

The gun had not left Bill's hand. It was still aimed at Doug's head. "I'm counting to three. You better spit out another name or you're going to get a bullet."

"I—um—I think Billy Ray Martin was a large donor. But he's a famous singer. You can't take him out. Is that what you're going to do? Kill him?"

"I'm not killing anyone. I just need their names."

"Something's really wrong here. No one has broken the law. Who is behind you? Who are you working for?"

"Better you don't know anything. I'm walking out of here. Your phone is tapped and everything you do is being watched. Don't try to call someone. Keep your mouth shut. If we find out you have talked, you're going down. Understood?"

Doug shook his head. The handkerchief was blood red.

"You know nothing. If you talk, you will be found dead and it will be claimed a suicide. So don't even let that thought sit on your mind for a nanosecond."

Bill grabbed his briefcase and threw the hatchet inside and zipped it up. As he walked to the door he turned back and looked at Doug. He had not moved from his desk. "You'll have to get that hand looked at. They will ask you what happened. You tell them you were working in your shop and turned on a saw. Or you were cooking and chopped off your finger by mistake. We are watching everything you do. So don't make a mistake by talking. You don't know anything, Doug. Absolutely nothing."

Doug was visibly shaken. He shook his head and stayed seated at his desk. Bill walked to his car, checking to make sure no one was around. He pulled out onto the main street and took his time going home, zigzagging around town. When he got home, he dialed the code and entered the information he was given.

It was late in the night when he broke out in a sweat and felt nauseous. He tossed and turned and finally got out of bed and drank a small glass of wine. The moon had moved from behind the clouds and its rays were pushing through the thin curtains of his bedroom. He sat on the edge of his bed with tears coming down his face. This was worse than anything he'd had to do in Afghanistan. This was America. His own country. And he found himself hating those invisible people who were controlling him like a puppet. One day he was going to cut the strings. One day real soon.

CHAPTER TWENTY-EIGHT

C hristmas in the Sinclair home was like stepping back in time. There were trees in every room, wreaths on the outside of every window in the front of the house, the roof was lit with white lights, and the lawn had a winter wonderland scene that stopped traffic for weeks. Sharon loved to decorate for the holidays and involved all of her children in the process. That included Bill, of course. He did it reluctantly at first, but after he saw the joy it brought, he eventually jumped in with more enthusiasm. The food, the gifts, the smells, and the sights all brought the family together under one roof for a few days, to celebrate the blessing of Christmas and to give to each other. To top things off, almost like an answered prayer of a child, it snowed most Christmases in Washington. So the lawn was piled with snow and everything standing was morphed in the white powdery dusting.

When they were young kids, the children would slide down the hills in the neighborhood on garbage can lids or on cardboard boxes. Snowmen were standing in every yard guarding the house while those inside watched for that magic sleigh and eight reindeer.

Secrets were kept, packages piled up around the trees, and all was well with the world.

This Christmas, Avery was carrying the first grandchild. Emily and Rob were settled into their marriage and were talking of children at some point. Everyone was keeping their eyes on them with smiles on their faces. It was time for children in the Sinclair household. The sound of little feet, the laughter. It was coming.

But for Sharon, it wasn't coming fast enough. She looked around the house, smiling. She'd done her best this year to make it beautiful. It was going to be a difficult time because of the obvious—Susan wasn't there with them. An empty chair was placed at the table so that they all would remember her. Somehow by setting a place for her at the table they felt as if she wasn't so far away. Sharon had always hung stockings across the massive fireplace for her children. Susan's was among the stockings hanging, full of their favorite candies, chocolates, and small items they might find interesting.

The aroma of turkey roasting in the oven brought Bill out of his study. "Hey, lady. You got something I could snack on until dinner is ready? What time are the kids coming over?"

"Around 5:30. Emily is bringing the pies. Avery is bringing cookies. And Jesse is bringing the eggnog and bottles of wine."

"Well, I'm starving. What do we have I can munch on?"

"I'll get you a sandwich to hold you over." Sharon went into the kitchen and grabbed a plate and made him a ham sandwich and poured a glass of tea.

"Aren't you going to eat?"

"For some reason, my appetite has been poor lately. Not sure why. It's a bit tough not having Susan around for Christmas.

Thanksgiving was tough enough. But I knew this would be more difficult."

"We all feel it, Honey. I have a lump in my throat that won't go down. I am sure the kids feel it. But we must try to have a good time tonight. We have other children and Susan would want us to be happy."

Sharon nodded but inside she knew nothing would make it okay.

"Are you ready for this, Sharon? All the kids being here. You've been pretty secluded since you came back from Anne's."

"I'll be fine. They're my kids. Yes, I'll be upset when I stare at the empty seat at the table. I bet I won't be the only one that sheds a tear. You think?"

"No. You won't be alone in that aspect. But I worry about how long you have grieved. How private your grieving is. I haven't cried either. I need to. I have been so busy with work that I have placed all those feelings way back somewhere. I guess I am accustomed to that. But you are not. You usually have them all out in the open. But not this. Not this time."

Sharon smiled. "I'm shocked that you would notice that much, Bill."

He reached over and touched her hand. "Do you know how long it has been that we have been together? Even held each other close?"

She looked down. "I know, Honey. I'm sorry. I have pulled away from you and I'm sorry. Please don't be angry with me. You know I love you. But my heart has been broken into a million pieces. I don't know how to put it back together."

He stood up and pulled her close to him. She resisted but he held her tightly. "Let me love you back. Let me heal your heart. I am strong. I have huge shoulders. And my love is enough for us both."

She leaned into him and quit resisting. He was sure he felt her give in. Maybe the healing would begin now.

Bill was counting on it. Because truth be known, he needed her, too. More than she would ever know. Because of what he was asked to do, he needed some sense of normalcy in his life. Some depth and closeness that would pull him back from the dragons that wanted to take his life away.

He also knew that Sharon would die if she knew what he was doing. The extent of destruction that he played a role in by taking lives or intimidating people to get what Command wanted. This was not what he was trained to do in the homeland. This was for terrorists. But he was being used, and he couldn't share it with her. Not yet, anyway.

The kids were coming in. He let her go, slowly, and went to greet the them.

"Dad! You look wonderful. How's Mother? Where is she? We haven't seen much of her since she got back from Aunt Anne's house." Emily was coming through the door with pies in both hands. Rob had another pie, and bags full of packages in the other hand.

"She's in the kitchen, Em. I know she'll be thrilled to see all of you. Go put your pies down and give me a hug." Bill moved to help Rob, who shook his head and walked towards the tree, set the bags down, and went into the kitchen with the pie.

"Dad? Hey! What's up? Gosh, it smells good in this house." Jesse was coming in with presents under each arm and a bag in one hand.

"Hey, Son. Come on in. Mother's outdone herself in the kitchen."

"That's nothing new."

Jacob and Paul and Avery were all together, carrying presents and tins of cookies. The house was filling up and it almost felt like old times. Almost. Bill greeted his sons and nodded towards the kitchen.

"Everyone is gathering in the kitchen where that aroma is coming from. I am starving; been that way all morning."

Jacob grinned. "I have been thinking about this meal all morning. How's Mother holding up? I know she is missing Susan today."

"She is, Son. She's hurting real bad. But our job is to make her smile today. Not to forget Susan, but to enjoy what we have here. This meal is a family tradition, and we all enjoy it. Go make her smile."

All three sons walked into the kitchen, grabbing bites of turkey and sniffing into the air, making Sharon laugh.

"Oh, get out of here! It's almost ready. Paul? Why don't you get the glasses filled with iced tea, and put plenty of ice in them. I hate hot tea. Jacob, please put the turkey on the table, and everyone else get out of the kitchen. How am I supposed to think?"

The group obeyed and left the kitchen, settling around the table, talking noisily about presents and expected snowfall. Sharon walked in with bowls of vegetables and Emily carried dressing and rolls. The table was covered in food that was steaming hot, making appetites soar.

"Mother, you have outdone yourself. Dad was right!" Jesse spoke with a mouthful of food.

"It feels like more this year, for some reason. Maybe because I am getting older. Not sure." Sharon smiled and nodded at Bill.

"You pray for us, Bill?"

"Of course."

The room was quiet as Bill prayed for the family. "Lord, this is a tough day for us all. We miss our Susan. But you have her now, so we are going to trust that she is happy. Be with us today, especially Sharon, as our hearts are heavy. We thank you for all that you have given us. Protect this family and keep us close. Amen."

And Christmas came and went. But the loss of Susan was everywhere. Unspoken but loud.

CHAPTER TWENTY-NINE

J esse and Maryanne were an item. It was getting pretty obvious to those around them that this might be a wedding kind of thing. Jesse was smitten; never dreamed he would find someone like her.

She was strong, even stubborn at times, and their tastes were not the same. Not even close. But somehow, in that world of romance, it worked. They had dated; they had eaten at every major restaurant in town. They had sat up and watched old movies and eaten bad pizza, drank a few beers, laughed until they were exhausted, and still came back for more. Soon, they were staying at each other's place and carrying clothes back and forth.

Someone needed to bring up marriage, but no one wanted to say it. It was a scary thing, getting married. It was so final. And Jesse knew he had to be dead sure before he brought it up. He wondered if they'd discussed everything that was critical to a deep relationship. The word *deep* even made him nervous. But it was there, just the same. And he wasn't getting any younger.

He'd watched Emily walk right into that marriage like it was nothing. She seemed to do it with such ease. But he would have been comforted to know that there had been some struggle, some hesitation that she'd felt before she just said the word "yes." He wanted a home and a family. He knew it was in his cards. But Maryanne was almost bigger than life. She was so pretty he just barely could look at her. To stare at her in the eyes made his knees weak. To share a life with her, well, it might kill him. The beauty of it, that is.

It was time to pick her up. They were going to a concert at the Civic Center downtown, and it was still cold outside. Spring was forever coming in Washington. But he was dressed to the nines and had his heavy wool coat and scarf; wind was certainly a constant in the winter. He pulled up to Maryanne's house and got out, excited to see what she was wearing. He was never disappointed.

He knocked on the door and when she opened it, she was still in her jeans. Crying.

"What in the world is going on? We are going to be late!! What's wrong?"

"I feel horrible. Can we just skip this thing?" She was standing there in her ripped jeans, her hair was wet, and her makeup was running down her face.

"I bought tickets. They weren't cheap. Maryanne, what is happening to you? You were all excited about going."

"Want to come in? I'm a complete mess."

Jesse stepped through the doorway. "I can see that."

"You're mad."

"I'm—" He paused. "I'm upset. I'm not mad. There's a difference. I was looking forward to hearing this band and I thought you were, too."

"I was."

"The Electric Light Orchestra. Who doesn't like them?"

"I know. I know. I just cannot go. I feel awful."

"What is it? A cold? Allergy? The flu?"

They sat down on her sofa and he hugged her. She wiped her eyes with a Kleenex and grabbed two more out of the box to blow her nose.

"My brother James, the attorney, has been in a terrible wreck. He's dead. We weren't that close, but it has upset me to the point that I feel almost immobile."

"Honey, I am so sorry. What happened?"

"I was called by a friend of his, who was at the hospital. He was in a bad car wreck; a semi plowed into him from across the median. I can only imagine the horror he felt seeing that truck coming at him."

"Don't think about that, Honey. I am sure it happened so quickly that he barely knew what hit him."

"He had his faults, but James was brilliant. Such a great personality. And he had my father's good looks—dark thick brown hair and blue eyes. You don't see that combination often. The women loved it."

"Sorry I never got to meet him, baby."

They both sat down on the sofa and Jesse pulled her into him. She cried and tears came into his eyes listening to her sobs. "We'll make it through this, Maryanne. I had to bury my sister and it was one of the toughest things I've ever had to do. But somehow, months later, I could see the light at the end of the tunnel. I'm here for you."

She sat up and wiped her eyes. "I'm a wreck tonight. I'm so sorry that this has ruined your plans for us."

"Don't be silly. What do you need me to do? How can I help tonight?"

"I think I need to be alone, strange as that sounds."

Jesse stood up slowly and pulled her up next to him, wrapping his strong arms around her.

"Whatever it takes for you to deal with this is okay with me. I'm just a phone call away. Will you let me know if you need anything?"

She kissed him softly and wiped her eyes. "Of course I will, Honey. Thank you for being so understanding. This is just such a shock to me. The last thing I thought I would hear tonight. I'll call you in the morning, I promise."

Jesse decided to go to the concert alone. Bad idea. The music was loud, which was no surprise. The crowd was massive, with elbow room only. But in the middle of all that crazy, he felt her absence. He knew she was home suffering, so he left in the middle, which he never did. And driving home it suddenly hit him that his bachelorhood was on the verge of death and he was dangerously close to doing the thing he'd scoffed at in his younger years. When all his friends had taken the dive and married their high school sweethearts, he had sat back with a smug look on his face. But now he was running towards it like a fool in love. Only it was true this time.

She was it. It felt right. He only hoped that life didn't get in the way, like it had tonight. It seemed like there was always something going on that kept the good part of life from happening. This time he was going to stick his foot in the door to make sure this chapter of his life didn't close before he had a ring on her finger. Oh yes, the ring. Maybe he needed to make a trip to the jeweler.

He slept that night with a smile on his face, feeling mischievous. But not so much that he forgot her pain.

CHAPTER THIRTY

In the spring, before any leaves even thought about showing their bright green tips on the barren trees scattered across Washington, Bill made a decision to tell Sharon about his secret life. Not the whole but part. It was getting more and more difficult for him to explain his whereabouts without her hitting him with twenty questions. He hated lying to her. Absolutely hated it. But up until now he'd had no choice. He was going to put her at risk; just the fact that she would know some of what was going on. But the way it was going now, his marriage was at risk. Whoever was in command of this nightmare was already threatening him. He knew it would only get more difficult as time went on. So even though he dreaded it, he was going to sit down with Sharon and have a serious talk. She might even freak out. But it was better for her to find out from him than wait until something horrific happened to him. She would never forgive him. He would be lucky if she understood his position as it was.

He had given great thought as to how and where to tell her. He was certain that his house and car were tapped. His personal cell, without question. He wasn't sure if they had put a tap in his shoes, so he was going to use extreme caution in how he told her. It was perhaps the most serious conversation they would ever have, short of learning their daughter had been killed in a car wreck.

Sharon had been to town all morning and was not expecting him home for hours. He could hear the surprise in her voice when she came through the door. "Bill? Is something wrong? What in the world are you doing home at this time of day? Are you sick?"

A smile danced briefly across his lined face. "No. I'm fine. Just got through early. How was your morning?"

She waltzed through the door and stared into his face. "We've been married a long time. I can't recall one time you came home early. Now you gonna tell me or what?"

He shook his head and took her hand. He was barefooted. He sat her down and took off her shoes. She looked puzzled but followed his lead. He put his finger to his lips and pointed to the door going out to the backyard. She nodded and walked through the door. It was still a little chilly outside, so she grabbed the afghan on the sofa on her way out and slung it across her shoulders. Bill grabbed two cups of hot coffee and followed her out. Once they were on the porch, Bill took her hand and led her out in the yard to a small gazebo. Once there, he pointed to the two chairs on the outer edge and they each sat down.

Bill could tell Sharon had no clue what was going on, and he knew what he was about to share with her would change everything between them. He had to do it in the right way. He looked at her and put his finger up to his lips to silence her. She nodded, somehow sensing that this was very serious. He stood up and checked the gazebo for a tap, looking underneath, on top and around all the sides. He could easily miss it, but he felt pretty sure it was clean. Still, all precaution had to be taken, or both of them could be dead tomorrow.

"Can I talk now?" Sharon was at the end of her rope.

"Hang on."

Bill moved his chair close to her and nodded.

"Sharon, obviously I have something to discuss with you. It has taken me a long time to decide whether or not to talk to you about this, but now I feel it's critical that I do. I hope you'll listen until I'm finished and then I want to hear your thoughts. Fair?"

She frowned. "I guess."

"Some time ago I got a call from the White House. I think it was the chief of staff; I am pretty sure I recognized his voice. I was told I was needed by the President to be a part of twelve men who would be asked to take care of certain situations at any given time. I could not refuse. I would not know who the other men were nor would they know me. We would act independently and were sworn to secrecy. If any of us talked I am certain we would be taken out. I cannot and will not tell you what I have been asked to do. It is critical that you never find that out. But the main thing I wanted you to know is that I will get phone calls at random times night or day, and I have to respond immediately. I have no choice. In the past I have used the excuse that a client needed me, because I could not get you involved. But because of recent circumstances, I feel it is time I tell you some of what is going on."

Sharon had a frightened look on her face, but she was a strong woman.. "I have to admit I suspected something. But I was nowhere close to the truth. I feared an affair, although that was a stretch. I am shocked that the President would ask men to do things that must be so horrific you cannot share them with your wife."

"It has gone on for years, Sharon. I don't even know how long this group has existed."

"So who calls you?"

"Someone who goes by 'Command.' I don't know who he is."

"And he gives you orders that you have to obey."

"I have to carry them out word for word. I cannot hesitate or make a mistake."

"And you're telling me that no one knows this group exists except a handful of people and they are sworn to secrecy?"

"That is correct. It has to be that way. Many lives are at stake. Including that of the President of the United States."

She sat back and took a deep breath. This was huge and he knew her mind was going ninety to nothing.

"There is a plan being carried out that has been in existence for a long time, through many Presidents. We are not told anything. But I do know we are not the first group enlisted to serve at the pleasure of the President."

"So to your knowledge, none of the twelve have committed treason?"

"I don't want to talk too much about the details, Honey. But I will say that one man has already lost his life because he joined another group that was working against the current President's agenda."

"He's dead?"

"Yes. And I don't want to be next." Bill sighed and stood up, pacing back and forth. "I hate sharing this with you because you won't be able to let it go. It will stay with you night and day and one of us needs to stay sane. It has nearly driven me to distraction having to keep all this from you."

He turned and stared at her face. "I was asked to take the man out but when I entered the building, I recognized him from when we were in Afghanistan. I couldn't shoot. We had a short conversation and made a weak plan for his escape from the building. He made it back to his house and I was going to provide him a passport to get out of the country. He was dead before morning."

Sharon winced. "So they took him out."

"It was almost as though they heard us planning his escape. I am afraid to make any move because they are watching."

"I sure hope no one can hear this conversation."

"Just remember that our phones are tapped, probably our house, cars, and I don't know what else. You cannot ever speak of this to anyone. You and I cannot talk about this without using extreme caution. You must not forget this protocol, Sharon. It's a life and death matter. No room for error."

"I understand. Even though it is terribly risky, I am thankful that you shared this with me. It answers so many questions I had about where you were going at night. All hours of the day or night."

"That is one reason I told you."

"Took you long enough, Bill." She smiled.

Bill reached over and kissed her softly. "We better go inside. I think they may be watching me closely to make sure I don't defect. We have to act perfectly normal. I want you to put this aside and go about your life and our life together as usual. Don't do anything odd that is out of character. It will be hard to set this aside knowing I am going to be put in dangerous situations. But we will have to trust that this won't last too much longer. I have no idea when they will release me from this commitment, but I reassure you I am being as careful as I can."

"I know you were highly trained as a Navy SEAL and are extremely capable or they would not have come after you. But that doesn't make me feel any better every time you leave the house. I still will have that fear that you may not return home."

Bill stood up and reached for her hand. "Come on, let's go back inside. Get your coffee cup and let's grab supper out tonight. When we come back home, just relax and forget what we've talked about. We cannot discuss this at the restaurant or in bed tonight. Any questions you may have in the future will have to be answered when we know we are totally alone, and tap free."

They walked inside and changed clothes, anxious to leave the house and enjoy a good meal. Before they entered the restaurant, Bill pulled her close to him. "Man, it feels so much better knowing we are on the same page again. I love you, Sharon. Now let's go enjoy our dinner and laugh. I don't remember the last time I laughed."

She squeezed his hand and they walked into Chase Steak House. Bill looked back for a second and saw a black sedan pulling away from the curb across the street. His heart rate kicked up but he hid it from Sharon. They would never be alone; not until his part in this nightmare was over.

And even then . . .

CHAPTER THIRTY-ONE

Paul was worn out from a long afternoon of baseball practice. He had worked up a sweat even though there was a cool breeze blowing. The games were going well; they were actually on a winning streak. When he walked through the front door he found Avery sitting on the sofa with a cold rag on her face. He rushed to her side, kneeling down to talk to her.

"Honey, what in the world is wrong? You got a bad headache or something?"

Avery had her eyes closed. "No. It's worse than that. I am having contractions. It's way too early for this baby to be born."

Paul got up quickly and pulled out his cell phone. "I'll call your doctor. He needs to know what's going on."

"I hate to bother him. That's why I'm sitting here, waiting to see if it will pass. But I sure don't want to deliver this baby at home."

"You better believe I sure don't want you to. I have no idea how to birth a baby. I'm dialing his number. We can't take a chance, Avery."

"Okay, I guess you're right. Let me talk to him, if you get him on the phone."

"Dr. Whittington, this is Paul Sinclair. My wife Avery is having contractions and the baby isn't due until May. Should we head to the hospital? Do you need to speak to her?"

"Put her on the phone, Paul. I need to ask her some questions."

"Yes, Dr. Whittington. They started about an hour ago. No, they aren't strong, but my back is killing me and the contractions are low. Not Braxton Hicks contractions. Low, almost like menstrual cramps."

"I think you need to take a trip to the E.R. and let them do an ultrasound on you. It always pays to be on the side of caution when it comes to a baby. Head that way, and I'll meet you there."

"Thank you so much, Dr. Whittington. I'm so sorry to bother you."

"I was late leaving the office anyway. See you shortly."

Paul got Avery into the car, pulled out the driveway, and sped off to the hospital. His head was spinning. "Did you do too much today? Did you lift something heavy?"

Avery had her head leaned up against the back of the seat, with her eyes closed. "I did nothing unusual. I felt weird when I got up this morning and the feeling never did go away. Then the contractions started a little while ago. I knew something was wrong. I don't want to lose this baby."

"I know you don't. I don't want you to, either. Let's hope it's just a dry run."

"Be quiet for a few minutes. I'm about to lose control."

Paul reached over and grabbed her hand. "It's okay, baby. We'll make it through this."

The E.R. was packed when Paul parked and ran in to get a wheel chair. He rushed back outside and helped Avery into the chair and wheeled her in. The nurse the front took his insurance card and another attendant wheeled her back to a room. It looked like they wouldn't have to wait long to see Dr. Whittington.

Avery was placed on a bed and covered up with warm blankets. She was shivering from nerves. Her mouth was dry so one of the nurses gave her some water. The place was full and people were everywhere. Out in the hallway on stretchers, in the rooms, and out in the waiting room. They were fortunate to have been taken back so fast. Suddenly Dr. Whittington appeared and his booming voice could be heard immediately.

"Hello, Avery. I'm here and there's nothing to worry about. We'll get a quick ultrasound and I will examine you to see what is going on. Are the contractions still strong?"

"They have not changed much at all since they started a few hours ago."

"Okay. Let's see what's going on."

The ultrasound showed that the baby had dropped. But he saw something else that was frightening. The baby was not fully formed.

Avery was staring at her doctor, watching his face closely. She somehow sensed that something was wrong. "What is it, Dr. Whittington? What's going on with this baby?"

He turned and looked at her and shook his head. "I did not see this on the earlier Ultrasound, but the baby is not fully formed. Your body is trying to abort this baby. I am so sorry, Avery."

Paul was so shocked he could not speak. But he somehow managed to stand up and grab hold of Avery before she burst out crying. .

"No! Not this baby. How could that be? I felt movement. I know I did."

"It is rare not to have caught this earlier. But in the first ultrasound the fetus is too small to see that much. I am so sorry, Honey. The child would not have lived through the birth. It is better for you to have this baby now instead of carrying it full term."

"I don't know if I can take this, Paul. We are losing our baby! Oh God, please help us."

Tears were streaming down Paul's face as he held his wife. One of the worst nights of his life. He never dreamed this would happen. He had feared the baby was coming too soon, but not for this reason. It was happening so quickly. And tonight their dreams for this child would be over.

Dr. Whittington pulled the door closed and spoke quietly to a nurse. "We need to get her ready for the delivery of this fetus. The child is not formed completely. Her body is trying to get rid of it." Paul could hear him talking to one of the nurses outside the room. He shook his head. Avery was taken immediately to a surgery room on the next floor and he walked beside her until they took her in the room. He dialed his father and mother quickly and told them the news.

"Dad, can you come? This is the worst night I've ever had. We are losing our baby. Can you and Mom come?"

"Sure, Son. We will be right there."

Paul walked into the room where they were preparing Avery for the delivery. It was going to happen quickly. That was the good news. The baby was already coming out. So much blood. He had never in his life seen so much blood. A nurse put a line in Avery's arm and gave her fluids, and the team was standing by to give her blood if she needed it.

"Son, do you want to stay in here, or wait outside?" Dr. Whittington spoke with a gentle voice.

"My parents are coming. I'll wait right outside the door."

"This won't take long and we will take her to a private room when we are through."

"I want to see the baby when it comes out. Will Avery be asleep?"

"No, she will be able to see her baby. A nurse will motion for you to come in when we deliver the baby."

Paul was sickened at the thought of delivering a dead baby. His baby. He looked up and saw his parents coming down the hallway. He ran to them and hugged his mother. Sharon had tears streaming down her face, but was obviously trying to stay calm for Paul.

"Come here, Paul. I know you are devastated. To find this out now is unbelievable. How is Avery?"

Paul wiped his eyes and looked at his mother. "She cannot even talk she is so upset. I hope she can handle this."

"She's a strong girl, Son. She will be fine. But you will have to be strong for her. This won't be an easy thing to get over. But you both can do it. She can get pregnant again and you can have a family. Keep that in the back of your mind, Paul. After you both heal, of course." Bill put his arm around his son's shoulder and looked at Sharon. She shook her head.

"I guess we better wait by the door. I told Dr. Whittington that I wanted to see the baby when it came out. A nurse will notify me when it is okay to come into the room. I want to be there for Avery, too. When she sees that child she is going to flip out."

"We all would, Paul. It's a tough thing."

A nurse stuck her head out the door of the operating room and motioned for Paul to step inside. "The baby has been born, and your wife is waiting for you."

When Paul entered the room, he noticed how quiet it was. No sound. The baby was wrapped in a blanket and Avery was holding it. He walked up to her and bent down and kissed the baby's head. The child was stillborn and very small. They did not unwrap the blanket but spoke quietly to each other about the still baby.

Avery looked up at him but her face was gray. No expression whatsoever. "It's a boy."

"Honey, he's beautiful. We need to name him. What do you want to call him?" Paul whispered to Avery.

She swallowed and wiped her eyes. "I think I would like to call him William after Dad. Is that okay with you?"

Paul nodded. "I like that. Can I hold him for a moment?"

Avery handed him the child, and the life drained from him. The main thing he kept thinking was how damn quiet it was in that room. It was a loud quiet. He could hardly stand the silence. He wanted the baby to cry; to make some kind of noise. But it was as still as a stone. William. He never lived outside the womb. But he would be remembered as though he had lived a lifetime with them.

CHAPTER THIRTY-TWO

"Emily"

I never thought a family could go through such trauma and come out on the other side. But survive we did. First the loss of our sister, and then this baby. They say things come in threes, but I was praying they were wrong. We couldn't take one more thing. I had not talked to Mother in a while and needed a good visit with her, but I was sort of dreading the emotion of it all. The funeral for a baby is not something I ever thought I could live through. I sure didn't want to rehash all that emotion with Mother. She was barely healed over Susan's death. If you ever do get over burying a child. So I decided not to bring up anything at all about any of it. We just needed to have lunch and visit and have a good laugh.

Even though we were spread out and not under one roof anymore, I did believe in my heart of hearts that we were a close-knit family that could weather the storms life gave us. But until you are hit with one, you don't realize what you are asking of each other. It's like the worst F4 tornado ravaging your family walls apart. The very inner core of it all. You cannot see that core, but it's there.

I've seen families torn apart from an unexpected death. Marriages ruined over it. But we keep standing. I believe we will stand. But how much hell can one live through and remain standing? I guess we will find out.

Rob and I were doing wonderfully well. I was actually proud of how we maneuvered through our honeymoon and the baby issue. We both grew closer on that trip and I think more unified. At least it felt that way for the moment. My family had quieted down about Rob, so we could be about our business of making our own nest and Rob could begin the long, long journey of becoming a healthy part of our family. He was cool about it. Very brave about Dad. Maybe that was one of the reasons I married him. The brave part. I needed that. I had always been sort of cocky about what I could put up with. But he was flat brave. Nothing shook him. I liked that. And I was so glad that one of us has that grand trait. I prayed it came through the DNA to our children-to-be. You don't see bravery anymore, except in the military, I realized. Those men are crazy brave. But the average person is so lost in their texting and Facebook that they have lost their grip on the real world. Real issues.

The phone rang. I thought she would never pick up.

"Hello? Mother?"

"Yes, Dear. How in the world are you? I'm so glad you called."

"Want to have a light lunch and a good laugh? We both need that."

"You couldn't have ordered a better day. What time you picking me up?"

"In fifteen minutes. You be ready?"

"I am ready now."

"See you soon."

Always loved that about Mom. She was always ready. One step ahead of us all. Someone needed to be.

⊰⊱

Roe's Kitchen was a small diner not too far from Mother's house, on First Street where huge trees lined up along both sides of the road and their bows hung over, making a delightful canopy that was a pleasure to drive through. The diner was old but felt comfortable and I figured that was just what we both needed. Comfort.

Mother was dressed in white slacks, a sign that spring had come. She looked a little tired but had survived with beauty intact. I, on the other hand, look disheveled, as usual. Thrown together. Rob said he liked that about me. I had beauty somewhere in me, but you had to search for it. The dark hair and blue eyes might get to you, but you had to get past that slight messiness of me to see it.

"You look nice today, Mother." Thought I would start on a good note.

"Emily, you say the nicest things. I know I look worn out, and I am. But the spring weather is trying to revive my spirits. I was hoping it showed."

"How is Dad?"

"Your father is doing well, considering he is the one who holds this family together."

"I always thought it was you."

"It may be, but I like to think it's Bill. I don't think I have it in me anymore. It's getting too heavy, if you know what I mean."

"We're not going there today, Mom."

"Agreed."

"This place is busy. And the smell is heavenly. What shall we have?"

"I am considering the chicken pot pie. I know it is getting warmer, but that just sounds good for the soul."

"I am going for a chicken salad on croissant today. With water of course. Although I would kill for a Sprite."

"Get it. Who cares?"

"So Dad is still really busy? Going out late at night?"

"He does have demanding clients. It's ridiculous how they control his time."

"He can't just tell them he is busy?"

"He is highly respected in his field, and I guess he just accepts it as part of the job. These are very wealthy clients he deals with. Not the normal Joe Blow down the street."

"I'm aware of that. It just seems odd that he goes out late at night."

I could tell Mother was holding something back by the look on her face, but I chose not to push it after all she'd been through. I was just hoping Dad wasn't having an affair.

She turned the tables on me. "So how is Rob doing? You guys settled in after the honeymoon?"

"Yes, very settled. It has been an adjustment living with someone but we are getting the hang of it."

"It's an adjustment having an empty nest, Emily. I never thought it would be this hard. All my friends raved about it when their kids left home. I thought I would love it, but the house is too quiet."

"You and Dad have more time together, right?"

Mother looked down and I saw something flash across her face. I'm not even sure what emotion it was. "Oh, we have our times. But he stays pretty busy. He has to make the money while he can. We aren't getting any younger, Emily."

I reached across the table and put my hand on hers. "Mother, you and Dad are doing okay, aren't you? I mean, he treats you right? "

She suddenly looked a little hard. "What do you mean? He is the sweetest man in the world. It's just that he is completely into his work. There is little time for anything else. But I think he is under enough pressure without my complaining that I want more time together. I did mention that we could travel a little. That would be fun."

"What was his response?"

"He said maybe at some point. So I wait."

"I would love to see you guys go to Europe or something. You have worked so hard raising all of us. It's about that time in your lives that you need to enjoy things."

"Not going to happen at this point. But I can hope."

"I didn't want to mention it, and I know we haven't been married very long, but I want to start a family before too long. I haven't said anything to Rob yet. I am going to wait a while. But I want you to know I am thinking about it."

"I hope you can, Emily. There is no good time to have a baby. You know that. So don't wait too long; do it while you are young."

"I will, Mom. And why don't you make some travel plans? At least get on the Internet and look around. See where you might want to go."

Mother looked out the window. I would have given anything to have known what she was thinking. I sat there watching her, wondering what was going on in her head.

"I think I'll have some peach cobbler for dessert! You want to split it with me?"

"Heavens, Mother. We both are going to get fat! But yes, I will take a bite or two."

"Emily, have you called Paul? Have you checked on your brother?"

I tucked my head down and shook it. "I'm sorry. I just don't have the nerve. I know he is hurting so badly but I don't know what to say. What do you say?"

"You don't have to say anything. Just go see him and hug him. He needs you."

"I hate what they had to go through. I wasn't going to bring it up. I know he is dying inside. I can feel it. We all died a little over that baby. Is he okay?"

"He and Avery will make it. But they both are miserable right now. The nursery is still there. Can you imagine passing that room all the time in your house?"

"I'll call. I know he probably is wondering why I haven't. We got too close there for a while. I backed away when he got married because it wasn't healthy. His wife would not have liked me very much if we had stayed that close."

"It's the twin thing. No one really understands it but you and Paul."

"I'm stuffed, Mom. You ready to go?"

She stood up. Suddenly she looked old to me.

"Yes, I am ready. Thanks so much for calling me today. It feels good to get out. And you look wonderful. I mean that. Marriage is agreeing with you."

I rolled my eyes. "Thanks, Mother. I'll call again soon. And yes, I will go see Paul. If you talk to him, tell him I'm coming over."

"I'll let you tell him yourself."

"Give Dad a hug for me. And tell him to slow the heck down. Life is too short."

Mother got a funny look on her face. "Shorter than you can ever imagine."

When we parted I was left with a funny feeling in my chest. She was holding back on me. But I didn't know what or how. I texted Paul that I was heading his way. I might as well get it over with. It would be good to see him and Avery. But if I was honest, I was a little afraid that if we spent too much time together, Avery might think we were getting too close again. I could read him like a book. He could read me. It was eerie. But nice at the same time. We almost breathed the same air. But when we were like that, there was no room for anyone else. We were like a two-person club, and no one else was allowed in.

I drove up to his house and he was waiting outside, which was unusual. I got out and ran to him. He hugged me and the connection swallowed me up. I pulled away because I could feel his pain. I knew I would. It had been a long time since I had allowed myself to really feel Paul. But he needed me now. So I stepped into it. I would just have to control how close we got. I think he was feeling the same thing.

"I was hoping you'd come by, Em."

"I know. I could hear you."

He looked at me and we were there. Oh, well. Being a twin was a blessing and a curse. But I had a feeling I wasn't going to psychologically figure it out at the moment. I jumped in with both feet, riding the pain in his heart like it was mine. If I had any doubts about whether I should get so involved in his life again or not, I just had to look at his face. I would not get over that smile. Not ever.

CHAPTER THIRTY-THREE

Call it the power of suggestion, if you will, but Jacob Sinclair couldn't stop thinking about Gail Bailey. Her name had been brought up so many times that it was stuck on rewind in his head. He really liked Jane. He didn't want another woman. But there she was, hung up in his mind, and he didn't know what to do to get rid of her. Gail was coming into the office today to see if there was a better deal on her car insurance and he found himself looking forward to seeing her. He sat at his desk pondering his dilemma when she walked into his office.

Could she be more beautiful? "Hello, Gail. Come on in!" He stood up and pointed to a chair on the other side of his desk.

Gail smiled. "Hey, Jacob. Thanks for seeing me on such a short notice. I need to find a cheaper insurance without compromising my coverage, if that is possible. I need to really watch my money for a while until I get more established on my own. I hope you understand."

Jacob smiled and nodded, thankful she could not read his mind. "I will do what I can to help you, of course. Let me pull up some rates on the computer and see what we have to offer."

Gail scrolled through her phone calls and put her phone back in her purse. He could see her out of the corner of his eye. She looked troubled, but he didn't want to ask why.

"We have another option here, but your deductible will go up."

"I assumed it would."

"I am sorry about that. But if you want a lower rate the deductible goes up accordingly."

"Same as health insurance these days."

"I can write you a policy with Sunshine Auto Insurance, and we will cancel your other policy immediately. I will need a check for the first six months, which is cheaper than paying by the month."

"That is fine. I will probably get a small refund back, anyway, from the original policy, right?"

"It looks like you will. It will come directly to you as soon as that policy is cancelled."

Gail signed the new policy and started to stand up to leave. "Thank you, Jacob, for being so helpful. It's been a rough time on my own and you have made things a little easier for me."

Jacob stood up and shook her hand. He held it a tad too long and caught himself just in time. "I'm always here if you need anything. "

She paused. He looked at her with a questioning look. "Well, I am headed to Starbucks for coffee, would you care to meet me there?"

His inner voice said no, but he totally ignored it. His stomach was in his throat so he could hardly get his words out. "Sure, I'll head that way now."

She smiled her golden smile, and his knees went weak. He was ashamed of himself but there was no stopping it now.

He had his keys in his hand when a text came through on his phone. He decided to ignore it. Knowing he shouldn't go, he walked to his car and headed to Starbucks, not knowing what to expect. Maybe just a short chat over coffee. Maybe not. But he was hoping it would put an end to his constant thinking. Somehow.

Starbucks was packed. Surprise, surprise. He ordered and sat down, waiting for Gail to show up. It didn't take five minutes and he spotted her at the counter ordering. He stared at her, wondering what she was like and what she wanted to talk about. She walked his way and took a seat across from him, smiling.

"Nice of you to do this. I know you're busy."

"Not that busy. You doing okay?"

"It's an adjustment being single again with a child. Lily is a good child but it is tough working and raising a child alone. And the dating thing is ridiculous. I don't even want to go there."

"It's tough dating even when you don't have a child. I've been dating the same girl for a while. There is no way I want to start over again." He surprised himself with that statement, considering he was sitting across from an adorable single woman.

"I don't blame you. Who is this girl, anyway?"

"She's a nurse. And a damn good one, too. I enjoy her and we seem to get along. I think she wants to move in together or better yet, get married. For some reason, I am hesitating. Not sure why."

Gail shook her head. "You men hate to take the leap. Freedom feels so good, why mess that up, huh?"

"I don't know if it's the freedom or just the fear of the unknown."

"Well, marriage is tough even if you love each other. I thought we did. But it didn't last."

"So what do you want, Gail? What are your goals? At least, short term."

"I'd like to settle down and be able to support my daughter. I need to heal from the divorce before I get involved with anyone else. I want to go slow, for Lily's sake. And really, my own, too."

"I think that would be wise. I've not had children yet, but it seems the right thing to do. She has enough adjustment dealing with the divorce. Not to mention bringing in another male."

"She seemed to like you, though. Right off the bat. I thought that was cute."

"She only saw me that one time."

"I know, but she remembers you."

Jacob turned red. "Well, that's sweet." He looked at his watch. "I'd better be getting back to work."

"Don't let that scare you away. She just thought you were nice, and that's saying a lot for Lily. She is so shy."

"I appreciate that. She is a very cute little girl. You are a lucky mother."

"Yes, I am. Thanks, again, for meeting me for coffee. It was nice just talking to someone. Maybe we can do this again?"

"Sure. Anytime. Let me know if you need anything. And have a great day, Gail."

He stood up to go just as she was standing up. Gail turned and hugged him and he smiled and walked to his car. She smelled like a field of flowers. Jane wouldn't wear perfume because of her work. He had forgotten how wonderful a woman could smell. He had forgotten what it felt like to have butterflies. And frankly, he had forgotten how it felt to actually talk to a woman and add to the conversation. Jane was such a talker that he usually kept quiet. It was nothing but a chat over coffee. But now it was going to stay with him for the rest of the day. He had to focus on work and that was a good thing. For if he thought too much longer about Gail, he would want to call her. And that was out of the question.

He glanced at his phone and saw that Jane had texted him twice. He texted her back that he was almost at work. She would not wonder. She trusted him completely. So why wasn't he happy with her? Why was he dragging his feet? And why did he like Gail so much? Because she was new? He didn't even know the woman.

He was too old to do this. His mind was split. He didn't like the feeling. It messed with his head and he began to second guess everything. Mainly he wondered if Jane was right for him. Jane felt like an old comfortable pair of shoes. Gail felt like a hot fudge Sunday. Or the first spring breeze. Dang it.

⊷⊶

Gail got back in her car and drove away, smiling. She just flat liked Jacob. She liked him right off the bat, just like Lily. And now she learned that he had a girlfriend named Jane. It sort of melted her enthusiasm over the coffee break they had shared, but maybe there was still hope if she waited long enough. It was time for her to heal. And if it was meant to be, it would happen. He seemed like a good man. She didn't want to pry. But maybe, just maybe, she would remain in the back of his mind for a while. Long enough to want to know more about her. She had the time to wait. But then there was Jane.

CHAPTER THIRTY-FOUR

The phone in Bill's pocket was ringing. He hadn't heard from Command in a few days. It was refreshing but he never could really relax. Probably not healthy. He pulled it out slowly and answered, noting that Sharon was in the kitchen cooking dinner.

"I have something I need to you take care of."

"And?"

"James Ferguson. His whole organization is at stake. He is building a substantial momentum against the President. Very powerful influence. He's got to go."

"You want me to take him out?"

"Get rid of him. Immediately. I'll send directions after we hang up. Do not get caught. Watch behind your back. This guy is very powerful and has people. He is never without guards. You just may not see them. Got it?"

"I'll take care of it."

"Bill, no mistakes here. No leaking. We hired you because you can do the job. But we are watching because we know it's getting to you."

"Anything else?"

The line went dead.

Bill shook his head. This was getting real old. Sharon stuck her head in the doorway and frowned. He hated those frown lines between her sweet eyes. They were all-knowing eyes now. She raised an eyebrow and he nodded. That was all they could do. No words. But he knew that she understood. He stood up and walked over to her and held her in his arms. He whispered quietly into her ear, always knowing he was taking a risk.

"Thank you for being here for me. For understanding the pressure. As soon as I can change things, I will. Until then, we are pretty much stuck."

She whispered back. "I know, Honey. I'm getting supper ready, but I know you may not be here to eat it. Don't worry about me at all. Now that I understand things, it is a little easier for me to see you go. But I do worry about your safety."

"We better change the subject. What's for dinner? Have you heard from Emily lately?"

"We're having chicken and yes, we ate lunch the other day. She's fine. I think she went to see Paul. He needs her."

"Those two are like a soap opera. But I am sure he has missed her."

His phone buzzed in his pocket. He knew then that his work was about to begin. His blood pressure shot up and he could feel the tension in his whole body. This whole thing was wrong and there was nothing he could do to stop it yet. Yet. One fine day he would blow this whole thing wide open.

He checked the phone. The message was clear; *157 South Winston, 9:00. A fifteen-minute window.* He hurried out the door, grabbing his gun and waving at Sharon. Dinner would have to wait.

South Winston was a warehouse district on the north side of town. Dark and dangerous at night. He parked a good way from the warehouse and slipped on his black mask. Trained better than anyone he knew, he still had sweat pouring down his back when he was about to walk into a bad situation. Fear was there, but he was trained to channel it to increase his energy.

He projected power when he came through the door with his gun out, ready to shoot. This time the door was locked. He had to use a flat, thin, narrow pick to open it, which could put him more at risk if any sound was made. Luckily, no one was in the main room when he came through the door. The room was half dark; a small light in a side room cast shadows across the empty space. He slowly crept along the wall to the far end where there was a room with a light hanging over a desk and a figure was sitting there bent over reading something. He assumed it was James Ferguson. He prayed it was. He raised his gun to shoot and a shot was fired from over his head. He ducked and saw James run out of the room and race out of the back doorway. He had no idea who had fired the shot, but his main directive had fled. He would not be able to complete his orders.

Bill walked around the back of the warehouse, watching for any movement. Another shot was fired, but it was random. No one could see him. He stayed hidden for a few moments, hoping to see any movement in the parking lot, which was surrounded by trees. He decided to take a run for the line of trees, keeping his hand on the trigger. He looked back just in time to see a shot fired from the top of the building. He aimed at where he saw the gun go off, and a man fell to the ground. He turned and continued into the trees; this was what he was trained to do. He would find the guy if he was in there. It was so dark he could barely see, so he decided to stand still and listen. He was trained to hear a leaf fall, and he knew James was afraid. He was running for his life, so he was almost certain to make a mistake. As he stood there, he could almost hear someone breathing very close to him. He squatted down and squinted into the darkness in a circle around him. He was hoping for a glisten from a belt buckle or button on a shirt. He decided to wait it out because he had a gut feeling James was standing near him.

Ten minutes went by and his legs were tiring in the squat position. But he didn't want to move. He wanted to create some kind of doubt in James's mind. So he waited it out for another twenty minutes and then he heard a crackling sound.

James was moving. He stood up slowly and walked several yards and then he saw a figure darting through the trees. Just for a second, any moonlight that had filtered through all the trees had shown down on James long enough for Bill to see him. He ran and tackled him and rolled him over on the ground. They were face to face in the darkness.

"James, what are you doing? Why are you running?"

"I knew you were here to kill me."

"Why are you working against the President?"

"Because so much is wrong. He is doing everything he can to take America down."

"But you know you are in danger by opposing him so outwardly. You are being blatant about it."

"The public has a right to know what is going on in the White House. They are fed lies by the news media. Half of what is being said is not the truth. Whoever you are, you know I am right."

"I was sent here to take you out. To stop what you are doing. You must be making progress for them to react so drastically."

"Frankly, I don't think they put much value on human lives. I think they take people out all the time without a thought. No hesitation whatsoever. If the public knew this, things might change. A mutiny of sorts across America. People would be afraid. They would panic."

Bill knew better than to get into a conversation with a target. It would make it harder to follow through with his orders. But he agreed, "They just might panic. But I think enough of them would want to fight back. It might start another war here." Bill loosened his grip on James' shoulders. "Sit up. Let's talk. I was supposed to take you out immediately. I am certain there are others watching me to make sure this happens. I can fire my gun into the air, but that doesn't mean they won't track you down and kill you. I allowed another guy to run and they killed him within twelve hours. You don't have much of a chance."

James sat up and rubbed his sore arm. "Go ahead and kill me. Because I am not going to keep quiet. I knew the risk when I began speaking out. This was bound to have happened sooner or later. If you let me run, I'll just keep on talking, forming a larger group that agrees with me. I'll get shot and you'll get into trouble for not following orders."

"What a crappy statement that is! It almost seems surreal. I still can't believe this has been going on for centuries in the government. Unknown to the public."

"There are many who suspect. But they have little concrete proof. You need to make up your mind pretty fast here or they'll come after us both."

Bill didn't know what to do. It felt like there was no way out. "If I let you go and aim my gun into the air and fire a few shots, where can you hide?"

"There's a cabin up north of here on a small lake. It's a fishing camp. I doubt they would look for me there. But I don't have any food there to exist on until I can figure something else out."

"I can get food to you. I'll send some people there with fishing supplies and have them leave food for you. But I want you to know I am being watched closely. I'll tell them I shot you down but there was a shooter firing shots at me. I took the shooter out and ran for my life. They are not going to like it at all and I will pay somehow. They are pretty ruthless. I am letting you go because I believe what you say is happening and I hate what I have to do. This is not what I was trained for in the SEALs. I am ashamed of it, actually. A friggin' nightmare."

"It's good to hear you are figuring out what is really going on. Even if you shot me, I would die knowing you understand what I was fighting for."

"I totally understand. All of the SEALs would agree with you. There are twelve of us doing this but we don't know who the others are. We cannot communicate with each other. My family is at risk. We better get going. We have talked too long."

Bill aimed his gun and shot into the air several times. The shots echoed in the quiet night. James stood up and ran. The cabin was a few miles away, but the darkness would help his escape.

Bill didn't have much hope as he walked of the woods. He didn't believe James would even make it to the camp. If James was caught and neutralized by someone else he was going to be in trouble big time. If James made it, then maybe it would buy them both some time.

Command was on the phone before he could even get back to his car. He had pulled off his mask and removed the black jacket. Sweat was running down his back. And there was a lump the size of Cuba in his throat.

"Is he down?"

"I shot him. But there was another shooter up on a roof somewhere that kept shooting at me. He nearly got me at the first shot. Where were you guys? I thought you were out there somewhere."

"I just need to know if you got the job done. My men were tied up on another job."

"That sounds pretty weak. I took him down, but I didn't stay around to see if he was dead. I kept waiting to hear the sound of your guns, but I heard nothing."

"This has a familiar ring to it, Bill. If he's loose, we'll catch him. And then we'll come after you."

"That sounds like a direct threat."

"Exactly."

The line went dead. Bill shook his head. How much longer could he play this game? Or die? He headed home, not knowing what to expect of the night. But he was tired and Sharon would be waiting. That was enough to give him the energy to get home.

CHAPTER THIRTY-FIVE

It was a foggy day and the clouds hung low in the sky as Bill drove slowly up the gravel driveway to the fish camp. Grass had all but taken over the road, so he had to keep a grip on the steering wheel so the car wouldn't veer into the tree-lined ditch on the right side of the road. He was hoping that the fog would make it more difficult if not nearly impossible to see him from the main road.

He got out of the car and moved along the edge of the house, looking around to make sure no one was following him. It would be nothing short of a miracle if they both made it out of this fiasco alive.

He looked through one of the filthy windows facing the porch and thought he saw James at the kitchen table drinking a beer. He eased up to the door and knocked. The door opened a crack and James stuck his head out precariously.

"Damn, you scared the crap out of me. Get in here fast. I doubt we are alone."

Bill slipped into the cabin and turned to look at James. "We don't have much time to get this figured out. I know for a fact that they are looking for you, either dead or alive. I told Command I shot you, but I don't think he believed me. They will hunt you down, and unfortunately for us, they are incredibly good at it."

"Figures. Well, I just need to hide out here a couple days and then leave the state. I have friends in other places. I am sure they will help me out. But I cannot promise I will let this agenda go, Bill. This country is in trouble. Someone needs to take a stand."

"I agree. But they won't go down quietly. And they will take whoever they can down with them."

"That goes without saying."

"But don't you speak my name to anyone. I cannot stress enough the importance of keeping my name out of the mix. My whole family will be shot point blank if they find out I let you go free."

"I wouldn't consider doing that, Bill. I appreciate what you have done and the risk you have taken. I just hope it is worth it for us both."

"I best not stay long. I brought food for about two weeks for you. When I leave, you are on your own, James. I pray to God you make it across state lines. But I wouldn't feel too safe until you got a little farther south or west. Make yourself as invisible as possible for a time."

"Thanks for the food and water. I have some whiskey that I found after digging around the kitchen. This place is a filthy mess. But it will do for now. It is remote, but that doesn't mean they can't find me. I'm not stupid. Just rebellious."

Bill allowed a grin to surface. "Leave soon. Don't stay anywhere too long. I assure you, they have ways of finding people. They sent me to kill you. The others they have hired are equally good at what they do, and they won't hesitate to kill. One day I am going to blow this whole thing wide open. But I have to get my ducks in a row first."

"I'm not sure there is such a thing anymore. With technology being what it is, there probably isn't a perfect time to let the secret out."

"I'm going to head out now, before someone shows up. Keep the flashlight usage down to a minimum. And sleep with one eye open. I will have no way of knowing where you are, but I am sure I will hear if they take you out."

James nodded. "Get out of here. And thanks for the help. I owe you my life."

"I hope that debt remains active for many years to come."

James smiled. They shook hands and Bill darted out the door and ran to his car, looking around as he started back down the grassy road.

Bill wanted to contact Sharon but thought better of it because his personal cell was most likely tapped. He had given up all his privacy to do what the President asked him to do. He hated it with a passion, and the hatred was building more and more every day. He needed to devise a plan to communicate with the press at some point. He would have to wait, but he wanted to research who the best reporter would be to set up an interview. This was down the road, of course. But it was something that gave him hope. He had to end this nightmare or die trying.

When he reached the house, the light was on in the den. Sharon was sitting in her favorite chair reading. He was so glad she was still up. He walked into the house slowly and put his briefcase down and laid his gun on the table. It was nice to be able to be out in the open with her. She looked up when he came into the room and smiled.

"Hello, Honey. I'm so glad you made it home. I've been worried."

He knelt down beside her and took her hand, and spoke in a soft voice. "Sharon, I despise having to put you through this. But it is still helpful that you know what is going on. Tonight was productive. I cannot go into what took place, but I will share it with as soon as we know that no one is listening. Have you had a good night?"

She watched him walk to the sofa and sit down, rubbing his eyes. Exhausted. "I am fine. Talked to three of the kids. Paul could not stop talking about how good it was for Emily to stop by. So they are tight, again. Avery is still a mess over losing her child. There are no words to make that easier."

"I'm sorry. We will do what we can to help them get through this. We should have the kids over—keep things as normal as we can around here."

"I'll set up a time and have them over for dinner."

"Sharon, I'm heading up to bed. Absolutely worn out. My mind has to be ready to work tomorrow. We have several big clients coming in and I want to prepare for them. I need to be crisp."

"You go ahead. I'll be up soon. Just want to finish this chapter I'm reading."

Bill laid his head down on the pillow and closed his eyes. One more time that he avoided killing someone. But his phone was going to ring. Command was going to be furious if they didn't locate a body. James had a red laser dot on his head; he was a dead man walking. But just maybe there was a chance in hell that James would make it over state lines. Bill wanted his own life back.

He wanted to know what "normal" was again. But for now, he needed to set this aside; compartmentalize it. Because tomorrow he was going to sign a contract with General Electric if he played his cards right. He smiled. He wished he was playing cards with the government, because he was damn good at it. But he was also a good shot. He had a sniper's aim. He could take anyone out if he wanted to. And right now, he could think of a few people he'd consider taking out.

He fell asleep before he whispered his thoughts out loud. And the man in the woods, hiding from the whole United States government, was up staring out of a window with a gun in his lap. He never heard the shot that hit him between the eyes. Neither did anyone else.

CHAPTER THIRTY-SIX

Bill woke with a crick in his neck and his phone ringing. He broke out in a sweat immediately and felt his blood pressure rising as he answered the call. The voice on the other end was one he had grown to hate.

"We found your man. I'm starting to wonder about you, Bill."

Bill swallowed the lump in his throat. He hoped the man on the other end of the phone didn't pick up the quiver in his voice. "So you did locate James?"

"Sure did. Hiding out in a cabin in the woods. You didn't know about that, did you?"

"Thought I nailed him with the shot I fired."

"You are one of the best snipers we have. How could you miss him? What's going on with you, Bill?"

"It's not me. I did what I was asked to do. No one told me there was someone on the roof that was trying to take me down."

"You were trained to deal with that."

"I'm no good to you dead."

"I'm beginning to believe you're no good to us alive."

"What kind of sarcastic remark is that?"

"You are slacking, that's what. This is the second time we've had to take someone out that you missed."

"I'm not perfect. And I have no control over the situation I walk into."

"We're giving you one more time. If you mess up again, then you're out. Or maybe I should say down."

"I didn't want this job in the first place. I was forced into it. I do the best I can, but that doesn't seem good enough for you."

"It isn't up for discussion, Bill. Do your job or you're out."

The line went dead before Bill could say another word. He put the phone down on the nightstand and sat up to get out of bed and make coffee. Sharon grabbed his hand and he turned to look at her.

"Not a good call?"

"Nope. But I will deal with it."

Sharon looked at him and shook her head. He forced a grin and slipped into some dirty jeans and walked into the kitchen. The floor was cold and his head was throbbing. Things were not going well at all. He really had hoped James would make it, but he knew the chances were slim. His stomach felt sickened by the news because he was sure that James was caught unaware.

Sharon followed him into the kitchen and they both grabbed their mugs and headed outside. The gazebo had become their place to talk. The only place that felt safe, but it was precarious at best. After taking their seats across from each other, Sharon spoke first.

"I'm almost afraid to ask you what the phone call was about. Do you feel like talking about it?"

"It's not good. I let another man go free, and of course they took him down. He didn't really have a chance, although I don't know how they found him so quickly. I took him some food. My car may have a tracking device on it. But then they would know

I helped him, and if they knew that for certain, I would be dead right now."

"Bill, this is serious."

"When I agreed to do this, it became serious."

"You didn't have a choice."

"No, I didn't. But now they own me. All of the family. If I mess up again, they will take us out."

"Isn't there anyone you can talk to?"

"I have no idea who I can trust."

"You have to think of something. There has to be someone in the government that doesn't bow down to the President."

"Oh, most of the Republican party tries not to. But that doesn't mean I could trust them with this information."

"So what's the next step?"

"I can't come up with something right now. It's going to take some thought and real planning. Our lives are at stake, Sharon. I'm not a magician. I have no hat to pull the rabbit out of."

"I know that, Bill. I also know we can't keep living like this. Under the gun."

He took her hand and kissed it. "You are the love of my life. I will protect you to my grave. But some things are bigger than we are, and this is one of them. I will vet some people and see if I can come up with someone I can talk to. I don't know right now who that would be. It might be an admiral in the Navy, one of the men who trained me. But you never know who is eating out of the same plate as the President these days. It just isn't so black and white anymore."

They both sat in silence, lost in their thoughts. The wind was blowing a cool breeze. The sun was up full blast in the sky. On all counts it was a beautiful day, but Bill was oblivious to any beauty around him. All he could think about was how he was going to handle the situation he was in. He had to go to work. His clients were going to be there shortly. He stood and motioned to Sharon that it was time to go inside and took her hand. They slowly walked inside, both worried about what was to come.

━┤ ├━

At his desk, Bill prepared to meet the bigwigs of Global Electric. He would be handling the accounting for the appliance and hospital equipment divisions. It would bring money into the accounting firm and begin a relationship with GE that could draw other large businesses. The move to a larger office had been right on target. He tried to get his mind off the morning conversation and get his head into the meeting at hand.

The CEO of GE came walking through his door, and Bill stood up to shake his hand. "Patrick Lathrop. Nice offices."

"Thanks, Patrick. Bill Sinclair. Please have a seat."

"I know you have discussed handling the appliance and hospital equipment divisions. I've read up on your company. You have quite a reputation, Bill."

Showing no emotion, Bill nodded. "I am excited to be taking care of those accounts for you, Patrick. We don't want you to worry about anything. We'll handle it all from day one. You will get reports monthly and we'll stay in close contact with you at all times. No surprises here."

"That's what we are counting on. No surprises. Our company is so large now that it has become increasingly difficult to manage all areas. There are loose ends that seem to pop up out of nowhere, and you get enough of that going on and the whole thing unravels."

"You're in the business of making money. That's the bottom line. And the bottom line is our friend. Our whole mission in life. You came to the right place."

"Say, Bill, I have a yacht I'm taking out Sunday on the Potomac River. Would really like for you to go. I need to spend some time with the man who is taking care of my money."

216

Bill was surprised but smiled and accepted the invitation. "Of course. It would be my pleasure. Been a while since I've been out on the water. Where do I meet you?"

"I keep my boat at the Captain John Beach Marina near the Occoquan River. If you'll meet me there at 8:00 Sunday morning, we'll have a go at it. Should be calm waters that time of the day."

Bill stood up and shook his hand. "I'm glad you came today. Hope I made you feel comfortable about our firm taking care of your financial needs. I think our reputation speaks for us. I'm sure you've done your homework so I'm not telling you anything you don't already know."

Patrick shook Bill's hand and smiled. "Look forward to getting to know you better, Bill. See you Sunday at 8:00 sharp."

Bill sat down at his desk in the quiet of his office and let his mind wander. His children were getting settled in their own lives. His wife could take care of herself. He had already made out a will and set up an irrevocable trust. His affairs were in order. He wasn't ready to die just yet. He would go down fighting for his own life and the lives of his family. But he also felt a loyalty to the other eleven men in the same ugly situation he was in. Something had to give. And soon. It was an election year and the current sitting President was more determined than ever to get his agenda carried out. He was doing a pretty damn good job of it, too. How could so many grown men turn their heads and let these things happen? How could the military heads tolerate what he was doing? And did they know about it? He had to find someone to talk to, before it was too late.

CHAPTER THIRTY-SEVEN

The forecast was for torrential thunderstorms all day. The phone had been ringing all morning with people cancelling their dental appointments. Apparently church wasn't the only thing that people skipped during a storm.

Jesse looked at his watch. He and Maryanne were supposed to go to his parents' home for dinner. It would be the first time since Christmas that the whole family would be together. He was anxious to see how Paul and Avery were holding up after the death of their child. No one had spoken of it in a while, and he didn't want to cause them more pain by bringing it up.

He had a ring in his pocket to give to Maryanne. Yeah, he was going to bite the bullet and propose. But he just hadn't decided when to do it. He made a business decision to head home early, since his day was pretty much shot.

As he was getting into his car, his cell rang. "Is the dinner still on at your parents?"

Jesse hesitated. "Um, as far as I know."

"It's so bad out. Would be a great night just to stay in."

"I couldn't agree more, but we haven't all been together since Christmas so I can't miss this dinner."

"Well, come a little early then. We can spend some quiet time together. I've missed you so much."

Jesse grinned. "Sure, I'll come early. I have a small gift for you, anyway."

"A gift?"

"Don't say another word. Just wait and see."

Jesse ran home and changed clothes, put on some of Maryanne's favorite cologne, and checked his hair. He grabbed the small blue box with a gold bow on it and drove to her house, so lost in thought that he nearly passed up her apartment. When he knocked on the door, she opened it with a big smile, and he sashayed into the room with a sheepish grin.

"What have you got behind your back?"

"Let's sit on the sofa. You're way too pushy."

She grabbed him and kissed him hard on the mouth. "Oh, I've missed you. Haven't you missed me?"

He knelt down on one knee and her mouth flew open.

"What have you done, Jesse Sinclair?"

He smiled. His eyes were fighting back the tears. He put his hand on her knee and kissed her lips. "Maryanne, I have fought this for so long in my life; not wanting to commit to anyone for any length of time. I have been a loner, a man who said he would never get married. And then you came into my life and nothing has been the same. All my efforts flew out the window like a scared bird. And you know what? I don't even care."

She was silent. He could tell she was about to cry. "Maryanne, I know we are not perfect. We will have our moments. But I am here today to ask you to marry me."

He took the ring out of the box and slipped it on her finger. It just happened to fit like a glove.

She threw her arms around his neck, crying in his ear. Whispering sweet things. "Oh, Jesse. You are so good to me. I am so happy. Thank you for doing this today. It could not have come at a better time."

"So the answer is yes?"

She pulled away and looked him in the eyes. "Yes. I will marry you. I will be your forever love."

They hugged and he pulled her up to him. "We have a few things to work out. Like the when, the where, and all that stuff. But at least we have this part done; we are in agreement that it has to happen."

"Are we ever one hundred percent sure of anything? I am as sure as anyone can be. I am eager to have you in my life and live with you, and have our children. I want a family as good or better than the one I was born into. But I mainly want to be a good husband to you."

"We have a lot to discuss."

"Yes, we do. But right now, we need to leave and go to Mom and Dad's house. They will be waiting for us. I don't want to be late."

"I'll get my purse. We are not saying anything just yet, are we?"

"No. Let's not announce it tonight. I would rather wait until we have our plans laid out."

"Agreed. So let's go. I'll try not to glow too much."

As soon as they walked through the door, Jesse smiled. The smell of his mother's cooking, the hum of people talking—it felt like home. His mother looked the same. She always did. Pretty but a little worn out looking. Maybe stress. His father always seemed to have everything under control. He never showed any sign of stress on his face, and he had a way of making the whole family feel as though everything would be all right. He hoped that gene was in his blood. He had never met anyone quite like his father. He admired him although he was a little intimidated by his strength.

Everyone gathered around the table, laughing and talking all at the same time. It could get a little noisy when they were all together. But that was what made it fun, and his mother never seemed to mind. In fact, the look on her face was pure delight.

"Dad, why don't you start the meat going around the table? I know the boys are starving."

Bill grinned and took a huge piece of chicken and passed it to Paul. While everyone was filling their plates with the massive amount of food that Sharon had on the table, the conversation stayed at a low hum.

"Emily and Rob, how are things going with you? Any plans of moving?"

"No, Jacob. We are staying put right now while Rob finishes school. But I think I'd kind of like to build. We haven't talked about it, but I think that might be fun."

Rob smiled slyly. "You realize, of course, that most marriages don't make it through the construction of a home."

She raised an eyebrow and stuck out her tongue.

"Paul, you two doing okay?" Emily turned her head to look at his face.

"I think so. As well as can be expected. It is too quiet around the house. And we need to talk to the doctor to see when we can try again to have a baby."

Avery kept quiet but nodded.

"Someone needs to have a child. I'm dying to have a baby around." Sharon laughed and shook her head. "If I could, I'd have one."

Bill's phone went off in his pocket. He shot a glance at Sharon and went into his office and shut the door.

"Your timing is impeccable."

"Sorry, but we have a group we need to take care of. The news is all over them and they are building in numbers. The head guy is Ted Taylor. You'll recognize him from his pictures all over the news. He's well known and in the public eye frequently. He owns television stations and who knows what else. A lot of power."

"When and where?"

"You'll get a text telling you the details. We want to take him out and then the group will fall apart. We will let you know where his car is. Do what you have to do."

"Oh, so I don't have to kill him."

"You have to make sure he dies."

"I will be waiting for directions."

"No error this time, Bill."

"Don't worry."

"It's your life, not mine."

"I understand."

He ended the call and sat down at the table as though nothing had happened. But Sharon knew. He waited for the text to tell him what to do next. He could feel the tension building as he waited. He smiled at the children and made small talk, but his there were tiny beads of sweat forming across his forehead. No one would ever know how much he hated this secret job. But one fine day everything was going to blow wide open.

CHAPTER THIRTY-EIGHT

Midnight was the perfect time to break into a car. Bill walked past the Cadillac parked on Eighth Street by Stanton Park, noticing the mass of shrubbery that would hide his movements. He was dressed in black and had his mask on, but he silently wished the car had been parked off a main street. The homeless were scattered, smoking their drug of choice, and not many cars were moving on the road. He cut back and knelt down beside the driver's side and felt underneath the car. There was a fog in the air and moisture had collected on the car. He needed to be careful. He was a master at what he did, but he always fell on the side of caution when handling explosives. When he was young he'd been fearless, but now there was a burning in his gut. A sick feeling that wouldn't go away. Command had given him precise orders to take Ted Taylor out. He didn't say how. So Bill had decided to attach an explosive device to the underside of the car. A few times while he was working, a car would drive slowly past the vehicle. He held his breath, hoping the black suit and face mask worked to keep him hidden.

The device was high-powered and the technology was unbeliev-able. It would be activated by his cell phone. And no one would be the wiser. Bill attached the unit and wiped the edges of the car to make sure there was no sign of his being there. He also dusted away his footprints and moved onto the grass when he was ready to leave. He would have to walk a block away and find a location to sit and wait for Ted to appear. He had no idea how long it would take, but he knew Sharon would understand if he didn't come home until morning.

He had parked his car away from the location, so sitting in the car was not an option. Walking along the quiet street, he found a bench in front of a local watch repair shop. He sat down, pulled off his mask, and looked at his watch. It was 12:45. He felt tired and wanted to lean back and doze off but he knew that was im-possible. He scanned the area and noticed that most of the home-less were bedding down for the night. It was a beautiful park and Washington at night just looked like any sleepy town. Everything was blurred by the lights and the water-laden fog and there was a slight halo around all the lights.

The scenery did not portray all the evil that lurked in the capi-tal city. Most of the population had no idea whatsoever that any-thing as sick as The President's Club even existed. The political arena knew things happened, but had become so hardened to it in order to save their positions that they became blind to the under-ground activity. What were at first horrendous acts of crime soon became the norm.

When Bill retired from the Navy, he'd felt free. He felt like Washington was home and a great place to live out the rest of his days. Until that one day he'd gotten a phone call that changed his life forever. And Washington became a noose around his neck.

Bill glanced at his watch again. An hour had passed. There were a few homeless men walking the sidewalk. It was extremely quiet. But then he noticed a tall figure walking under the street-lights, holding a woman's hand. He was dressed in a suit and had a hat on. He squinted to see if it was Ted, but it was so dark he couldn't tell. The man walked with a strong gait and held himself erect. Bill watched to see if he was headed for the Cadillac, and it looked like he was. Sweat beaded up on his brow as he waited to see if the guy was going to open the door of the car on the passenger's side. He didn't want to have to kill the woman just to get to Ted, but it looked like they were both going to get into the car. This was a moment when he wanted to be able to make a call to abort the mission and wait for another time to catch Ted alone. But Command would not see it that way. He, and whoever the "others" were, did not care about the loss of life of innocent people. The woman was guilty by association.

Ted leaned his companion against the car and kissed her. He grabbed her arm and she pulled away. Then Ted did something that made the hair stand up on Bill's arm. He slapped her hard across the face and she screamed and ran. That move made it a lot easier to kill the man.

Bill watched carefully as Ted started the car and drove down the street to a red light. The roads were quiet. No one was around but the homeless men who had filled themselves with cheap beer and were dozing against some of the shadowed buildings. Bill turned on his phone and clicked on the red button. It took exactly two seconds and the car exploded, shooting pieces of metal into the air in all directions. What was left of the vehicle was on fire. The sound was so loud it echoed for blocks, and in the distance Bill heard the sound of a siren.

It was time for him to disappear. He walked to his car and drove slowly home, feeling better about what he'd done, but also realizing that this was how men rationalized their killing. He knew it was wrong, no matter how disgusting Ted Taylor was. No matter how many people he had mowed down to become a business tycoon.

The house was quiet. Bill shed his clothes, allowed them to drop on the floor near the bed, and slipped under the cool sheets. He was utterly exhausted, both mentally and physically. .

Sharon stirred and reached for his arm and pulled him up next to her.

"Are you okay?"

"I am now."

"Was it bad?" She spoke in a low whisper.

"It's always bad."

"I've been worrying about you ever since you left."

"I'm home now, Honey. And it feels so good."

She patted his arm and snuggled into him. His thoughts ran rampant about the aftermath of the explosion. This event would be all over the news. People would be shocked to hear Ted Taylor was dead. And he, Bill Sinclair, would have to live with this the rest of his life. He would be the only one besides Command who would know. He didn't know how he would ever be able to let the press in on what was happening without going to prison himself. And the other ten men might suffer. But it had to stop. One of them had already been taken out for trying to escape the Club. But he wasn't going to escape. He was going to turn traitor on the United States government. He was sweating lying under cool sheets. He needed sleep so badly but it would not come. At least, not yet. He had so much to work through, and it meant risking the lives of his wife and all of his remaining children.

He guessed there would be an investigation going on for the next few months. But he hoped nothing would be found except perhaps remnants of an explosive. What else was going on in the government that the people didn't know about? And how in the world did he arrive at this place in his life by becoming one of the exceptional snipers of his time? A Navy SEAL that couldn't be taken down and never lost one of his men. All that work for nothing.

And then he had a thought. *What if I could take the President out?* And would that stop the nonsense going on or just move it to another party? He had to figure it out. All angles. It would take him some time, but he was good. And he knew it.

He felt Sharon next to him and gritted his teeth. He had to take care of this before he lost the one person in the world he could trust. He fell asleep in spite of the words running through his mind and the sound of sirens still whining in the distance.

CHAPTER THIRTY-NINE

The one hundred fifty-six foot yacht was on Pier 54 and nearly took up the whole slip. The water had a slight chop but The Grand Slam would not feel a thing. Patrick Lathrop was standing near the stern when Bill walked down the pier to the boat. He was shocked that the yacht was so large; he wasn't sure what he'd expected, but it wasn't this massive boat in front of him. He smiled and waved at Patrick, who greeted him with a big smile, showing a mouth full of white teeth. He was dressed casual and seemed to be in a great mood. Bill boarded the Slam trying hard not to look so impressed.

"Morning, Bill. So glad to see you! Come on board and have a seat with me. It's a perfect morning to be out here and I think you'll enjoy yourself. The chef has fixed us a nice breakfast and this will give us time to get to know each other."

Bill shook his hand and sat down in the large dining chair and looked around at the crew and the other boats out on the water. "This yacht is so big I almost want to call it a ship."

Patrick laughed a deep laugh that rippled across the water. "It's a beauty, all right."

"Do you take it out often, Patrick?"

"We use this more than we should. It's addictive. Especially when the weather is good. And right now it is perfect."

Patrick took a long drink of his Bloody Mary. "So how long have you been with the firm?"

"Many years. I've been a CPA for as long as I can remember. I loved numbers as a kid and still do today."

"I admire your tenacity. I could no more sit at a desk all day for anything."

"It's not so bad. I meet wonderful people and it is great to work at a job where you can change someone's life. Money is the center of so much of our lives. Managing it and understanding the ins and outs of the tax laws is so important. Especially to large companies."

"Yes, we've had our share of audits. That's why I wanted your company to take care of us."

"We'll do a great job for you, Patrick. Don't you worry about anything."

They both got quiet for a moment and ate the perfectly prepared eggs benedict and fresh fruit. Bill took a bite out of the blueberry muffin and a swallow of hot coffee. The chef had outdone himself.

"This breakfast is delicious. I didn't realize I was so hungry. But food always tastes better on the water." Bill swallowed the last bite of muffin and egg.

"Yes, it does. So tell me a little about yourself. Surely you've done something besides numbers."

Bill sat up straight and smiled. "Of course I have. I was a Navy SEAL and spent some time in Afghanistan. Did a little sniper work while I was there."

"I see. Did you enjoy that part of your service to your country?"

"Well, I don't think any of us enjoy war time. But I always try to excel in what I do."

"Did you ever have to kill civilians?"

"Not sure where you're headed with this, but we tried hard not to ever kill innocent people. I am certain air strikes sometimes took out more than just the enemy. But that's hard to control. You're always going to have some casualties that you didn't count on."

"I served in the Navy, myself."

"Really? That's interesting. It's a good way to grow up and become a man, to find out what kind of man you really are. Or want to be."

"Not heard it put that way before, but yes, it makes a man out of you one way or the other."

The water was kicking up a bit but it was still a perfect day. Bill was enjoying the excursion and the conversation.

"So do you keep guns at home, Bill? Left over from your SEAL days?"

"I have a few. I don't hunt anymore, so it's mainly for personal protection."

"I keep a few myself. With the way our world is going, you may need that gun to protect your family."

"That's exactly how I feel, Patrick."

"It looks like the government is making some pretty crazy deals with Iran. Every time I watch the news there's something radical going on. How do you feel about where this country is going?"

"I really don't like to discuss politics with my clients, but I'm not too happy about it."

"I didn't mean to push. Just wondering which side of the proverbial fence you are on."

"I'm a conservative, for sure. But the world is headed in a different direction. Not to change the subject, but do you fish much?"

Patrick laughed. "Good segue, Bill. I do fish when I have the time, but things have gotten out of control with Global Electric. We are a huge company and our hands are into so many areas of industry that it's hard to sleep at night. Another reason why we need you."

"I've never had a hobby of sorts. I find that cutting grass is therapy for me. I know that sounds funny, but I can lose myself totally while mowing. I would love to find a sport I enjoyed. But I work so much that my down time is spent with my family."

"I get that. Well, we are going to head back to shore, Bill. I don't want to tie you up all day; just wanted to get to know you better."

"I have enjoyed every second. It was refreshing to be out on the water and get away from life for a few moments"

"Sounds like you have your hands full."

"I have a large family, and it's hard to keep up with all that drama!"

"Look at your calendar and see what you have open for next week. I'll email you the file for the books for the hospital and appliance divisions. So make the appointment after you've had a chance to check things out."

Bill shook his hand and stepped off the yacht onto the pier. For some reason, and he wouldn't know why until later, he'd felt uneasy about where the conversation was going. The questions about guns and killing innocent people threw him completely. This was a very wealthy man, running a monster of a company. *Why did he want to know about my having a gun?* The whole thing smelled funny, but he was not sure in what way. He would have to really keep himself in check when it came to Patrick, until he had the man figured out. It was a great boon for the business to get this man on board. Who knows? It could lead to even more business with Global Electric if he played his cards right. But he still didn't know who he could really trust.

He climbed into his car and sat there thinking about the whole morning. He might be blowing things out of proportion but he usually could trust his gut feelings. This was a business relationship and he planned to keep it that way. He just wished Patrick would have played his hand. He was fishing for something. Bill wasn't sure what. But there was definitely a lure on the end of that line.

CHAPTER FORTY

Eloping had its pros and cons. Jesse and Maryanne had decided to take the dive and get married, even though it was going to upset the whole family. Maryanne had no parents, but Jesse sure did. Very involved parents. And most, if not all, of his family probably thought he would never marry. He was going to surprise them all, but not in the traditional way. They had planned a quick trip to Kiawah Island, a few miles from Charleston. He was excited. He would have loved to have taken her to Paris, but since they were sneaking off and spending only two nights there, they chose a closer rendezvous. Maryanne wasn't as nervous as he was, because she had no one who was going to freak out at her quick marriage. Jesse, however, had a retired Navy SEAL for a father, and he would not let this go easily. He would hear about this one trip for the rest of his natural life.

They were heading to the airport, luggage in the back seat. His receptionist had moved all his appointments so that he was free for the next few days. It felt weird, sort of like he was skipping school and running away with the girl next door.

Jesse reached over and patted her knee. "I'm a little nervous about this. How about you?"

"I'm excited. I wouldn't say I was nervous. But it's a huge step we're taking, and I do feel the weight of our decision."

"It's one of the most important decisions we will ever make in our life together. I feel great about that part of it. Just hoping my family will understand."

"We have to remember while we are standing in front of them all like the firing squad, that it is our life. We made this decision because we are ready. We didn't want to spend thousands for a stupid wedding. I think that's a smart decision, if you ask me."

"I'm certain "smart" won't be the word that comes to their mind."

They both laughed. "No, I'm sure it won't. But we both know what we are doing. I'm sure after the initial shock they will come around."

"I guess we'll find out soon enough. It feels funny running away like this. It's sort of freeing, if you know what I mean."

"I agree. Breaking traditional rules is always freeing to me. At least when it doesn't hurt anyone but me if it doesn't work out. So when will we tell them?"

"I think it's best we wait until we are married. Maybe our second day there. That way Mom can plan the party."

"Sounds right. I wish I could see their faces. That would be worth millions. Instagram hits would go off the chart."

Maryanne looked out the window, quiet for a few moments. Then she turned to look at Jesse. "Did we talk about children?"

Jesse glanced at her, with one eye on the road. "Kids? I'm not sure we did."

"Well? How do you feel about that?"

"Um, we're not even married yet. I think we should wait."

She smiled. "Come on. What do you feel about us having children?"

"Honey, I love kids. Of course I want your children."

"How many?"

"Does that need to be decided right now?"

"Well, no."

"Good. Let's just let things happen naturally. I'm sure we will be having a baby at some point. I would like to get used to having you around first. That's going to be a huge adjustment."

She hit his arm with her small fist. "Oh! You can be a jerk sometimes."

"Well, I'm not used to underwear hanging off my shower rod or makeup all over the counter. And I know how you keep your apartment. Perfectly coiffed. We bachelors are not so tidy, you know."

"You will be when I get you trained. My girlfriend says that she just trained her husband. Now he's perfect."

Groan. "Train? I'm not your dog."

"No. But you have lots to learn."

"And I imagine you do, too. We men can be pretty complicated."

She burst out laughing. "This is a funny conversation. Are we almost there?"

"Yes. And I cannot wait to get there and have the ceremony. Did you write your vows?"

"I did. They are very short. I hope yours are."

"Mine is nearly one sentence. I was stuck."

"As much as you talk, I wouldn't think you'd have any trouble."

"I'm not sure what to say. I'll be yours forever. That's about it, right?"

"Oh, let's not put too much effort into this vow. It's only the rest of our lives."

"Such a small thing."

They pulled into the hotel parking lot, laughing.

"Let's take our luggage inside and check out our villa. It overlooks a lagoon, with a short walk to the beach. I think you will love it."

"Sounds like heaven. I could use the respite from the world."

"It will feel like we have dropped off the world. This place is amazing."

Jesse checked in at the front desk and got the key to the villa they rented. When they opened the door, Maryanne was blown away. It was like a little paradise.

"Oh, Jesse! This is perfect."

There was a small living room with linen covered furniture, lush palm trees in two corners of the room, and the refrigerator was full of orange juice, fresh brewed raspberry tea, and all types of food. On the island were a box of donuts and an arrangement of mixed flowers. She looked around and saw chocolates lying on their pillows in the bedroom.

"Not bad for such a quick decision, huh?" Jesse grinned, sitting down on the sofa.

Maryanne sat down next to him and blew out a sigh. "I'm so glad we did this. Just you and me and the local pastor. It's so quiet and peaceful."

Jesse walked over to the open door and looked out over the lagoon. There was a nice breeze blowing through the room and somewhere off in the distance they could hear some music.

"Let's go see where that music is coming from." Jesse reached for her hand.

She smiled and jumped up. "Sounds romantic." She kissed his lips.

"Mmmm. Maybe we should stay in here."

"No way. I'm ready to see what's going on out there, and maybe get a bite to eat."

They walked over to the clubhouse where they found a small group of musicians playing all genres of songs. People were gathering around and the smell of fresh fish cooking floated in the air. The food was included in the price of the room, so Jesse and Maryanne filled their plates with fresh fruits and fish and hushpuppies, slaw, and rolls. The iced tea was sweet with a touch of wine infused into the mixture of lemons and limes. An unusual blend but it worked well with the atmosphere. They found a table in the back of the room that had a thatched roof over it, and tasted the food they had piled onto their plates. People were dancing and laughing. It couldn't have been a nicer atmosphere to start their honeymoon.

"I feel a bit guilty that we are having so much fun here while our family is home unaware of what we are about to do."

"Do you feel like you should call them now and let them know where you are?"

"I don't know. I just hate for them to miss this lovely occasion."

"Let's finish our meal and then we can decide whether or not to call them, okay?"

Jesse sat back and relaxed, trying to just enjoy being with Maryanne. He never thought he would come to the place where he would be absolutely in love with someone, enough so that he would want to spend the rest of his life with them. But Maryanne had really snagged him early on. It felt good to be wanted and to also know this was the one.

The breeze had gotten a little cooler, which made it really enjoyable. He reached for her hand and she smiled. She got up and pulled him towards her and they danced across the room, mixing in with a few other couples. Soon the room began to fill up but Jesse didn't notice, because he was so wrapped up in Maryanne.

He failed to see his mother and father across the room dancing in the crowd. Nor did he see Paul and Avery, and Emily and Rob. Soon they were all on the floor and suddenly Jesse realized that his whole family was around him. He pulled away from Maryanne and grinned.

"What have you done, woman?"

"I could tell you wanted them around. So I made a phone call to Paul. He made this happen for you."

Jesse waltzed over to Paul and gave him a bear hug. "Man, it's good to see you guys!"

"Thanks, Jess. We were so happy to hear the news. We all are just glad to be included. It would have been a shame if you guys had run away and married without our getting to see this big event."

Sharon and Bill came over and everyone started talking at once.

"Son, there's no way I was going to allow you to marry without your mother getting to witness it."

"Dad, we just wanted a quiet wedding and then have a party when we got back. But this is wonderful. I was really missing all of you."

"So let's drink and dance and enjoy this night. For tomorrow you and Maryanne will tie the knot and all of us will have to go back home."

CHAPTER FORTY-ONE

Morning came quickly and Maryanne was up washing her hair and getting her dress ready. Sharon had come in to help her with the dress. Avery and Emily helped with her hair. She looked like a China doll when they were done. Her dark hair was silky and her dress snow white. She could have been a model for any major magazine in the world. All the family was wondering how in the world Jesse had gotten this girl to marry him. She was a little nervous but mainly just wanting to get it over with. She wanted to be Jesse's wife.

"Sharon, do I look okay? I wanted to surprise Jess with this dress. He's never seen it."

"Are you kidding? You'll take his breath away. How do I know that? Because you take ours away."

Maryanne blushed. "You're being too kind."

"Kind, nothing. It's the truth. You look stunning."

Emily walked up to her and pushed a lone strand of hair out of her face. "I just don't know what you see in my brother, but I do want you to be happy. If you ever need to talk to anyone, just call me. I'll always be here for you."

"Your brother has been nothing but wonderful to me, Emily. He is my Superman. He is always there for me and so understanding. I adore him."

"That's all that matters then." Emily looked at Avery and grinned. "I felt the same way when Avery married Paul. Only I knew Paul to the bone."

"I remember that day, for sure. You were so worried I wouldn't last with him, because he has so many little things that he is adamant about. Having to eat with nothing touching on his plate. I thought I would die the first time he said that to me in a restaurant." Avery smiled.

They all laughed, easing the tension in the room.

⊷ ⊶

The men were having a similar conversation. Only everyone was wondering how in the world he had snagged such a beautiful woman.

"Dad, I just fell in love with her. Can I help it if I am irresistible?"

"I haven't seen that side of you, Son. But if you say so."

"I would have lost that bet, for sure." Jacob laughed.

"You're not always right, Brother. That just shows you don't really know me." Jesse popped him on the back.

"I know you too well. I almost want to warn her about your moods."

"You'll look odd with a black eye at my wedding."

Bill stepped in, holding back a chuckle. "Come on, guys. Are you ready for this, Jesse? Are you nervous?"

"A little. But I just want it to be over with. I'm ready to start our life together."

"That's a good thing. Because it's going to happen faster than you realize. It's a commitment for life that you are making. No more chasing girls. No more anything. It's you and Maryanne now."

"I'll be fine with that, Dad. I have no interest in any other woman. We have a great relationship and can talk about anything. I like that about us."

"You'll need that, Son. Life is tough and you will go through more things than you can imagine. Stay strong. Have faith. And never give up on her. No matter what."

Paul shook his head. "Oh, you will go through things, all right. Avery and I have fought over the dumbest things since we got married. Everything seems bigger. More important. But you have to keep it light, or you will never make it, Jess."

"All this advice. Where's your faith in us? We are two consenting adults. I probably should have eloped just to spare myself all of this nonsense talk."

Bill laughed. "Okay, Son. It's time to head to the ceremony. Keep your emotions in check. When you see her in her wedding dress, I'm warning you, it can take you down."

Jesse walked into the room and saw the pastor standing at the front of the chapel waiting for them. He took his place at the front and turned to see Maryanne walking in. His Dad had been right. She was breathtaking and he felt a little weak in the knees. She walked up next to him and he took her hand for a moment, squeezing it tightly. She nodded and smiled. She was shaking like a leaf.

The pastor began the ceremony quietly." Jesse Sinclair and Maryanne Millhouse, you are about to pledge the most sacred vows that one person can make with another. As you stand before your family and God, you must give careful consideration to that which you are promising. You are accountable to one another for as long as you both shall live. These vows are as binding in adversity as they are in prosperity.

Jesse faced Maryanne and swallowed hard. He spoke in a quiet voice. "Maryanne, I have never felt surer of anything in my entire life that I want you to be my wife, my forever love, until I die. I feel you are a gift to me, and I will fight to protect you and us, with every breath that I take. You fulfill me in so many ways that we have only begun to touch. I am thankful for your life, and will cherish you and honor you for the rest of my life." He put a ring on her finger and stepped back.

Maryanne took his hand and smiled. "Jesse, I have loved you even when I wasn't sure who you were. I love how we can talk about anything, how we share so many beliefs, and how we are so open with each other. I promise to love you, to cherish you, and help you become your best you for as long as I live. I want to walk beside you, hand in hand, no matter what we face, into eternity."

She slipped his ring on his finger and they turned to face the pastor. "I now pronounce you man and wife. Now go and live your lives under the covering of these vows. God be with you both."

The family was crying and ran to surround them, hugging them and throwing flower petals up in the air. It was a lovely private wedding; just what Jesse wanted. Maryanne was lovely in her dress and he could tell she was thrilled that the family was there. That was the surprise of his life, other than her accepting his proposal. He took her hand and they walked through the crowd to the dinner that was waiting for the whole family. Maryanne and Jesse sat at the head of the table and the family sat around them, laughing, talking, and toasting to the couple until they ran out of words.

"I can't believe you guys were going to elope." Emily grinned at her brother.

"It was a thought, for sure."

"Thought? We had it all planned before I stepped in and made a phone call to your mother." Maryanne grabbed his arm and laughed.

"I thought it was kinda cool, actually. We would save ourselves a ton of money and come home to enjoy a great party with the family."

Sharon stepped into the conversation. "I'm so glad you made that call, Maryanne. I would have hated to have missed this."

"It happens only once in a lifetime, so I thought it worth letting you in on it. I think it turned out very well."

Jesse looked at his father. "Dad, how have things been since we all left home? More time for you and Mom to spend together?"

Bill grinned and nodded, swallowing his last bite of steak. "Pretty much, Jess. As much as my work will allow."

"You guys take it slow. Make it fun. It will get hard soon enough." Paul shook his head and winked at Jesse.

"I figure if I can drill on her mouth and not get punched in the nose, then I'm pretty sure we can work through anything!" Jesse laughed and looked at Maryanne. She was blushing.

Jesse squeezed her hand, thinking of how lucky a man he was to have found her.

An hour later, the table was cluttered with leftover food and empty dishes and the family was preparing to leave. Sharon and Bill hugged their son and new daughter-in-law, wishing them the best.

"You two enjoy this day together, and know we are always here for you. Life takes over quickly, so keep close to each other. It will take all you have to stay together so build a strong foundation."

"Mom, you don't have to be so serious." Jesse hugged her and smiled. "We're gonna be fine."

"Oh, I know you are. But you just never know what might come up. We already know that after losing Susan. Your father and I have lived through some tough times and it looks like we are not done yet."

Bill nudged Sharon and frowned.

"What does that mean, Mother? Is everything okay?"

Sharon caught herself and forced a big smile. "Oh, don't pay any attention to me. I just want you both to be happy. Now we are on our way. Let us hear from you soon."

Jesse and Maryanne watched as the family left in their separate cars. "What in the world was that all about?" Maryanne looked at Jesse with worry in her eyes.

"I have no idea. But I bet we find out soon enough. I really don't know what she meant, but I hope it wasn't serious. They've been through enough already. Dad seems strong enough so I don't think it is his health."

"Are you kidding? He's built like a tank. It's her I'm worried about."

"She'll be fine. My mother is a strong woman. Whatever it is, she can handle it." But Jesse wasn't so certain anymore. He'd not seen his mother like that, ever. He took Maryanne's hand and they walked back to their villa. It was a beautiful ceremony and he was going to make the best of their time together, in spite of the insinuation of dark times ahead.

CHAPTER FORTY-TWO

Patrick Lathrop was a man of his word. Bill had been sent the files through email on the two accounts that GE wanted him to provide accounting services and audits. It took him a while to go through everything, mainly because he was looking for errors in previous years that might just save the company some money. Bill had an eye for errors and nothing slipped by him. But he was still pondering the visit he'd had with Patrick. Both of the businesses were running smooth as silk, but they were losing money. Especially the medical supplies account. So he looked for skimming, since most of the purchasers were using Medicare as the form of payment. Medicare fraud was rampant. What he found were several employees skimming money from the Medicare payments. They tried to hide it but were not very good at it. He was surprised that someone hadn't seen it already. Mistakes right under the company's nose.

As he was going over the accounts, Patrick walked through his door and sat down in a red leather chair on the other side of his desk, smiling like he owned the place. He looked at Bill over his glasses.

"Morning, Bill. How's it going?"

"Well, as mornings go, I guess this one is going okay. You are out and about early."

"No grass grows underneath my feet, Bill. You will learn that about me"

"I believe I already have."

"I know you just received the files, but have you had time to glance over them? Have you seen any obvious errors?"

"The companies seem to be running perfectly, but I have found some glaringly obvious theft."

Patrick sat up, alarmed. "What do you mean?"

"There are some employees, I don't know who yet, who are skimming profits from Medicare purchases. It is unbelievably common in businesses like yours where most of the buying is done through Medicare. No wonder that program is broke."

"Most of my people have been with me for years. They are loyal to a fault."

"Well apparently several are not. It is too much for one person to skim, so I would say it is at least two but possibly a group."

Patrick stood up, shaking his head. "This is outrageous. Now who do I trust?"

"That could be a problem, Patrick."

"And how in the world do I locate the rats?"

"They are pocketing the money. You would have to have access to their computers. I can help you with that."

Patrick sat down and stared at Bill. It was obvious that he was troubled. But Bill could tell there was something else on his mind. He had no clue what.

After a few uncomfortable moments of silence, Patrick spoke. "How do I trust you, Bill?"

"What do you mean, Patrick? Do you doubt what I've found?"

Patrick shook his head. "No, not at all. But how does one trust anybody?"

Bill nodded at the solemnity of that statement. "I understand that question totally.

"Do you, Bill? Do you really know where I am coming from?"

"I can't say I know that, Patrick. But I know in my own life that there is really one person I can completely trust and that is my wife."

"What about your kids?"

"They love me, but I don't know if they are even capable of keeping a secret."

Patrick laughed. But it was hollow. Bill suddenly saw a side of Patrick that piqued his interest.

Bill pointed to a pad and picked up a pen. "If you are going to talk to me about anything serious, we would need to meet somewhere. I do not trust the walls in here."

Patrick grabbed the pad. "What about your home?"

"Not there, either."

"Then I think we are on the same track here."

Bill raised his eyebrow. "You set the time and place. Perhaps on your boat. Or maybe an unattached location. Somewhere you don't usually go." He passed the pad to Patrick.

"Exactly. I will give that some thought and get in touch with you. What is the best way to reach you where no one else has access?"

"Now that is a problem."

"Sit here. I will be back shortly."

Patrick got up and left without another word. Bill sat in his chair, rocking back and forth. He was struggling to put this all together. Something was going on here that had a familiar ring to it. But he didn't want to surmise anything before he heard Patrick's thoughts. He wanted to think that he had just met another of the twelve, but Patrick didn't seem cut out for something like that. Whatever it was, Patrick felt the need for extreme privacy, and it appeared that the option was very narrow as to where that place would be.

Forty-five minutes went by while Bill sat in his office quietly, thinking. Patrick walked through the door, closing it, and sat down. He didn't speak a word. He handed Bill a phone and wrote on a pad on the desk. *Because we do not know if this office is private or not, I am giving you a cell phone that you will use only to contact me. My number is in your phone. Do not let anyone else know this phone exists. I will call you tonight with a time and place for us to meet. I don't know how you will do it, but make sure no one knows where you are going.*

Bill nodded. He stood up to shake Patrick's hand. "I'll check into the matter of the theft, Patrick, and let you know anything else I find. Somehow you need to find a way to check your employees' computers to see who is talking to whom. We need to get on top of this. Thanks for stopping in. I will be talking to you soon."

Patrick nodded and shook his hand. He took a second to look at Bill right in the eyes and then he turned and walked out. For a moment the room went cold and Bill sat down, shivering. He needed to be fully prepared to hear what Patrick was going to tell him. But he had no idea at the moment what that was going to be.

He dove into the files, hoping to catch other errors so that he would have something more solid to tell Patrick. He had a feeling there would be some people losing their jobs because of this discovery. It should have been noticed a long time ago. Bill knew nothing about Patrick but he knew he was going to get the opportunity soon.

He left for lunch, calling Sharon to meet him at the Roti Mediterranean Grill on Pennsylvania Avenue. The traffic was bad at noon; everyone headed out to grab a fast lunch somewhere. That was an oxymoron—there was no quick lunch to be found at noon. He pulled up into the parking lot and took the last parking spot, looking quickly to see where Sharon could possibly park. He got out and walked into the café and Sharon was sitting at a table waving at him. He grinned and walked towards her.

"How in the world did you beat me here?"

"I was running errands when you called so it didn't take me any time at all to get here."

"I'm glad. Look at the crowd! We'd have never gotten a seat so quickly."

"You sounded urgent when you called. Is anything going on you wanted to talk about?"

"I just wanted to spend some time with you, Honey. It always makes me feel better if I see you during my busy day."

Sharon looked at him and nodded. She knew he had changed directions. She wrote on a pad she took out of her purse. *"Did you get a call?"*

He wrote back. *"I got a visit from Patrick Lathrop. It was very interesting."*

They ordered their meals and Sharon wrote another short note.

"Is something wrong? Did you find out about his companies? Was he upset?"

"Nothing like that. I am not sure what he wants to discuss, but I have my own ideas. I will catch you up on things as I get more information."

She nodded. "This meal is delicious. I won't fix a heavy meal tonight. I have some charity work to do this afternoon and then home again. Are you working all day?"

"That depends. Not sure. I may talk to Patrick again today. I'll let you know if I am going to be later than usual."

He picked up her hand and kissed the palm. She blushed. It was her favorite thing that he did when he wanted to show her he loved her. And at the moment, he felt like she was the only person in the world he could talk to. She knew him. She understood all of it. If he ever lost her, he would not be able to breathe.

CHAPTER FORTY-THREE

The evening dragged as Bill waited on that second phone to ring. Bill sat on the porch watching the moon shining through a few stray clouds, wondering where the meeting place would be. It was tough not being able to talk to Sharon at the house. They had to change into new clothes and remove their shoes every single time they wanted to talk about the Club. He leaned his head back and closed his eyes. He was tired of the strain.

Just as he was about to doze off, the phone rang in his left pocket. "Patrick?"

"Yes, Bill. Glad this works so well. It may be our only way to talk. I found a place we could meet. Somewhere I never go. I'm sure you know where Lincoln Park is. Let's meet there at 11:00 tonight. I won't keep you long."

"See you then, Patrick."

He walked into the house and sat down in the living room where Sharon had settled on the sofa. She smiled and touched his face. He would have given anything to talk to her. But he knew he couldn't so he smiled and kissed her.

"I may have to leave later. But I won't be gone long."

"Okay, Honey. Let's just sit here and watch a movie and relax for a few hours. We never get to do that."

Bill grabbed the remote and surfed through the channels until he found *Something's Gotta Give* and they sat back for two hours laughing and enjoying a movie they had seen three times before. It felt so good to escape for a moment.

"Jack Nicholson is some actor. The face of evil and the face of a broken man. He can play any part."

Sharon nodded. "Kind of like you. You wear several hats yourself."

He looked at her. "I wish I could wear only one."

"I know you do. Soon, maybe."

"Wish the kids were here tonight. I was thinking about Susan today. How much she is missing of our lives."

Sharon pulled away and wiped a sudden lone tear that had let loose from her eyes. "I think of her every single day. I loved her so much. She was so much like you."

"I hate it when you say that because she was so much more."

"She did have your personality. And she was brilliant."

"The accident haunts me to this day. Unanswered questions."

"What do you mean, Bill?"

"Oh, nothing really. Just hoping it was an accident."

Sharon stared at him, frozen. "You mean—?"

"I have no idea. No proof. But only suspicion. A possibility."

"I would have never thought of that. What put that in your head?"

Bill glanced at his watch. "I need to go. It's a good time to stop that conversation before we get in too deep. The walls have ears." He whispered in her ear.

"I'll be up waiting for you."

"I'll be home as soon as I can."

The short drive to Lincoln Park was nerve-wracking. Bill pulled into a parking place and noticed that the place was empty. Dark.

He got out of the car, scanned the area, and walked slowly to the first bench he saw that was surrounded by trees and low shrubbery. His eye was on any car that drove past, which wasn't many at 11:00 at night. Patrick couldn't have chosen a better place.

Bill sat back and waited, his mind running rampant with thoughts about the conversation that was about to take place. He kept checking his watch and taking a swallow of coffee in the mug he'd brought from the house. He had changed into new clothes and new shoes. It seemed like forever before he spotted Patrick walking his way. He was both relieved and nervous.

Patrick shook Bill's hand and sat down, looking around nervously. "We can't be too careful, you know. Hard to ever be one hundred percent sure that no one is watching or listening."

Bill shook his head. "I've covered my end. I'm wearing new clothes and new shoes. I've told no one. So what's on your mind, Patrick?"

Patrick leaned back and blew out a sigh. "Bill, what do you do when you are not at work?"

"That's an odd question out here in the dark at 11:00 at night."

"I have to go through these simple questions before I can talk about why I am here."

"I spend time with my family."

"So no outside activities?"

"What do you mean by outside?"

"Are you involved in anything else?"

"No."

"We have established that you own guns, but you do not hunt, correct?"

"What do you do in your spare time, Patrick?"

"I'm asking the questions."

"Well, we need to cut to the chase here."

"I have to find out if I can trust you, Bill."

"How in the world are we going to get to that point?"

"It is critical that we do." Patrick was looking at Bill as if he wanted to read his thoughts.

"How do I know I can trust you?"

"We both are sitting here late at night with someone we hardly know."

"If it weren't so serious it would be comical."

Bill thought he saw Patrick smile.

"I told you, Bill, that I was in the Navy. I was a SEAL, too. I also was a sniper. You and I have the same background."

"Did you know that about me when you came to McCloud, Kenner, Jones, and Sinclair for financial assistance?" Bill said.

"I did my homework. It wasn't too difficult to find out."

"So why the questions if you've already vetted me?"

"Trust is the key to our whole relationship. I have to know we are on the same page. And I can't stick my neck out and then find out we are not."

"I feel the same way, Patrick. I am beginning to wonder why you called me here."

"While in the Navy I was privy to information about the United States government."

"And?"

"I was wondering if you knew anything about a club?"

"That's pretty vague. What type of club?"

"Connected to the government."

"I've heard about it."

"What do you know about it?" Patrick didn't give an inch.

Bill was getting nervous. He couldn't tell which side of the fence Patrick was sitting on.

"I've heard rumors."

Patrick rubbed his face. Bill could see he was getting frustrated.

"I'm talking about The President's Club, Bill."

Bill froze for a moment. Patrick had actually said it out loud. *Now what?*

"What are you trying to find out from me, Patrick? Just say it. We are beating around the bush and we are getting nowhere. Just trust me and tell me what it is you want to know."

"We need to get this thing wrapped up. Our being so close to the White House isn't a good thing."

"So get to the point. I need to know if we are on the same side of this thing. It's driving me nuts."

"Are you a member of that club?"

Bill sighed. There it was. The question he wasn't sure he should answer.

"Are you?"

"No, I'm not. But I know all about it."

"I'm one of the current twelve. Well, eleven now. One of us has been taken down."

Patrick jumped up and almost shouted, but caught himself. "I knew it. I just knew it. So how do you feel about it? The killing and torture that goes on?"

"It is ruining my life. I have no life, actually. I hate what I am being asked to do. The safety of my family has been threatened. I'm not even sure they didn't cause the accident that killed my daughter. It's sick what our government is doing in the name of justice. And as I understand, this has been going on for years."

"Do you know any of the other eleven?"

"I have no idea who they are, but I did recognize one of the twelve. I was asked to take him out because Command said there was a leak. But as soon as I opened the door to shoot I saw his face and knew who he was. I helped him escape that night but the government shot him the next day. That also happened with someone they asked me to kill who was working on an agenda to stop the President. I helped him and they took him out. So they are watching me like a hawk. They see me as a weak link."

"That is a hell of a position for you to be in. What are they telling you?"

"Do you work for the government, Patrick?"

"No way. But I am aware of this club and what it has done for centuries. It has changed in some ways, but the agenda remains the same."

"They are telling me to do things that are inhuman, just to show they are in charge. Things I don't want to do. If I don't do them, I will be taken out."

"They threatened you?" Patrick sounded shocked.

"All the friggin' time."

"That's hard to believe that something so powerful has existed underground all these years and no one has ever attempted to blow their cover. I have wanted to do it for years, but I knew it would take more than one person to accomplish that."

"It is so sick how they have this set up, with Command calling all of us, one at a time, to commit murder or torture someone into giving us information. It goes on all the time. And everyone turns a blind eye."

"So how does it work?"

"Before I tell you, how did you find out, anyway?"

Patrick sat back and took a deep breath. "You may not believe this, but one of the twelve from years past confided in me and I was sworn to secrecy. Don't ask me why, but when I vetted you, I just knew you were a prime target for them. I took a huge risk talking to you about this. And so did you."

"No joke. We both could die over it. They are good at what they do. They hire the best of the best. So we can never be certain, even if we are very clever in how we hide our conversations and meetings, that they are not watching or listening."

"We've been here long enough tonight."

"I agree. Let's pick up this conversation another time. But not here. We can never meet in the same place twice."

"Remember you have that phone with you at all times. If you ever need to talk to me, ring me. I will be available to you 24/7.

From time to time, we will ditch these phones and get new ones just as a precaution. Nothing is overlooked. I know you are an expert in covert, so this shouldn't be a problem for you. I am not one of you. But I know how to be careful."

"I would give almost anything to get rid of the pressure I feel all the time. The constant knowledge that the phone will ring in my other pocket and I will have to kill some poor soul or torture them. Suddenly a human being just disappears from the face of the earth. What is amazing is that the public does not question it. We make it look like an accident or blow them to pieces. There is never a trace of them left, either way. I have to live with that, Patrick."

"I couldn't do it. And I am sorry you have to."

"Nice to talk to you. To know I can trust you a hundred percent."

"We have to stay on our toes, Bill. I run a mother of a company. We are huge. But I never lose sight of the small stuff. Watch yourself. Do not mention my name to anyone, except in reference to the work you are doing for me."

"I usually do not speak about my clients to anyone."

Patrick stood up and shook Bill's hand. "We'll talk soon. Get some rest, Bill."

Bill sat back down and waited for Patrick to reach his vehicle and pull out of sight. Then he walked to his car several blocks away and drove home, totally exhausted but with a smile on his face. Maybe, just maybe, there was a way. But it was bigger than he or Patrick. They were going to need a friggin' core group to figure this one out.

CHAPTER FORTY-FOUR

Sharon was sitting up waiting on him when he came in the house. He had hoped personally that she was already asleep, because he had no idea how they could even begin to discuss what just took place in Lincoln Park while sitting in their house. The walls had ears. He knew it wasn't a safe place. He wasn't even sure about the backyard gazebo. He had checked it several times, but he never felt dead sure it was clean. The fact that he was still breathing told him it was probably okay, but he was nervous just the same.

"Honey, I was so worried I couldn't sleep. I decided to wait for you here in the living room. I watched another movie while you were out."

He leaned over and kissed her. She smelled like lavender. He suddenly wanted to be with her and clear his mind of everything he'd just been through. But he knew she wouldn't go for it. She had sat up all this time and she wanted to know what was going on. She deserved that.

"I really didn't expect you to be up."

"Can we go outside? It's so nice and quiet out there."

He took the hint. Well, it wasn't much of a hint. Pretty obvious what she wanted.

"I'll be out in a moment."

Sharon walked to the door, took off her clothes, put on a new robe she'd purchased, and walked barefooted out to the gazebo. It was a pain but it had to be done to have any privacy. Bill came behind her in a new undershirt, shorts, and no shoes. He had taken two Cokes out of the 'fridge and walked behind her to the gazebo. He checked all the places a tap might be but found everything barren. They sat close together, and sipped their Cokes in the quiet of the night.

"You won't believe what I'm about to tell you. I almost don't want you to know, so in case you were ever interrogated, you wouldn't have to lie."

"I need to know what you are going through. I want to be a part of that secret life you live, because otherwise, I feel so shut out. So separated from you."

He reached over and grabbed her hand. "Honey, I don't even want to live this private life. I hate it. But as it is, I have no way out." He leaned over and whispered into her ear.

"Sharon, you would not believe the conversation I had tonight with Patrick Lathrop. First of all, he's a nice guy. A straight-up kind of man who doesn't mince words. I really like him. He's got money, but he still can get down to the nitty-gritty with you. We met in Lincoln Park, which shocked me, as it is located so close to the White House. It was dark and no one else was around. But I was still nervous. It took some time to trust each other but we each finally gave up, I think. He wanted to know if I was one of the twelve. He knew about the President's Club. He isn't part of it, but he wants to blow it wide open like I do. We just don't know how to go about it. I had no idea we would talk about this. I was nervous as heck. So was he. Both being ex-Navy SEALs, we came from the same core of beliefs. The SEALs stick together. So that is where the trust came from, in my estimation."

"How in the world did he find out about the club?"

"My question exactly. An ex-club member told him. I would love to be able to talk with one of those men. I just don't know who they are and he's not going to tell me that information. That man, whoever he is, doesn't want it known that he spoke about the club."

"I can understand that. So how did you leave it?"

"We had been in the park too long, so we agreed to meet again soon."

"That had to be hard to stop the conversation right when you just discovered who you both were."

"We could have talked for hours. But we lack privacy in our everyday lives. There is hardly a place where we can talk. Because he spoke with an ex-club member, he could be a target that someone is watching. We don't know that for sure, but Patrick feels unsafe to a point. He has a lot of influence. He knows tons of people and has made a huge fortune. These thugs know he could influence a lot of people and also find out information he shouldn't know."

"That makes you have to be even more careful and aware of your surroundings."

"Exactly. There is almost a red dot on my forehead, as it is."

"I don't like the sound of that."

"You and the rest of the family also have that red dot. But they are mainly watching me."

"Where do you go from here, Bill?"

"I wait to hear from Patrick. He will call me and tell me where to meet him. In the meantime, I am certain I will be given another order from Command. I dread it like the plague. But I have to behave like it's just business as usual for me. I can't let on that anything is different in my life. Luckily, Patrick is a client of mine. So my meetings with him can be explained if need be. I am certain now that Patrick planned it this way. At first I feared he was checking me out for Command. To see if I would be loyal. I guess there is still a chance of that, if you want to know the truth. I can't be sure until we talk more that he isn't one of them. My gut feeling says no, but I have been wrong before."

"I'm glad you said that and not me."

They laughed but it was a guarded laugh. "I am going with the feeling that he is being honest with me. I certainly was with him. It felt so good to talk to him, but I didn't go into detail about anything I had done. That can wait. He really didn't ask tonight. I am sure the next talk will be more detailed."

Sharon yawned and stretched. "I know you are worn out. Are you ready to go to bed?"

"It feels so good to talk to you about all of this. But I am scared to death that they will find out. I don't know how, but in saying that, I really don't know where they are. We would never find out how they are listening to us. They are so good at it now that it's nearly impossible to do anything that they won't know about. A drone could be overhead. That is why Patrick and I need to be very careful. We can't let one thing slip. He spoke of that tonight before he left the park. We also can't meet that often or they will find out. He is my client so we have that to fall back on. But the cell he gave me will come in handy for short conversations."

"I think we should call it a night. I know you are strung out, Bill. I don't know how you are walking around carrying all of this inside of you. Thank heavens we have found a way to talk. But that is even limited. I feel like you are sitting on a time bomb."

Just as they both stood up to walk inside, Bill's phone rang. And this time it wasn't Patrick. It was Command. Bill shook his head and glanced at Sharon. She walked inside and left him at the gazebo so that he could concentrate.

"We have a job for you."

"I'm listening."

"There is a conservative group that has formed and is growing rapidly. With the election around the corner, we need to find out what their agenda is. The head guy is Martin Wilson.

He's a loud mouth and spreading lies like crazy against the President. We need this reelection. Either scare him out of moving forward in his agenda or take him down. Things are slippery right now; if we are going to win the election, then some of these groups need to be stopped in their tracks. There are a few incidents that don't need to get out to the public. If they do, we are done."

"So you want me to scare him or take him out?"

"Depends on what he says to you. You have to see if he is willing to come off his high horse and slow this thing down. Or you will have to end it."

"I'll take care of it."

"No mistakes. We still have our eyes on you, Bill."

"I'm aware of that."

"I don't think you know the extent of it."

"Is that a threat again?"

"Call it whatever you want."

"Is that all?"

The line went dead. Bill knew the contact information would come at any moment on the phone. He walked inside with his shoulders carrying more weight than he could bear. Martin Wilson was a loud mouth, but he wasn't a bad guy. To take him down would just about rip Bill's stomach out. He didn't know if he could handle it, but if he let the guy slide by, his own life would be in jeopardy. Or his family. He really didn't have a choice.

The text came through at midnight. Bill was sound sleep. Sharon heard the phone go off and nudged Bill awake. He reached under the pillow and read the message and laid his head back down on the pillow. Sharon slipped her hand into his and snuggled up against him.

She has no idea how much I need her. Now I have to pull from all my SEAL and sniper training to focus on Wilson like a cougar hunting his prey. Bill realized that the closer he got to being able to tell his story the more difficult it was to carry out his orders. People were going to get hurt or even lose their lives before this was all over.

He tossed and turned for an hour before his brain shut down. He needed the rest for several reasons. He had to be able to think out a list of scenarios. He had to be prepared for anything that could happen and the list was endless. And there was no room for error. Not one slipup.

CHAPTER FORTY-FIVE

"Serendipity." That was the word Jacob was trying to think of. Seeing Gail Bailey was serendipity. A wonderful thing happening at an unexpected time. Only it was messing up his world. She stopped in at the oddest of moments to say hello. Not the normal hello. But the hello with chocolate chip cookies. He leaned over his desk to tackle a stack of paperwork, and just as he was getting started he glanced at the doorway and she was standing there holding two tickets in the air, smiling. It was the smile that got him. Not the tickets. And his curiosity got the best of him.

Before he could speak, Gail held up her hand. "Now don't tell me you have tons of work to do. I know it's early and you just got to work. I just stopped by to show you these tickets to a baseball game. Not sure if you like that kind of stuff, but I love baseball."

"Are you kidding me? I love baseball. Let me see those tickets." Gail was smiling as she handed them over to Jacob.

"The Washington Nationals are playing. That's great. I'd love to go."

"I'm not going to keep you any longer. Just let me know if there is going to be a problem with you getting away."

Jacob raised his eyebrows. "I'll be fine. Thanks for coming by. I do need to get to work."

She was gone. It was that simple. But now it was complicated. He had no idea how to get away from Jane. He was going to hurt her for sure. And if he broke it off she was going to freak out. The problem was he really liked Jane. He felt comfortable with her. And he barely knew Gail. He suddenly had a mother of a headache and reached into his bottom drawer for an Excedrin. She had really complicated his life. He was so attracted to her he couldn't think straight. But was she worth giving up Jane? And how did one ever make that determination? He'd been with Jane for quite long time. But oddly he couldn't see himself marrying her. Why?

His head was spinning and now he couldn't concentrate on finishing the contracts he had in front of him. He couldn't allow Gail to make his work suffer. He was moving up in the company and that mattered to him. He had worked hard to gain the respect of his boss, and no woman was going to change that effort. But on the other hand, he was at a life crisis point and needed to make the right choice.

He got up and walked out of the office and headed to Starbucks for some coffee and time to think. Not that he had to make the decision today. But if he wanted to go to the game with Gail, he was going to have to talk to Jane. He hated lying. He felt sick. He wanted to call Paul, but what a slamming he was going to get from that guy. Paul was not the one to talk to when you were doing something stupid.

He pulled into the parking lot and got out of his car, noticing what looked like Jane's car parked three cars over. His heart started racing. He wasn't quite ready to have that conversation with her, especially while sitting in Starbucks. He couldn't decide whether to go in or not.

Finally, with a knot in his stomach, he opened the door and stepped inside. The place was packed with people ordering coffee and sitting at the tables talking. He glanced around and saw her in the corner sitting with a man he didn't recognize. She didn't see him, so he sat down where he could watch what was going on. He was surprised at how he felt about seeing her with someone else. There was a tightening in his chest but he tried to stay calm and see where this was going. The place was getting noisier so there was no way he could hear what they were talking about. He was trying to give her the benefit of the doubt, as the man could easily be a coworker. Ten minutes later they were still laughing and talking, and suddenly the guy reached over and touched Jane's hand. What surprised Jacob was that she didn't pull away.

As time passed, Jacob knew he was going to have to get back to work. He couldn't stay there all morning watching Jane. But he was dying to know what she was up to. So he settled into his seat and drank his coffee, and he kept his eyes on her. He suddenly felt like his decision was being made for him, right before his eyes. Maybe she wasn't happy, either. She'd never said anything to him about wanting out. Or given him an ultimatum. He had dragged his feet on the subject of marriage. And now he was sort of glad about that. Marrying her had just not felt right, even though he did love her.

The man kept his hand over Jane's and their heads were closer together. He wondered what would happen if he just walked over. He wouldn't know what in the world to say and he knew he would hear a valid excuse for why she was there with another man. He was frozen. So he just sat there another fifteen minutes waiting.

Finally, his answer came. And it hit him right in the gut. Jane stood up to leave and the man came over to her and kissed her right in the middle of Starbucks. She kissed him back and they walked out together. She never turned her head to the left or right. She could have easily have seen him sitting there in the corner. He sat there holding his coffee in his hand, trying to decide what to do and then he picked up his cell phone and sent her a text. He walked to the door and watched her look at her phone. The man was standing next to her by her car as she opened the text. What she read was; "I see you have decided to end our relationship. I wish you the best, Jane."

She glanced quickly around and saw his car parked down from hers. She looked at the door and saw him standing in the doorway. He could tell she was upset. The man took her arm and opened the door to her car. She climbed in and Jacob could tell she was crying. He wondered why she was upset if she really liked this new guy. She started her car and pulled away, and the gentleman got into his car and followed her.

Jacob didn't want to know where they were going. It was over. He felt a little sick walking to his car. But things had a way of taking care of themselves. Maybe Gail had been put in his path at the perfect time. Maybe he and Jane were going to end the thing, anyway.

He went back to work and finished all the contracts, leaving work with a feeling of relief. At least he didn't have to be the one to end a long relationship. At least they hadn't gotten married too quickly, before they found out it wasn't going to work. His cell rang. It was Paul. He dreaded the conversation, but oh, well.

"Hey, man. What's up?" Jacob was sweating already.

"Just had you on my mind, dude."

"That's nice. What you been doing?"

"I was going to ask you that."

"Work. That's pretty much it for me."

"How's Jane?"

"Why you asking about her?"

"Lighten up, Jacob. Just wondering how you guys are."

"I don't really know at the moment."

"What's that supposed to mean?"

"It means I don't know."

"Did something happen?"

"Looks like it did."

"Would you talk to me in complete sentences instead of riddles?"

"You just caught me at a bad time, is all."

"You want to stop by my office and talk?"

"I'm pretty busy today."

"Come on, Little Brother. I do care, you know."

"I saw her just a moment ago in Starbucks with another man."

He could hear Paul sigh. "What the heck does that mean?"

"It means he kissed her and she kissed him back. So I'd say we might be done here."

"Damn. I'm sorry, Jacob. That sucks. And you had to see it happen. I know that hurt."

"It was more of a shock, I guess. But I was going to end it, anyway."

"Now we're getting somewhere. Have you met someone? Wait a minute. Is that Gail Bailey still in your life?"

Jacob's mouth was full of cotton. Dry as a bone. "She has stopped in from time to time about insurance, if that is what you mean."

"Is she the one who is pulling you away from Jane?"

"If you have to know, she is the one who is making rethink my whole relationship with Jane."

"That's deep."

"Too deep to discuss on the phone."

"I had no idea. Maybe that is why you've been on my mind."

"I cannot imagine."

"Listen, man. You can talk to me anytime. Just be careful with that girl. I have an odd feeling about her. Make sure she is who you think she is. Don't just jump in over your head. She already has a daughter. You know nothing about her life before she came here."

"I think I am old enough to figure out how to get to know someone. I'm not one of your students, Paul."

"I didn't mean to insinuate that. Why are you always on edge when we talk?"

"Because you treat me like a kid. I'm tired of it. I got to run, man."

"Let me know what I can do, Jacob. I really do care about your life."

"I didn't get that impression all these years."

"I guess we picked on our younger brother too much."

"That may be why I have the exterior of a rhinoceros when it comes to talking to you."

"Take it easy, big guy. I just called to see how you were doing. I had no idea all of this was going on."

"It was just going on a few minutes ago. Before that, I was your same boring brother. Now I have cut Jane off. I sent her a text and watched her open it. I think she was upset, but she didn't know I was watching. I am sure we will have a conversation at some point. But right now things are pretty raw for both of us."

"Just let me know how things go. I'll try to stay out of your hair."

"That would be new."

"Bye, Little Brother. Talk to you soon."

Jacob put his phone down on the seat next to him and drove home. He felt sick inside because of what he had seen. But deep down he knew it was the best thing that could have happened. He didn't want to be the one to hurt her. And now it was done. He really needed to heed Paul's advice and get to know Gail better, though. No point in jumping into another relationship when he barely knew the woman.

He walked into the house and sat down on the sofa, leaning his head back and closing his eyes. His mind was racing. He had so many thoughts running through his brain that he didn't know what to do first. So he dozed off, hoping when he woke up some or part of the nightmare he just lived would go away.

He didn't see the text that came in from Gail Bailey. But when he woke, he saw the flashing light on his phone and clicked to see what the message was. Sometimes you can be blind even with your eyes wide open.

CHAPTER FORTY-SIX

H is plan was to scare the guy to death. Not to kill him. Bill knew how Martin Lewis was because he was always in the news spouting off about issues he was against. Everyone knew him, which made it very difficult to get close to him. Close enough to hurt him or even surprise him. Bill was good at this; he was trained to do covert missions. He'd taken out villages in Afghanistan. But to sneak up on this guy was going to take some planning. He didn't want to hurt anyone else, although Command would not care. He just wanted the job done.

Martin wasn't married. That was a good thing at this point. He did have a woman on his arm at every event or any photograph. But after surveying his house, it appeared he was home alone most of the time. The gossip was that he was a very private man about his personal life but there was always a way to find out who a person really was. Bill had people he could call. So he reached into his address book on his phone and found a guy named Pete Jennings, who was always ready to do some spy work.

"Pete, Bill Sinclair. How in the world are you, man?"

"I'm doing great. Been busy as a one-armed paper hanger, though. What you need, Bill?"

Bill laughed. "You know I never call you unless I really need something done that is critical."

"That's true. Who is it this time?"

"A guy named Martin Lewis."

"That loud mouth we see on the news all the time?"

"Yep, that's him. I need to know everything you can find out about him."

"When you need this?"

"Yesterday."

"Stupid question on my part."

"Just get what you can and let me know ASAP. I got someone breathing down my neck for the info."

"Will do."

"Send me the bill. I know you will!"

"I'll get back to you shortly on this."

Bill sat back in his chair and smiled. He knew he would have the information in about an hour. The guy worked at lightning speed and his methods were untraceable as he dug up the info.

In the meantime, Bill needed to decide about how to hurt the guy. To wake him up to the fact that he was being watched by people who did not approve of what he was doing. He knew he needed to slow him down. To make him hurt somewhere so badly that he stopped rolling with his agenda.

Bill knew he was a good enough shot to just take the guy's knee caps out. That was pretty painful. But he was afraid that would only anger Martin. His thought was to take one of his hands off. So he was positioning himself to possibly wire the door handle on the driver's side of the car, so that when Martin reached to open the car door, there would be an explosion that would take his hand off. Not wound it. Take it completely off.

One hour later to the minute his cell rang. It was Pete with good news. "Bill, I got something for you."

"I'm all ears."

"This guy is pretty clean for such a creep. But he does have a young niece living with him from time to time. She is fifteen years old. Want me to load that house with cameras to see what's going on?"

"Yuck. I hate to step into that but it might be something we could use if my plan fails."

"I'll get on it right away. He has pretty tight security, but I think I can manage to get a few cameras in the house so we can find out what you need to shut him down."

"Thanks, Pete. I thought you might find a criminal record or something he'd buried in his past. Keep checking. This is pretty serious."

"I'll do it. You'll get a text from me when the cameras go in."

Bill frowned. So the explosion had to work. This other plan of Pete's was a little weak. The young girl was his niece. Surely there wasn't anything sick going on with her. Losing his hand would get his attention for now, so the Bill was going forward with that plan immediately. The loss of his hand would also stop anything happening to that young girl, so he was killing two birds with one stone.

Bill had access to any explosives he would need, so that wouldn't be an issue. He gathered the information he needed to requisition the explosives. They would be at his doorstep in less than forty-five minutes. Meanwhile, he wanted to study the movements of Martin Lewis so he would know exactly when to attach the explosive to his car.

When Sharon got home he told her he was going out on a job and left dressed in black. Not his usual attire when he was doing covert—this time he just wore a black cap, black pants, and a t-shirt. He was going to park somewhere near Martin's home to see what security he had around the house and also check out the surrounding area. He wanted the explosion to just affect Martin, not any neighbor, so he needed to see how close the houses were. His target lived in Woodland Heights, a prestigious neighborhood, so most of the houses had plenty of room on either side of the house. The lots were large and most houses had some type of privacy fence. Luckily, Martin's home was at the end of a cul-de-sac, so he was tucked back in some wooded area which would help hide him while he set up the explosives.

Bill watched the house for hours to see what activity was taking place. Martin appeared to be alone for the day, with no interaction with the neighbors. He knew he would have to watch for several days before he attached the explosive to be as certain as he could that he wouldn't hurt anyone else but Martin.

Bill shuddered to realize how cold he was acting. He despised having to do this but for now the steps he was taking were as automatic as a robot's until he could get the job over with. He had subtracted his emotions from any actions he had to take, because otherwise he would not be able to carry out his job, and the lives of his family were at stake.

As he waited, he got a text that Pete had already gotten the cameras in place. Martin had been gone for thirty minutes, and in that short of a time Pete had been in and out of the house. The guy was something else. Bill could always count on him to get the job done. But this might have been record time even for Pete. Bill knew Pete would let him know if anything of importance was on the camera. Even some drug use would be huge.

Bill continued his surveillance of the property for the next few days, checking to see who the visitors were, if anyone stayed overnight, and if Martin ever had interactions with the neighbors. It did seem that he lived a very private life except for what was seen in the news. This helped Bill in factoring the time he would place the explosives on the car door. Martin seemed to have a habit of leaving the house around 8:30, perhaps to get a morning paper and coffee somewhere. So Bill planned to attach the explosive around 4:00 AM so that there would be no surprises. This had to work. There couldn't be one single mess-up or he would be ashes the next day. He was certain of it.

He went to bed beside Sharon around 10:00 PM, telling her to make sure he woke up at 3:00. She set the alarm and placed it on her side of the bed. At 2:45 he sat straight up in bed, rubbing his eyes. It was an old inner habit of his to awaken before the alarm went off. He absolutely detested the sound of an alarm, maybe from his time overseas. Who knew?

He put on his clothes quietly so as not to awaken Sharon and left without a sound. He had the explosives in the car and the wire to attach them to the door. He wore a mask this time and had also brought with him some spray paint that he would use on the sidewalk in front of Martin's house so that the police would think the instance was gang related.

He parked around the corner from the house and walked to Martin's house, cutting through trees so as not to be seen. Just in case. It was still dark so he was pretty sure he was covered, but he always had to think out of the box. He knelt down by the car and began attaching the explosive, which was small but powerful.

He heard a sound and stopped breathing. He rose up and noticed that it was the neighbor's dog that had gotten out somehow. He was running towards Bill, carrying a bone. Bill decided to ignore him and it worked. The dog didn't hang around long and ran away. That could have been a disaster, Bill thought, as he struggled to get the wiring hidden. Nothing could be seen in the broad daylight; he had to make sure of that.

At nearly 4:30 he was done. He erased any smudges on the door handle and fingerprints on the car, even though he had tight-fitting gloves on. He left no stone uncovered. He felt like Superman as he sneaked away from the house.

If he stayed in his car to watch the explosion, he would have to move his the car closer to the house.. But he didn't want any neighbors out at that time of morning to remember seeing a black sedan. So he left the car where it was and hid in tree branches in the woods next door to Martin's house. It was a perfect place as long as that dog didn't get out again. All he needed was a barking dog at the base of the tree he had climbed. He would have liked to have left and gone back home to bed, but arriving here in this location at 6:30 or 7:00 he would have taken a huge risk in being seen. So he had to tough it out and wait in the trees until Martin went out for his paper. He found himself dozing off several times so he pulled out his phone to see if Pete had texted him again. Nothing. He was accustomed to long waits during his days as a SEAL, so that didn't bother him. But he was anxious this time, worried that the explosive might not be enough to do the job. He could only hope that nothing would happen to change Martin's schedule.

At 8:30 sharp, Martin Lewis walked out the front door in wrinkled jeans and a pullover shirt, leaned down to pet a stray cat walking by, and walked towards his vehicle. The neighborhood was still quiet. There was one car that drove down the street but not towards Martin's house. Luckily, his being in a cul-de-sac kept the traffic down to zero. Bill watched as sweat dripped down his back. He was warm but mainly he was nervous. This had to work.

Martin stood by the car lighting a cigarette, which Bill had not taken into account. He took a few puffs and switched the light jacket onto his left arm while he reached for the door handle with his right hand. Bill shook his head. Just as soon as Martin pulled on the handle, the explosion went off, making a huge noise and knocking Martin off his feet. He was out cold for a several minutes. The neighbors on his right side came running out of their house to see what the noise was all about. They undid their gate and came over to Martin's yard, and found him writhing on the ground, holding his arm. His right hand was gone. Bill could hear them talking to him, but could not tell what they were saying. He climbed down out of the tree and slowly moved out of the woods and walked to his car. He could hear police sirens already moving closer to the neighborhood. He got to his car and pulled away, unnoticed by anyone.

His plan had worked. Martin Lewis had lost his right hand. Now all he had to do was wait and see how this affected the movement against the President. It would be all over the news before the day was out. There would be reporters on the scene in moments. Somehow those wolves found out about any event that happened. He headed home and when he got to his house, Sharon was up fixing breakfast. He sat down at the table, rubbing his eyes, and yawned.

"I'm starving."

Sharon looked at him and winced. "What?"

"Have you looked at yourself? You are worn out. Your hair needs cutting, your eyes are bloodshot, and I don't think you have shaved in three days. You look like a gangster."

Bill rolled his eyes. She had hit the nail on the head.

CHAPTER FORTY-SEVEN

"Emily"

I don't know when it started, but I knew it was there. During the last few times I visited Mom and Dad I had noticed that something had changed between them. On one hand they were closer than ever before. But I felt a tension in the air that I couldn't put my finger on.

It was upsetting to say the least. Home was where I gathered my strength. I couldn't allow that to be torn apart. Rob and I were planning on becoming parents and I needed something solid to come home to, so I could prepare myself for what was going to be required of me. I was such a planner, a detail person. I could never just let things happen. Only I was about to with this baby. I wanted to be calmer, more laid back than usual, so that it would be fun and not such a detailed task.

Dad seemed tired and more preoccupied than ever. I wanted to talk to him but was afraid of coming across as too nosy or intrusive. There was a battle of wills going on between us at all times. I would say we were even on all counts and today was no different. There was tension in the air and I didn't put it there.

My trip this time to the house was to tell them that Rob and I were going to plan on having a baby. We were getting serious about it and I was excited. I knew Mom would love it, but it could take me a while to get pregnant. I walked into the kitchen, realizing it was early, and found the two of them eating breakfast. Late for them to be doing that, but I asked no questions.

"Well, look at the two of you. Dad, you look like a hobo or something dragged in from outside. What in the world have you been doing lately?"

He looked up, "guilty" practically written on his face, but his eyes tried to lie. "I'm just tired, Honey. What a nice surprise, having you walk in here early in the morning. Why aren't you at work?"

"I could ask you the same question."

"Touché."

"I had the morning off and decided to come here to let you guys in on the wonderful news that we're going to be trying to have a baby. We really want one and hope it happens soon!"

Mom looked up with a sudden smile. It was real, but not, "Oh, Honey! I am thrilled to hear that. I thought you were going to wait awhile."

"We have thought about it and want one now, while we are young. I know there is never a perfect time."

I noticed Dad wasn't into the conversation, which wasn't all that odd, but I felt like he was so preoccupied. "What do you think about all this, Dad?"

He looked up like he'd just walked in on something. "I think it's grand. You ready for that? A child? Not easy these days with what is going on around us."

"I know, Dad. Just be excited for us."

"How is old Rob taking it? I'm surprised he wants to have children."

"How would you know what Rob feels? You didn't like him in the first place."

"I had my opinion, but you didn't pay attention to it."

Mom stepped in to save me. "Now, Bill. Give her a break. She loves Rob and I am happy for the both of them."

"Oh, Sharon. I am, too. It's just been a heck of a week for me. Emily, I am sorry if I don't sound too excited. I'm just tired."

"I noticed you looked tired. Wasn't going to say anything but I'm worried about you."

"That's new, isn't it?"

"Dang it, Dad. What's going on with you, anyway? Why are you working so hard? I don't know another CPA that has to go out at all hours of the day and night for clients. It sounds weird to me."

"I have some strange clients."

"They must be hoodlums."

He looked at me with a look that I cannot describe. "No, they're just rich, I guess. Very rich."

"Okay. Well, Mom, I hope you guys have a good day. I can't stay long; just wanted to stick my head in and share the news. I'm so excited and hope it happens fast. It's funny, once you decide, you can't wait for it to happen."

"I'm thrilled, Emily. And don't pay any attention to your father. He just slept on the wrong side of the bed last night. Irritable. You know how men are."

"I do. But I would love just once for Dad and I not to get into an argument when I come over. I hope he doesn't do that with my child. The poor thing won't ever want to come over here."

Dad stayed silent. I could tell he was far away. I just wish I knew where he was. I left the house feeling like Mother was covering for him. Was he ill? Was he selling out to his partners? Was he delivering drugs in the middle of the night? I didn't know what to think. And I probably wouldn't ever know. Looking back at my childhood, he'd always had a grouchy side. I thought the SEAL training did that to him. Maybe I was being too hard on him. He'd been through a lot in his life and was highly respected in the military. But he always rubbed me the wrong way. And I did the same to him. It was odd, because I might have been the one who needed him the most. And I couldn't get there to save my life. Still, I loved him to death.

Back home, I walked into my house with a frown and the weight of the world on my narrow shoulders. Rob had come home to get his laptop and cell. He was always forgetting something. "You see your parents? How'd that conversation go?"

"You know. Mother was great, Dad was grouchy."

"So it went well! That's great to hear." His sarcasm was on point.

I smiled. "I don't know why I set myself up for a disappointment with him."

"That's normal, Honey. He's your father."

"He's not going to change."

"When we have our baby, we are going to be so swallowed up in that joy that your dad's sour attitude won't penetrate us."

"I love hearing you say things like that. It really sounds like you are so happy about having a child of our own."

"Once I accepted it, now I can't wait."

"I feel the same way."

He walked over and kissed her as he was walking out the door. "Honey, don't let him spoil our excitement."

"I am worried about him, Rob."

Rob paused, scratching his head. He glanced at his watch. "Do you want to talk about this now?"

"No. You go to work. I just sense something. I wish I knew what."

"We'll talk later. You got to work today or what?"

I laughed. "Yeah. I am headed in now. I had the morning off."

He waved and shut the door. I fixed my hair and stared at myself in the mirror. I loved my parents and the way they'd brought us up. The way they loved us. I wanted to do the same for my own kids. I felt safe, cared for. And they gave us every opportunity we could want to try new things, to keep learning. They offered us new experiences. They showed us the world. About to be a parent myself, I saw how huge that really was. Dad was wonderful but he wasn't around all that much. I guessed that was normal for a father who worked all the time and was in the military. He was always on some secret mission. *Now that he and Mom are alone, their needs cannot be that large. And he still works himself to death. I could be dreaming. I could be hormonal.* But something in my gut said something wasn't right.

I got up and picked up my purse and walked out the door. Work would keep me busy and Rob would be waiting for me when I got home. I had to keep my mind focused on my own world. Mother would have to manage her own. Once I moved out, that was it. I cannot watch over her anymore, I reminded myself. I bet she never knew I was doing that. Hovering around her. Loving her. Making sure she was okay. She thought I was just annoying her. But I was protecting her from whatever I feared myself.

I realized I knew less than I thought I did about life. About the world. About men. So for the moment, I decided to focus on my own life and what I dreamed of. And I was sure not going to share my dreams with Dad. Because he would definitely shoot them down like falling stars on a clear night. And I was not in the mood for a dreamless life just yet.

CHAPTER FORTY-EIGHT

Plastered on every channel was the blaring news that political activist Martin Lewis cheated death by escaping an explosion at his home, with the only damage being the loss of his right hand. The police had stated that it was probably gang related based on the typical graffiti all over the sidewalk in front of his house. Reporters were lined up at the hospital, waiting for the opportunity to get information from Martin firsthand. The front page of the newspaper was covered with his photograph and a full page story of the accident and all that Lewis represented, including the agenda he had against most of what the President was doing in the White House. The police held no suspects in the crime and had no comment other than it was still being investigated.

So even though he'd lost his right hand, he still received plenty of attention through every media known to man. Bill sat back on the sofa and watched as the fiasco was told in fifteen different ways by the news reporters. It was almost like they couldn't tell the story fast enough. He had already received a call from Command congratulating him on a job well done. However, he was notified early on that he still might have to take Lewis out if things didn't quiet down with that whole group. Lewis knew tons of people and wasn't on this bandwagon alone. He had built up quite a following so there was no guarantee that this movement would just come to a screeching halt.

Sharon sat down beside Bill, amazed at all the publicity this accident was receiving.

"You would think the President had been shot with the amount of coverage this is getting."

"That's exactly what this guy wants."

"Do you know him, Bill?"

"No. Not personally. Everyone knows who he is."

"Was this gang related?"

Bill shook his head.

She looked into his eyes and lowered her head to her hands. "Oh, no."

He put his hand on her leg and whispered. "Honey, don't even think about it. There is nothing we can do now."

She turned her head and looked at him. "I don't even want to know," she whispered.

"I know you don't. And you don't have to know. This is one time it has gotten publicity. Most times you don't even hear about it. People die and nothing is said on the news. They just disappear into thin air."

"How can that happen? What about their families?"

Bill whispered again. "They are probably paid off to keep their mouths shut."

"We are turning into Nazi Germany."

"Or the old Soviet Union. This is on our own homeland. Going on right under the noses of the American people. And no one seems to notice. Partially because they're not informed."

They were talking in a very low voice. But Bill knew it was risky as hell.

"How can it be stopped, Bill? How will you ever stop it?"

"Let's see what Patrick Lathrop has up his sleeve. I think he may be a Godsend."

"I sure hope so. You cannot do it alone, that's for sure. If we live through this and you and Patrick pull this off, then America has a chance. But we don't know how many people are involved in this huge cover-up."

"I have carried out some pretty serious covert in my lifetime, but this may be the worst yet. Because we are supposed to be a 'land of the free,' governed 'by the people for the people.' But it has turned into a friggin' nightmare. The government has taken over so many areas of our lives that the forefathers would not recognize it anymore. People for the most part are blinded very easily. I'm talking about intelligent people. It is a slow thing that happens and it begins to weaken the foundation we stand on. Slowly but surely the government has moved into our lives and is now trying to control the morals of the world by never having any boundaries. There are no rules of the land anymore. It's getting blurred by the 'rights of the people.'"

"I feel sorry for you, having to carry this weight on your shoulders. Not to mention I am terrified what will happen to you or to us."

"Emily is worrying me. I fear she will figure this out. She's a smart cookie and yesterday I felt her studying me. She is trying to figure out what I'm doing. The boys are, too."

"We cannot let this be known—not yet, anyway."

"However, they are at risk, like you are. I have no idea what 'they' will do with my family if they ever suspect I am a traitor. If you could hear the voice of Command you would hear someone who can be ruthless. But that just means that whoever he answers to is putting pressure on him to get the job done at all costs. They will stop at nothing to get their way. That is not a good trait for our government to have unless it is positioned against our enemies. We cannot allow this nation to turn against itself. I feel we are weakening. We have no borders. We are becoming so diluted that we will no longer be the same nation you and I experienced as children.""

"We could go on and on. But right now we have to focus on the task before you, Bill. When will you hear from Patrick?"

"At any moment. Especially with what has just taken place. I think he will call me tonight, if you want to know the truth."

"Can I get you anything? What are your plans today?"

"I will go to work like I always do. Business as usual. I will let you know if Patrick calls."

"No one can tie this to you, right?"

"Not the police. I guess a small part of the government knows I was involved. But only a very few. Maybe two people. When this thing blows apart, I just want to be alive to see it happen."

Sharon nodded and got up, touching his shoulder as she walked away.

Bill watched her, thinking that he hated never knowing if this was going to be the last time he saw her. It was almost like he was still a SEAL. He was a dead man walking for that whole time in Afghanistan. Now that he was home, it still felt like there was a laser pointed at his head all the time.

Bill drove into work thinking about what he saw on the news. He would have given anything to know what was going on in Martin Lewis' head about now.

His cell rang and it was Patrick. No surprise. "You free to talk, Bill?"

"I'm in my car. I'll call you back when I get to the office."

He quickly hung up and set the phone in his shirt pocket, pulled into traffic and drove to work as fast as he could without getting a ticket. Police were everywhere. When he reached the parking lot he parked and walked into the front lobby where he took a seat at one of the plush sofas and dialed Patrick's number.

"Okay. I can talk freely now."

"I don't want to risk it with you having your work attire on; there could easily be a bug somewhere."

"Where do you want to meet?"

"Waterfront Park on Water Street. At noon."

"See you then."

Bill's heart was racing. He wondered what Patrick would have to tell him. He hoped there was a group of people who were behind this effort to expose the President's Club. He knew they could leak it to *The New York Times*, or *Wall Street Journal*, or the *Washington Post*. It would blow wide open with just a one-liner leak. But Bill could not have it traced back to him. He was so looking forward to the day when he was free again. He was sick and tired of being owned by the government and wanted his freedom and safety back. But it wouldn't come without great effort and caution. One tiny word gets out and he won't live to see the freedom come. He also wondered about the other ten people stuck in the President's Club. So many questions and all he could do was wait. But he wouldn't have to wait long because he would talk to Patrick in a few hours.

As soon as he got to the office, the whole staff was buzzing about what had happened with Martin Lewis. He, of course, acted shocked like they were. But inside he felt sick. There was an uneasy feeling inside of him, almost like he feared they would see blood on his hands. He was screaming to come out of hiding, but he could never tell anyone what he'd seen or done. They wouldn't believe most of it, anyway.

CHAPTER FORTY-NINE

The house was quiet and Sharon had nowhere to be, so she sat with her coffee out on the porch, listening to the birds that always nested in the trees in the early part of the day. The sun was bright but there were clouds that were moving across the sky, giving a few unexpected moments of shade and a slight coolness to the air. She was grateful for this quiet time after Bill had left for work.

She needed to think about things. She had a huge burden on her shoulders and she had been sworn to secrecy. However, she also knew her children were at risk, so she debated whether or not to hold a family meeting and just tell them everything, or wait until something horrible happened and then they would resent her for not telling them the truth sooner. She looked back over her life with Bill, smiling at all the years of love and laughter centered around the table at their meals together. So many memories found in that small space in the house. Even though the children griped about having to come for dinner now that they were grown, they all slipped into that familiar give and take of conversation that flowed during the meal. The banter was like a sweet song and she wanted to hear that until the day she closed her eyes for good.

Jesse, being the oldest child, had not been around much to pick up on the changes in his father. If he did, he never mentioned it. But Emily was moving closer and closer to finding out the truth. She had been the last one to leave and had grown very close to her father, even though they were at odds most of the time. It was a love/hate relationship but it was very strong. It would almost be freeing to be able to share it all with the children. But that may have been a selfish thought and she wanted to do the right thing.

She laughed at that one thought. "The right thing." Because the government wasn't even close to doing the right thing. They were like a locomotive with no brakes rushing down a mountain pass. Watergate had happened because someone got caught. Not because it hadn't been done before.

This club that existed was purely for the residing President to control opposition that had formed against his main agenda. It had existed for years; who knew how long. No one was talking about it; everything was kept hidden. But the power and strength of it was as strong as ever. Amazingly so. She despised the hiding and felt like she was being part of what kept that fire alive. Everyone involved knew that if any air got to the flame, it would consume the whole plan and everyone involved in it. So secrecy was critical. The surprise factor was what made it work.

When she thought of Bill, there were parts of him that she would never know. She adored him and he was a strong, goodhearted soul. But inside, deep inside, there was a man that she did not recognize that could carry out horrific acts for a purpose that even he might not believe in. He was so trained to obey orders that he hardly hesitated. After he had left the service, she had thought that might have changed. She was wrong. It had only been sleeping, like a giant waiting to be awakened. She wondered if in some sick way he enjoyed it only because it was what he had eaten, slept, and drunk for so long. He had honed his skill, and ironically, that is why they chose him. But would he be able to let this go once and for all, when it all hit the fan? He was growing tired and he was growing older. That would be the blessing in all this. Maybe it all would fall into place with this meeting with Patrick Lathrop. She was puzzled as to how he even found Bill in the first place, unless he was part of the group that supported the club. Nothing made sense and everything made sense. It was a crazy time in their lives and she had to find a way to cope with it.

Suddenly she felt like she was going to suffocate. She walked inside the house and looked around. Were they watching her? Were there hidden cameras in all the rooms? Where were the bugs hidden? She started going through her clothes and shoes trying to see if she could find anything. She looked at all the lampshades and windows and every piece of furniture they owned. She was almost like a mad woman, roaming through the house, feeling the tops of door jambs and going through papers on his desk. She wanted to know it all, but she realized that Bill kept nothing in the house that could be found to tie him to the club. He carried that phone with him all the time. She did find two things that looked like computer chips that she flushed down the toilet. They may have been nothing but it made her feel good to get rid of them. She was exhausted from dealing with the constant worry and wondering. Her whole life had narrowed down to what Bill was doing at the moment. She feared for his life, and for the lives of her family. But she was strong and would remain by his side till the end. No matter what.

The phone rang and she answered it in the kitchen.

"Mom? You doing okay?" Emily sounded happy.

"Yes, I had a few moments this morning to relax and enjoy the birds outside. What about you?"

"I'd like a lunch with you today. Think you could make it?"

Sharon grimaced. She was going to get questioned by Emily, she just knew it. "Oh yes, I'd love some time with you."

"Good. I'll meet you at The Bread Line at noon."

"Okay, Emily. I look forward to it."

Noon was not the time to eat lunch in Washington. The Bread Line was packed. People were waiting in line when Sharon got there. But Emily was savvy to the eating habits of the work force. She had come early to get a table. She was waving at Sharon when she walked through the door. The smell of fabulous food was floating in the air. It was impossible not to be hungry with all those aromas floating around.

Sharon took a seat across from her daughter, halfway dreading the conversation that she knew was coming. But there was no point in dodging the bullet. It was a talk they probably needed to have to calm Emily's curiosity.

"Mother! You look rested. How are you?" Emily was her usual cheerful self.

Sharon nodded and smiled. "I'm fine. How are you and Rob?"

"Oh, full of ideas and nothing at all."

"Still planning on having a baby?"

"Yes. Let's order and then we can talk."

They both poured over the menu quickly and ordered, waiting for the waitress to bring them the iced tea. The place was filling up fast.

Emily placed her hand over Sharon's and took a deep breath. "Mother, I have been meaning to ask you about Dad."

"He's doing great. Just working too hard."

"Exactly. Don't you think he needs to slow down a bit?"

"Might as well be talking to the wind, Emily. He has a mind of his own."

"All men do. But I am worried about him. Going out at all hours of the night, stressed. That can't be good for him."

"I'm sure it isn't."

"And another thing; what is he doing out late? Why would any client call him at 10:00 at night and need to talk to Dad? Why can they not discuss it on the phone? Something seems odd to me."

"I don't ask questions, Emily. If he wanted me to know, he would tell me."

Emily sighed. "Mother, that doesn't seem like you at all. You would never have allowed this when we all were home. Do you know something and you just aren't sharing it with me?"

Sharon looked at Emily. Her face was stone. "Some things are better not known."

Emily gasped as the waitress placed food before them. "Oh, gosh. What in the world does that mean?"

"It simply means that maybe I don't want to know."

"Is he having an affair?"

"I doubt that."

"That is what it feels like. Or he is doing drugs? Selling drugs? He has been stressed out. Is money tight?"

Sharon held up her hand. "Emily, slow down. Your father would never sell drugs. He was a Navy SEAL, of all things. You are letting your imagination run wild."

"Well what the heck is it? You are driving me crazy. I lived there not that long ago. I know Dad. These phone calls are just strange."

Sharon ate some of her salad and gazed out the window. There just was no good answer to her questions.

"Emily, you need to relax about this. I appreciate that you are concerned about your dad, but right now, we have to trust that he is doing the best he can do on this job. He has a ton of pressure on him and quite a few clients. Now, let's talk about you having a baby."

CHAPTER FIFTY

A t precisely twelve o'clock, Bill was sitting on a bench wait-ing for Patrick Lathrop to appear. It wasn't ten seconds later that he showed up with his gentleman's grin and handshake. Bill stood up and grabbed his hand and sat back down. He felt con-spicuous even though he had no real reason to feel that way. There were plenty of people in the park; it wasn't like they stood out in a crowd. It was a hot day and Bill was already perspiring. Some of it was nerves. Well, most of it. Patrick seemed cool as a cucumber but he wasn't the one under surveillance.

"Good to see you again, Bill."

Always the nice guy, Patrick is true to form. "Same here, Patrick."

"Any news I need to know about, other than your handiwork was splashed all over the newspaper and television?"

"So you saw it, huh?" Bill wiped his face.

"I have never seen so much coverage in my life."

"Nothing I'm proud of."

"I know you aren't. That had to be tough."

"I can't think about it when I am doing it. It is just by rote."

"How you holding up?"

"I'm getting sick of having to do these things. These are innocent people who are just getting in the way of the President."

"It's been going on for a long time. Now we are going to have to devise a plan to stop it."

"I'm worried it's bigger than the two of us," Bill admitted.

"It is. But there has to be a way. No one has even tried yet."

"I'm worried about my family, Patrick. The deeper I get into this, the riskier it is for my family."

Patrick put his hand on Bill's shoulder. "I've got that covered already."

Bill turned to look at him. "What does that mean?"

Patrick leaned back on the bench and looked out across the park. "I told you that I have people."

"And?"

"I have your family covered. I have men watching your whole family. No one will ever see them. You will not know they are even around."

Bill jumped up angrily. "What have you done, Patrick? Do you know how dangerous that is? If Command finds this out, he will kill us all."

Patrick stayed strangely calm. "Relax, Bill. Sit down. They will never know. These people are experts. They know what they're doing. Trust me, will you?"

"I don't even know who is watching me from the other end. I have no idea where the bugs are, or if it goes beyond that."

"You will never know that. But they will also have great trouble every locating my men. I know what I am doing, Bill. You've got to trust me or we can't go forward. "

Bill sat back and watched kids playing across the park. He was worn out with the worry.

"Do you know how much I hated taking that man's hand off?"

"Just be thankful you didn't have to kill him, Bill. I know it's tough, but we need to focus on how to blow this thing up. Short of taking out the President, there has got to be a plan that we feel will work, but will also not put your family in danger or the other men in the club."

Bill sat up straight. "Is there any way possible to find out who the other men are?"

"I already know who they are, Bill."

Bill leaned forward and whispered. "Damn. Are you serious?"

"I have studied this for a good while. Once I was privy to the information about the club, I started digging into every branch of the military. It was pretty obvious once I saw that they chose you."

"If it was that easy, then how come others have not figured this out?"

"You have to remember that an ex-club member told me and swore me to secrecy. He could have been killed for telling me. But I think he also knew I might have the wherewithal to do something about it. And that came into fruition when I met you."

"This is getting thick. Have you contacted the other men?"

"Not yet. It isn't time. But I have people watching them. There are more people than you realize who want this massacre stopped."

"You have a group of people who already know about this?"

"Bill, this is bigger than you think. There are people in Congress who know about this but have chosen to turn the other way. They have an agenda and that is what they are pushing for. And remember this has been going on for quite some time. People grow numb to it. It's just something that happens so that things get taken care of. Deals are made. People look the other way. It happens all the time."

"I'm shocked that so many know about it."

"Look, Bill. I'm a very wealthy man, and I have some very wealthy friends. Good men. And they believe in this country. Or what this country used to be. It is slowly slipping away. And what you're being made to do and the threats that go along with it have to stop. We are going to come up with something."

"In my estimation, it had better be soon. I don't know about the other men, but they are on top of me big time. They are pressuring me and threatening me about my family all the time. I'm not sure they didn't have my daughter Susan killed. I will never know that. I think it would be impossible to prove."

"They cover themselves pretty well. And some of the judges are in their back pocket. You know how that goes."

"So, changing the subject a bit, when do I tell my kids that they are being observed?"

"Not yet. I don't think it's time to do that. But I will let you know. I mean, you have a say in this, Bill. I cannot tell you exactly what to do. But we both know that the more people who know, the higher the risk of Command finding out. Someone will slip and talk. And then the whole thing will explode."

"I don't want to ruin the chance of our being able to end this monster."

"For now, keep quiet. I know it is tough, but telling your children this right now, in my opinion, would not be in the best interest of our goal."

"I agree. Just wanted to run it by you."

Patrick grabbed his hand and shook it and stood up to leave. "I will contact you again. In the meantime, take care of yourself. Don't push so hard. And know that there is light at the end of the proverbial tunnel."

Bill nodded and smiled a weak smile. "I'll wait to hear from you. Thanks for the talk, Patrick. You amaze me every time we talk."

Patrick walked away and Bill sat on the bench for a while, thinking. What was going on behind the scenes was way over his head. He had no idea that Patrick would know so much about the Club.

That there would be a group of people, wealthy people, who would stick their necks out to stop this sick control that the President had over people. What was happening to the world? To America? How did we get so sick inside our own borders? He had always stayed away from politics and immersed himself in the SEALs. He loved those men and they had become family to him. Now, being involved in this mess made him wish he'd never retired from the Navy. But he was getting too old to keep up the pace. And this was aging him at the speed of light.

He stood up and looked around. It was incredible that a conversation could take place so close to the White House and no one knew. But he had to face the fact that other people were watching him. Even then, as he stood in Waterfront Park. He was placing so much trust in Patrick Lathrop, a man he barely knew. He hoped before God that this man wasn't part of the wicked plan. He hoped he was trusting the right man. He hoped.

CHAPTER FIFTY-ONE

"Emily"

The sun was setting over the tops of the houses, casting shadows across the yards. It was a hot, difficult summer and my work load was heavy. The lawyers in the firm were piling up my desk with cases and forms and filing. My mind would not stop thinking about my father. The stress on Mother's face was increasingly visible. I picked up the phone to dial Paul's number. It would be fun to see him again and talk to him about my concerns.

"Hey, you. What's going on in your world?"

"You don't want to know. You busy tonight?"

"No, actually Avery has a meeting with a women's group tonight. I will be home alone."

"That's dangerous. Can I pop in for a chat?"

"I don't recall us ever having just a chat before. It's usually a long drawn-out conversation with plenty of drama."

"Well, have it your way. I'll bring the popcorn."

"Come on over. I'll be here."

I hung up the phone, smiling. So thankful that we had re-established our connection after a dry spell. I knew I would be able to talk to Paul and he wouldn't overreact. Jesse and Jacob were in their own worlds and I was almost certain they had no clue what was going on at home. They were about as observant as a dead fly.

I hurried out of the office, clocking out and straightening my desk. No one cared. But it was a habit of mine. I got in my car and drove slowly over to Paul's. There was a silver Tahoe behind me that seemed to be following me. I laughed. Paranoia kicking in. But they did turn every time I did. As I pulled into Paul's house they drove past me and kept on going. I let it go and walked into the house like it was my own. I found Paul with his feet propped up watching the news.

"Mind if I grab something to drink?"

He grinned. "I know you are already standing in front of the 'fridge looking for something to eat. What's the point in asking?"

"Just trying to be polite. What's yours is mine, right?"

"Appears to be that way, yes."

"How you been?" I sat down on the sofa next to his chair and leaned back against a soft pillow. I followed suit and took my shoes off and rested my feet on the coffee table. This didn't go unnoticed by Paul. He shook his head.

"Busy. Just plain busy. Getting ready for school to start again. Practice is already going full force. Lost some good kids last year after graduation. These new kids are hard to teach. They think they know everything and they know nothing."

"You love every moment, so I don't want to hear it."

"I do love it, but I can still gripe about these new kids. You work so hard to build a tight team that plays together and knows what the heck they are doing. Then graduation hits and you lose half your team. It sucks."

"And how long have you been doing this? It ain't no surprise, is it?"

He laughed at her slang, which she didn't use often. "Yeah, yeah. I hear you. Now what did you come over here to talk about? It wasn't my football team, I know that."

"You're so smart. I'm amazed at your intuitiveness. I am worried about Mom and Dad. Have you seen them lately?"

"Nope. I really haven't had the time. It's about time for one of those dinners. I'm sure we will be getting a call from Mom soon."

"I've had lunch with her recently. She looks so stressed out. I really feel something is going on with Dad. She won't say anything. I've pried as much as I can without being blunt. She said he wasn't having an affair. I'm not so sure. His work hours are ridiculous. I just think he is not telling her everything."

"Don't you think that is between the two of them? I sure don't want them prying into my personal life."

"Nor would I. But these are our parents. I am worried Dad is into something dangerous. Like drugs or something. And I just noticed someone seemed to be following me on my way here."

Paul sat up and looked at her with amazement. "Are you kidding me? Emily, have you lost your mind? Are you too bored in your job? Why are you looking for things? There is nothing creepy going on with our parents."

I sat up and glared at him. "Paul, I know you don't take me seriously, but who else am I going to talk to about this?"

"I don't know. And what do you expect me to do about it, if there is something going on?"

"Why don't you visit with Dad and see what you think? Ask him about his work. Talk to Mom and see if you notice the stress she is under. I mean, they should be having a great time now since we all are gone. My moving out left them with all the time in the world to be together and enjoy life. It seems like Dad is working harder now than he was when we were home. And he just disappears for hours. Mom doesn't even really know where he goes. Doesn't that sound like he is doing covert or something?"

Paul sat back and thought a few moments. She could almost see his brain working like hers. "I guess it does seem strange. I'll pop in for a visit and see what I can find out. I'm sure they aren't going to just tell me everything. But if I sense what you are feeling, I will let you know."

"Don't wait too long, Paul. I am feeling urgent about it. And Mom is going to get tired of my asking her what is wrong or what is going on with Dad."

"You can be annoying, that's for sure."

"Oh, stop it. And what do you think about that Tahoe following me?"

"If you keep seeing it, then I'll think something about it. Right now you are so on edge that I am afraid you are overreacting about everything."

"Maybe."

"Just settle down. I'll go over there in the next few days and see what I see."

"Thanks. You and Avery still trying for another baby?"

"Not yet. She's just not ready after losing our baby. I don't blame her and don't want to rush her. But I do think the sooner we try, the better we both will be."

"Rob and I are trying. I told Mother. Wouldn't that be cool if we had our babies during the same month?"

"Silly, do you think we live in a parallel universe? You better head home before it gets dark. And just watch out for yourself. Let me know if you see that Tahoe on your way home. And thanks for stopping by. I love having you around. It feels like old times."

I got up and hugged him, jumped in my car and backed out of the driveway. When I pulled out onto the main highway I thought I saw the silver Tahoe again. But the sun was going down fast and

I couldn't really see the color. And besides, there were a zillion Tahoes on the road nowadays. People were either driving a truck or SUV. Still, I couldn't stop feeling like someone was there. I hoped that I found out soon.

CHAPTER FIFTY-TWO

"Emily"

The smell of Mother's cooking was worth a million dollars and even though I provoked her to have us all over for a meal together, it felt good to be home again. Dad seemed to be in good spirits and for once Mother looked rested and happy. I helped set the table and greeted Paul and Avery when they came in with arms full of desserts. Paul looked at me and I nodded. He knew this was for him. I was hoping against hope that there would be a five-minute window where Dad and Paul could be alone and talk. Not that anything would come from it, but at least we were going to give it a shot. I decided that I was going to be helpful to Mother, mainly because of my sensing that she might have a lot on her plate at the moment. The boys were in their normal form of bickering back and forth. I guess it wouldn't be home if they didn't fight a little.

"So, Jesse, how's the world of dentistry going?" Jacob had decided to get the first stab.

"I guess you wouldn't know. You haven't been to the dentist in years, Jake."

"You kind of ruined me on that."

"And how's that?"

"Knowing what you put your hands on when you were young, it's just hard to believe people are allowing you to have your hands in their mouth."

Jesse smiled. "They have no idea, do they?"

Dad interrupted the banter. "Jacob, how's your business going? You building clients?"

"Trying to, Dad. I have a Rolodex full of names. We actually have been very busy with car insurance. It seems people are buying new cars left and right."

"I was wondering about the sale of homes. I keep seeing sold signs in the yards as I drive through town."

"I think sales are up this year, Dad."

Mother came in with the roast and potatoes, and we all quieted down. The food was so good you didn't want to ruin it by talking too much. We all served our plates and were just about to dive in when Dad got a call. He reached into his left pocket and pulled out a cell phone, left the table, and locked himself into his study. I looked at Paul and he nodded. He waited a few minutes and got up from the table and headed towards the study, looking behind him to see if Mother was going to stop him. She just raised her eyebrow and kept on eating. I felt nervous all of a sudden, hoping against hope that Dad would open up to Paul, if there was something to be told.

⟨⟩

Paul knocked on the door and walked in. His father was sitting at his desk shaking his head. He stuck the cell phone back into his pocket and got up, looking at Paul.

"Can I help you, Son?"

"What the hell is going on, Dad?"

"What do you mean? I got a phone call and had to take it here in the study."

"Something isn't right, Dad. Every single time we eat dinner here, you get a phone call and have to leave early. Mom says you have clients that are needy, but I'm not buying it. What is going on in your life?"

Bill turned away and looked out the window. He had a distant look on his face.

"Paul, I have two jobs. You know I'm a CPA, but my other job is classified and I cannot discuss it with you. Now, you need to relax and not worry about anything. I appreciate your concern, but I can't go into anything with you or the rest of the family. I want to reassure you, though, that everything is fine."

Paul stared at his father for what seemed like a long time. "Why don't I believe you, Dad?"

"I don't know, Son. I haven't given you any reason not to trust me."

"Are you back in the SEALs?"

"No, I'm not."

"Are you working for the FBI?"

"No. Look, Paul. I can't let you interrogate me. I have no answers for you. You are just going to have to trust me. It's classified. That's all I can tell you."

Paul shrugged and walked out of the office. He felt frustrated because he wasn't hearing all of the story. But he knew better than to push his father. At least he found out there were two jobs going on and the secrecy stemmed from the second job being classified. He hoped that would satisfy Emily, but he had his doubts that she would let it go that easily. When he walked back into the dining room and sat down, she gave him the eye.

⋙ ⋘

"Well?" I jumped right in.

Jacob then dived in head first. "'Well' what?"

"I'm talking to Paul."

"What are you two up to?" He wasn't going to stop.

"Nothing. Now stay out of it, Jacob. What did you find out, Paul?"

"Not much."

"What do you mean, not much?"

"Just that. He said he was working two jobs. One of them was classified."

I looked at Mother and raised my eyebrow. My voice was getting loud.

"Mother, is that true? Is Dad working classified again?"

"Yes. I didn't see any reason to tell you children. It's not like he hasn't done this before."

"We thought he was through with that." Paul stuffed his mouth with food that was getting cold.

"I don't think a SEAL is ever really through." Mother cleared some of the empty dishes from the table.

Jesse spoke with his mouth full, which annoyed me. "I thought he was done with that covert stuff; isn't that why he became a partner in the CPA firm?"

"It is. But things change. Your father knows what he is doing. Now you need to let it go. He isn't going to talk about it to you, so just let it go."

I looked at Paul and shrugged. "I guess that explains why he gets up and leaves at all hours. Every time we are all together, he has to leave early. It makes us all wonder, Mother. We aren't kids anymore. If something is going on, we need to know."

"Everything is fine, Emily. The less said the better, actually. Now who wants dessert?"

Dad walked into the dining room and took his place at the head of the table. "I want some pie and two cookies. I really didn't finish my meal."

"I thought you were done with covert work, Dad?" Jesse stared his father down.

"I thought so, too, Son."

"So why did you jump back in?"

"They needed me, so I said yes. I really didn't have a choice."

"You always have a choice. At least that's what you have always told us."

"Not this time, Jess. Not this time."

"When you got out of the Navy you said you'd had your fill of covert. Now you're right back in it. And you're not getting any younger, Dad." Paul had a worried look on his face.

"I thought this would be a time when you and Mother spent time together and travelled. You haven't done anything since I left." I was really upset about the whole covert thing.

"And how can you do covert here in the US?" Jacob was obviously struggling with the idea, just as we all were.

"I can't talk about it, kids. You guys have to accept that answer. I cannot say any more about it."

"Are we in danger, Dad?" I stuck my neck out.

He looked at me with a frown. "Emily, stop it. I've said all I am going to say about it. You guys need to relax and know that if I can ever tell you more, I will do it. Now help your mother clear the table. She outdid herself again with such a wonderful meal."

We all got up and helped her clean up the dishes. I felt guilty in a way, pushing him so hard. But it felt like he was hiding something. Or that there was more to the story. But I realized, like Paul, that we were not going to get anything else out of him tonight. Not this night. And it left us all wondering what that phone call was about. I felt unsettled. I hated that feeling.

CHAPTER FIFTY-THREE

The stars were shining bright and the moonlight lit up the gazebo where Bill was waiting for Sharon. He sat back in his chair and blew out a deep breath. He hated that last phone call. He figured it was coming after watching the news. Sharon came out the back door barefooted and wrapped up in a blanket. He wanted to take her away from all of this. He was scared to death that it could all backfire and they could all lose their lives. But for now, for tonight, he just relished the sight of her. She was so lovely in the moonlight.

"What a nice dinner. Sorry for the twenty questions from the kids."

"I'm surprised they waited this long to ask."

"What are you going to tell them, Bill?"

"For now, nothing. Patrick said the more who know, the higher the risk of someone slipping."

"I realize that. But they are at risk now, right? People are watching them from both sides."

"I can't even allow myself to think about all that. I just try to forget they are out there. We have to focus on the business at hand, which is planning our next move."

"Speaking of moves, what is your next move?"

"You mean the phone call tonight?"

"Yes."

"Basically, they want me to blow up a building with a few people in it. Martin isn't going to stop. It slowed him down, but his group is even more fired up. The agenda still stands."

"So they want all of them dead?"

"Command said it would be easier to just take out the building. To make it look like an accident. I'm not sure how I will do it. It has to be explosives or they will have time to escape. This is really making me sick. I can't tell you how tired I am of doing this. Innocent people. I hope to God I don't know any of them. I won't know until the papers print the deceased. How will I live with this, Honey? How will any of us live with this?"

Sharon stood up and leaned over to hug him. "I know it must be terrifying. I hate that you have to make these decision, Bill. No one should have to do that. The only good thing is that it may be coming to an end. Oh, I hope it does."

"We can't count on ending the club. But I would like the rest of America to know it exists. I want out. And I want the other ten out. They have to be going through the same kind of hell."

"I am sure they are."

Bill leaned in and lowered his voice even more. "Sharon, there's something I haven't told you. And it cannot go anywhere. For now, you and I are the only ones who know what I am about to tell you. When I first accepted this position in the club, I decided that I would keep records on every covert operation they sent me on. Every single person I had to kill or torture. I have them on a couple of thumb drives and have put them in a location that only I know.

I need to share it with you so that if anything happens to me, you will get them to the right persons."

Sharon was crying, holding her head in her hands. "You mean you have recorded your actions? You have recorded the deaths and torturing that you had to do? Oh, Bill! That is awful! I never want to see them! I understand that they might come in handy, but I don't want anything to do them."

"Calm down, Sharon. I have no intention of ever showing you what is on those thumb drives. I did it to protect myself in case this thing blows wide open. There will be investigations and I have to have proof or it is just my word against theirs."

"So at some point you will turn it over to a reporter?"

"Only a highly reputable reporter with good credentials. Because this is so horrendous, it needs to get into the right hands. I am sure Patrick will have someone in mind. I have been doing some research myself. I don't know what will happen when this all comes out, but I do know that if we have all the information we need, someone's head is going to roll."

"Will the President fall?"

"Probably not. He will be protected at all costs. But those under him who knew about this; they will take the hit. You realize that this has been going on for a long, long time. It didn't just start with the current President."

"Are you saying every President has used it?"

"I doubt that some of them did would like to think that some didn't. But politics gets a little slippery. Sometimes it could have been used when the President at that time didn't know it. He was not privy to that information because he was being protected."

"I despise politics. And I wish you were not involved in this at all. I don't know how you sleep at night, Bill. I don't know if I could do it."

"You forget all the training I've been through. I had to be able to sleep at night no matter what I did during the day. We were dealing with the enemy then. Not innocent people. I had no problem sleeping when I had put down the enemy. Because they were about to take us out. Someone was going to die."

"So what is your next move?"

"I wait to hear from Patrick. He has a group of people that he is conferring with. I have no idea who they are. Money people. Influential. I don't know how much he tells them, but I have to believe that he trusts them explicitly."

"When you do decide to tell the world, I don't know how anyone will protect you, or us, for that matter."

"Don't you worry, Honey. We all will be given immunity if this hits the fan. Let's try to stay calm until I know what the plan is and when this thing is going to go down. You have been wonderful through this whole thing and I want you to know I realize how difficult this has been for you."

"I hate hiding things from the kids. But it's heartbreaking watching you having to deal with the stress. I can see what this is doing to you, Bill."

"It won't be long now. We better go inside. I don't know who the heck is watching us, but I guarantee we are not alone out here anymore." He turned and looked at her. He whispered low in her ear. "Under my chair at my desk I have cut a section of the carpet and lifted a small area of the floor up. I placed a metal box there with the thumb drives. In case something happens to me, you have to get these to Patrick." He looked at her and she nodded, frowning.

Once inside the house, Bill went into his study and got on a new iPad he had just purchased. It had not been in the house before that evening so he knew it was clean. But he would have to carry the iPad with him at all times, so he had purchased the smallest one Apple made. He got online and studied the most famous, out front reporters. The ones always on television and in the newspaper talking about the most current events. He had nailed about four of them: Bob Lancaster, Jill Harris, Mose Hale, and Harry

Osner. These were the top four that he could find that might be able to handle the job.

He was nervous and excited at the same time. Emotions were running wild. But this was a dream he never thought in a million years could happen. He wasn't exactly sure how he would ever have gotten out of the President's Club alive. But if Patrick was the man he appeared to be, then things just might fall into place.

He still had a fear deep inside that Patrick could be one of them. One could not be too careful. At this time, Bill still was in control of the information he had recorded. He planned to keep it that way until his next conversation with Patrick. All he could do was wait.

CHAPTER FIFTY-FOUR

The text waiting on Jacob's phone was the worst thing in the world he could read. He never saw it coming. Gail Bailey had bailed out. Her words were short and to the point. She was moving back to Memphis to try again with her ex-husband. The one who had beaten her up. The one who had left her. He'd heard that women were drawn back to their abusers. Well, he found that out firsthand. He was shaking when he read the text. He had ended it with Jane, or rather, was forced to end it when he saw her kissing her new boyfriend. But Jacob was weakened by Gail coming into his life. He was taken by her, just like Paul had warned. And now she was gone. Just plumb gone.

He waited to text her back, because he wanted to say the right thing. Well, what he really wanted to do was blast her with every word he could think of. But he would regret it and right now he didn't feel like regretting anything. He just wanted some peace in his life after having the shock of his life.

So he pulled out his phone, after a few days had gone by, and sent her a text back. It wasn't ugly, but it was to the point. He told her to send him her new mailing address for all the insurance she had purchased. And that he wished her well with her ex-husband who had left her stranded with a child.

He did not hear back for several days. But she did finally send him her new address and a big apology for leaving so suddenly. He winced when he thought of Lily, whom he had grown to adore even in the short time he had known her. People come and go. And right now everyone was going.

Sitting at his desk, he determined that he was going to get that manager job or die trying. He had been distracted by Gail and now that was all gone. So he could focus on his work and the job at hand. He was tired of being the sibling that struggled and was made fun of all the time at family dinners. He didn't want to be the brunt of someone else's joke. He wanted to be his own man. It would take some time but he was determined to make his life different.

Paul had hit the nail on the head with Gail. He'd only seen her once but had her figured out. How did he do that? She was so nice, so pretty. Why couldn't he be more like Paul? But he wasn't and he wasn't ever going to be. He was the shorter son, the one who was slower, and the one who took the longest to learn anything. But his strong suit was that when he finally did focus on something, he got it. He wasn't going to quit. So right now, that was his aim. The manager job. He cleaned up his desk, looked into his Rolodex, and began dialing the phone numbers of people who were possible leads for insurance. Some already had one or more policies with him, but maybe they needed something else. It was worth a try, and he was going to spend his whole day dialing the phone.

Halfway through the day he looked up and Paul was standing his office. Not the conversation he wanted to have. But there it was, whether he liked it or not.

"Hey, Brother. How's it going?"

"Great. Having a great day."

"I just had a moment and decided to see how things were, because I know you are going through a tough time. Have you heard from Jane?"

"Not a word. I guess she got the picture."

"We all really liked her, Jacob. She was a nice girl."

"Yes, she was. But apparently I wasn't enough for her."

"That's not really a fair statement, because you were turning towards Gail Bailey, too."

"Touché. Well, that's over with now."

Paul raised his eyebrows. "What do you mean?"

"Just what I said. It's over with."

"What happened with her? Do you mind telling me?"

Jacob frowned. "Would it matter if I did?"

"Probably not."

Jacob sighed. "I got a text from her saying she was going back to Memphis to try again with her ex-husband."

Paul gasped. "Are you serious?"

"Dead serious."

"That's crazy. Did she say why?"

"No. And it doesn't matter why. I know the guy is a jerk; he abused her. She told me one night when we were out eating together. I guess that's par for the course."

"Now what are you going to do?"

"I'm going to get my head into my work like I should have been doing all along. If I had been, I might still have Jane. But maybe that was going to happen, anyway."

"You were a little sluggish on the marriage thing, right?"

"Yes I was. But now I'm glad. I'll be fine. It will take some time getting used to, but I am certain that pouring myself into work right now is the right thing to do."

Paul stood up. "I couldn't agree more, Jacob. Just know I'm around if you need someone to talk to."

Jacob nodded and watched Paul walk out the door. *That went well.* Better than he'd expected. He glanced at the Rolodex and picked up the phone. He was determined to make a sale that day.

He was on the phone talking to a lady about health insurance and had turned his back on the door, leaning on the credenza behind his desk. Two men wearing black walked in, put a black cloth sack over his face, and grabbed him, phone and all, and picked him up. They pulled so hard the phone cord came ripping out of the wall and the phone in his hand fell to the floor.

No one heard. He was alone in the office, which was a rare thing. He had no idea where he was being taken, but he kicked and fought all the way out the door.

Paul had just left Jacob's office and Jacob prayed his brother was still around. He felt hopeless and scared to death as they stuffed him into the trunk of their car and drove away, screeching their tires. It happened in broad daylight, in the blink of an eye, when no one was around.

His mind was racing ninety miles an hour. *What do they want from me? Who in the world are these men?* He didn't know where they were taking him or what they wanted. But he felt sure he was going to die. His whole life played before his eyes and he realized suddenly that he had wasted most of his life being ridiculously stubborn. He had rebelled against any advice his father had given him. He wanted to do it all his own way. His mother would panic. They had already lost a daughter. How could he get out of this?

He began to feel around the trunk with his feet to see if there was anything that would help him escape, but there wasn't much room to move his legs. He could hear a muffled conversation but nothing else. He did have his cell phone but they had tied his hands so it was worthless to think of calling someone for help. His only recourse was to wait and see what they wanted. But the waiting was not going well. Sweat was pouring from his body. It was hot in the trunk and he was dying of thirst. He was more scared than he'd ever been in his entire life.

The car stopped and the two men got out of the car and opened the trunk. They pulled him out with difficulty and stood him up. "What do you want?" He asked the same question over and over.

They would not answer. Neither of the men said a word. They simply picked him up and threw him over a railing; he felt it with one of his feet as he went over the side. He was floating in slow motion downward towards what, he didn't know. *I'm headed towards either land or water. I'm going to die, either way.*

It was split seconds but it felt like a long time. When he hit water he sank fast, struggling to hold his breath. He hadn't known when to take a deep breath, so he didn't have enough air in his lungs to keep him alive until he found a way to get his hands loose from the ropes they had wrapped around them.

The bag came off his head so he tried to open his eyes. The water was murky. He was running out of air. His lungs felt like they were going to burst. He blacked out into nothingness and floated close to the bottom.

CHAPTER FIFTY-FIVE

Somewhere in that murky water was a man struggling to see. Struggling to find the body of a young man who had been thrown over the side of a bridge. He squinted and thought he saw a dark motionless figure floating in the water. He grabbed the body and pushed off from the bottom. They both went upwards quickly and he pushed the face of the young man above the water, hoping he would gasp for air. But he was limp.

Bill Sinclair was trying to save his son from dying. He had received a panicked call from Paul, screaming into the phone that two men had kidnapped Jacob from his office. Paul had been in his car talking on the phone when he saw the men in black shove Jacob into their trunk. He followed the car and kept his distance, calling his father to let him know where they were headed. He had to stay back because there weren't that many cars on the road. The bridge was not on the main road. They knew what they were doing.

Bill raced at lightning speed to the location Paul described, found the bridge and Paul's car, and dove in. He didn't take the time to talk to Paul. He knew his son would be dead if he didn't get to him quickly. The men had already driven off as soon as they dumped Jacob over the rail, so they were nowhere to be found.

But as he dragged his son to shore and pumped water out of his lungs, his only thought was getting air into the lifeless body. The next thing he'd do was find out who the thugs were that nearly took the life of his youngest son.

He blew air into Jacob's mouth, struggling to revive him. Time seemed to stop as he did CPR on his son's chest. It was nothing short of a miracle that the young man came back to life. Jacob had nearly died; his lungs were full of water. A few more minutes and it would have been too late. Bill leaned over his son, who was sputtering water out of his mouth, shaking all over from the sheer terror of what had happened.

"It's okay, Jake. I've got you. You're okay now. You're okay."

Jacob could barely talk. "Dad . . . they tried to kill me. . . .Who were these people? What did they want from me?" He managed to croak.

Bill tried to calm his frightened son. "Don't even worry about that. Just take some deep breaths. I'm going to get you home. It's going to be okay, Son."

Paul came rushing down the embankment to help Bill carry Jacob up a steep incline to the road.

"Let me help, Dad. You can't do that by yourself."

"I'm glad you are here. This embankment is too steep."

Jacob was shaking and ashen, but he was a fighter. "I can walk some, Dad. Let me put my feet down and it will make it easier for us to make this hill."

A few times Jacob went to his knees and Paul grabbed him up. Bill went ahead of them so he could pull Jacob up to level ground. As soon as they got to the road they put Jacob in the car and took off, heading towards home.

When they walked into the house, Sharon was in the kitchen cooking dinner. She peeked around the corner and screamed.

"Bill! What happened to Jacob? Is he okay? Paul, why are you here? What's going on?"

"Calm down, Sharon. Jacob has been through hell. We need to get him changed into some of my clean clothes. Sit down so I can catch you up on what's happened."

He put his arm around her and hugged her. "We've been through a very fragile, harrowing situation. I don't want you to freak out, Sharon. But two men kidnapped Jacob and threw him over a bridge into deep water with his hands tied. He was drowning when I got to him. Luckily for him, Paul was still sitting in his car in the parking lot when the men kidnapped him. He'd just had a short visit with Jacob and was making a few phone calls in the car. He saw the whole thing go down. But we don't know who the men are and I need to make a quick phone call to Patrick.

"Things are going to change, Sharon, faster than we had planned. Someone was supposed to be watching Jacob and the rest of our kids. But somehow these men got through, anyway. So I don't feel safe anymore. Can you sit here with Jacob while I go make a phone call?"

Sharon was crying and Bill saw the anger in her face. "I can sit here. But Patrick better tell us what the hell is going on! He was supposed to have us surrounded. It doesn't look like he did his job very well, does it?"

"I don't know what happened, but I will find out. I'll be right back. Just sit tight."

Bill's hands were shaking when he dialed Patrick's number. Things had come down to the wire quicker than he'd planned. He knew better than to plan in the first place. He was taught to be a step ahead of his enemy, but right now it was difficult to tell who the enemy was.

Patrick answered on the third ring. If he'd been standing in Bill's office, Bill would have punched him in the face. "Before you say a word, Patrick, I have to tell you I am extremely disappointed in you and at the moment I am not sure I can trust anything you are going to say to me. My son was just kidnapped and thrown over a bridge. He nearly drowned. It was a stroke of luck that Paul had just visited Jacob and saw what went down or the boy would be dead by now. What in the hell happened to all that security you promised?"

Patrick did not wait for the words to stop before he jumped right in. "Bill, hold on a second! Three of my men were shot so that explains how the kidnappers got to Jacob. Nothing I can say will compensate for what you have been through with your son. But we are going to have to step up the plan right now. We cannot wait another day. Somehow they got wind of either you talking to me about the club or heard you and your wife talking."

"They are coming after me next," Bill insisted. "I can feel it. Obviously my family is not safe. I have checked the gazebo numerous times before we talk. I find it hard to believe they heard us. But that is a moot point now. We know they know something or this would never have happened. We need to have a talk. And only God knows where that safe place is that we can talk without getting killed."

"I know you are angry and upset. I don't blame you for a second. But I had men on your children. These men know what they are doing. But somehow they got caught unaware. I don't like that. Let's meet in your office parking lot in my car. I will come in a rented limo so I know it will be clean. We can lay out our plan of action without fear of being heard. I am so sorry, Bill, about your son. Is he okay now?"

"After I pumped a lake of water out of his lungs. Yeah, he's going to be okay. But my children will not trust me now. They are all going to be terrified. And my poor wife. She is at her wits' end. We need to bring this thing out in the open and it needs to happen fast or we'll all be dead. You included."

"I will meet you at your office in twenty minutes. But Bill, I need to take care of your family immediately. They need to be moved to an unknown location. I have a lodge in the Catskill Mountains that would be the perfect place for them to be secluded. Get your family ready and tell them to drive to Leesburg Airport and I will have my private jet waiting for them. The lodge is stocked full of food and everything they will need to be comfortable. Don't delay, Bill. Tell them to pack a small bag and head in that direction within the next thirty minutes. When I meet you, we can discuss further details."

Bill hung up the phone and walked back into the living room. He was fired up and could hardly speak, but he flipped a mental switch and got into his training mode. This was no different than any covert he had done in the past in some ways, but his family was involved this time. He took Sharon and the boys outside to talk, sitting Jacob down on the porch. He was still weak from the near drowning.

"Sharon, you and Paul and Jacob listen to me. This is the most critical conversation we will ever have in our lives. There are people who want to take me out, and unfortunately, my family, too. Because of what I am doing for the President, it's all classified. I am sure they think there is a leak, and that leak is me. So I have a target on my head, but they are including you in that target. Sharon, you need to call Emily and Rob and get them over here immediately with bags packed. I want Avery here, too, and Paul, you can inform everyone of what is going on. As soon as everyone is here, load the vehicles and drive to Leesburg Airport where there will be a jet waiting for you. You will be taken to a lodge in the Catskill Mountains and it will be protected as if it's the White House. Guards everywhere, a heavy duty fence, and surveillance cameras everywhere. You will be safe until you hear from me."

"What about what you shared with me yesterday?" Sharon asked.

Bill walked over to Sharon and pulled her aside. "I have all of that with me now. I am meeting with Patrick in twenty minutes and then he will know everything. I made copies of it which are where I told you yesterday. If anything happens to me, you know what to do."

"I never thought it would happen so fast."

"I am surprised it has gone on this long. Hurry and get the kids ready to leave. Don't waste any time packing too much stuff. This is temporary, Sharon. It won't be long before things will go back to a new normal."

He kissed her and hugged his sons. "I am so thankful you are okay, Jacob. Stay strong. Your mother will need you and Jesse to help with things at the lodge. I will stay in touch. Keep your phones on and take your chargers. Sharon, I have you a new phone. It's lying on the kitchen counter. Take that with you and ditch your old one. I love all of you. Please understand that I am doing the best I can do to protect all of us."

Bill jumped into his car, knowing that at any moment he could be killed. He was so worried about his family he could hardly think straight. But it wasn't the time to get emotional. He had to remain calm and think logically and realistically. He had to think like a criminal and think fast.

As he pulled up to the office, he saw Patrick's vehicle. He slammed the car into "park" and jumped into the back seat of the black Mercedes. Patrick was already rolling and it was obvious to Bill he knew what he was doing.

"Bill, we don't have much time. I trust that your family understands the urgency of getting to the airport. We don't want anything to happen to them. I know they will be safe at the lodge and well protected."

"They are on their way now."

"Our plan is equally critical. Every single thing we do now has to be acted out with precision. There can be no mistakes, no stone unturned. This isn't a practice run, Bill. We both have wanted this opportunity to blow this thing up but now we are being forced to.

That puts us at a disadvantage because that's when most people screw up. We don't have that prerogative."

Bill paused. "There's something you don't know, Patrick, which should make our case simple."

Patrick stared at Bill. "What? There's something you haven't told me?"

"Right. When I accepted the call from Command to join The President's Club, I decided right then that I needed to cover myself. I recorded every conversation I had with Command and every act of violence I had to commit because of their orders. I photographed all victims that I killed or tortured. And all of this is on two thumb drives that I have with me now. I made copies and they are hidden in a secure location that only my wife knows about."

Patrick looked astonished but he kept his voice low. "Are you kidding me? Bill, this is music to my ears. How brilliant! I am amazed you had the wherewithal to do that under such pressure. I am not sure we can use the taped conversations in a court of law, but it will give fire to the reporter you talk to."

"I have researched and I feel Harry Osner is the man I need to contact. He seems to lean to the conservative side and not with the establishment. I know what he writes may not be who he is. But we have to choose someone fast, because there is no time."

"Let's head to New York to *The Post*. I'll put a call in to Harry Osner to see if he is in, or how we can reach him. This is an emergency. I hope he sees it as such."

As the black sedan pulled away from his office, for the first time since he could remember Bill was genuinely afraid. But he knew he could never let that fear show or he would be devoured.

CHAPTER FIFTY-SIX

The private jet landed at Leesburg Airport and the whole family was escorted to the plane. Their luggage was loaded and all the passengers were told to buckle up. Inside the plane, it was plush and very comfortable. They were served beverages and small snacks, and the pilot told them to relax, that they would reach their destination soon.

Emily was staring out the window. She was furious and confused. All this time she had been right about her assumption that something was going on. She had never in her greatest imaginations dreamed her dad's second job would end up with his family hiding like this. Their lives were threatened. Her father might not come back home.

⊨‡ ‡⊨

Sharon was not sure what she could tell them now because Bill had not given her the okay. She knew the whole family was wondering what in the world he was involved in that would cause this much stir.

The boys were sitting near her and Jacob was leaning back in the seat with his eyes closed. He looked exhausted from everything he'd been through.

"Mom, can you shed some light on this mess? Why are we being hauled off to a hidden location? Who is after Dad?" Jesse asked in a low voice.

Sharon rubbed her eyes and shook her head. "Son, I am not sure I can talk about any of it right now. Perhaps when we get to the lodge I will be able to ask Bill if it is okay for me to open up to you children about what has been going on in his life. But until then, you've got to trust me. And your father."

"This is ridiculous. Is it the military that is putting pressure on Dad? Why would he take a position now, at his age, with such high risk and security level? That doesn't even sound sane."

"I know, Jess. No matter what you are thinking, no matter how long you try to figure it all out, I assure you that you won't guess what hell he's been through, and why. So let it go for now. I realize you all are angry and afraid. Worried about Dad. But right now, we need to pray and remain as calm as possible. Patrick Lathrop is being kind to move us to this location. We will be taken care of until this all gets settled. I am not sure what we will end up with as far as your father is concerned. But all we can do right now is wait."

Emily shook her head. "I'm not too good at sitting back and waiting. You know that. I am fuming because Dad wasn't honest with us from the get-go. I know I am running my mouth and probably shouldn't. But this is so serious. We all could have been harmed. Look what happened to Jacob? Maybe if we had known about it, Jacob would have been more prepared. He almost died, Mom."

"Don't you think I realize that, Emily? Come on. I am dead sure your father has done what he could to protect his family. But you have to realize that things are not always like they appear. Give this a rest until I hear from your father. Then, maybe I can share what is going on."

Emily rolled her eyes. "I'm so tired of hearing that I could scream."

"I'm tired of saying it, believe me. I want things to go back to normal but it's going to be a while. So we need to be strong and patient. That will help your father most of all."

The lodge was everything Patrick had said it would be. Sitting back in a stand of trees and surrounded by a tall metal fence, the stone and wood lodge was tucked in and hidden from the world. Inside, the high ceilings made it feel even larger. The family walked through the whole building, looking at all the rooms and settling into the bedrooms with their luggage. The living area had massive leather sofas and chairs, a huge fireplace, and windows across the back that looked out on a lake. The bedrooms had large headboards and thick soft blankets. Sharon checked the refrigerator and it was stocked full of food. The pantry was also well stocked with everything you could ever want to eat. The tension lifted and her children began to talk and laugh about being hidden from everything. They had left their jobs with very little explanation. Hopefully, they would all have a job when this came to an end. But somehow, their daily lives seemed far away. This whole experience was surreal.

A man dressed in a white chef's shirt and black pants walked into the living room. Everyone was startled. They thought they were alone in the house.

"My name is Michael and I'll be serving you dinner in an hour. Would you all like to take a shower and get comfortable?"

Avery and Paul nodded and headed to their room. The others followed suit, and Sharon went upstairs to her room, hoping to text Bill. She took a quick shower and changed into some blue jeans and a white blouse. She sat on the bed and looked out the huge windows that went from floor to ceiling, and sent Bill a short text to see if he would respond. She waited for a few minutes and laid her phone down on the bed and leaned back to close her eyes for a moment. She was so tired of worrying. It was getting to her and she missed Bill. She knew he would be going to a reporter but she didn't know how he would be received. The information he was going to share was mind-boggling. She only hoped that whoever he spoke with would believe what he said and would see the imminent danger they were in. Something drastic was about to happen and it was a nightmare not knowing what that thing was going to be.

Suddenly a text came through. It was Bill. "Honey, I cannot talk right now. I hope you are safe. We have arrived in New York. I will keep you posted."

She sent a quick text back letting him know they were all safe and at the designated location. At least she had heard from him and knew he was okay. At any second he could be taken out. She knew how dangerous it was. She could almost feel it in the air, even at the lodge.

She got up and went downstairs to see if dinner was ready. Michael came out of the kitchen and announced that dinner was served, and the family sat down, overwhelmed by all the food.

"I feel like we're being treated like celebrities." Maryanne smiled. "I have been so concerned about Jacob since we arrived at the house and boarded the plane."

"It does feel that way. But things are way too serious for us to totally relax here." Sharon nodded to Maryanne and took a bite of the fish.

"We've been through a lot this year and I have a feeling it's not over yet. But we have to stick together and trust that your father knows what he is doing."

After the rich dinner and dessert, they all gathered into the living room. Michael walked into the living room with them and sat on the arm of the sofa.

"I realize all of you are frightened and have been through enough already. I hope your stay here will give you a break from the worry. I want you to know that we are surrounded by an electrical fence, surveillance cameras are everywhere, and there are about twenty armed men on duty, guarding the premises. But just in case there is a break in security, I want you to know there is a hidden room. Please follow me into the hallway."

They all followed him cautiously into the long, wide hallway. Michael pointed to a button on the wall.

"This button opens up a portion of this wall." He pressed a well-hidden button and a section of the wall opened up. Inside was a large room with everything they would need to survive if they had to stay in the room for a period of time. There was a small kitchen, water, heat, air conditioning, a closet-sized bathroom, and plenty of ammunition and guns.

"I hope we do not have to use this room because that would mean that the enemy had broken through all the guards and security measures we have installed. I doubt that can happen but we prepare for the worst. If that happens, you push the button and all of you get into this room. Once inside, push the button on the inside wall and the wall will close back up. No one will ever know you are in here. It is totally sound proof and lined with steel."

"Patrick has thought of everything. Does he fear for his life?"

"One can never be too prepared." Michael answered very quickly and briefly.

"I guess you're right. I never thought about needing anything like this."

"When large amounts of money are being passed around, protection is high on the list of things you want to have. He deals with all types of people. Some of them are very short-sighted and short-tempered."

"I hope we never run into them."

"I assure you, I feel the same way."

"Thank you for showing us the room. It does make me feel safer here."

"I want you to ask me for anything you need. I am here at your disposal. But do not go outside. Do not try to leave. Just stay here and enjoy the privacy. Mr. Lathrop has worked hard to protect you and we don't want to jeopardize that protection in any way."

"I think we understand the perimeters of our being safe here. Thank you so much for the wonderful meal and the information you have shared with us. Do you carry a gun, Michael?" Sharon had a solemn look on her face.

Michael raised his shirt on the right side and showed the gun he wore on his hip. "We all are armed here. I will protect you, Mrs. Sinclair. Don't you worry about that."

Sharon nodded and moved everyone back into the living room. After Michael left, Emily spoke up.

"I am beginning to get a grasp of just how serious this really is, Mother."

"It's beyond anything all of us could imagine."

"What I don't understand is why Dad is involved in such a horrible situation. And he put us at risk, also."

"That information is not available to you just yet. But one day you will know it all. Let's turn on the television and relax, or you can all go to your separate rooms to do that. I just want to get my mind off things until I hear from your father. I'm sure what he is going through right now is probably one of the worst times of his life. The scariest. We need to remember that. If he gets out of this alive, it will be nothing short of a miracle."

They all went to their rooms, ready for some rest. It had been an exhausting day both physically and emotionally for all of them. Jacob and Maryanne, especially. He was worn out and still shaken from the near drowning. His body was sore.

Sharon went to her room and finally allowed herself to cry. She had held it in for so long, but here, away from home, she let it all go. Her heart was broken and her trust in what she thought was a trustworthy government was gone. She just wanted Bill home safe and sound.

She knew when she laid her head down on her pillow that Bill was in the most danger he'd ever been. But it could also save hundreds of lives. So there it was. The yin and the yang of it. Her eyes closed but sleep did not come. She couldn't be sure that the love of her life was still breathing. And somehow her staying awake kept him alive.

CHAPTER FIFTY-SEVEN

B ill Sinclair sat in the middle of a dark parking garage on 40 Clinton Street. He was leaning against a concrete post, hoping against hope that he wasn't followed. He was waiting on Harry Osner to show up. His heart was racing and he could hear his heartbeat in his ears. He was sweating and his mind was going in ten directions. He blew out a deep breath and looked around. No cars in sight. He felt in his pocket for the two thumb drives. He hoped against hope that those two small pieces of plastic would save his life and the lives of the other ten men involved. He didn't know Harry Osner, but he'd read all he could about the man. From what he had heard from Patrick, the guy was tough. He didn't sway easily. And this was a matter of uttermost importance and secrecy. Right under the President's proverbial nose. He knew but he didn't know. Tricky.

Finally, a man arrived in a white Nissan. He was short and stocky. A hat was pulled down over his face, so Bill could not be sure it was him. He didn't move from where he was sitting until the man started walking towards him. Bill slowly stood up, dusting off his pants. There was little sound in the garage. It was late. It was eerie to be standing there waiting on a man he had never met, putting his hope in such a small thing. And a less-than-an-hour conversation.

The gentleman spoke in a low, deep voice, and shook Bill's hand. "Harry Osner. Now get in my car so we can talk. It isn't all that safe standing in a dark parking garage this late at night in New York City."

Bill slipped into the passenger seat and closed the door. He trusted a stranger at a time when he could trust no one. "I appreciate you coming out at this time of night to see me."

"Let's put it this way. You got my attention."

"I guess I did. Believe me, this doesn't happen every day in my life."

"What do you have for me, Mr. Sinclair? You sounded like it was urgent."

"I'm here to tell you about something that is going on that violates the Constitution, the Bill of Rights, and the values that this nation is founded on."

"You have my ear."

"Do you understand the danger in what I am about to tell you?"

"I can only go on what you have told me so far. We don't have all night, so let's get to the point. Don't be afraid to talk to me. That's why I am here."

"I served in the Navy as a SEAL and I retired from the Navy several years ago. I was done with covert and taking lives. I had done my time."

"I can appreciate that."

"I got a call one day that shook the ground I was standing on. From someone called 'Command.' I was told it actually came down from the chief of staff to Command. But I have no idea who Command is. He told me that I had been selected to become a member of The President's Club. They had vetted me and I was perfect for the job. They said I had no choice but to serve at the pleasure of the President. So I had to say yes. At that time, I was not aware of what the club stood for. But I had a feeling it wasn't good."

"I'm listening."

"I was told by Command that there were twelve of us. But I would never know who the other eleven were. And they did not know each other. Everything was shrouded in secrecy. I was sent a private cell phone and that is how we communicate. The rules were that I would receive a call from Command with a covert operation I had to take care of alone. I had no choice. I would receive a text telling me where, when and who. I had to go totally black, and if I got caught they would not save me. I was on my own to take care of the job at hand."

"And that job was?"

"Sometimes I had to kill someone who was going too strongly against the President's agenda."

"And other times?"

"Other times I had to interrogate them, to the point of torture if needed, to get information from them or intimidate them enough where they would back down from their own agenda."

"What kind of torture?"

"I have used waterboarding, stabbing their hand, taking their hand off with explosives, you name it."

"How many times were you called?"

"I lost count."

"Did you ever not follow through?"

"Yes. A couple times I recognized the person. The first was someone I had served with in Afghanistan. The second man I helped to escape. But they took him out, anyway. He never made it out of Washington."

"Any others?"

"Yes. One of the twelve was thought to be a leak. And that cannot be tolerated. So I was asked to take him out. He was one of the men I had done covert with. When I called out his name, he knew I recognized him. But even though I let him go, he was killed trying to escape."

"How did they treat you after the mission failed?"

"They threatened my life and the lives of my family. I lost a daughter and cannot prove that it was them who took her out. A car accident not far from my house. Something wasn't right about it, but I will never be able to prove it."

"What has caused it to escalate to this point?"

"I think they believe I am talking to someone. So I have moved my family to a designated location where they cannot be harmed."

"What proof do you have that this President's Club exists, Bill?"

Bill was shaking, but he was determined to get all the information out as clearly as possible. It had to be right. He pulled the two thumb drives out of his pocket and held them up so that Harry could see them.

"When they forced me to join the club, I decided immediately that I would tape all conversations with Command, photograph every killing, and record all information about each covert action I was forced to do. All of it is on these thumb drives. I have made copies for my own sake. Because no one would ever believe this is going on right under the noses of the people. And we twelve have had to kill or wound innocent people. The freaky thing is that apparently this club has been going on for a long time. This isn't the first President to use it to his advantage."

Harry rubbed his eyes. He looked tired but he was obviously intrigued by what Bill was telling him. He had made notes and recorded the conversation.

"You have proof of this? I cannot do anything just on your word alone."

Bill put the thumb drives in the palm of Osner's hand. Harry stared at them as though he didn't know what to do.

"I am willing to give these to you, but I do not want you to reveal the source of this information unless I get total immunity. I have a source that knows the other ten men involved in the club. We have not spoken to them yet, but I bet they will be willing to testify against the government if they also receive immunity. None of us wanted to be involved in anything like this. It undermines everything we stand for. Everything we were taught in the military."

Harry was quiet for a moment. "Well, this tops any other private meeting I've had in my life, and let me tell you, I've had plenty. I've been told things I wish I hadn't been told. But this is right up there in the top ten."

"Something has to be done now. We are in danger of losing our lives as we speak."

Harry took the thumb drives and shook Bill's hand. "I'm proud of you coming forward like this. The risk is too great for me not to act on this information. But as I say that, I realize they could also take me out. Secrecy is imperative until I have all my ducks in a row. We cannot say anything about this meeting to anyone. Or I will drop it like a hot potato. You understand?"

"I sure do. But how do I know you will act on this, Harry?"

"I would not have met you here in a dark parking garage if I was not willing to act. However, I have to think this thing through. I will need to talk to a lawyer. I have one that I trust implicitly. It's critical that this is done right. In the right order. You can't make mistakes, but I sure can't print them yet. I have to know all the information you give me is one hundred percent accurate. We can't just point fingers without having all the facts."

"All that is on the thumb drives is real. Accurate as it can get. Raw footage. You won't want to see what is on there, but I want you to look at it. The world needs to know that when someone suddenly disappears that is involved in dealings with the government in any shape or form, it needs to be looked into. It will always be broadcasted as a suicide or accident. No one will ever know it was a planned death."

"That is a cold, hard statement."

"But it is true. Another thing to remember; we have had to take out innocent people to get the one they want. They have no regard for the innocent. Hell, they all were innocent, for that matter. The ones they want are the ones going against what the President wants. The others were just around for the ride. You can't believe how cold they are when they want something done. I have no choice in whether or not I obey their orders. I will die if I don't. It's the worst form of intimidation. Run like the Mafia. I hate it and want out so badly I can taste it."

"I hope we can get you out, Bill. I am sorry for what you men have suffered at the hands of our own government. It sounds so harsh, but it is despicable. Hard to wrap my mind around it, that something like this club exists right under our noses."

"And that it has gone on unnoticed for years." Bill paused. "Listen, Harry. We can waste no time getting this out. Action needs to be taken immediately. I will take care of getting my source to contact the other men involved in the club. We will let them know that you will be working on getting us all immunity for our testimonies. I want my life back, if that is even humanly possible."

"I am sure you do, Bill. I will get on it immediately. I won't print this story until we know you have immunity. How can I contact you? The same phone I used before?"

"Yes. This phone is untraceable. I will be waiting to hear from you."

⊶ ⊷

Five seconds after Harry pulled away, a black sedan pulled up and Bill climbed into the back seat. Bill had been wired so that Patrick could hear the whole thing.

"That went well. Don't you think?"

"It was okay. I was nervous as hell, though. I want this to work, Patrick."

"It's our one shot to get the news out about the club. I know those other men will want it to happen. They have to be as sick of it as you are." Patrick said.

"Speaking of those ten men, you need to approach them to see if they would be willing to testify if they receive full immunity."

"I have been busy while you were meeting with Mr. Osner. My attorney has spoken with the federal judge and he has given you and the ten other men involved in the President's Club total immunity and anonymity."

"Are you serious? That fast?"

"I have spoken with a few of the ten. They are willing to testify if they can remain anonymous. I told them their testimony is critical. We have to have all ten to make an impact, I think."

"I agree. I wish one day that I would be able to meet the other men involved."

"That probably will be happen, Bill. If we can find a safe location."

"So we are ready for Harry to go to print with it?"

"Yes, sir. So Harry can go forward with the article. Hold on to your hat. Because heads are going to roll, Bill. Heads are going to roll."

CHAPTER FIFTY-EIGHT

The building that Martin Lewis was in, with fifteen other people, went up in smoke right on national television. Some bystander was filming the whole thing as it exploded. Bill sat up in bed, hidden in a condo in New York City with everything but Rottweilers surrounding him for protection. He had ignored the phone call from Command last night. He knew they had to know his whole family was gone. They didn't know where. But they knew he was on the run. It made his blood curdle to think of what they would do to his family if they found them. Or him, for that matter.

The private phone had not rung again since he missed the one call. He picked up his phone and called Harry to let him know that Patrick had covered some ground since their conversation. Having immunity was huge.

"Harry, it's Bill. I got some great news."

"Let's hear it."

"We got to a Federal Judge and he gave us immunity and anonymity. All ten of us. So you can go to print with the information I gave you."

"Has Patrick contacted the other ten men?"

"He has spoken with most of them. They are in agreement that this has to stop. None of them want to be involved with this horrific underground movement."

"Bill, once this comes out, we don't know what will happen. It will take on a life of its own. No one will know it was you who leaked us the information. No one will know who the other ten men are. But someone in the government knows. Just be prepared. Don't leave any stone uncovered. And make sure that all the men tell the truth. This will be one of the most pivoting moments in your entire life."

"I'm totally aware of the solemnity of the situation. But it can't be worse than blowing someone's brains out who didn't deserve to die. I don't know how any of us sleep at night. It's worse than war. And all war is hell."

"I'll keep in touch. Let me know if you have to change phones."

"Will do. I look forward to reading the headlines."

Just as soon as he hung up with Harry, his phone rang again. "I'm on fire this morning, Bill," Patrick said. "This thing is going to roll real fast. Are you ready?"

"How can you possibly get ready for something like this? I know I want to be with my family. How soon do you think that can happen?"

"I don't know for sure. When this news hits the paper, that is when you will be in the most danger. Your family is safe. But I want to move them one more time to another house I have in Colorado. We can never be too careful. If they put two and two together about you and me, then they might start hunting down all of my properties to see if that is where you are hiding."

"There is going to be so much going on that they won't have time to think. This will catch them blindsided. I know they are not expecting you to go public and they sure don't know you recorded everything. That was a brilliant move on your part."

"We will see how brilliant it is. In the end, all I want is my life back, and I know the other men want that, too. But ultimately, we don't know if the President's Club will be gone for good. I don't trust politics anymore. Some men will stop at nothing to get their way."

"Stay put until you hear from me. I will contact the other ten men to let them know the article is going to be published. All of you need to prepare to testify. Keep your wits about you, Bill. This is going to move very quickly."

Bill was dying to hear his wife's voice. He hung up the phone and called Sharon. He was dying to hear his wife's voice.

"Bill? Oh my gosh! I've been waiting to hear from you. I was afraid to call because I wasn't sure what you were doing. Are you okay? What is going on?"

"Take it easy, Honey. I've missed you, too. You wouldn't believe how fast things are moving now. Patrick has pulled off a friggin' miracle. He went before a federal judge and presented our case, and the judge has given us total immunity and anonymity so that we can testify without revealing our identities. So all of the other men are on board, Sharon. They all want out of this nightmare."

"And the reporter? Did you speak with him?"

"Harry Osner was amazing. Very direct in his approach. But he sized up the situation and knew it was a chance of a lifetime for him as a reporter. This will blow his career off the map."

"When will the article hit the paper?"

"As soon as he can get it written. He has to make sure it is one hundred percent accurate. I am sure I will get a phone call to clarify certain things, but he is ready. I hope the world is ready. It's going to cause hell in the White House, but it needs to be cleaned up."

"I just want our lives back, Bill."

"Hold on, Sharon. It will happen. By the way, Patrick is going to move you and the kids to another location in Colorado. I know the kids will love that. You will be covered up in security, so don't worry. I am a little vulnerable here in New York. Not sure what my next move will be, but I will let you know."

"I'll tell the children. Be brave, Bill. We are with you."

"I love you, lady. Thanks for being by my side through this mess. I promise you this will be the last time we have to live like this. If we have to move to another country, we are going to have a normal life."

"I live to see you again."

Bill's phone rang off and on for the next two days as he went over facts and situations with Harry. Harry was going to be thorough. This was only going to happen once. One article. One day on the front page of *The Post*.

"It has to be exactly right," Harry told Bill. "True on every point. But I also don't want to leave out anything. I want it all."

To Bill, Harry seemed like a hungry animal picking off bits of meat on a carcass—for Harry, the meat was information that would take the guilty parties down. Like David and Goliath, he had his slingshot pulled and was holding the biggest stone he could find. But the giant had never been taken down like this before. It would shake the foundations of the White House. The horror was that it needed to be done. Men needed to be held accountable. Bill hoped it would work. He prayed all this wasn't in vain. At the very least, he wanted out, and for his family to be safe. There was not one hundred percent in any of this. But it was the only shot he had. And Harry held the slingshot in his hand. Bill was the one who had handed him the deadly stone to throw.

Lying back on his bed waiting for the next call, he thought about all of his missions he'd been a part of while serving the country he loved so much. He never regretted once what he had to do to defend America. He never wished he didn't have to fight for the freedom of others. But when he thought of what he had done for the President's Club, he felt a tightening in his chest. He felt sick in his bones. It was so wrong. So sick. He was amazed it had lasted so long through the centuries. Why hadn't someone leaked it to the press before? Was it stupid of him to think he might get away with this and live? Was it the fear that drove those other men to silence for the rest of their lives? Even the one who had spoken to Patrick still wished to remain in the dark. Invisible. He was still afraid.

The oddest thing was that all of the men who had served in the club were the same men who were willing to give up their lives for their country. But in this one thing, revealing what was going on underground in the White House, they were not willing to die to let the secret out. That said a ton about what the government or a few men in the government held over their heads. *Death is death. How bad could it be?*

CHAPTER FIFTY-NINE

B ill awoke on the fourth day to someone knocking on his door. His heart was racing because he had not had a visitor since he arrived on the top floor of the towering building. He looked through the peephole and saw it was one of the men hired to guard him. He opened the door slowly and the tall, hefty man held out a newspaper. Bill's stomach dropped to the floor. His knees went weak. He broke out in a sweat. He gathered enough strength to sit down on the edge of the bed and opened the folded newspaper. The words nearly jumped off the page they were so large. WHITE HOUSE MURDERS UNCOVERED. Bill could hardly swallow. He squinted to read the first few lines of the article.

Unprecedented corruption has been uncovered in the White House. Innocent people have been murdered or tortured at the hands of twelve of our most valued ex-military who were working at the pleasure of the President of the United States, with no option but to obey. Led by an unseen Command they were given tasks and had to obey with no recourse. Error was unforgiveable. The formation of the President's Club took place centuries ago, but has remained active underground, hidden from the American public. Now these brave men, minus one who lost his life for daring to separate himself from the club, are willing to take a stand and end this horror once and for all. This is nothing short of heroism on the part of these men. They risked their lives serving our country, which they loved and were willing to do, but when they retired from the military with great honors, they were drafted into the President's Club by intimidation and threats to their families and their own lives.

The alleged corruption started with the President and chief of staff. It is unknown at this time who else is involved in these horrific crimes to American citizens but all of this will surface in a court of law when these eleven men testify to the crimes they were forced to commit.

Bill could read no more. His hands were shaking and he had a multitude of emotions running through his body—relief, fear, anger, and a sense of accomplishment. This was the beginning of the end for the President's Club. But he knew he was still in danger. So were all the men. Especially now that this article had gone to print. His phone rang and he jumped up to answer it.

Sharon's voice was full of excitement. "Bill, have you seen the newspaper? I just read it online. I can't believe what you brave men are doing to expose the corruption. I am so proud of you! How do you feel seeing it all in print for the world to see?"

"I am both proud and scared. Because I am not sure what the President will do now that he has seen this. Of course he will deny all of it. But he isn't aware of the thumb drives that I have. And the testimonies of all the men will just add to what I have already said to Harry Osner."

"Bill, we all are here thinking about you. Your children are so shocked at what has been going on for years. It is difficult for them to grasp."

"I wish they didn't have to know."

"Do you know when we might see you?"

"It will be a little while, Honey. Depends on when the attorney general of the Justice Department uses military force to arrest those who are at fault. Like the chief of staff, the head of the National Security Council, and anyone else that knew about this."

"Do you think that will take long?"

Bill grinned. "No, Honey. I don't. I think now that this has hit the papers, things are going to roll. Patrick said the same thing. I need to be careful because I feel they might come after all of us in the club. We are not safe right now, because this is the first time any news of the club has gone public."

"I am so worried about you."

"Let's trust that the security surrounding me is sufficient. Patrick seems to think it is. I have to trust him, Sharon. He is all I have."

"I will keep this phone next to me. Please let me know what is going on. I don't feel free to call you all the time. I know you are alone in the condo, but I never know if you are on the phone with someone. I don't want to interrupt."

"You are never interrupting. Just hang tight. I will be calling you often to let you know any news."

Bill sat back on the sofa and closed his eyes. This was what he had wanted for so long, but it felt like he'd just jumped off a tall building with no parachute. What a glorious day in history for this to all be brought out into the light of day! No more hiding. No more secrets from his family. The government had gotten so secretive and corrupt that no one knew what was going on. Now some of it would be known. But no telling what remained hidden in the bowels of the White House.

Where did America go? And how do we save her? The questions sat in his head like the headlines on the newspaper he had just read. He could imagine the shock going around the world with those headlines. He almost winced at the knowledge that foreign countries would know about this. However, lying had been a game for centuries between countries. This wasn't new.

A text came through on his cell from Paul. "Dad, we all are so proud of you. I had no idea what all you have been going through. How did you do it, Dad? How did you hold up under such pressure?"

"Son, I did what I was trained to do. Only this time it was wrong. So wrong. I don't know how to tell you about the nightmare I have lived, but one day you will know it all."

"I know it may not mean anything, Dad, but I'm here for you. If you need someone to talk to that you can trust."

Bill smiled. His eyes watered. "You have no idea what that means to me, Paul. I am so very tired of the hiding. The blood. The danger. I am ready to come home."

"We are ready for that to happen. We have missed you so much. Take care of yourself, Dad. It's not over yet."

"You are correct. It's not over. I just hope it can be over at some point."

"What do you mean, Dad?"

"I mean, I hope there isn't a laser on me for the rest of my life. I don't know if they will tolerate this, even though it is public information now. They could hire anyone to take us all out, the eleven men that are left who are testifying. I am one of those men. I'm not sure we will ever be totally out of danger."

"That's not very encouraging after all you have been through to get this out."

"It's part of the politics that most people don't think about. They can always find you. And they can always make it look like an accident. Just like I did, Paul."

"Just know you can talk to me, Dad. I won't keep you."

"You will be the first to know if anything comes up."

"Bye, Dad."

"Bye, Son."

Patrick rang next. Bill was surprised he had waited this long.

"Hey, Bill! We did it! It's hard to believe that the worst is over. I have been on the phone with the other ten men. They are very nervous about this article. They all were full of questions about what is next. How do you feel?"

"I'm dealing with it pretty well. But I fear for all our lives. Even yours now."

"It's a precarious time, Bill. But it had to be done and it feels so good. Think of all the men before you who couldn't do this. Or wouldn't. We have cracked the system. At least in this one area. Now the whole world will know. If you or any of the men get killed, everyone will know who did it. The word *accident* won't come into play anymore."

"I'll still be dead, though, won't I?"

"I'm taking care of you. And all the men. They are surrounded by security. They would have to drop a bomb on each one of you to get to you. And that's not going to happen. It's too late now. I am certain the attorney general will have those men responsible for the crimes arrested immediately. They will be prosecuted. I wouldn't doubt that the President denies any knowledge of it. But we know he is involved."

"You have spent a lot of money on this project, Patrick. I don't even want to think how much this security level costs."

"It is nothing next to the joy I get from exposing the evil that is going on. And freeing up eleven men's lives. Just think, Bill. You'll be able to rejoin your family soon and live a normal life. And work on my books again."

"Oh yes, the Medicare theft. Did you really not know that was going on?"

"It is already being fixed as we speak. I knew something was happening. But I wanted to know you and it gave me an opening that I jumped through to find out if you were part of this club."

"I kind of thought that was your angle."

"Well, it worked. I really like you, Bill. There aren't many of you left on this earth."

"That may be a blessing, Patrick. You have done so much with so little credit."

"That goes for all of you men. Think of what you've lived through, Bill, that no one will ever know. It is part of life. But we learn and go forward. It is what makes us men."

"I thank you for all you've done to help me bring this about. I know the other men are so relieved. Please let me know when anything takes place as far as the courts are concerned. I know the television stations will eat this up. I will cut mine on shortly to see when the rat race begins to see who can report what first."

"They are like wolves, the media. I hate it, but we used it today for our benefit. It worked, too."

"Talk to you soon."

"Stay in your room Bill. I'll let you know when you can see your family."

CHAPTER SIXTY

S ometimes, not often in politics, justice slips through the fingers of the ungodly attorneys and those who committed the
crimes are punished. In this case, this one time in history, the
White House administration crumbled before the eyes of the nation. It was both refreshing and terrifying.

Bill and the other ten men gave unprecedented testimonies
behind closed doors in gory detail of what they were required to
do. They left no stone unturned. Relief was seen on the faces of the
men who had held so much in, but their identities were protected
so that they could start a new life. It was a harrowing time for the
United States. Something so deadly had been hidden for so long
that it took a while for the average American citizen to realize how
long the thin crooked arms of evil stretched. The news media did
their job, telling the story in ninety different ways. But they never
found out the names of the twelve men, no matter how much they
pried.

On a Saturday night, in the middle of November, when cold winds were beginning to blow in the capital city, eleven men sat around a table toasting each other for the victory they had thought would never come. They discussed briefly the difficulty they'd had in following through with the orders of Command. But it was an unspoken decision that they not talk about the horrors they'd inflicted on the innocent. Nor did they speak about the information that was gathered through torture. It was a unanimous decision for all the men to lay it to rest in the ground, along with the first member of the club who had been taken down by the hands of the government. He was a hero to the eleven men. But to the nation, all twelve men were seen as heroes. It was going to be difficult to set aside what they had been through and what they had done and go back to a normal life, or what they hoped would be normal. Their families would have to take all the truth in, work through the knowledge they'd acquired, and then move forward to a better day.

Bill enjoyed finally meeting with the men, seeing their faces, and knowing he'd played a huge role in setting them all free. Patrick walked in and the men welcomed him with open arms.

"I just wanted to sit in for a few moments and relish in the victory we all share. This is something that should go down in history and be written up in history books. People will talk about this at their dinner tables. It shows every person that doing the right thing pays off in the end. Yes, lives were lost, but we were determined to push through. To find a way where there was no way."

"We owe you so much, Patrick, for the time, money, and energy you put into this whole thing. We could not have made it happen without you." Bill put his arm around Patrick.

Patrick sat down and the room got quiet. All the men knew Patrick had something to say that they needed to hear. "Men, here are the facts that we have to look at. The chief of staff, the secretary of state, the man we knew as 'Command,' who was really a pissed-off retired admiral, and the head of NCS got life for their part in this murder fiasco. The President got off because he denied any knowledge whatsoever of the President's Club. We all know he knew. But as far as we could make it happen, the club is dead, for all purposes. Now, having said that, none of us can be certain that it won't rear its ugly head again. It has lived through centuries, so this may not end it for good. Because of that doubt, I will have security on you for a long time, but that cannot last forever. But I ask you to never turn your back to the possibility that when you are not looking you could be caught. Don't turn your back to the wind. I hate to think it is for the rest of your life, but it just might be. I realize in saying that that you may never have a normal life again. I am sure you felt that way when you returned from covert in Afghanistan. But this is supposed to be your home. You should be safe here, but you are not. At least, not totally.

"So I am giving you fair warning; be aware of your surroundings at all times. Don't relax so much that you miss the most obvious clue that you are being watched or that someone has a bead on you. I don't know how else to put it. That means your families, too. Teach them about safety. Teach them to look around them for any strange person or situation that just doesn't feel right. Your best option is to move out of the area where you sense a threat, but they can always find you. So don't think for a moment that you are safe."

One of the men spoke up. "So just because we got justice done this time, doesn't mean that it is really over. We aren't going to ever have a normal life."

"I know you don't want to hear it. But the political field breeds corruption. Selfishness. And unfortunately, there are men who will stop at nothing to get what they want. That is how this started in the first place."

Bill spoke up, his forehead creased with exhaustion. "I don't know about you guys, but I am sick of all of this. I would move overseas in a New York minute if I thought it would help. I don't like my family feeling unsafe. I hate to tell them that for the rest of their lives they are going to have to worry. In my estimation, the best thing for us to do is to live out our lives normally. Yes, we can take precautions, but I don't think we need to get paranoid about it. We all will carry a gun as long as we live. We can teach our sons and daughters how to handle a gun. But other than that, for me and my family, I am going to try to blend into society as best I can without making my family feel like they have to always be looking over their shoulder."

Several men spoke up. "I agree with Bill. The best revenge we can have is to live a normal, happy life. We have been robbed of that for so long. It would almost be like punishment if we have to live on the edge, always looking back."

Patrick wiped his face and took a long drink of beer. "I know it seems unfair. But realistically, the President's Club could rise back up with no problem. Not with the current President, but we are in an election year. Depending on who wins the election this year, it could lay dead or return. I guess we just have to wait and see."

The men soon dismissed themselves, shaking hands, hugging, and wishing each other the best. But looming over their heads was the suggestion that they might never be free. And that put a somber note on the victory that had taken so much work to accomplish.

———

As they left the room, Patrick could see that they were all thankful to be able to go back to their families and not have anything more to hide. He would keep the security at a certain level and hope that would be enough to keep these brave men safe. He had the money. He had the desire. But he didn't have all the answers.

CHAPTER SIXTY-ONE

B ill Sinclair did exactly what he said he was going to do. He and Sharon relished every day they had together. He did not fear; he did not look over his shoulder. But everything Patrick had said was always sitting center stage in his mind. He went back to work, gaining more clients than ever, mentoring the young employees he'd hired. He did the work of three men and never complained. He was closer than ever to his sons and Emily. And the babies were being born one right after another to carry on the Sinclair name.

One afternoon in May, he had purchased four tickets to see the Washington Nationals play the Detroit Tigers. He was excited and so were his sons. It was the first time they'd been able to get away and be together since they had all been sequestered in Colorado. Even though that whole fiasco was not discussed often, they all had been changed greatly in the passing of it.

The boys had a greater understanding of who their father was but Emily was not so clear on it. She remained a little distant at times, trying to figure out the whole picture. The real man. She asked her mother many questions and also sat with her father, trying to figure out how he could do what he had been forced to do. He knew she was struggling. But he also knew there was no explaining it.

On game day, it was warm, but not too warm. The breeze was perfect for sitting in the stands watching their favorite baseball team. The atmosphere in the stadium was pure excitement. The smells of popcorn and hot dogs always made them hungry. As they waded through the crowd they bought all the food they could possibly eat and then some. The stands were filling up fast and they hurried to find a place where they could see the whole field. Bill was enjoying this time with his sons, and they spent the first few minutes talking about the players and their stats. When the game started, Bill leaned back and just took in the sights and sounds. When the Nationals scored a homerun, the crowd went wild.

Bill looked around watching the faces of the people around him, and it was then that he noticed someone who looked out of place. He was dressed in black from head to toe. Everyone else was casual. Jeans and a baseball cap. This man stood out. He looked like a businessman but there was something odd about him. Bill couldn't put his finger on it, but inside his gut, he knew something wasn't right.

He kept an eye on the guy off and on during the game. His sons saw his face and his whole demeanor change.

"What's wrong, Dad?" Paul asked, frowning.

"Nothing, Son. Just squinting because of the sun. It's pretty bright out here today."

Paul didn't accept that answer. "You worried about something? I can see it on your face, Dad."

Bill looked at Paul and shook his head. He didn't want them worrying. But he noticed all of the boys looking around without being obvious. There was an odd tension in the air.

In the ninth inning, the Nationals were winning 9 to 7, and Bill stood up to stretch. He noticed that the man was gone, and he spent most of the remainder of the inning scanning the crowd to see if he could spot him. It made him upset that he even had a doubt about the man. It was ruining his time with his sons. He didn't want to think about snipers anymore. He didn't want to live ducking and in fear of that shot he wouldn't hear that might take him down. It had felt so good to step back into a normal life and lose himself in his work again, and his children. But this man, this guy in black, had looked too out of place and it stuck in Bill's gut. He just couldn't shake it off.

As they walked out of the stadium, Jesse brought it up again. "Dad, what are you doing looking around the stadium at the crowd? Are you looking for someone? Is something wrong?"

Bill made them all stop when they got to the car. He turned and looked at them and they could see that he was dead serious.

"I saw someone today. I have not felt this way since the trial. But something was wrong. He was too out of place. I cannot say for certain, but I felt him watching me. You might say I'm paranoid, but I don't think so. I have not been wrong before."

"What do we do, Dad? Do you see him out here anywhere?"

"We do nothing right now, Jess. But now I will be looking over my shoulder until I am certain I'm not being followed."

"I thought we weren't going to live like that." Jacob had a frown on his face as he climbed into the car.

Bill got in the driver's side and started the engine. They were quiet on the way back to the house. But all of them were thinking about the same thing. Some time had passed since the trials. They had almost forgotten the feeling of fear that had swallowed the whole family up. But now, because of this one man that Bill had seen in the stands, it was back. The worry. The watching.

Bill pulled into the driveway and got out, walking into the house looking for Sharon. She came around the corner of the kitchen with a dish towel in her hands. She took one look at Bill and stopped in her tracks.

"What is it, Bill? You look like you've seen a ghost."

"Maybe I have, Sharon. Maybe I have. I sure hope so. Because it if wasn't a ghost, then this whole damn thing has started back up again."

She sat down on the sofa and put her face in her hands. "I thought it was over, Bill. They are in prison for what they've done. I thought it was over."

Bill stood up and walked over to the window that looked out on the front of their house. The boys were in the kitchen laughing and talking about the game. He saw a black sedan drive by the house slowly. His heart raced as it passed the house and drove off quickly.

"Honey, I hate to say this, but I don't think it will ever be over."

EPILOGUE

"Emily"

I guess life does go on, even after some of the worst events a family could experience. My parents lived to be old. And that was an achievement, let me tell you. My father had to live on the edge his whole life, carrying a gun, watching behind his back. It caused us all to live that way. But we managed. We kept on keeping on.

Our children are grown now and I have lost my brother Paul to an illness the doctors could not explain. Of course I have felt lopsided without him. I talk to him even now. But in the back of my mind I wonder if they caused his death somehow. We all think that, but it is unspoken.

I guess the significant thing in all of this is that our family has stuck together. I am ashamed of our government and how it has lost its thread. It no longer seems true and loyal to the people. I will have a difficult time ever believing things aren't happening underground that none of us know about. I understand covert because of my father. But not on our own land, with our own citizens. The lies are so thick that even those who spoke them have lost their way in the web they have woven. *Politics.* That word could be removed from the English language for all I care. What I want are real people caring about the good of the whole. A people's government.

I remember the graciousness of my mother. How she stood next to my father no matter what. I have tried to pattern myself to be like her. I could not have ever dreamed that I would want to be like my father. We fought all my young life. But now that I am older, I see. I understand who he really was. He was a hero. A silent hero. He carried the weight of a horrible secret so that we wouldn't have to know how really ugly things were.

This new understanding tends to color my carefree childhood memories and messes with what I thought our lives were. But I think as we reach adulthood, it pretty much does that, anyway. We wake up to reality and the grown-up world, which isn't as Alice and Wonderland as we thought it was.

I have grown tougher in my years. I don't cry as often. But Rob is wonderful and has turned out to be the best husband a girl could want. Dad wouldn't agree, of course, if he were alive. But he didn't want to ever admit he was wrong. I laugh thinking about that.

I just wanted you to know our family made it through. We survived. Not without anger or fear. But we didn't allow all that to ruin our lives. Our father saw to that. He wasn't going to let them win.

America is a beautiful land. With beautiful people. We just let government get too big. I will remember how she was, and hope that she will get strong again. I have a flag flying in my front yard, attached to an old oak tree. But I will also remember the love my mother and father had. It was magnificent. It was what we all yearn for. Something that lasts. Like God. Like our country. America.

—Yours, Emily Sinclair

We the People of the United States, in Order to form a more perfect Union, establish Justice, insure domestic Tranquility, provide for the common defense, promote the general Welfare, and secure the Blessings of Liberty to ourselves and our Posterity, do ordain and establish this Constitution for the United States of America.

AUTHOR'S PAGE

 Nancy Veldman is an author, pianist, and watercolor artist who lives in Destin, Florida with her husband, Richard. They have four children, ten grandchildren, and one great grandchild. She has written over one hundred songs and has produced ten piano CDs which are available on Magnoliahouse.com, iTunes, and Amazon.com. She is also an author and is currently working on her eighth novel. Nancy owns a gift shop in Sandestin, Florida called Magnolia House, and for twenty-four years it has been a gathering place where people come from all over the world to hear her music and shop for home accessories and jewelry. Her love of people comes through all of her art, music and books, but also in her work with the homeless and those less fortunate. She loves reading, walking, exercise, the laughter of her grandchildren, and eating cupcakes! Please visit her website, www.magnoliahouse.com, to learn more about her and the Magnolia House. You can listen to her music and videos on YouTube. She welcomes your emails at nancy@magnoliahouse.com.